CATHERINE:
A TIME FOR LOVE

CATHERINE:
A TIME FOR LOVE

Juliette Benzoni

Catherine Series No. 5

This edition published in England in 2020 by
Telos Publishing Ltd,
139 Whitstable Road, Canterbury, Kent CT2 8EQ
www.telos.co.uk

Telos Publishing Ltd values feedback. Please e-mail us with any comments
you may have about this book to: feedback@telos.co.uk

ISBN: 978-1-84583-983-3

Catherine: A Time for Love © 1968, 2020 Juliette Benzoni

Original title: *Catherine, et le Temps d'Aimer*

Cover art: Martin Baines
Cover design: David J Howe

The moral rights of the author have been asserted.

British Library Cataloguing in Publication Data.
A catalogue record for this book is available from the British Library.

CONTENTS

This edition dedicated to Linda Compagnoni Walther

PART I

THE PILGRIMS TO COMPOSTELA

1: The Dominican Abbey of Aubrac

The mist thickened every minute, winding its long grey tendrils round them like a damp shroud … How long had they been wandering like this over these lonely grassy uplands, the occasional hollows of which brimmed with grey-green water? It seemed like hours and hours! But there was nothing to suggest they were drawing near their next halting place. The wind had risen, raging from every corner of the vast plateau, momentarily tearing the mist aside, after which it closed round them more stiflingly than ever.

Catherine walked along in the midst of the pilgrim band. Hunched, head lowered beneath her huge hat, she struggled to hold down her flapping cape and leaned heavily on her staff for support. She had discovered during the five days since leaving Le Puy how useful a staff can be when one is crushed by fatigue. Especially now, when she was supporting a fellow pilgrim, Gillette de Vauchelles, with her free arm. This was the woman whose haggard face and racking cough had caught her eye at the Easter Mass. Gillette was a widow of about 40, of gentle birth and exquisite manners. But her tragic expression spoke of an incurable grief. She was gentle, melancholy and deeply religious. Seeing her struggling along, gasping for air at that altitude, Catherine felt bound to go to her assistance. At first Gillette had refused.

'I shall be a burden to you, my sister. You have enough troubles of your own.'

This was true enough. The strain of the day's march was beginning to tell, and Catherine's feet, in their crude leather shoes, were painfully blistered. But she knew her companion was in dire need of help, so she smiled gently at her.

'I am all right. Besides, two of us can manage better than one.'

Leaning against each other, they continued the weary march, which grew more exhausting with every passing hour. They had left the barns of Malbouzon at daybreak with the intention of reaching the priory of

Nasbinals by nightfall. It was but twelve leagues distant. But then the mist had come up, and soon after that they had been forced to recognise that the path they were on was not the right one. There was no cairn of stones to show that they were on the right way. So the pilgrim leader had assembled his companions together.

'We have to follow this path now, wherever it may lead,' he said. 'If we leave it, we are liable to find ourselves going round in circles in the mist. It is bound to take us somewhere, and in any case the wisest thing is to put our trust in God!'

A murmur of approval greeted this remark. It was translated for the benefit of the many Swiss and Germans who walked at the rear of the band, and they all seemed to approve of the leader's decision. He seemed already to have established complete dominance over his heterogeneous pilgrims. He must have been about 45 years old. Catherine really didn't know quite what to make of him. She knew, because she had heard people talking about him, that his name was Gerbert Bohat, and that he was one of the richest burghers of Clermont, but nothing about the man accorded with his reputation. He was tall and thin, with the face of an ascetic. Yet his clean-shaven, tormented face seemed to carry the stigmata of every human passion. The usual expression in his grey eyes was an arrogant one, but from time to time Catherine had seen a look of uncertainty bordering on fear flash through them. His manner was icy, and while he might display some of the qualities of a leader of men, Catherine had the definite impression that Gerbert Bohat detested women. When he spoke to her it was coldly, almost rudely, whereas he was capable of friendly behaviour toward the other pilgrims. But when the time for prayer came, Catherine found that the man's spirit could take fire …

Since the moment when Gerbert had decided to lead his troop along this unknown path, they had walked and walked. When they reached an ancient bridge spanning a rushing stream they thought at last they had found a landmark.

'That is the Bès river, and this is the Marchastel bridge,' Gerbert said. 'We must keep straight on. We won't stop at Nasbinals after all, but at the Dominican abbey of Aubrac. Courage!'

These words cheered everyone up. One man, who had made the pilgrimage before, said that they would be much better off at the abbey than at Nasbinals. The guest-houses in these solitary regions knew how to treat exhausted travellers. They set off again, singing. But as the mist gradually closed round them again, the voices fell silent, and once again it seemed as though the merest chance guided their steps.

From time to time the mist would lift long enough to disclose the hazard of a peat-bog, a sudden gorge or the greyish hump of a hill, but for most of the time they were walking blindly, eyes on the ground, searching for the right path. And now the approach of night redoubled their danger. Were they going to have to halt there in the middle of this deserted countryside, spend the night in this icy wind drifting with snowflakes? In the last days of March, ice and snow are not uncommon in the desolate wastes of Aubrac. Despite everything, despite the terrible weather and her painful feet, Catherine's courage did not fail. She would have endured ten times worse for Arnaud's sake.

Suddenly Gillette de Vauchelles stumbled and fell forward so heavily that Catherine was dragged down with her. This gave rise to a bit of agitation in the column, and a moment later Gerbert Bohat was standing beside them.

'What's going on here? Can't you look where you are going?'

His tone was abrupt and stripped of compassion. Catherine answered in the same style. Tired as she was, she was in no mood to put up with the Clermontois' bad temper.

'My companion is worn out. This endless road … if you can call it a road! And this mist …'

Gerbert's thin lips curved in a contemptuous smile. 'It's only five days since we began this pilgrimage. If this woman is ill she should have stayed at home. A pilgrimage is not a pleasure jaunt. God demands …'

'God demands,' Catherine broke in curtly, 'that we should show mercy to others and pity for their afflictions! Where's the great merit in undertaking this long penance when one is in perfect health? It would be better, sire, if you offered your arm instead of these reproaches!'

'Woman,' Gerbert interrupted, 'no-one wants to know your views. I have a difficult enough task – to lead this band of pilgrims safely to the Tomb of the Apostle! Any of your companions here will help you.'

'Might I point out that I called you "sire"? I am not accustomed to hearing myself addressed as "woman"! I have a name: I am Catherine of Montsalvy!'

'What you have above all is an intolerable arrogance! Here we are nothing but a band of sinners on the road to repentance.'

The man's scornful and sermonising tone was all it needed to make Catherine's temper, already near breaking-point, explode.

'It becomes you well to speak of the pride of others, brother,' she cut in, deliberately emphasising the word 'brother', 'since this appears to be a subject with which you are perfectly acquainted … if one can judge by the warmth of your fellow-feeling!'

A flash of rage lit up Gerbert's grey eyes. His glance met Catherine's, but she refused to look down. She even felt a sort of savage pleasure in the man's obvious exasperation. It was time he realised once and for all, that she was not going to submit to his dictates … This was the message that could be clearly read in Catherine's violet eyes. Gerbert did not misunderstand.

Instinctively he raised his arm with its heavy staff. One of the other pilgrims hastily intervened, seizing his arm and forcing it back to his side.

'Now then, brother! Calm yourself! Remember that you are dealing with a woman, not a varlet! Zounds, the rough manners you have in this wild Auvergne of yours!' said the pilgrim, in a rallying tone of voice. 'Wouldn't it be better if you concentrated on getting us out of this damned mist that pierces to the marrow? The spot seems ill-chosen for a dispute. Meanwhile, I can help Dame Catherine with our sister here as far as the next halt … that is, if there is another one!'

'She will get all the attention she needs at the abbey,' Gerbert muttered as he returned to his place at the head of the column.

'I'll believe in this Dominican abbey of his when I see the roofs!' Catherine's defender remarked as he helped her up with poor Gillette, whose knees were collapsing under her with weariness. 'We shall have to carry this woman,' he went on, casting a questioning look round him. Catherine smiled gratefully at him. She hadn't noticed him before, and she was surprised at his unexpected appearance for a pilgrim. He was a young man, thin and of medium height, with brown hair, but there wasn't a line of his face that in any way corresponded to one's notions of how a pious pilgrim should look. There seemed to be not a single regular feature in what was, nonetheless, an unusually expressive countenance. He had fleshy lips with a long, prominent nose, flattened at the bridge; small blue eyes set deep beneath bleached brows; a square, strong-willed chin; and a mass of precocious wrinkles. His features were coarse, but in his vivacious expression and lively glance were signs of native intelligence, while the mocking lines of his mouth suggested an irresistible leaning toward irony.

Becoming aware of Catherine's silent scrutiny, he gave a curious grin that split his face from ear to ear, doffed his large pilgrim's hat – which he wore cocked elegantly over one ear – and bowed so low as to dust the ground with it.

'Josse Rallard, fair lady, at your service! I am a Parisian, a gentleman of fortune, and though I am on my way to Galicia, it is as much for the accomplishment of a vow as for the pardon of my many and numerous sins … Hey, you there! Who will help me carry this woman as far as the guest-house?'

There was no response from those nearby. Clearly, the pilgrims felt they had enough troubles of their own. They were weary, soaked through. Many of them were shivering in the icy wind. No-one felt equal to taking on this additional burden. Catherine told herself that they looked like a frightened flock of sheep, and could not repress a feeling of scorn. Was that the sort of helplessness that was to prevail among these penitents? By now the band was just about to start off again, headed by Gerbert Bohat, when Josse pushed his way through the people around him and went up to a man hunched up beneath his pilgrim's hat, and struck him on the shoulder.

'Come now, aren't we both Parisians after all! Pride is a wicked sin, brother, especially in a pilgrim! Dame Catherine, may I introduce Messire Colin des Épinettes, a distinguished jurist and scholar whom I am delighted to discover among us. Now, brother, you take hold of Madame this side and I'll take the other. It isn't right that Dame Catherine should wear herself out when we are there to help.'

The furious look on the 'distinguished jurist's' face made Catherine want to laugh so much that she forgot her weariness for a moment. She could almost swear she heard him growl.

'Devil take you and your viper's tongue!' he snarled as his fellow citizen; but all the same he put one of Gillette's arms round his neck, while Josse did the same with the other, and in this fashion the poor woman barely touched the ground. Catherine took charge of her staff and bundle, light enough in all conscience. The pilgrims meanwhile were complaining of the length of the march, and the darkness. Some of them feared falling into a bog and were imploring Saint James to safeguard them in their present peril.

'Be quiet,' Gerbert's imperious voice rang out somewhere in the crowd in front of them, 'or, if not, sing!'

'We haven't the heart,' someone said. 'Why not admit that we are lost?'

'Because we aren't,' answered the leader. 'The abbey cannot be far now …'

Catherine opened her mouth to express her own doubts on that score, but just then, as if to lend weight to Gerbert's words, the faint sound of bells reached them through the mist. Bohat gave a triumphant cry.

'The bell for lost travellers! We are on the right path! Onwards!'

Brandishing his staff like a standard, he rushed off in the direction from which the sound had come, and the pilgrims followed him as best they could.

'Let's hope he has some sense of direction,' Josse grumbled. 'Mist is very deceptive.'

Catherine didn't reply. She was cold and terribly tired. But the noise of the bell grew louder and clearer every minute. Soon a faint yellow glow appeared through the mist. Gerbert Bohat greeted it like the sign of a personal victory.

'That's the fire the monks light at the top of the belfry. We have arrived.'

Suddenly the mist lifted and Catherine, with a feeling of relief, saw a mass of dark, squat buildings rise up before her. The black outlines of an immense and ancient tower, a massive belfry crowned with flames and a high nave supported by flying buttresses seemed to stand sentinel over the flock of large, dark buildings with their few windows and doors.

The guest-house, standing on the last fold of the vast plateau, looked exactly like a fortress. Revived by the sight, the pilgrims began shouting with joy, and the tumult even succeeded in drowning the heavy, leaden notes of the bell tolling just above their heads. Then the gate slowly creaked open to allow three monks, carrying torches, to rush out and greet the pilgrims.

'We are God's travellers,' cried Gerbert at the top of his voice. 'We seek shelter.'

'Come in, brothers, you will find shelter here.'

As if it had been waiting for the pilgrims' arrival, the show now began to fall thickly, dotting the immense yard of beaten earth, where the nostrils were assailed by a strong smell of stables. Catherine leant against a wall, exhausted. Doubtless she would have to spend the night with her companions in a dormitory. And yet, without quite knowing why, she felt a longing to be alone with herself this evening for a little while. Perhaps it was because this strange journey was disorientating her, for all her courage. She felt uprooted amongst these people; their aspirations and vows were foreign to her. What they all wanted was to purify themselves at the Apostle's tomb, assure themselves after a fashion of a stake in Paradise while they were still alive. But she? Certainly she hoped God would vouchsafe an end to her Calvary, and the cure of her beloved husband, but this was only so that she might see 'him' again, rediscover his love, kisses, warmth, everything that made up the living reality of Arnaud. There was no high spirituality about her quest — she was searching for an earthly, carnal love, without which she felt she had not the strength to live.

'We must separate here,' Gerbert's voice cut in briefly. 'Here are the ladies who will take care of the women. Men, follow me!'

At this, four nuns issued from a nearby building, dressed in black like the monks, their sombre costume relieved by a white wimple.

Josse Rallard and Colin des Épinettes handed the barely-conscious Gillette to two of them. Catherine approached. 'My companion is exhausted,' she said. 'She needs rest and care. Have you got a room where I could look after her?'

The nun looked at Catherine with annoyance. She was one of those sturdy country women who fear neither man nor beast. She laid Gillette upon a stretcher fetched by one of the other nuns, signed to the latter to take one end while she seized the other, and only then deigned to answer Catherine.

'We have only two rooms, and they are occupied by a noblewoman and her ladies. This woman arrived here ten days ago with a broken leg and is unable to leave yet.'

'I quite understand. But couldn't she send her women to sleep in the dormitory and give us one of her rooms?'

Sister Léonarde did not trouble to suppress a grimace, which might have been a mocking smile, and shrugged her hefty shoulders.

'Personally, I wouldn't like to run the risk of asking her. She is … well, let's say, she's not an easy character! She is a great noblewoman, it seems.'

'Yet you don't look as if you would be easily overawed, sister,' Catherine said. 'However, if you are afraid of the lady, I am quite willing to approach her myself.'

'I am not afraid,' said Sister Léonarde. 'I just can't stand shouting, and nor can the Mother Superior. And the Lord has endowed this woman with the most terrifying voice.'

As they spoke, the stretcher, with Catherine following behind, had passed through the little low that which led into the part of the guest-house reserved for women travellers. The few remaining women pilgrims brought up the rear. They found themselves in a vast kitchen with a stone-flagged floor, where a smell of wood smoke mingled with the sharp tang of sour milk. Strings of onions and pieces of smoked meat hung from the low, darkened ceiling. Cheeses drained on trays of plaited willow, and in front of the gigantic chimney two nuns stood, sleeves rolled back to the elbows, tending to a massive black cauldron full of cabbage soup.

They put the stretcher down before the fire, and Sister Léonarde bent over the sick woman.

'She is very pale,' she said. 'I will give her a cordial, and meanwhile they will make up a bed for her …'

'Tell me where this lady is to be found,' said Catherine, who was determined to get her own way, 'and I will speak to her. I too am a noblewoman …'

Sister Léonarde laughed aloud this time.

'I already guessed as much,' she said, 'if only from your stubbornness. I will go and speak to her myself … but I know in advance what the answer will be. You take care of this poor woman!'

She started across the huge room. Catherine bent over Gillette, who was slowly regaining consciousness, but then she paused, started after Sister Léonarde, and stopped again. She was considering whether or not she could safely leave Gillette when one of the other women came up.

'I will look after Dame Gillette,' she said. 'You go and see to the other matter yourself.'

Catherine smiled her thanks and sped after the nun. She caught sight of the woman in the distance, hurrying down a long, damp corridor and then knocking at a door, which opened to admit her.

The lady with the broken leg undoubtedly did possess a mighty voice, because when Catherine herself paused at the door, she could hear her bellowing.

'I need my women to take care of me, sister! You surely don't expect me to send them to the dormitory at the opposite end of the building? Devil take it, a bed is a bed, wherever it may be!'

Sister Léonarde made some reply that Catherine could not catch, possibly because she was too preoccupied with the effort of placing that strangely familiar voice, which now could be heard swearing roundly.

"Od's bodkins, sister! Must I put it more clearly? I intend to keep my two rooms!'

Catherine could not stop herself. She opened the door and entered the room, which to be sure was both small and low-ceilinged, a great bed with faded hangings and conical chimney taking up almost all the available space. But once inside the door, she stopped short, struck dumb with surprise …

Propped up in the bed on a mountain of pillows sat a massive and powerful figure of a woman, before whom the sturdy Sister Léonarde paled to insignificance. The lady's thick white hair still showed some streaks of red, and her complexion, heated by anger, was a fine brick red. She was covered by a mass of blankets. A sort of cape, lined in fox fur, was flung round her shoulders, but one fine white hand protruded from the wide sleeves and was now extended in a threatening gesture toward the nun.

The creaking of the door as Catherine entered had distracted the lady's attention. Vaguely perceiving a feminine shape in the doorway, she swirled round in a fury.

'What's this? People stroll in and out of my room now as if it were some public meeting-place! Who is this woman?'

Choked with emotion, uncertain whether to laugh or cry, Catherine stepped into the room so that the firelight enveloped her.

'Only me, Dame Ermengarde! Have you forgotten me, then?'

For a moment the old lady was helples with astonishment. Her eyes popped open, her arms fell to her sides, her mouth parted soundlessly and she grew so pale that for a moment Catherine was quite alarmed.

'Ermengarde?' she asked anxiously. 'Don't you recognise me? Have I frightened you? It's me, it's …'

'Catherine! Catherine! My darling …'

The words were uttered in a positive roar, which made Sister Léonarde jump. The next moment, the nun was obliged to restrain her impetuous patient, because Dame Ermengarde, forgetful of her injury, was on the point of leaping out of bed to greet her friend.

'Your leg, Countess!'

'The Devil take my leg! Leave me alone! 'Od's life, Catherine, is it really you? Can it be possible? Ah, it's too wonderful!'

She struggled in the sister's grip as Catherine ran toward her and embraced her. The two women kissed and clung to each other. Catherine's eyes were wet with tears of joy.

'Yes, it's too wonderful … It's a miracle! Oh, Ermengarde, it's so good to see you again. But what are you doing here?'

'What are *you* doing here?'

Ermengarde gently pushed Catherine away, and then held her at arm's length and examined her closely.

'You haven't changed ... or hardly at all! As beautiful as ever – even more beautiful perhaps? Different, though, less eye-catching perhaps ... but so much more heart-breaking! Let me see, I would say you were fined down, etherealised. It's devilish hard to see how you could ever have sprung from a draper's shop!'

'Countess,' the nun intervened crisply, 'I beg of you to refrain from all mention of Messire Satan under this holy roof! You are forever calling upon him!'

Ermengarde turned and gazed at her with unfeigned astonishment. 'Are you still there, then? Ah yes ... of course, this business of the rooms. Very well then, go and turn out those lazy women next door, put them into the dormitory and move your patient in there. Now that I have Madame de Brazey with me I need no-one else! And we have much to discuss!'

The nun pursed her lips a little at finding herself so cavalierly dismissed, but she bowed and left the room without another word. The slamming of the door behind her was the only indication of her resentment. The Countess watched her leave the room, then she shrugged and creaked heavily over the bed to make room for her friend beside her.

'Come, sit beside me, my love, and let's talk! How long is it now since you left me to take the city of Orléans by storm?'

'Five years,' Catherine replied. 'Can it really be five years? Time passes so quickly!'

'Five years,' Ermengarde echoed slowly, 'that I've been trying vainly to discover the whereabouts of a certain Dame de Brazey. The last I heard of you, you were at Loches, lady-in-waiting to Queen Yolande. Aren't you ashamed of yourself?'

'Yes,' Catherine admitted, 'but time went by without my noticing. And now, dear Ermengarde, you must get out of the habit of calling me de Brazey. That's no longer my name ...'

'What is, then?'

'The best name of all: Montsalvy!' the young woman declared, so proudly that the Countess suppressed an involuntary smile.

'So, you won in the end? It has been written somewhere, Catherine, that you should constantly surprise me. What alchemy did you resort to, to tame the intractable Messire Arnaud?'

Catherine's smile vanished at the mention of her husband's name. A line of suffering appeared at the corner of her soft mouth, and she looked away.

'It's a long story' she murmured. 'A sad story ...'

The Dame de Châteuvillain fell silent for a moment. She studied her friend, touched by the grief she glimpsed there, the strength of which emotion she instinctively guessed. She did not know what to say next, afraid of wounding Catherine further. After a moment she said with a rare gentleness:

'Call one of my women. She will help you take off those wet clothes, and see that they are dried and others are found for you. They will be a bit large, but warm. Then they can bring us some supper and you can tell me all about it. You look exhausted.'

'Yes, I am,' Catherine said, with a faint smile. 'But first I must see to one of my companions, the one who so badly needed a room to herself.'

'I'll give orders.'

'No,' said Catherine, 'I must see to it myself, but I'll be back in a minute.'

She stepped out into the corridor just as Gillette was carried into the next-door room, the one Ermengarde's two attendants had vacated. The woman who had promised to look after Gillette was there too … She smiled at Catherine.

'They say you have found an old friend here,' she said. 'If you like, I can take care of your companion tonight. She is no trouble.'

'But I don't want …' Catherine began. 'You need to rest!'

The other woman laughed.

'I'm stronger than I look, now! I can sleep anywhere; on a stone, in the rain … or even standing up!'

Catherine studied her with interest. She was a young woman of around 30, small, dark and thin, but with a healthily sunburnt skin and strong white teeth. She was poorly but neatly dressed. As to her face, her slightly tip-tilted nose and large expressive mouth gave her a look of gaiety that Catherine found appealing.

'What's your name?' she asked softly.

'Margot! But they call me Easy Margot … I … I'm not a very desirable sort of person,' she added, with a humble frankness Catherine found touching.

'Tush! All we pilgrims are brothers and sisters, and you are worth as much as any one of us … But thank you for your help! I shall be next door. Call me if you need me.'

'Don't worry,' said Margot. 'I shall manage quite well on my own. Anyway, what poor Gillette needs most is some good hot soup and a night's rest … whatever our leader may say, trying to get rid of her now as he is!'

'What did he say about her?'

'That he wouldn't allow her to travel with us tomorrow because he didn't want to have to drag a lot of sick people all the way to Compostela.'

Catherine frowned. This Gerbert seemed bent on imposing his will on the rest, but she determined there and then that this would not be allowed.

'We'll see about that,' she said. 'Tomorrow I'll have this matter out with him. Unless our sister wishes to stay here, I shall see that she leaves with us!'

She flashed a last smile at Margot, who was gazing at her in admiration, and returned to Ermengarde's room.

It was late that night by the time Catherine finished her tale, but in the Romanesque courtyard of the guest-house the bell for lost travellers still sounded regularly. It provided a strange counterpoint to Catherine's narrative and seemed to under-line its tragic quality. Ermengarde heard her out without so much as breathing a word, but once Catherine finished, she sighed and shook her head.

'If anyone but you had told me all this, I wouldn't have believed the half of it,' she said. 'However, it seems you were brought into this world for an uncommon destiny. And I can see you sailing through the most appalling adventures. Compared with that, your turning up here in pilgrim's guise is the merest anecdote ... So here you are. then, on the road to Compostela. But what if you don't find your husband there?'

'Then I'll go farther, if need be. I'll go to the ends of the earth, because I know I shall have no peace or respite till I have found him again.'

'And supposing that instead of being cured of his leprosy he has only succumbed further to the disease?'

'I shall stay with him nonetheless. Once I have found him again, nothing, no-one, will ever part me from him! You know very well, Ermengarde, that he has always been my only reason for living.'

'Alas, I know it only too well! And all this time I've had to watch you getting into these terrible situations and flinging yourself into such horrifying adventures, I've found myself wondering if God was really to be thanked for placing Arnaud de Montsalvy in your path.'

'Heaven couldn't have made me a more wonderful gift!' Catherine cried so agitatedly that Ermengarde raised her eyebrows and remarked, casually:

'To think that you might be ruling over an empire! Did you know the Duke Philippe has never forgotten you?'

Catherine changed colour and brusquely pulled away from her friend. This mention of the old days hurt her.

'Ermengarde,' she said quietly, 'if you want us to remain friends, don't ever mention the Duke Philippe to me. I want to forget that whole part of my life ...'

'Well, I must say you've got a deucedly accommodating memory. It can't be so easy!'

'Perhaps not! But ...' Catherine's voice cleared suddenly, and she came back and sat beside Ermengarde and asked her gently: 'I'd rather you talked of my family, my mother and Uncle Matthieu. It's so long since I had news of them! That's if you know anything about them.'

'Well, of course I do,' Ermengarde grumbled. 'They are both well, but they find it harder to go without news than you seem to! I thought they both seemed much aged last time I went to Marsannay. But they are both in good health.'

'My ... defection didn't upset them too much?' Catherine asked, with a touch of embarrassment.

'It's a bit late to be thinking of that!' the old lady commented, half smiling. 'No, it's all right, don't worry,' she added hurriedly, seeing Catherine's face darken. 'Nothing unpleasant has happened to them. The Duke is not so unjust as to make them suffer for his disappointment in love. In fact, I'm inclined to think that he hopes your desire to see them again will bring you back to Burgundy one of these days. So he would hardly be so foolish as to send them away to exile. Anyway, I think he wants you to know what a magnanimous man he is! Your uncle's fortune is appreciating nicely, what is more, which is more than can be said for the Châteuvillains'!'

'What do you mean?'

'That I'm under something like sentence of banishment myself. You see, my sweet, I have a son who resembles me. He has had enough of the English and of feeling uncomfortable in his role as a Frenchman. So he went and married young Isabelle de La Trémoille, who is the sister of your friend the former Lord Chamberlain.'

'I hope she isn't anything like him,' Catherine exclaimed, horrified.

'Not in the least – she's quite delightful! But the result was, my son sent back his Order of the Garter to the Duke of Bedford and openly revolted against our own beloved Duke. Consequently the ducal army is even now besieging our castle at Grancey, and it struck me suddenly that it was high time I travelled about and saw a bit of the countryside. I should have made the most exasperating hostage. Thus it is you find me on the open road, travelling toward Compostela in search of a future salvation that is beginning seriously to enter my thoughts. But I bless this happy accident that gave me a broken leg and kept me here. Otherwise I should have been far away by now, and might never have seen you ...'

'Unfortunately,' Catherine sighed, 'we shall soon have to part again. Your leg will certainly keep you here a few days longer, and I must leave tomorrow with my companions!'

The Dame de Châteuvillain's naturally florid colouring veered to red brick.

'Don't be so sure of that, my beauty! Now that I've found you again, I'm not letting go of you again so easily! I shall leave with you. My people can carry me on a stretcher if I can't manage a horse, but in any event, I shan't stay here a minute longer than you! And now, what about some sleep? It's late and you must be tired. Lie down beside me; there's room for two.'

Catherine did not need to be asked twice. She slipped into the bed next to Ermengarde. The thought that she could be travelling from now on with Ermengarde's sturdy optimism to keep her company filled her with happiness and confidence in the future. The dowager was indestructible. Once before, on the death of little Philippe, Catherine had believed her spirit broken. She had staggered from the blow, grown old overnight. Her spirit seemed to have deserted her ... and now here she was again, travelling the open road, more vigorous and formidable than ever! Certainly the journey would be easier with Ermengarde, and a great deal pleasanter!

The fire was sinking. The Countess had blown out the candle and the little room was deep in shadow. But Catherine could not help smiling as she thought of Gerbert's face the next day, when he beheld the imposing lady on her stretcher and learned that he might now count her amongst his pilgrims. That was a meeting that would be well worth seeing.

'What are you thinking about?' Ermengarde said suddenly. 'I can tell that you aren't asleep yet!'

'About you, Ermengarde, and about myself. I'm lucky to have met you at the beginning of this long journey.'

'Lucky? It's I who am lucky, my dear! Here have I been bored to death, for months – what am I saying, for years! Thanks to you, I sincerely hope my life is now about to become a little more animated and amusing. I needed a change, Heaven knows! I was falling to pieces, and now I'm cured!'

And as if to confirm this miraculous resurrection, Ermengarde instantly fell asleep, and soon her stentorian snores drowned the melancholy tolling of the wayfarers' bell.

In the ancient Roman chapel of the guest-house, the pilgrims were repeating, after the Abbot, the words of the ritual pilgrims' prayer:

'O God, who sent Abraham forth from his own land and safeguarded him in his travels, grant the same protection to these your servants. Support us in danger and ease the rigours of our journeys. Be to us as a shade against the sun, a cloak against the rain and wind. Sustain us in weariness and defend us against all perils. Be to us as the staff that guides our feet and the port that receives the shipwrecked travellers ...'

But Catherine's voice did not join in the prayer with the rest. She was still mulling over the harsh words she had exchanged with Gerbert Bohat, just before coming into the chapel for the Mass and prayers that preceded their departure. When he had seen the young woman appear with Gillette de Vauchelles, still looking very pale, leaning on her arm, the Clermontois had gone white with anger. He had rushed toward them so impetuously that he did not notice Ermengarde bringing up the rear, leaning on two crutches.

'This woman is in no state to continue the pilgrimage,' he said curtly. 'Naturally she may hear the Mass, but I propose to leave her in charge of the nuns.'

Catherine had vowed to herself that she would be gentle and patient in the attempt to mollify Gerbert, but at this she felt an instant stirring of anger that suggested it would take little to make her lose her temper completely.

'And whose decision was that?' she asked with unusual gentleness.

'Mine!'

'And by what right, may I ask?'

'I am the leader of this pilgrimage. I make the decisions!'

'I think you are making a mistake. At the outset of our journey you were deputed leader of our band by the Bishop because you struck him as a worthy man, and because you had already made this journey once before. It is true he appointed you as our guide – but not as our leader in the sense in which you seem to understand the word.'

'Which is to say?'

'That you are no more a captain than we are soldiers! Be content, brother, with guiding us on our way, and don't bother yourself too much with the rest of us! Dame Gillette wishes to continue her journey, and she shall do so!'

A ray of anger that Catherine had learnt to recognise, glittered threateningly in the man's grey eyes. He took a step toward her.

'Do you dare defy my authority?' Gerbert demanded in a shaking voice.

Catherine did not flinch; she even managed a cold smile.

'I'm not defying anything: I'm simply refusing to recognise your right to impose your will on the rest of us. Anyway, you needn't fear that Dame Gillette will cause you any trouble; she will make the rest of the journey on horseback.'

'On horseback? And where do you propose to get a horse?'

Ermengarde, who had been following the conversation with interest, decided that this was the moment for her to intervene. She clattered over to Gerbert.

'I have some horses as it happens, and I am giving her one. Have you any objections?'

This interruption appeared to give the Clermontois no pleasure at all. He frowned and looked at the old lady with evident distaste.

'Who is this?' he asked. 'Where have you sprung from, my good woman?'

It was an unwise move. The Dame de Châteuvillain went bright scarlet. She leant heavily on her crutches and drew herself up to her full height, which manoeuvre brought her face to within a few inches of Gerbert's own.

'It rather behoves me to inquire, my boy, where a coarse-mannered lout like you might have sprung from! Forsooth! You are certainly the first person who has ever addressed me as "good woman", and I would advise you not to be so rash as to repeat the experiment, unless you would like my men to teach you better manners! However, since I propose to join your band for the rest of the journey, in order to travel with my friend the Countess of B … of Montsalvy, I am prepared to tell you that my name is Ermengarde, Lady and Countess of Châteuvillain in the country of Burgundy, and that the Duke Philippe himself weighs his words carefully when he speaks to me. Now have you anything further to add?'

Gerbert Bohat hesitated, obviously restraining himself with some difficulty from making a sharp answer, but the old lady's peremptory manner seemed to have impressed him despite himself. He opened his mouth, shut it, shrugged, and at length said: 'I have not the power to prevent you joining us, much as I should like to, nor to stop your taking this woman with you, since you are going to provide transport for her.'

'Thank you, brother,' Gillette said gently, with a weak smile. 'You see, I have to get to the Apostle's tomb … I absolutely have to, so that my son might recover his health.'

Catherine, whose sharp eyes had not left Bohat's face, seemed to see the anger recede from his eyes like an ebbing tide. A look, almost of regret, passed through them. He looked away.

'Do as you please,' he said curtly.

He went off but, in passing, Catherine met his eyes. This man was now her enemy, she was certain of that. But what she couldn't understand was the curious expression in his face when he looked at her. There was cold anger there, resentment too, but something else besides. And Catherine could have sworn that this other thing was fear.

She was thinking over all this in the chilly chapel, amid the not very musical din of voices proclaiming their trust in the Lord. What was there in her that could possibly inspire fear in a man as self-confident as Gerbert Bohat? … Since no answer to this question suggested itself immediately, Catherine decided to postpone that line of thought till later. It was quite likely too that Ermengarde's vast experience of human nature might come in useful in solving the mystery.

She left the church mechanically, like the others, accepted the piece of bread that the monk in charge of these matters was doling out to each departing pilgrim, then took her place among the rest. She had refused Ermengarde's offer of a horse. Sister Léonarde had skilfully dressed her blistered feet, and she now felt able to walk.

'I'll ask for help when I find I can go no farther,' she told Ermengarde, who was being assisted to mount by two of the nuns. Gillette had been installed on a quiet hack that till then had carried one of Ermengarde's women. The two maids, who together with four men-at-arms comprised her retinue, were made to ride on one horse and took their place at the back of the band, among the few other pilgrims who were making the journey on horseback.

The gates swung open before the pilgrim band, who were heartened by a night of rest and comfort. Snow and fog were but a memory. The sun shone in a clear blue sky, and though the air was still cool and fresh, there were signs of a fine warm day to come. Beyond the walls of the old guest-house, the road, now broadened to a wide stony track, plunged down to a grassy basin that led by degrees into the deep Lot valley, wreathed in a soft blue mist.

Josse Rallard and Colin des Épinettes had stationed themselves, by tacit agreement, one on either side of Catherine. The latter seemed to have lost his gloomy expression of the day before. He gazed over the countryside, which sparkled in the morning light, and gave a great satisfied grin.

'Ah, nature,' he confided to Catherine, 'what a magnificent spectacle! How can we live in stinking cities when there is all this fresh, unspoilt beauty all around us!'

'Especially when there are so many impossible women in the aforesaid cities,' Josse added, with an amiable smile at his companion. The good citizen of Paris, however, seemed not to appreciate this sally. He grew suddenly sombre, shrugged, and stepped out ahead of the other two. Catherine looked questioningly at her companion.

'Why is he cross?' she asked. 'Have you said something unkind to him?'

Josse burst out laughing, winked at her and slung his bag cheerfully over his other shoulder.

'If you want to get on well with the excellent Colin,' he whispered, 'take good care to avoid talking to him of women in general and his own wife in particular.'

'Why is that?'

'Because she is the most frightful harpy God ever flung into our midst; and the only reason our good friend, who has nothing of the knight errant or paladin about him, has entered upon the rigours of this pilgrimage is to escape from her. He has everything a man could want: health, money, a good name. But, alas, he also has Dame Aubierge, and I really think that to get out of her clutches he would be ready to venture as far as the Egyptian Sudan. I am sure that given the choice between a slave's fetters and his armchair in the Rue des Haudriettes, he would choose the fetters!'

'As bad as that?' Catherine cried. 'Does she quarrel with him the whole time?'

'Worse!' Josse exclaimed in a tragic voice. 'She beats him unmercifully!'

Just then, Gerbert, at the head of the band, struck up a psalm to walk to, and at this Josse began to sing a drinking song, which had the merit of being a great deal livelier.

2: THE RUBIES OF
SAINTE-FOY

They completed the difficult journey between Aubrac and the holy city of
Conques in two days, travelling through the Lot valley and the narrow
gorges of Dourdou. Twenty long leagues broken only by a short night's rest
at Espalion, in the former Knights Templars' fort, which was now in the
hands of another order of soldier-monks, that of St John of Jerusalem, who
did their best to succour the weary pilgrims. Gerbert Bohat seemed driven
on by a sort of rage, and refused to listen to the complaints or sighs of his
band.

For Catherine, these two days were positively infernal. Her blistered foot
hurt her cruelly, but she still obstinately refused to continue on horseback.
She had the feeling that if she did not complete this journey like the poorest
of pilgrims, as a penance, God might not take pity on her. She offered up her
sufferings for Arnaud's sake, that the Lord might heal him and then allow
her to find him once again. To obtain a joy as great as that she would gladly
have walked over burning coals …

Nevertheless, had it not been for the aid of an elderly Knight of St John,
who had taken pity on those small, blistered, bleeding feet, at the time of the
ritual washing of feet that the kneeling monks performed for the pilgrims,
and tended them, Catherine would have been obliged to end her journey
there and then, or else to resort to some means of transport. The soldier-
monk had dressed her raw places with an ointment compounded of tallow
fat, olive oil and spirits of wine, which had worked miracles.

'It's an old horseman's recipe,' he had told her, smiling. 'The young men
of our order whose thighs and buttocks are too tender-skinned for long rides
make great use of it.'

He had even given her a little, in a small jar, and the ointment had
proved itself excellent. In spite of everything, however, by the time the little
village and its immense abbey came into sight, clinging to the steep slopes of
the narrow Ouche valley, Catherine was on the verge of collapse. She gave
the most cursory glance at the fine basilica before which her companions all

flung themselves with one accord upon their knees.

'You are at the end of your tether,' Ermengarde hissed at her. 'Now don't take it into your head to follow the others to the abbey – which is full up anyway. There is an excellent inn here, it appears, and I have every intention of spending the night there.'

Catherine hesitated at first, fearful of Gerbert's sarcastic reaction, but the pilgrim leader merely shrugged.

'Stay where you wish. The abbey is full already, and I am not too sure where I can find lodging for us all. Everyone will have to fend for himself. So, do as you wish. But don't forget the High Mass and the procession we shall be making after it, as well as the various prayers and other offices.'

'When will we be leaving again, then?' Catherine inquired anxiously.

'Not till the day after tomorrow. You don't seem to realise that this is one of the high places of the Faith, my sister, and well worth a day of prayer!'

With this he bowed curtly, turned on his heel, and set off toward the abbey gates, ignoring Catherine's protests. Despite the fatigue of these long stages on foot, she would gladly have pressed on at still greater speed, halting for the barest minimum of time along this road that her beloved husband had travelled. Spending a whole day here seemed an appalling waste of time, even if it were to restore her strength.

'Such a waste of time,' she murmured, giving her arm to Ermengarde, who had just been helped down from the saddle by her ladies, not without some difficulty. The Dame de Châteuvillain was likewise tired by the hours spent on horseback, and she was as stiff as a board. But she had lost none of her spirit.

'I'll wager I know what you are thinking, my dear,' she said gaily as she led Catherine through the entrance to a large inn, the buttressed walls of which gave it something of the look of a fortress.

'What, then?'

'You would give a lot to be able to mount a good horse tomorrow, leave all these Paternoster-sayers to their own devices and gallop like the wind toward that town in Galicia where you believe there is something waiting for you.'

Catherine did not even trouble to deny it. She gave a smile of infinite weariness.

'It's true, Ermengarde! The slowness of this pilgrimage is killing me. Just imagine, we are still so near to Montsalvy that I could easily slip across to embrace my son. But I set out on this pilgrimage as a pilgrim and I don't intend to cheat God. Unless something turns up along the way, suggesting that I must seek Arnaud elsewhere, I shall carry on to the end of the road, with my companions. And besides, it is as well to be numerous. The road is dangerous, beset by bandits, and it is wise to travel in strength. With your women and men-at-arms, there would be only seven of us. And even then, there's no knowing if we should be as many as that all the way, for I see one of your men has run away already.'

This was indeed the case. When they had left Espalion at dawn, Ermengarde's escort had no longer consisted of four men, for one of them had been missing. But, to Catherine's surprise, the old lady had seemed not unduly put out. She had merely shrugged.

'Burgundians don't like travelling,' she had said. 'And the idea of going to Spain did not appeal to Saulgeon. He must have preferred to return home.'

This unexpectedly philosophical attitude had intrigued Catherine. She knew Ermengarde, and the strictness with which she treated her servants, too well not to find her reaction incomprehensible. Had the formidable old lady changed as much as that?

The inn at Sainte-Foy welcomed the Dame de Châteuvillain with all the honour due to one of her rank. Ermengarde had an extraordinary knack for getting herself the best service. Though the hostelry was crowded, she instantly obtained two rooms, one for herself and Catherine, and one for her women and Gillette de Vauchelles, whom she definitely seemed to have taken under her wing.

The travellers downed their supper quickly and silently. They were all weary. But whereas Ermengarde climbed into bed the moment she entered her room, and quickly fell asleep, Catherine lingered for a time at the window that looked out over the little square. Her heart was too heavy for sleep. Besides, it was not so important to sleep well that night, since they would not be leaving the next day.

Sitting on the little stone ledge below the window, Catherine let her eyes wander over the strange, colourful spectacle down below. As often happened in these pilgrim centres, a troupe of tumblers and jugglers had taken up position outside the church porch itself, and were performing their tricks there before some assembled villagers and a handful of pilgrims who were going to have to spend the night sleeping on the ground. There were musicians among them who played the viol, lute, harp and flute. A thin lad, wearing a costume half green, half yellow, was juggling with flaming torches. Meanwhile, a storyteller sat at the foot of one of the two Roman towers, draped in gaily coloured rags, deep in the midst of recounting some adventurous exploit, forefinger raised and a look of inspiration lighting his face, to a ring of girls and boys. A little farther off, a slender girl dressed in scarlet was dancing barefoot, leaping to the rhythm of the music, in front of the high stone façade where a majestic figure of Christ, proud and angular, raised a hand in blessing over a multitude carved in stone. The torchlight seemed to bring to life the figures carved in the prodigious Last Judgement over the tympanum, like characters in a drama. Gilded and painted as they were, it all resembled the illuminated pages of some rich and rare Gospel.

The elect looked as if they were about to take off for the celestial regions, while the damned seemed to grimace all the more agonisingly amid grinning devils in the torments of Hell.

The magic of the scene moved Catherine, and she reflected that this was the very spot where she would be joining the road that Arnaud, and then poor Gauthier, had taken. One after another, the Knight in the black mask, together with his skinny Squire, and the great blond Norman must have alighted before this noble porch, and mingled for a moment with the crowd, which just now lay dreaming beneath the stars ... Catherine had only to close her eyes for an instant to conjure them up quite vividly, the fleeing leper and the child of the northern forests. Where were they now? What had become of them, and what traces of them was she likely to find, speeding in their pursuit with only her frail woman's resources? For not only did Catherine find it impossible to admit that Arnaud was lost to her forever, she also refused to believe in a dead Gauthier. There was something indestructible about the giant. Death could never have struck him down like that, in his prime, at the height of his powers. She would not succeed in laying him low for many years to come; not till her valet, Old Age, had worked his vile will on that granite body.

Suddenly Catherine's reverie was interrupted. She had just recognised Gerbert Bohat watching the entertainment in the crowd below. She saw him go up to the dancer in red. The girl, panting from her exertions, was just on the point of passing a tambourine round in the crowd when the Clermontois seized hold of her. Though the incident took place at some distance, Catherine had no trouble in making out the gist of their dialogue. Gerbert's hand first pointed at the girl's low-necked, sparkling dress, then at the great Christ carved on the church façade, and his meaning was crystal clear. He was reproaching her for giving a performance in front of a church wearing clothes he judged immodest. And it seemed that this tall black figure standing over her frightened the young girl, because she raised her arm as if fearing to be struck.

But soon Catherine began to feel vaguely alarmed. Gerbert's puritan zeal seemed not to the liking of a group of young peasants who, until this incident, had been listening to the storyteller. They saw nothing wrong in dancing in front of the church and undertook to defend the dancer. One of them, a sturdy lad whose powerful build reminded Catherine a bit of Gauthier's, seized Gerbert by the collar of his tunic, while three more advanced upon him threateningly and the girl's shrill voice began to insult him ... In a moment Gerbert Bohat would find himself in a sorry way.

Catherine could not have explained the impulse that prompted her to act as she did. She really had no sympathy for this man, whom she considered harsh, sardonic and pitiless. Maybe she acted as she did only because she needed him to guide her as far as Galicia ... But, in any event, she went running from the room, rushed out into the courtyard where Ermengarde's men were drinking a last cup of wine before retiring to bed, and summoned the Sergeant.

'Quick!' she commanded. 'Go and help the pilgrim leader! The crowd will tear him to pieces! ...'

The men picked up their arms and ran out. She followed them without quite knowing why, the soldiers having no need of her. Perhaps she just wanted to see how Gerbert would react. As it happened, the whole incident blew over rapidly. The three Burgundians had broad shoulders, massive fists, features hardened by years of fighting, and gleaming weapons. The crowd parted before them like the sea under a ship's prow, and Catherine, hurrying along in their wake, found herself standing beside Gerbert in the abbey porch. The crowd were still mumbling and growling, but they were falling back now like an angry dog threatened by the whip. Slowly they dispersed, and most of them returned to watch the minstrels. who were already back to their tricks.

'You're safe now, messire,' Sergeant Béraud told Gerbert. 'Go back to sleep now and let the poor folk enjoy themselves: they're not doing any harm.' Then he turned to Catherine. 'Lady, we have done as you wished. Shall we escort you back to the inn?'

'Go back without me,' she answered. 'I'm not sleepy.'

'If I am not mistaken, I owe this intervention to you,' Bohat said dryly as the men-at-arms departed. 'Did I by chance call to you for help?'

'You are much too proud for that! On the contrary, I think you would happily have let yourself be lynched. But I saw you were in difficulties and I thought ...'

'When women start thinking ...' Bohat sighed, with a look of such contempt that Catherine began to lose her temper. This man was not merely strange, he was frankly hateful. She didn't hesitate to tell him so.

'I grant that they often do foolish things, especially when they take it into their heads to save the life of a remarkable masculine mind. Truly, messire, I beg you to accept my regrets and apologies. I would have done much better to have sat peacefully at my window and watched them hang you from the abbey gateway, after which, certain that you had died a Christian death for the greater good of the faith, I would have gone to bed, first saying a prayer for the repose of that great soul! Still, now the worst has come to the worst, I shall leave you. Goodnight, Messire Gerbert!'

She was just about to leave when he detained her. This volley of sarcasm seemed to have astounded him, and when Catherine turned, she saw that every trace of anger had gone from his face.

'Forgive me, Dame Catherine,' he said hoarsely. 'It is true that if you had not helped me these poor people would have taken my life. And I should be grateful to you. But,' he added, as the violence crept back into his voice, 'it is hard for me to thank a woman, especially since my life is an intolerable burden to me. If I did not fear God I would have put an end to it long ago!'

'Putting others into the position of taking it for you is a trick that wouldn't have fooled God for a moment. I might add that your crime would be doubly evil in that case, because to your own secret intention would be added the evil you had driven innocent people to commit. As for your thanks, don't feel obligated. I would have done the same for anyone.'

Gerbert did not answer, but as Catherine stepped out in the direction of the inn, he began to follow her, stooping a little. Suddenly he seemed loath to leave her, and Catherine could not understand this new whim. Then, since he was silent, she spoke up:

'You hate women, don't you?'

'With all my heart, with all my soul … They are the pitfall into which men are forever falling.'

'Why this hatred? What have they done to you? Have you no mother?'

'She was the one pure woman I have ever known. All the rest are but filth, wantonness and falsity.'

Catherine might well have felt insulted by this harsh verdict. Nevertheless, she felt nothing but pity, because behind Gerbert's hatred she sensed a torment that dared not declare itself.

'Have you always hated them?' she asked. 'Or …?'

He did not let her finish. 'Or is it that I have loved them too much? In truth, I believe it is that. It is because I have carried the accursed craving for woman in my blood that she is my long-standing enemy. I hate her!'

A candle flame flickered on the shop counter where holy images and relics were for sale, illuminating for a moment the tall pilgrim's face and hands, one of which was holding his black cloak. His features glowed with the most sombre passion, and his free hand trembled. A rebellious instinct made Catherine pause.

'Look at me,' she ordered,' and tell me if you really think of me as filth, wantonness and falsity …

She stood still in the golden light, presenting her delicate face with its golden halo – freed from the dark hood of the day – waving softly round it. Heavy ringlets tumbled about her neck, giving her back something of the queenly coronet of former days, twice sacrificed. With a faint smile she contemplated her companion, now ghastly pale. He seemed turned to stone, but a statue with eyes of flame.

'Come, Messire Gerbert, answer me!'

At this he made a frightened gesture, like a man trying to ward off a diabolic vision, and fell back into the shadow of the abbey wall.

'You are so beautiful you can only be a demon sent on purpose to tempt me! But you won't get the better of me, do you hear. You won't get the better of me! *Vade retro Satanas!*'

A sort of holy terror seemed to have seized him, and he was about to run away. Catherine realised that it would never be possible to reason with this man; he was sick to the very soul.

She shrugged; her smile vanished. 'Don't talk nonsense,' she said tiredly. 'There is nothing diabolic about me. You seek peace for the soul, but I am looking for something else ... But this thing I seek is not within your power, or that of any other man to confer upon me, except for one alone.'

Gerbert could not resist asking: 'Who is this man?'

'I don't think that concerns you, Messire Gerbert,' Catherine said with a sigh. 'Goodnight.'

And this time she set off for the inn without his making any attempt to restrain her. The night was peaceful, and the sounds of day in the little town were being extinguished one by one. A bell tolled somewhere. A dog started barking. Catherine felt weary now, and vaguely depressed. She had hoped to lighten the tension between herself and Gerbert somehow, but now she saw this was never to be. This man carried a secret with him that it was not in her power to pierce. And all her attempts to humanise him were useless. So why bother?

The next day seemed endless to Catherine. She spent most of it tending her blistered foot, but she still had to attend all the extra ceremonies with the other pilgrims. Yet there was too much impatience in her for her to be able to pray calmly.

She had knelt for interminable moments gazing at the barbarous, magnificent gold statue of Sainte-Foy, wreathed in incense, sparkling with precious stones more thickly encrusted than flowers on a meadow in spring. It was a strange, almost terrifying statue, with its implacable face and staring eyes, like some fantastic apparition, and Catherine stared at it with a kind of fear, unable to visualise in it the little 13-year-old girl saint who had once been martyred for her faith. To her it looked more like a fearful sort of idol, and its fixed dilated eyes oppressed her.

Still, it was said of her that she had the power to set prisoners free. Irons, chains, manacles and fetters were piled behind her, a moving expression of gratitude. However, Catherine felt stifled in this dark church amid these prostrate worshippers, prisoner of an impatient love from which nothing could release her.

She had pins and needles in her knees from so much kneeling, and this reminded her of the endless prayers she had been obliged to recite by the side of her sister Loyse, Notre-Dame of Dijon. She stood up, turned and found Gerbert Bohat's eyes full upon her. He looked away at once, but just had time to catch in them that strange half-fierce, half-fearful look that she had noticed before. Catherine sighed wearily.

'You shouldn't get angry with him,' Gillette's gentle voice whispered beside her. 'Gerbert is an unhappy man.'

'How do you know?'

'I don't know it, but I feel it … He suffers torments; that is what makes him so harsh.'

In spite of her resolution and good intentions, Catherine could not bring herself to follow the long procession that was to carry the statue all round the town and thence into the drought-stricken countryside. She returned to the inn and joined Ermengarde, who was still in bed. The dowager watched her come in with the ghost of a smile.

'Haven't you had your bellyful of Paternosters yet, Catherine? When are you going to be reasonable and take my advice and my horse? Do you really want to go with this band of pilgrims when we could travel so much faster?'

Catherine folded her lips tightly and threw a sidelong glance at her friend as she folded up her cloak.

'Don't keep on about that, Ermengarde. I've already given you my reasons. The road is dangerous; it is best to travel in numbers to deter the bandits.'

The old lady stretched and yawned widely, then sighed. 'For my part, I'll wager that good fast horses are a better way of escaping from brigands than sore feet. What is more, I warn you that if we go on much longer like this, you will go out of your mind … and me too!'

In her heart of hearts Catherine agreed with Ermengarde, but she did not want to admit this. She was convinced that if she didn't continue her journey with the pilgrims to the bitter end, God would hold it against her and punish her by preventing her finding Arnaud. But the Dame de Châteuvillain had always known how to read what lay behind her friend's pretty, expressive face. She murmured:

'Come now, Catherine, give God credit for a little grandeur of soul – don't think of him as some base merchant who is interested only in driving a bargain. What of his clemency?'

'I put great trust in that, Ermengarde; but nevertheless we shall continue our journey with the rest!'

She spoke decisively, in a tone that brooked no argument. Ermengarde realised this, and a sigh of discouragement was her only reply.

The procession round Sainte-Foy proved altogether efficacious, because it was raining buckets at dawn the following morning when the pilgrims resumed their journey and left Conques amid the usual pious chants. Catherine was back in her usual place between Josse Rallard and Colin des Épinettes. She stepped out bravely, refusing to see Ermengarde and her mounted attendants who were following. The Countess had somehow managed at their last stop to procure two new horses, one of which carried one of her chambermaids while the other trotted along riderless, with Sergeant Béraud holding the leading reins. Catherine was quite aware that this particular animal was destined for herself, but she preferred to ignore the fact.

The road climbed steeply up the hill toward the Lot valley and Figeac. And the rain didn't help matters. It blurred the countryside, blotting out the soft pinks of budding heather, dripping from every leaf, streaming into the eyes and making the coarse frieze pilgrim cloaks sodden and heavy. Fine and gentle one minute, painfully stinging when driven by a whiplash of wind, it cast a dreadful gloom over that severe countryside, a heavy melancholy that seemed to crush Catherine's very soul. There was no singing that morning. Gerbert walked ahead, stooped, head bowed, never once turning round.

Suddenly, just as they reached the top of the hill, they heard cries behind them.

'Stop … stop, for God's sake!'

Gerbert did turn round this time, and the rest with him. Lower down the slope they saw three breathless monks running as best they could. Every now and then they stumbled over a stone or tuft of heather, but this only made them cry out the louder and signal more frantically.

'What's up?' Colin mumbled irritably. 'Have we forgotten something, or can those holy men be intending to join us?'

'That would surprise me,' said Josse Rallard, who watched them approach, frowning. 'They aren't carrying anything and they haven't any staffs.'

'Then it must be that they want us to remember them in our prayers at the Apostle's tomb,' Colin remarked piously. But his companion threw him such a withering look that he checked his fancies. By now Gerbert Bohat was striding swiftly back to meet the new arrivals. He joined them not far from Catherine and her companions, so that she did not miss a word they were saying. Anyway, short of breath as they were, the three monks were shouting loud enough to crack the rocks.

'We have been robbed! Five big rubies have been stolen from the cloak of Sainte-Foy!'

An indignant, angry uproar greeted this piece of news, but Gerbert was already retorting, with instant aggressiveness:

'That's an abominable deed, but I still don't see why you have come running after us to tell us the news! I trust you don't suppose that one of us is your culprit! You may be holy men, but we are God's pilgrims too!'

The tallest of the monks wiped his broad pink face with an embarrassed air, and gestured helplessly.

'The black sheep of the Devil may sometimes be hidden among the best of us. The mere fact of joining a pilgrimage does not in itself constitute a guarantee of saintliness. There have been cases …'

'We weren't the only pilgrims at Conques yesterday … or whenever the theft was committed. I admire your Christian charity, which prefers to attack some poor pilgrims rather than that rabble of tumblers and jugglers who were performing in front of your church the other evening.'

Catherine repressed a smile. Gerbert seemingly still had his adventure very much on his mind. But the monk looked more unhappy than ever.

'They all left the town yesterday morning, as you must know, and when the statue appeared at the procession yesterday, it was intact, not a stone was missing.'

'Are you quite sure?'

'It was I myself and the two other brothers here who were given the task by the Lord Abbot of making sure of the statue's condition before returning it to its niche. I can assure you that not a single stone was missing. This morning, five large rubies have gone … and you were the only strangers to spend last night in the town!'

A silence followed this evidence. Everyone held their breath, convinced of the monk's logic. Gerbert, however, refused to admit himself beaten. Catherine could not help admiring the courage and stubbornness with which he defended his little flock.

'That doesn't prove that we are guilty! Conques may be a holy city but it is still a city, for all that, populated by men who could be guilty of evil deeds.'

'We know our own black sheep, and the Lord Abbot has been taking care of them since this morning. My brother … it would be so much simpler to prove that none of you has taken the missing jewels!'

'What do you mean?'

'That there are only three of us, but if you were willing, it would not take us so long to search you.'

'In this rain?' Gerbert answered disdainfully. 'And would you take it upon yourselves to search the women?'

'Two sisters are following close behind. Ah, here they are,' said the monk, who seemed to have an answer to everything. 'And there is a little shrine, not far away, where I think we could install ourselves. I beg of you, brother. The glory of Sainte-Foy and of God is at stake!'

By standing on tiptoe, Catherine managed to make out two nuns hurrying along the path, as wet and breathless as their companions. Gerbert did not answer straightaway; he was thinking – and the young woman, indignant though she might feel at the news that a holy relic had been robbed, could share his thoughts. This search must deeply disgust him. And this further waste of time must annoy him as much as it did Catherine herself … A moment later he gazed round him.

'What do you think, brothers? Are you willing to submit to this … this disagreeable formality?'

'The pilgrimage enjoins humility upon us,' said Colin sententiously. 'This humiliation will be good for us, and Saint James will add it to the list of our merits!'

'Of course,' Catherine cried impatiently. 'But then do let's hurry up. We have already wasted far too much time.'

The band of pilgrims went across to the little stone shrine, which stood a bit farther on, just at the shoulder of the hill. From there the whole city of Conques could be clearly seen, but no-one was in a mood to admire the view. They would have to stand for some time under the heavy rain.

'I must say, these journeys in large numbers are great fun,' Ermengarde commented ironically, riding up just then beside Catherine. 'These good monks are keeping watch over us as if we were a flock of black sheep. I trust they don't expect me to let myself be searched!'

'You must allow it, my dear friend! Otherwise they will suspect you, and in the mood my companions are in, they might do something unpleasant! Oh … how clumsy you are, brother!'

The last part of this remark was addressed to Josse, who had stumbled over a stone and fallen so heavily against her that they both fell on their knees on the wayside.

'I am very sorry,' the Parisian replied, looking deeply contrite, 'but this track has more holes in it than a mendicant friar's habit! I hope I haven't hurt you?'

He helped her solicitously up to her feet and brushed the mud off her cloak and dress with such an apologetic air that she hadn't the heart to be angry.

'It's all right,' she said, smiling sweetly. 'I don't imagine this will be the last time!'

Then she went and sat beside Ermengarde under the porch of the little chapel. The nuns had just gone in. It had been agreed that the women would be examined first so that the sisters might return the more speedily to their convent. But meanwhile a few men of good will, Gerbert among them, were letting themselves be searched out of doors. Luckily the rain was beginning to lighten.

'The countryside is beautiful,' Catherine remarked, pointing at the vast panorama in grey, green and blue that unrolled below them.

'Ah, yes, the countryside is beautiful!' Ermengarde repeated mockingly. 'But how I wish it were farther behind us! Ah, there's one of my women coming out now! It's our turn. Help me up, will you!'

Leaning against each other, the two friends passed into the chapel. It was cold and damp in there, and unpleasantly musty, and the old lady could not help shivering, in spite of her warm clothes.

'Hurry up, you two!' Ermengarde told the nuns unceremoniously. 'And don't be frightened, I've never eaten anyone yet,' she added slyly, seeing their anxious faces. They were both of them still young, and visibly overawed by this powerful woman who spoke with so much assurance. But they proceeded to search her minutely nonetheless, while Ermengarde pawed the ground impatiently. After that, the older of the two turned to Catherine, who stood waiting her turn.

'Now for you, sister,' she exclaimed. 'First, give me that purse hanging from your belt!'

Wordlessly Catherine unfastened the solid leather pouch in which she carried her rosary, a little money, the dagger with the sparrow-hawk crest that she was never without, and the carved emerald given to her by Queen Yolande. The deliberate plainness of her attire did not allow of wearing so valuable a jewel on her finger, but she did not want to be parted from it nevertheless. Especially not since she was travelling into Spain, whence the Queen had originally come herself, and where her coat of arms might be of some assistance, as Yolande had suggested herself.

The nun emptied out the contents of the purse on the narrow stone altar and, catching sight of the dagger, flashed a sidelong look at Catherine.

'A strange thing for a woman who is supposed to need no defence but prayer!' she remarked.

'That dagger is my husband's,' the young woman answered dryly. 'I always carry it with me, and I have learned how to defend myself with it against bandits!'

'Who would doubtless be greatly interested in this!' the nun added, pointing to the ring! A flush of anger rose to Catherine's cheeks. The thinly veiled insolence of this woman exasperated her and she seized at this chance of shutting her up.

'Queen Yolande, Duchess of Anjou and mother of our Queen, gave it to me herself. Have you any objection to that? I am ...'

'Oh a great lady, I have no doubt,' the other woman said, smiling sarcastically. 'That's quite obvious when one sees these. What have you to say to this, noble lady?'

As Catherine looked on aghast, she unfolded a little cloth that the young woman had not observed till then. Against its grubby whiteness there sparkled, like five drops of red blood, the magnificent rubies of Sainte-Foy ...

'What's this?' Catherine cried. 'I have never seen them before. Ermengarde!'

'Witchcraft!' the stout dame asserted. 'How did those jewels get there? It must ...'

'Witchcraft or not, we have the jewels,' the nun cried. 'And you will answer for this theft!'

She seized Catherine by the arm and dragged her from the chapel, shouting.

'Brothers! Stop! We have the rubies. And this is the thief!'

Red with shame and anger before the barrage of inquisitorial eyes suddenly turned upon her, Catherine tore herself out of the nun's dry hand.

'It's not true! I didn't steal anything! I don't know how those jewels got into my purse! Someone must have put them in there!'

She was interrupted by a growl of anger from the other pilgrims. She realised, with terror, that they didn't believe her. Enraged by the rain, the delay, the accusation weighing over them, all these good people were on the point of changing into so many wolves. Panic swelled in her. She stood there while the menacing circle closed in on her and the hate-filled woman bellowed beside her that she must be taken back to Conques, handed over to the Abbot's judgement, hanged ...

But that was as far as the good sister got, because just then, Ermengarde, who had come hobbling across on her crutches, seized her by the arm and shook her like a plum tree.

'Stop this yelling,' she roared. 'Come now, my girl, are you quite out of your mind! Accusing a noblewoman of theft! ... Do you know who you are talking about?'

'A thief!' the woman shrieked, quite beside herself. 'A wanton who carries a dagger upon her person together with the fruits of another theft. This ring that she claims Queen Yolande gave her –'

Once more she was silenced. But this time Ermengarde's beautiful hand had struck her across the face with all the strength its owner could command. Her five fingers were left imprinted on it in red.

'Let that teach you a little courtesy and moderation, my sister,' she cried, heavily emphasising the word 'sister'. 'Dear Lord, if all the convents are peopled with harpies like you, God must be somewhat uncomfortable with his brides!'

Then she raised her voice and cried: 'Hello, there, Béraud and you others! To arms!'

Before the astounded pilgrims dreamed of stopping them, the three Burgundians spurred their horses into the middle of the circle formed by the three women with the chapel at their back. Béraud calmly drew his sword while his men started fitting arrows into their huge bows. The pilgrims followed these threatening preparations in total silence. Ermengarde smiled broadly.

'The first to move will be cut down at three paces,' she said harshly. Then, suddenly changing her tone to one of amiability: 'Now that the odds are a little more evenly disposed, by all means let us talk!'

Despite her threat, Gerbert Bohat had stepped two paces forward. One of her men drew his bow, but Ermengarde stayed him with a gesture, while

Gerbert raised one hand.

'May I speak?'

'Speak, Messire Bohat!'

'Is it true the rubies were found on this … this …?'

He did not dare use the word, but Catherine was stung to fury nevertheless.

'Oh yes! Yes, brother!' she replied. 'But before God and the threat of eternal damnation, I swear to you I have no idea how they came there!'

'Lies!' cried the nun.

'Ah, I shall lose my temper in a minute,' Ermengarde growled. 'Be quiet, woman, or I cannot answer for you, or for myself. Now continue, Messire Bohat!'

Gerbert came forward but did not lower his voice.

'On the one hand there is evidence … *flagrante delicto* … and on the other this woman's word alone …'

'Brother,' Ermengarde cut in impatiently, 'if you persist in referring to Dame Catherine in this fashion, I shall cut your tongue out. May I know what your intention is?'

The man's hard gaze did not falter. He directed it contemptuously at Catherine, who trembled with rage, and then turned back to his friends.

'The one sensible thing is to hand … Dame Catherine over to the holy monks, so that they can take her back to Conques and to the Abbot's judgement –'

'Where she would be lynched by the crowd before even getting as far as the abbey! No, messire, she is not going back to Conques. Her word may not be enough for you, but it is quite enough for me, because I know her well. Now, listen closely: you have your rubies back, that is excellent. Take them, sir monk, give them back to your saint … with this to make amends for your trouble …'

As she spoke, she tossed a heavy purse to the nearest monk, who caught it in mid air. 'As for ourselves, you will let us depart in peace!'

'Or else?' Gerbert asked heartily.

'Or else,' said Ermengarde calmly, 'we will cut our way through!'

'You are few in number!'

'Maybe so, but we have weapons, and courage! Each of my men is worth ten. So the odds are equal. It is possible we might be at a disadvantage, but I don't think so. And in any case, our deaths would cost you dear. Not many of you would be left to continue the journey safely toward Compostela. Catherine, ask our good sister to return what belongs to you.'

'Never!' cried the nun, who was clearly determined not to give up. 'This jewel too is certainly the spoil of some theft. It must be given to the Abbot as well.'

With an impatient sigh, the Countess snatched the purse from her, made sure it contained everything it should, and handed it back to Catherine without a word. Then, turning to one of her women, she ordered:

'Amielle! The horses! Leave Dame Gillette de Vauchelles the one she is riding on ...'

But Gillette stepped forward resolutely and stationed herself beside Catherine.

'I will go with you. I believe in Dame Catherine's innocence. No criminal would ever be as kind as she is!'

'And I believe in her too!' cried Margot. 'I want to go with you too. Besides, Dame Gillette has need of me.'

Ermengarde started to laugh.

'Take care, Messire Bohat, or you will soon find yourself all alone!'

'That would surprise me. These good people have no desire to continue their journey in company with a woman suspected of theft, who might well bring God's curse upon us all. Go ... since it is not possible to deliver the guilty woman up to justice without shedding innocent blood. We want no more of you!'

He stood facing the band of pilgrims, who huddled closer together as if to avoid all contact with Catherine. Some of them crossed themselves ... Catherine could have cried with rage. And when she looked at Gerbert, standing very upright in his dark clothes, heavy staff in hand, she felt like screaming. She felt branded by shame as by a red-hot iron. While Ermengarde signed to her to mount the riderless horse, she cried:

'How can I leave without proving my innocence, without ...'

'If there were the slightest chance of your doing so, I would advise you to return to Conques,' Ermengarde replied, 'but these folk would not leave you time to do so. They are obstinate bigots. As for you, my dear, when one bears a name like yours, one need not concern oneself with the opinion of clods like these. Come, into the saddle with you!'

Somewhat soothed by the contempt, quite equal to that Gerbert had shown, vibrating in the old lady's voice, Catherine placed her foot on Béraud's hand and sprang into the saddle ... The crowd parted before the little band, which included Gillette and, sitting pillion behind her, Margot, happy as a child on holiday ... Every face was turned toward them with fear and disapproval, at which the Countess shrugged impatiently. But as she passed before Gerbert Bohat, Catherine reined in her horse and cried out, very loudly:

'You condemned me unheard, Messire Bohat. In your eyes, one is condemned as soon as suspected. Is that your idea of justice and equity? When I've sworn on my eternal salvation that I've not touched the jewels, couldn't you have believed me? Anyone could tell you that I returned to the inn before the procession and left it again only ...'

'Now why waste your time arguing with these people. They are all as stubborn as mules,' Ermengarde cried impatiently.

Nevertheless Gerbert looked up at the young woman and murmured in a colourless voice:

'You could have had an accomplice. If you are innocent, go in peace, but I do not see how that is possible. As for me ...'

'As for you, you are only too pleased to have found a pretext to stop me travelling any farther with you, aren't you?'

'Yes,' he said frankly. 'I am glad! No man can think seriously about his spiritual salvation while you are around. You are a dangerous woman. It is fitting that you should leave us.'

Catherine gave a bitter laugh. 'Thank you for the compliment. Continue your pious journey, Messire Bohat, but remember that the dangers you shun will always be there till you find enough spiritual strength to resist them. Something tells me we shall meet again, if only at Compostela!'

This time Gerbert said nothing. But he crossed himself so hastily and with such real terror that Catherine almost laughed in his face. However, Ermengarde had taken Catherine's horse by the bridle and was dragging her off.

'That's enough, my dear. Now come!'

Catherine followed her friend docilely, and then, taking her horse's reins, she set off at a canter across the short plateau between them and the Lot valley. The rain, which had stopped completely, now started falling again, but gently, slowly, almost apologetically, too fine to be a serious nuisance. Despite herself, Catherine looked around at the empty spaces with a sort of rapture. She felt the urge to spur her horse, break into a gallop and rediscover the exhilaration of a headlong ride into the wind ... But Ermengarde's weight and her injured leg would not permit her to indulge in such antics. She would have to keep to this peaceful pace for some while longer.

Behind the riders there arose the sound of singing, carried across to them by the south wind:

'Maria, star of the sea,
'Brighter than the sun,
'Lead us through this dark valley,
'Lead us: *Ave Maria* ...'

Catherine gritted her teeth, instinctively gripping her horse between her knees. She had the absurd impression that this song was another, still more positive way of rejecting her from the pious throng. Was it to protect themselves from the curse they felt she had brought upon them that the pilgrims were calling upon Our Lady so fervently?

Gradually, as the distance lengthened between them, the song grew fainter, and finally died away altogether. Ermengarde had spurred her mount forward to join Catherine, and now the two women rode along for a while in silence. But suddenly Catherine, who had been brooding silently over her humiliation, noticed that a broad smile had spread over her companion's imposing countenance. She felt that Ermengarde was savouring her triumph, and cried furiously:

'I suppose you are happy now? I'm doing just as you wanted now – in fact, I'm almost prepared to believe you put those jewels in my purse yourself!'

The dowager did not seem offended by her friend's sharpness. She merely said:

'I only wish I'd had the foresight and imagination to think of it! I'd certainly have tried something like that. Now come, Catherine, stop looking so angry. You will get to Spain twice as quickly now, and God can hardly be angry with you, since it isn't your fault. As for the dangers ahead, I somehow think we shall be perfectly equal to them. Look … see how the sky is clearing ahead of us. The clouds seem to be rolling away from our road. Doesn't that strike you as a good omen?'

In spite of her annoyance Catherine couldn't help smiling.

'I should have remembered, my dear Ermengarde, that you have always had the gift of keeping heaven on your side … or at least making everyone believe that it was. All the same, I'd dearly like to know how those cursed rubies came into my possession and who could possibly have stolen them!'

The answer to this question presented himself that very evening; exhausted and breathless from his exertions. Catherine and her companions had reached Figeac, where they had rooms in the largest inn of the town, opposite the magistrate's court, and the ancient Hostel de la Moneda. Catherine and Ermengarde were both tired, more from the morning's adventure than from the day's riding, which had not been unduly arduous. They let the other women go off to the church for vespers and stayed in the inn courtyard, sitting under a great plane tree, where a magnificent and quite unexpected sunset was slowly fading. No less unexpected was the man who suddenly appeared and fell on his knees before Catherine, imploring her forgiveness.

'I stole the rubies,' Josse Rallard declared, quite distinctly but not too loudly, because of the servants passing to and fro in the inn yard, carrying baskets of linen. 'And it was I who slipped them into your purse when I pretended to fall and we tumbled down together. I've come to beg your forgiveness.'

While Catherine, too thunderstruck to speak, sat gazing in astonishment at the exhausted and dusty-looking man kneeling humbly at her feet, Ermengarde made a superhuman effort to drag herself up from the bench where she was sitting and reach for her crutches. Having failed to do this she roared:

'And you calmly come and tell us about it ... without even the grace to blush? Well, my lad, I shall have to hand you over to the magistrate without delay; no doubt he will have a length of spare rope for you. You there!'

But Catherine silenced her with a restraining hand on the arm. Her violet eyes were fixed on the man's strange greenish ones, and his features, which were a curious blend of brutality and refinement.

'Wait a minute. I want him to answer two questions first!'

'Question me,' Josse said, 'and I will answer.'

'First of all, why did you do this thing?'

'Steal the rubies? Lady,' he said, shrugging, 'I see I shall have to tell you everything. My only reason for taking the high road to Galicia was to place a comfortable distance between myself and the gentlemen of the watch who await me at Paris with a length of stout rope. I used to dwell in the Court of Miracles, but lately I have been unable to leave the place, because I was becoming too well known. So I decided it was time I saw a bit of the country ... I knew opportunities would turn up along the way ... And when I saw that statue all of gold, all set with jewels, I thought to myself that no-one would ever notice if I removed a few, whereas my own old age would thereby be comfortably provided for. The temptation was too much for me.'

'That's all very well, but having committed your crime, why let me be accused of it?' Catherine cried. 'How could you do such a thing? You must have known I could have been hanged for it!'

Josse shook his head vigorously, apparently undismayed. 'No, the risk you ran was much smaller than mine would have been. I'm only a poor creature, a mere beggar! But you are a great lady! And they don't just hang ladies like that. Besides, there was your friend here. The noble lady had the means of defence ... men-at-arms. I knew she would fight for you tooth and nail. But no-one would have intervened on my behalf. They would have strung me up from the handiest tree, and never mind a trial. I was dreadfully frightened ... so frightened my guts were all twisted. I thought it would be some time before anyone noticed the theft, and then no-one would suspect the holy pilgrims, and in any case we should have covered quite a bit of ground by then. When I saw the monks coming, I knew all was lost, so ...'

'So you passed the booty on to me,' Catherine finished calmly. 'And supposing things had turned out badly for me?'

'I swear before God, whom I believe in despite everything, that I would have given myself up. And if they refused to believe me, I would have fought to the death for you!'

Catherine was silent a moment, weighing his words with unusual gravity. At last she said:

'Now the second question. Why have you come here now? Why confess?

I am free, perfectly safe, and so are you. But in coming here you were staking everything – you were not to know how I would react, if I would hand you over to the authorities.'

'It was a risk I had to run,' Josse said coolly. 'I didn't want to stay with those bloodthirsty bead-tellers. I had had enough of Gerbert Bohat and Messire Colin. Once you had left, the journey wasn't interesting anymore, and ...'

'And I dare say you told yourself,' Ermengarde sneered, 'that the Queen's emerald might compensate for the loss of the rubies? You don't keep your eyes in your pocket, do you?'

But Josse again refused to be drawn. With his eyes fixed on Catherine's he added: 'If you believe that, Dame Catherine, denounce me without more ado. What I wanted to say to you was this: I wronged you to save my own life, but I am very sorry for having done so. I have come to offer you my services by way of reparation. If you will allow me to, I will serve you, and defend you ... I am a beggar, but I am strong and I can wield a sword like a gentleman. On roads such as these, one can always do with a strong arm. Will you then pardon me, and take me on as your servitor? I swear to serve you faithfully, 'pon my eternal soul ...'

Once again, silence, with Josse on his knees, motionless as he awaited Catherine's answer. Far from feeling angry, she found herself oddly touched by this bizarre youth whose his flagrant dishonesty was allied with strangely elevated sentiments and undeniable charm. The most outrageous remarks when he spoke them seemed perfectly natural. Nevertheless, before answering, she looked up at Ermengarde, who sat with lips tightly folded, likewise silent, but ominously so.

'What would you advise, my dear friend?'

The dowager shrugged crossly. 'What do you want me to say? You seem endowed with all the talent of the sorceress Circe, who changed men into pigs. But apparently you perform the opposite trick. Do just as you want – but I already know what you are going to say.'

As she spoke, Ermengarde leant across and grasped her crutches, pulled herself to her feet, refusing Catherine's assistance, and stood there triumphantly. Catherine was alarmed to think she might have offended her friend, and asked her anxiously:

'Where are you going, Ermengarde? Please, don't be cross with me ...'

'Where do you think I'm going?' the old lady grumbled. 'I'm going to tell Béraud to scour the town for another horse. This lad runs well enough, no doubt, but not fast enough to keep up with us all the way to Galicia!'

After which, precariously perched on her crutches, like a ship listing out on the open seas, Ermengarde de Châteuvillain made a majestic departure from the inn courtyard.

3: An Envoy from Burgundy

A fortnight later, Catherine and her escort had reached the foothills of the Pyrenees, and were crossing the Oloron torrent over the ancient fortified bridge at Sauveterre. The voyage hitherto had been without incident, because most of the country they crossed belonged to the powerful Armagnac family and was free from English brigands. The English strongholds were situated mostly in Guyenne, and since they had little wish to embroil themselves with the Count Jean IV of Armagnac, whose policy toward them had been strangely accommodating for some time past, they took good care not to trespass on his domains.

Passing through Cahors, Moissac, Lectoure, Condom, Eauze, Aire-sur-Adour and Orthez, Catherine, Ermengarde and their followers had at last reached the mountains that separated them from Spain. But Catherine's patience was wearing thin. Since they had parted from Gerbert Bohat's pilgrims, Ermengarde seemed suddenly to have lost all eagerness to reach her destination. Only a short while back she had been inciting Catherine to greater haste, triumphantly proving how much faster they would progress once they had left the slow pilgrim march behind, and now here she was apparently taking a malicious pleasure in slowing down!

At first Catherine had not suspected what was going on. They had had to spend a day at Figeac procuring a horse for Josse Rallard. Then they had stayed two nights at Cahors; it had been a Sunday, and Ermengarde had assured her that it brought bad luck to travel the holy pilgrim ways on the Lord's Day. This had seemed plausible and Catherine had restrained her impatience out of friendship. But when the dowager insisted on staying at Condom for a local festival, the young woman couldn't help protesting.

'You seem to forget that I'm not making this journey for pleasure. Festivals don't interest me in the least! You know how eager I am to reach Galicia, Ermengarde! What is all this talk of local festivals?'

Ermengarde did not lose her temper but maintained, with all seriousness, that too much mental strain was bad for the body and that it was wiser, even when one was in a hurry, to take one's time a little.

Naturally Catherine would have none of this.

'In that case I might just as well have carried out my original vow and remained with Gerbert Bohat!'

'You forget that it was no longer your decision whether you remained with the pilgrims or not, my dear!'

Catherine glanced curiously at her friend.

'I don't understand you, Ermengarde. You seemed so anxious to help me, and now, all of a sudden, you seem to have changed your mind?'

'I am counselling moderation only because I have your interests at heart How do you know you aren't heading for bitter disappointment? In that case, why be in such a hurry to get there?'

This time Catherine did not answer. Her friend's words voiced her own constant anxieties too accurately not to fall painfully on her ears. This whole adventure was rash and foolhardy, as she well knew, and this was not the first time she had reflected how slender her chances of finding Arnaud must be. Often at night, in the darkness, during those dark, heavy hours when the mind falls prey to tormenting thoughts and it is impossible to still the beating of the heart, she lay wide awake, outstretched on her back, eyes open, trying to stifle the voice of reason that prompted her to give up, return to Montsalvy and devote herself courageously to her son for the rest of her life. She was often on the point of abandoning her enterprise; but when day dawned and chased away the depressing phantoms, Catherine found herself more determined than ever to follow her dream: to find Arnaud again, if only for a moment, speak to him again. Then ...

But it was particularly dismaying to receive nothing but scepticism and counsels of prudence from her friend, just when she was most in need of encouragement. Ermengarde had never liked Arnaud, she had always known that. She approved of his lineage, his courage and talents for war, but she had always been convinced that Catherine would find only pain and disenchantment at his side.

All the same, as her horse's hooves rang over the cobble-stones of the bridge that clear morning, Catherine's heart was full of hope. Deaf to the thunderous roar of the foaming torrent below, she had eyes only for the immense mountains before her, their pointed peaks, capped with glittering snow, towering up into the sky. As a child of the plains, who had never known anything more awesome than the milder summits of Auvergne, she found this gigantic spectacle a formidable and at the same time exhilarating barrier. It seemed as though one could never find a path through. She could not help murmuring aloud:

'We'll never be able to get through those mountains.'

'Oh, yes we will,' said Josse Rallard. He was riding beside her, as he had been wont to do ever since they left Figeac. 'The way across comes into sight as one climbs higher.'

'But,' she added sadly, 'if your foot slips or you get lost up there in that terrifying country, you wouldn't stand much chance of getting out alive ...' She was thinking of Gauthier, whose gigantic form, which had seemed so indestructible, could well have been swallowed up by these same high mountains. Catherine had until then had high hopes of finding him again, but that was because she had never seen mountains such as these before. How could she hope to snatch their prey from giants like these?

Josse did not know what she was thinking, and the look he gave her was both curious and uneasy. But he seemed to sense that she was in need of encouragement for he said cheerfully: 'Why so? Didn't you know that this was the country of miracles?'

'What do you mean?'

With a brief backward glance at Ermengarde, who was engaged in paying the toll on the bridge, Josse pointed to the foaming waters below. 'Look at this river, Dame Catherine. You might suppose that no-one who fell into it would stand a chance of emerging alive. And yet, almost three centuries ago, the King of Navarre ordered that his young sister Sancie de Béarn be thrown into these very waters, bound hand and foot. She was accused of having tried to murder her own child. She would be judged innocent only if she came out alive ...'

'A judgement of God?' Catherine cried, gazing at the seething water in alarm.

'Yes, a judgement of God! The young Countess was a frail creature and her hands and feet were stoutly bound. She was thrown in from the top of this bridge, and no-one here would have given a sou for her chances. But the waters carried her safe and sound on to the bank. People declared that it was a miracle; but, to my mind, that sort of miracle can happen anywhere. If God wills, Dame Catherine, that is all that is needed. And then what do mountains, the fury of the elements or the cruel weather matter? All you need is faith ...'

Catherine didn't answer, but the grateful glance she bestowed upon her improvised squire proved that he had struck home and that he had already discharged some of his debt of gratitude to her. Now she contemplated the sun kindling the distant white peaks with perfect composure.

She rode on a while without speaking, lost in thought, her eyes fastened on the rosy incandescence that seemed to rise to meet the heavens. Josse had allowed his horse to drop behind once more. Then she suddenly heard him cough. She jumped and turned to look at him with wide, absent eyes.

'What is it?'

'Perhaps we should wait for the Dame de Châteuvillain. She is still on the bridge.'

Catherine reined in her horse and looked back. There indeed was Ermengarde, apparently engaged in a lively conversation with the Sergeant in command of the guard. She shrugged.

'But what can she be doing? If this goes on we shall never reach Ostabat tonight.'

'If Dame Ermengarde could have her way,' Josse answered calmly, 'we shouldn't get there by tomorrow night either!'

Catherine raised her eyebrows and threw a startled glance at him. 'I don't understand. What do you mean?'

'I mean that the noble lady is doing everything possible to delay your journey. It's quite simple: she's waiting for someone.'

'For someone? But who?'

'I don't know. Perhaps it's the Sergeant who left us so suddenly after Aubrac. Hadn't you noticed, Dame Catherine, that the good lady your friend keeps looking back?'

The young woman nodded. She had in fact observed this habit more than once. Not only did Ermengarde seem in no hurry to reach Galicia now, but she was forever casting impatient backward glances. An angry flush warmed Catherine's cheeks. She was not going to let herself be managed any longer, however good Ermengarde's reasons might be. The Countess was still chatting on the bridge. Catherine spurred her horse:

'Onwards, Josse! She can easily catch us up. For my own part, I have decided that I want to spend tonight at Ostabat. And it is too bad if we outdistance Madame de Châteuvillain. I refuse to go on wasting time ...'

Josse's wide mouth stretched in a grin from ear to ear as he spurred his horse after Catherine's.

The ancient guest-house at Ostabat, half stronghold, half hospital, had lost much of its former prosperity. The hard times, and above all the war that had ravaged the kingdom of France for many years past, had slowed down the pilgrimages. Pious folk hesitated a little longer before entrusting themselves to routes that the threat of English and French brigands, together with the usual perils of the road, had made doubly dangerous. One needed to be in dire straits spiritually, or quite stripped of worldly goods, to undertake a voyage from which many travellers never returned. And the great bands that had once passed before the ancient hospice standing at the junction of the three great high roads from Auvergne, Burgundy and the Ile de France, were now reduced to a few groups of pilgrims already alarmed by what they had encountered along the way, and rendered still more uneasy by the thought of the mountain perils ahead, not least of which were the notorious Basque bandits, not to mention the timid mountain guides who offered their services only in order to lead trusting travellers the farther astray. More than one robber-baron had his fortified tower on the flank of the great mountain and lured there all these travellers with their staffs and cords.

'With a little luck,' Ermengarde had confided to Catherine, 'we should have the guest-house to ourselves, and be able to make ourselves comfortable.'

But when the young woman, together with Josse, crossed the threshold, she was surprised to find a good number of horses there already, being rubbed down by well-dressed grooms. There were also several pack-mules and ten or so soldiers seated round a good fire, where a large piece of meat was roasting. In short, it looked like the travelling equipage of some considerable nobleman! The guest-house doors were open and monks could be seen bustling to and fro, doubtless attending to the needs of their distinguished guest, while a great fire crackled in the chimney.

'It doesn't look as if we need fear that we shall be too much alone,' Catherine muttered in annoyance. 'I wonder if there's a spare cell for us?'

Josse had no time to speak. A monk was approaching.

'Peace be with you, sister. What can we do for you?'

'Give us board and lodging,' Catherine answered. 'But there are more than two of us. The rest of our party follows behind, and I am afraid ...'

The old man gave a smile that creased his face into a thousand lines. 'Because of the nobleman who arrived here a little while ago? Never fear. The house is large, and its hospitality is open to you. Will you dismount? One of the lay brothers will see to your horses.'

But Catherine was not listening. She had just caught sight of an officer standing at the stable door. He was still in full armour, wearing an armorial tunic over his cuirass. Despite the deepening gloom, there was no mistaking the arms on that heavy silk garment. Catherine knew them only too well: they were the arms of the Duke of Burgundy!

She felt herself grow pale, and a cloud of confused thoughts whirled through her brain. Come now, it wasn't possible for Duke Philippe to be here! This escort might be that of a great lord, but it was scarcely imposing enough for the Great Duke of the West! And yet there were the lilies and ducal bars, the sabres of the Golden Fleece ... that Golden Fleece that had been founded in her honour a long time ago!

Her look of distress and rigid pose attracted the attention of the old monk, who gently shook the horse's reins. 'My child! Are you unwell?'

Without moving, eyes still glued to that disquieting coat-of- arms, Catherine demanded: 'This nobleman who has just arrived ... what is his name?'

'He is a personal envoy of Monseigneur the Duke Philippe of Burgundy.'

'An envoy? To whom? To what country?'

'How should I know? No doubt to the ruler of Castile, or the King of

Aragon, unless it might be the King of Navarre. But you seem very agitated, child. Come. You will feel better for some rest.'

Feeling somewhat reassured, Catherine decided to dismount, just as Ermengarde and the rest of the band rode into the guest-house yard. The Countess seemed in a very bad temper. Scarlet in the face, lips set in a tight line, eyes blazing, she called out angrily to Catherine.

'Now then, my dear, what are you playing at? We've been galloping after you for hours now, without being able to catch you up!'

'I am tired of wasting time, Ermengarde,' the young woman replied dryly. 'There are too many people along the road whom you seem to enjoy chatting to. I was afraid I might not reach this holy place by tonight, so I rode on ahead.'

'All the same ...' the Countess began. But the words died away on her lips and her grey eyes flashed. She too had just recognised the arms on the officer's tunic. Her lips under their faint shadowing of moustache spread in a broad grin.

'Ah, it looks as if we shall have a little company here,' she said, with a gaiety that did not escape Catherine. 'Friends no doubt.'

Catherine smiled coldly. 'Friends? I would advise you to avoid any nobleman who bears that coat of arms, my dear. Have you forgotten that you are banished, and on bad terms with Duke Philippe?'

'Bah!' said Ermengarde with a fine carelessness. 'We are a long way from Bruges and Dijon now. Besides, I still have some loyal friends in the Duke's Court. And in any case, I have never been faint-hearted, as you know. I like to look things in the face!'

The Dame de Châteuvillain lifted up her long, purple velvet skirts, revealing long narrow feet encased in solid boots, and set off toward the door where the officer still stood watching the approach of this imposing personage and apparently not the slightest bit impressed by her.

'Tell me, friend, who is your master?'

'Ambassador of my Lord the Duke of Burgundy, Count of Flanders, of ...'

'Spare us the list of the Duke's titles, I beg you. I know them better than you do, and anyway, I don't want to stand here all night. Tell me who this ambassador is.'

'Who are you to ask questions like these, lady?'

Before the Countess's fine, brick-red cheeks could purple with rage, a slender but firm hand drew the officer aside while a still youthful man, dressed in russet leather with a sobriety not without elegance, appeared on the threshold. His head was bare and his short-cropped blond hair was threaded with grey. The firelight disclosed a narrow face with lips so thin they looked as if they had been drawn with three fine strokes. A long, straight nose surmounted them. Two icy blue, slightly protuberant eyes fastened on the furious dowager, but within an instant their expression changed: a smile chased away the look of boredom on the regular features, while the lacklustre eyes began to sparkle.

'My dear Countess! I was beginning to fear that I had already missed you ...'

A discreet, peremptory gesture from the old lady cut short this speech, but too late: Catherine had not only heard the unfortunate remark, but had seen the gesture too. She stepped out of the shadows, and went up to her friend:

'And me, Jan, were you afraid you might have missed me too?'

The painter Jean van Eyck, Gentleman of the Chamber to Duke Philippe of Burgundy, and his secret ambassador in many instances, did not trouble to keep up a pretence. The delight on his face was both genuine and sincere. He sprang forward, both hands held out to that slender figure.

'Catherine! ... You! Is it really you? I'm not dreaming?'

He was so obviously overjoyed that Catherine felt her mistrust thawing a little. They had been great friends in the days when she had ruled over the court of Burgundy and over the heart of its Duke. She had sat as model more than once to this great artist whose genius she admired as much as she appreciated his loyalty. Jan had even been somewhat in love with her, and had not tried to hide his feelings. In spite of everything, Catherine could not help feeling pleasure; the sort of pleasure one finds in rediscovering an old friend after an absence of many years. She had only good memories of him and the long hours she had spent posing in front of his easel. They had been peaceful, gentle hours, with the exception of the very last – the one when she had heard news of the illness that had stricken her child by Philippe, then in the care of Ermengarde de Châteuvillain. She had decided to leave Bruges never to return, and Jean van Eyck himself had departed at almost the same moment for Portugal to seek the hand of Princess Isabelle on behalf of the Duke. Then life had swept Catherine up in its remorseless current. It was six years since she had last seen Van Eyck ... Spontaneously she placed her hands in his.

'It is I, my friend ... and it gives me great pleasure to see you again! What are you doing so far from Burgundy? I gather you had a rendezvous here with Dame Ermengarde!'

She glanced, in speaking, at her friend, and noticed that she coloured perceptibly. But Van Eyck seemed unperturbed by her remarks.

'Rendezvous is an exaggeration! I knew Dame Ermengarde was travelling to Compostela in Galicia, and since my mission takes me along the same road, I hoped I might be able to travel with her.'

'Has the Duke sent you to my Lord Saint James?' Catherine asked, with an irony that the artist instantly registered.

'Now, now,' he said, smiling. 'You know quite well that my missions are always secret. I haven't the right to discuss them. But let us go inside now. Night has arrived, and it is cold at the foot of these mountains!'

Catherine was to retain a strange, unreal and at the same time uneasy memory of that evening, spent beneath the ancient vaulted ceilings of the great hall where, at this stage of their pilgrimages, the faithful had crowded for so many centuries past. She sat at table between Ermengarde and Jan, listening to their conversation without taking much part in it. How could she? The affairs of Burgundy, which they were discussing, were so remote from her now that they did not interest her in the least. Even the ducal heir, the young Charles, Count of Charolais, who had been born to the Duchess Isabelle some months earlier, aroused no more than a flicker of interest in her, though he appeared to be a subject of passionate concern to these two Burgundians. All that belonged to a world now quite dead to her.

But though she might not have paid much attention to their conversation, she was nevertheless keeping a sharp eye on her two companions. Earlier on, when she had left her cell to go to the great hall, Josse had been waiting for her, still as a statue in the darkened cloister. She had jumped in alarm as he stepped out of the shadows, but he had put a finger hurriedly to his lips. Then he had whispered:

'This lord from Burgundy … 'tis he the noble lady was waiting for!'

'How do you know?'

'I heard them talking earlier on, in the herb garden. Be careful! He has come here for you!'

He had no time to say more, because just then Ermengarde appeared, flanked on the one side by Gillette and on the other by Margot, who appeared fascinated by the grand lady's imposing personality. Further explanations had to be postponed till later. In any case, Josse had melted back into the shadows like a ghost. But during the frugal meal of chickpeas, milk and apples, she was thinking about what he had said, and her eyes went constantly from one face to the other: from the long, calm face of Van Eyck to the animated, highly coloured face of Ermengarde. Ermengarde seemed happier than she had been for days, and Catherine told herself that Josse must be right: she *had* been waiting for the painter. But in that case, what connection could their meeting have with Catherine herself?

But she was not the woman to leave such an irritating question unanswered for long, and when Ermengarde got to her feet after the meal, yawning cavernously and stretching her tired limbs, she decided to move straight into the attack. After all, until the contrary was proved, the painter was her friend. It was up to him to prove it!

When the fat Countess had left the room and Van Eyck went to fetch a candle to escort her, Catherine detained him:

'Jan, I must speak to you!'

'Here?' he said, looking uneasily at a group of mountain folk in one corner of the great hall, who sat in a circle on the ground round a dish of chickpeas they were slowly devouring.

'Why not? Those people don't speak our language. They are Basques. You can tell by their wild eyes and dark faces. They aren't paying any attention to us. Anyway,' she added with a thin smile, 'what makes you suppose that what I'm going to say could interest anyone here?'

'Ambassadors are careful … by definition!' Van Eyck replied, with a smile strangely akin to Catherine's own. 'But you are right: we can speak safely. But what about?'

Catherine didn't answer straightaway. She went slowly across to the massive chimney, where the fire was gradually sinking, leant her arm against the chimney-breast and pressed her forehead against it. She let the fire caress every particle of her body. She loved fire for this strange dual nature that allowed it to be at once the best friend and worst enemy of man. Fire warms cold bodies, cooks bread and lights the way on a dark night, but fire also destroys and ravages, tortures and kills … Whenever she felt that she was going to have to do battle, Catherine liked to have fire near her.

Jean van Eyck respected her silence. Besides, his painter's eye was captivated by the long, slender black silhouette etched against the fiery hearth. The line of Catherine's dress clung to her body with anatomical precision. Her delicate profile looked as if it had been stamped in gold, and the long lashes cast a touching shadow over the huge violet eyes. The painter told himself, with a shiver of aesthetic pleasure, that this woman had never been so beautiful! Life and suffering had robbed her of the freshness of extreme youth, but had refined her. All at once her beauty had become more human and more unapproachable. She had the radiant purity of a celestial being, and yet the physical attraction that radiated from her was almost unbearably powerful.

'If the Duke were to see her again,' Van Eyck mused, 'he would prostrate himself at her feet like a slave … or else kill her!' But he didn't dare go too deeply into his own feelings. Only one thing stood out clearly from the confusion of his thoughts: a passionate, overpowering desire to record that tormenting beauty in one more picture! It seemed to him suddenly that his latest work, the double portraits of a young burgher called Arnolfini and his wife, was unexciting compared with the portrait he could do of this new Catherine. He was so deep in these thoughts that Catherine's first remarks made him jump.

'Jan,' she said softly, 'why have you come here?' She didn't look at him, but she forestalled the objections she knew this would call forth. 'No,' she said firmly, 'don't trouble to lie to me! I know a lot already. I know that Ermengarde was waiting to see you, and that this meeting concerned me in some fashion. I want to know why.'

She abandoned her pensive pose and turned to face him. Her great eyes fixed on him questioningly. Once again the artist found himself trembling at the spectacle of so much grace and beauty.

'Ermengarde was not waiting for me particularly, Catherine, but for some messenger from Burgundy. It was mere chance that it happened to be me ...'

'Chance? Do you suppose I've forgotten all Duke Philippe's little ways? You are his favourite secret envoy ... not a mere messenger! What have you come to say to the Countess?'

'Nothing!'

'Nothing?'

Van Eyck gave an amused smile, and went on: 'No, nothing, my dear. I have nothing to say to her.'

'Have you anything to say to ... me?'

'Perhaps. But I won't say it yet'

'Why not?'

'Because the time isn't right!'

As she knitted her fine brows together, the painter went up to her and took her hands in his.

'Catherine! I have always been your friend ... and I would have given anything to have been more! I swear to you on my honour as a gentleman that I am yours still, and that I would not harm you for anything in the world. Can't you trust me?'

'Trust? All this is so peculiar and confusing! How did they know, in Burgundy, that I was with Dame Ermengarde? Did the Duke's astrologer read it in the stars?'

At this the painter burst out laughing. 'You don't believe a word I say, and you are quite right. It was Dame Ermengarde who sent back the news. She sent a messenger ...'

A cry of anger interrupted him. 'She did? She dared do that? And she calls herself my friend?'

'She is your friend, Catherine; but she is your friend, and not your husband's. You see, she sincerely believes, and always has, that you have made a grievous error, that you will never find happiness along the road you are now travelling. And you must admit that fate seems on the whole to have been in agreement ...'

'It's not her place to judge these matters! There is one thing she will never understand: my love for my husband! Of course at the Duke's court they give the name love to a whole range of feelings, among which desire rules predominant. But my love isn't like that at all. Arnaud and I are but one being, one flesh! I suffer his pains, and if I were to be cut to pieces, each piece of me would still proclaim "I love Arnaud!" ... But neither Ermengarde nor the Duke could ever begin to understand feelings like those!'

'Do you think not? Not Dame Ermengarde perhaps. She is purely maternal and loves you like her own daughter. But what torments you is that she feels something similar for Duke Philippe. She has never spared him her criticisms or the rough side of her tongue, but she loves him like a mother; and her heart bleeds because she is now in banishment as the result of her own son having taken up arms against the Duke. She hoped to please the Duke by speaking to him of you. It's her way of proving to him that she still loves him. As for him!'

Catherine stiffened angrily. She threw back her blonde head and cut in: 'What right have you to suppose I want to hear about him?'

Van Eyck ignored her interruption. He turned, took a few steps away from her and went on hoarsely: 'Your departure wounded him terribly, Catherine ... and I know that the wound still bleeds! No,' he went on quickly, 'don't say anything, because I have nothing more to add. Forget everything on your mind and remember only this: I am your friend, and it is solely in this capacity that I shall be travelling with you tomorrow. Don't try to read anything more into it! Now goodnight, lovely Catherine!'

And before she could make a move to detain him, he opened the door and vanished.

4: Roncesvaux

The ancient Roman road stretched from below the half- dilapidated ramparts of St-Jean-Pied-de-Port, steadily uphill for eight good leagues, as far as the Bentarté pass. The road was narrow and dangerous, made slippery by the fragments of old paving-stones that still covered it in patches, and that the cold of these high altitudes rimed with a thin coat of ice. It was steep, too, and cut through a countryside that seemed to grow more and more bleak till it was almost as bare as the sky above. However, Catherine and her companions had chosen this route in preference to the easier one of Val Carlos on the advice of the magistrate of St-Jean, because it passed through relatively safe country. A brigand-chieftain, Vivien d'Aigremont, held the valley road with his savage bands of Basques and Navarrese. Not that the Burgundian soldiers escorting the Dame de Châteuvillain, plus those protecting Jean van Eyck, were not powerful, well armed and capable of ensuring that they travelled without too much danger. But from what they had heard of the blind ferocity and primitive brutality of Vivien d'Aigremont's men, it seemed that they would prove powerful enemies, and in any case their numbers were much greater. So on the whole it had seemed wiser to take the high road.

As they climbed, the cold grew more intense. A bitter wind swept to and fro across the giant peaks of the Pyrenees, sometimes dispelling, sometimes bringing long scarves of icy mist that hid even the nearest rocks. No-one had uttered a word since their departure at dawn. They were too preoccupied with where to put their feet next; they had long since decided it was safer to dismount and lead their horses by their reins in case of a fall.

The long, silent cavalcade strung out along the side of the mountain looked, in this swirling grey light, like a procession of phantoms. Even the weapons had grown dull with the damp air. Catherine heard Ermengarde muttering crossly behind her, struggling painfully along with the assistance of Gillette and Margot.

'Accursed weather and accursed place! Why couldn't we take the lower road like the Emperor Charlemagne before us? I'd rather deal with a pack of brigands than clamber along a path more suited to a mountain goat! Galloping about on the rocks at my age like an old ewe! It's ridiculous!'

Catherine had to smile. She half turned and called: 'Now, Ermengarde, don't grumble! You wanted to come this way.'

She had not breathed a word to the old lady of her talk with Van Eyck. What was the point? Ermengarde would not have understood why Catherine regarded her action as a sort of betrayal. She had clearly believed, in good faith, that she was acting for the best and for Catherine's welfare. And, after all, the painter and his well-armed escort provided a useful addition to the little band in these dangerous parts. Finally, whatever the mysterious message might be that Van Eyck had promised to deliver when the time was 'right', she knew that he was quite powerless when it came to trying to alter her resolution. All the same, Van Eyck's secretiveness and silences irritated her and piqued her curiosity. Why this almost official style of travel, the rank of ambassador, the men-at-arms, if he had come merely to pass on a message?

But Catherine knew Jan well enough to know he would not speak till the moment was right. The best thing was to wait ... But if she had walked in silence since morning, weighed down by a sadness she could not shake off, examining the breathtaking heights, the black chasms between the white peaks, it was not on his account but Gauthier's ... It was here he had vanished, in a setting on the scale of the giant she had believed indestructible! But what man of flesh and blood could hope to prevail against these giants of stone and ice? Catherine had never imagined that countryside like this could exist. And she realised now that until this minute she had been hoping against all hope and reason, in the teeth of all the evidence, that her faithful servitor would have emerged triumphant from this last battle and that she would find him somewhere, miraculously safe and sound. She had needed to come as far as this to realise that there would be no miracle ... But as she toiled up the steep, difficult path, leading her horse behind her, Catherine's thoughts were not on her present discomfort. She kept imagining that she saw the towering, strapping figure of her erstwhile companion stepping toward her out of the mist, with his confident smile and grey eyes that seemed to hold all the blind fury of the old Nordic gods together with all the candour of a child. And Catherine's throat became tight with pain and she had to close her swimming eyes for a moment. Then the kindly giant's shade vanished again, to rejoin Arnaud's stricken but arrogant form in the depths of Catherine's sore heart. For a moment she suffered so cruelly that she was tempted to lay herself down there, on the icebound rocks, and wait for death ... Only her pride and a force greater than her distress made her keep going, pushing on and on without any of her companions suspecting the drama unfolding within her ...

When they reached the Bentarté pass, daylight was fading. The wind blew in such savage gusts that the travellers could only proceed bent almost double. The climb was over, but to proceed along the summit they still had to follow a road that crossed over a series of saw-toothed peaks ... The sky hung so low and threatening that Catherine felt she might touch it merely by putting out a hand. Someone behind her spoke.

'In clear weather one can see the sea from here, as well as the frontiers of the three kingdoms of France, Castile and Aragon.'

But this did not interest the young woman, whose weariness was beginning to drag her down. In this deserted place there were hundreds of crude little wooden crosses placed there by earlier pilgrims, and Catherine stared at them horrified. It was as if she were journeying through a cemetery. Her eyes were dimmed by weariness. Her feet hurt and her whole body shuddered with the cold. Her hope of seeing Arnaud again had to be a powerful one to carry her through so many trials.

The rest of the journey as far as the lower peak of Ibaneta, and thence to the refuge of Roncesvaux, was a Calvary for Catherine, made worse by the oncoming darkness. When at long last they came within sight of the celebrated monastery, built many centuries earlier by the Bishop Sancho de la Rosa and King Alfonso-the-Builder, the moon swam clear of cloud, and its cold light streamed down on a group of low-roofed buildings with thick walls and stout flying-buttresses huddled at the foot of the Ibaneta pass. A square tower stood over them, and the road passed under a low archway into the ancient monastery. Everything around was powdered by hoar-frost, and this gave it an aspect of unearthly beauty; but Catherine had reached the limit of her strength and none of this meant anything to her. She saw only one thing: lanterns passing to and fro beyond the gate, carried by human hands, and to her these lanterns spelt life, warmth ... Gritting her teeth, she made one last effort, and got as far as the guest-house; but once there she collapsed onto a mounting block, incapable of taking another step. Van Eyck and Josse, at last aware of her exhaustion, had to carry her inside, half fainting. It had been a long time since anyone had heard a grumble out of Dame Ermengarde, who had been hoisted, like a great sack, onto her saddle.

Catherine sat on the immense hearthstone of the pilgrims' hall with a goatskin about her legs and a bowl of hot soup in her hands, and slowly felt the blood returning to her face and her interest in life reviving. There was a great crowd of people packed into the low-roofed chamber, with its smoke-blackened vaults: pilgrims returning from Galicia, their robes sewn with the emblematic shells and their eyes full of the pride of those who have accomplished their vows; muleteers driven by night and the threat of wolves and bears to seek refuge there; Navarrese peasants in black, often ragged tunics that bared their legs, and filth-encrusted feet in hairy skin shoes that left their toes uncovered; and lastly soldiers of fortune in battered armour. To and fro amid this crowd, rendered silent by weariness, passed the black robes of the monks. On their breasts, just over the heart, they wore a red cross terminating in a sword below, symbolic of their dual role as monks and soldiers. For the Augustine fathers of Roncesvaux still had to draw their swords from time to time to their captives from the mountain bandits.

They distributed bread and soup to all alike, paying no more heed to the elegant ambassador of the great Duke of the West than to the poorest Navarrese. Catherine reflected that their harsh features looked as if they might have been quarried from the native granite, and had little in common with the round plump faces of the monks of the plains ... Ermengarde sat beside her, snoring, sleeping with her back propped against the hearth. The others were eating or, overcome by fatigue, already asleep on the floor where they sat. In the distance they could hear wolves howling ...

Suddenly the door opened, and with it came a gust of icy wind. Two monks entered, their heads protected by large black hats pulled down over their hoods, carrying a stretcher on which a human form lay rolled in a blanket. The door banged to behind them. Several heads were raised as they entered, only to drop again: a sick man, a wounded one or even a corpse were common enough sights in these pitiless regions. The monks pushed forward to the hearth.

'He had gone astray,' one of them explained to the Prior who came over to greet them. 'We found him near Roland's breach.'

'Dead?'

'No. But very weak. And in a sorry state! He must have fallen victim to brigands who stripped and maltreated him. Thanks be to God, they left him alive.'

As they spoke, they lowered the stretcher down before the fire. Catherine pressed closer to Ermengarde, to make room, casting a perfunctory glance at the sick man as the monks uncovered him. Then all of a sudden she started, stood up and bent over the unconscious man, examining his wasted features. She rubbed her eyes, believing that weariness must have brought on hallucinations. But no, there was no room for doubt.

'Fortunat!' she breathed, her throat suddenly constricted with fear. 'My God, Fortunat!'

An impulse stronger than any weariness flung her down beside the litter, gazing upon this phantom, the first glimmer of hope that had shone in her darkness for a long time. This man knew where Arnaud was ... but what if he were to die before telling her?

One of the monks stared at her curiously.

'Do you know this man, sister?'

'Yes ... oh, Lord! I still can't believe my own eyes! He was my husband's squire ... and now I find him here, alone, ill ... What can have become of his master?'

'You will have to wait a little time to question him. First we must give him a cordial, to revive and warm him, and then give him something to eat. Let us attend to him!'

Catherine moved away regretfully and sat down again on the hearth. Jean van Eyck, who had observed the scene, came up to her and took one of her hands. It was icy cold … The painter felt her trembling.

'Are you cold?'

She gestured that she was not. In any case, her shining eyes and cheeks, flushed with nervous excitement, proved the contrary. She was in a state of appalling agitation, unable to drag her eyes away from the thin, motionless form that the monks were vigorously rubbing while the Prior held a little flask to the pale lips.

'Oh, God, let them be quick!' Catherine said to herself. 'Can't they see this is killing me?'

But the vigorous treatment Fortunat was receiving seemed to be having its effect. The blood was stealing back into his ashen cheeks, his lips moved, and in a moment he opened his eyes and gazed steadily at the men who were tending him. The Prior smiled at him:

'Are you feeling better?'

'Yes … that's better. I've been far away, haven't I?'

'Quite far! You must have been attacked by bandits, I think, and left for dead.'

Fortunat made a terrible face, which grew worse as he tried to sit up.

'Those brutes battered me like devils. I thought all my bones were breaking … Ah, I'm aching all over!'

'That won't last long. They are just going to give you a good bowl of soup, and some ointment that will allay your pains.'

As the Prior got to his feet, his eyes met Catherine's. She read this as a sign and, unable to control her impatience a moment longer, stepped forward. Once again the Prior bent over Fortunat.

'My son, there is a person here who wants to speak with you very urgently.'

'Who can that be?' The Gascon turned his head and propped himself up a little. All of a sudden he recognised Catherine and lifted himself up on his elbow while his thin face crimsoned.

'You! … Here? I don't believe it!'

In one movement she flung herself down on her knees beside the litter.

'Fortunat! You are alive. But where is Messire Arnaud?'

Without thinking, she laid imploring hands on the squire's arm. He shook her off brutally and his thin bearded face twisted in a diabolic grin.

'Do you really want to know? What difference can it make to you?'

'What difference … to me …? But …'

'What do you care about Messire Arnaud? Didn't you betray him and abandon him? What are you doing here? Has your new husband, the handsome blond lord, tired of you so quickly that you are reduced to running about in search of adventures already? That would just suit you, of course!'

A two-fold exclamation of anger passed from Catherine's lips as she knelt there bewildered, staring uncomprehendingly at the Gascon's hate-twisted face. The Prior and Jean van Eyck protested simultaneously in high indignation.

'My son, you forget yourself! What sort of language is this?' cried the one.

'This man is mad!' said the other. 'I'm going to knock his lying words down his throat!'

But Catherine sprang rapidly to her feet and laid a soothing hand on Jan's arm, already at his dagger, while she gently pushed the Prior away with the other.

'Don't worry,' she said. 'This concerns me alone. Don't get involved, please!'

But now Fortunat's malicious eye fell upon the painter who stood there pale with anger.

'Yet another knight errant, I see! Your new lover, Dame Catherine?'

'Enough of this insolence,' she said harshly. 'Father, and you too, Messire Van Eyck, be so good as to leave me alone. I repeat, this concerns me alone.'

She felt her temper rising and controlled it only by a superhuman effort of will. All around, the various pilgrims who understood French were pressing eagerly forward, but the Prior held them off as best he could. She went back to the litter, bent over the man stretched out there and calmly folded her arms.

'Why, you hate me Fortunat! Now that is something new!'

'Is it?' he said, with a malicious glance. 'It's nothing new to me. I have hated you for months, years now! Ever since that accursed day when you allowed him to go off with that monk. Your husband, the man you were supposed to love!'

'I obeyed his orders! That was what he wanted!'

'If you had loved him you would have kept him with you by force! If you had loved him you would have taken him to some remote place where you would have tended him till you died of his illness!'

'While I don't grant you the right to sit in judgement over me, God shall be my witness that, far from doing as I wished, I could have asked for no sweeter fate! But I had a son! His father insisted that I stayed with him!'

'That may be true. But in that case why did you go rushing off to Court? Was it also in obedience to your husband that you found consolation in the arms of Seigneur de Brézé, that you sent him to break Dame Isabelle's heart

… and Messire Arnaud's too, and that you finally married him?'

'That's not true. I am still the Lady of Montsalvy, and I defy anyone to question that! Messire de Brézé was guilty of wishful thinking. Have you anything else to reproach me with?'

Almost without their realising it, their voices were rising, taking on the violence of a passionate dispute. The Prior noticed many heads turning toward Catherine and tried to intervene. 'My child, wouldn't you prefer to continue this dispute in a more private place? I can have you shown into another room, you and this man …'

But she refused with a proud gesture. 'That won't be necessary, Father. I don't mind who hears what I have to say, because I have nothing to reproach myself with. Now then, Fortunat,' she went on, 'what else were you going to say? I'm still waiting.'

The squire began speaking, hoarsely, with a look of inexpressible loathing on his face. 'You are the cause of all his sufferings! Have you any idea of the torments he has undergone since the day you rejected him? All the days without hope, and nights without grace, with only the terrible knowledge that he was a living corpse? I know this, because I loved him. I went to see him every week. He was my master, the best, bravest and most loyal of knights!'

'Who denies that? Do you think to teach me the virtues of the man I love?'

'Your love?' Fortunat sneered. 'You give that to others! But I loved him truly, with devotion, respect, all the best there was in myself!'

'I don't love him? Why am I here then? Don't you realise that I am going to look for him?'

'You are looking for him?'

Fortunat fell silent abruptly. He stared at Catherine with malicious glee, and then, suddenly, burst out laughing. It was an insulting, fierce laugh that told Catherine far more clearly than any curses could have done just how implacably the little Gascon hated her!

'Very well, then, fair lady, search away! But he is lost to you … lost forever! Do you hear? *Lost!*'

He shouted this last word as if he feared Catherine might not have grasped the whole desperate meaning of what he had said. But it was unnecessary. Catherine had understood. She even staggered a little under the brutal blow, but she was able to summon up enough strength to push aside Jean van Eyck's proffered arm.

'He … is dead!' she said in a colourless voice.

But Fortunat burst out laughing again. 'Dead? Far from it! He is happy, free of you, cured …'

'Cured? My God! Saint James has wrought a miracle!' This time it was she who shouted, but with a dazzled fervour that the little Gascon hastened to destroy. He shrugged irreverently, which made the Prior's brows knit together angrily.

'There hasn't been a miracle. Though I revere Saint James, I have to tell you that he did not heed Messire Arnaud's prayers. Why should he, anyway? Messire Arnaud didn't have leprosy.'

'Not ... leprosy,' Catherine stammered. 'But ...'

'But you were mistaken, like everyone else, come to that ... You can't be blamed for that. When we left Compostela, Messire Arnaud still believed himself to be a leper. He was dreadfully disappointed ... despairing ... He longed for death, but he didn't want to die to no purpose. "The Moors still control the kingdom of Granada, and the knights of Castile are in perpetual conflict with them," he told me. "That's where I must go. God, who has refused to cure me, will grant me the favour of dying in battle with the Infidel." After that we travelled south. We crossed mountains, deserts ... and at last we reached a city called Toledo ... That's where everything changed!'

He paused for a while, as if savouring a particularly agreeable memory. His ecstatic smile was too much for Catherine.

'What do you mean ... everything? Come now. Speak!' she said curtly.

'You can't wait to find out, eh? You'll be sorry you were in such a hurry to know though, I swear to you. In fact ... but then, I can't wait to see you broken either. So, listen well: when we reached this city on the hill, we found the cortege of the Ambassador of the King of Granada there, who had been sent to visit King John of Castile and was now on his way back to his own country ...'

'My God! My husband had fallen into the hands of the Infidels! And you dare rejoice?'

'There are ways and ways of falling into someone's hands,' Fortunat remarked craftily. 'The way that befell Messire Arnaud is far from unpleasant ...' Abruptly the Gascon sat up and, turning a fiery eye on Catherine, continued in a voice full of triumph: 'The Ambassador was a woman, Dame Catherine, a princess, the sister of the King of Granada ... and she is more beautiful than the day! I have never beheld a more dazzling creature! Nor had Messire Arnaud!'

'What do you mean? Explain yourself!' Catherine commanded, her mouth suddenly dry with apprehension.

'You don't understand? Why should Messire Arnaud refuse the love of the fairest of princesses when his wife had abandoned him for another? He was free, after all, free to love – especially since there was gratitude as well as admiration in his feelings for her.'

'Gratitude?'

'It took the Princess's Moorish doctor three days to cure Messire Arnaud. He wasn't suffering from leprosy, as I have already said, but from some other malady, one easily cured but the name of which I have forgotten! It is true that it resembles that other accursed disease ... but now Messire Arnaud is cured, happy ... and lost to you forever!'

There followed a long and terrible silence in which it seemed as if all these folk, most of whom did not know her, were trying to hear the beating of Catherine's heart ... She still had not made a sign, or uttered a word ... She too hearkened as pain and jealousy, slyly, slowly ate their way into her soul ... She had the impression of living through some dreadful nightmare from which it was impossible to wake ... A dreadful, unbearable picture formed at the back of her mind: Arnaud in the arms of another woman! All of a sudden she felt like screaming, crying aloud to relieve the agonising sting of jealousy. Like a healthy animal confronted with sickness for the first time, she was helpless against this novel form of suffering. She longed to close her eyes, but pride forbade this. She flashed a terrible look at the Gascon and spat out:

'You are lying! How can you expect me to believe such a tale? My husband is a Christian, a knight ... he would never renounce his faith, his country, his King, for an infidel! And I am a fool to listen to you, foul liar!'

She controlled herself with difficulty, burying her hands in the folds of her robe. For two pins she would have struck that face so hideously deformed by spite and loathing ... Fortunat did not seem to be in the least impressed by her anger. He even seemed pleased by it!

'Lying? You dare to suggest I'm lying?' Slowly, his small black eyes fixed on Catherine's, the Gascon raised his right hand and solemnly swore: 'I swear on the salvation of my immortal soul that at this very moment Messire Arnaud knows love and happiness in the palace at Granada. I swear ...'

'Enough!' cut in Ermengarde's powerful voice from somewhere behind Catherine. 'God dislikes His name being called upon merely to wound another human being! You have disgorged your poison, my lad ... that's enough now! ... Tell me one thing, though: how comes it that you, the faithful servitor, should turn up here? Why are you risking your life wandering the roads when you too might be finding joy in the arms of some fair Moorish maiden? Hasn't your Princess got a maiden lovely enough to detain you? Why haven't you stayed with your master, sharing his happiness?'

The imposing red silhouette and imperious accents of the dowager seemed to awaken a glimmer of fear in the squire's eyes. She was like a rock ... The Gascon seemed a little intimidated. He looked down: 'Messire Arnaud told me to go! He wanted me to return to his mother, knowing she was ill and suffering, to tell her the good news – that he was cured, that ...'

'That her son, one of the King's captains, a Christian knight, had forgotten his obligations and vows for the black eyes of a houri? Fine news for a noble lady to hear! If Dame de Montsalvy is anything like I imagine her to be, news like that would kill her outright!'

'Dame Isabelle is dead,' Catherine said sombrely. 'Nothing can touch her now. And your mission is accomplished, Fortunat … You can go back to France now, if you wish, or return to your master …'

A look of cruel curiosity appeared on the Gascon's thin face.

'And you, Dame Catherine?' he asked eagerly, 'what will you do? I don't imagine you intend to go and win your husband back now? You wouldn't get anywhere near him anyway … Christian women there are all sold into slavery, and work under the whip, or else they throw them to the soldiery to amuse themselves with … unless they decide to kill them with cruel tortures! The best thing for you, believe me, would be a good convent somewhere and …'

The words finished in an incomprehensible splutter. Ermengarde's strong and beautiful hand had seized the man by the throat, so that he couldn't breathe.

'I've already told you once to be silent,' the dowager growled. 'And I never repeat something twice.'

But Catherine herself had not deigned to reply, almost as if all this were nothing to do with her. She turned away, cast one glance over all the anxious faces straining to see her, and then walked slowly to the door, the black folds of her cloak sweeping over the straw-scattered floor. Jean van Eyck tried to follow and called out to her:

'Catherine, where are you going?'

She turned toward him, smiling faintly.

'I need to be alone for a minute, my friend … I think you know how I feel. I'm just going to the chapel … let me go!'

She left the room, crossed the yard and went out through the archway that gave onto the pilgrim route. She wanted to go to the little chapel across the way. Earlier on, before supper, they had shown her the great church, but she had found it too rich, the Virgins too bejewelled, too much gold, too many strange objects surrounding the stone figure of the crucified Christ, so haunting in itself that it had obsessed Bishop Sancho the Strong. She yearned for a small, simple place where she could be alone with herself and with God. The little chapel, which abutted onto a sort of cave where pilgrims who died on the journey were buried, seemed the ideal place.

Apart from the statue of the saintly traveller with its oil lamp burning before it, the chapel contained nothing but a stone altar and worn, uneven flagstones. It was cold and damp in there, but Catherine was oblivious to these physical details. She felt, suddenly, what it must be like to be dead … Now that Arnaud had betrayed her, her heart no longer had any reason to go on beating.

For the sake of an unknown woman, the man she had loved above all others had broken, at one cruel stroke, all the bonds that united them. Catherine felt as if a part of herself had been amputated – the best, essential part – leaving her bereft and alone in a boundless desert. Her hands were empty, her heart empty, her life all devastation. She sank heavily down upon her knees on the cold stone and buried her face in trembling hands.

'Why?' she sobbed. 'Why?'

She knelt there for a long while, not thinking, not praying, unconscious of the cold seeping into her body. She didn't even feel the need for tears. In this dark, cold chapel she felt as if she were buried alive, and yet she had no wish to escape. Over and over again, the one agonising thought echoed in her head: 'he' had abandoned her for another woman … After swearing to love her as long as breath remained in his body, he had opened his arms to an enemy of his race, his God even … and doubtless he was now whispering to her the very same tender words to which Catherine had once listened, trembling with passion … Would she ever succeed in dragging that tormenting thought from her mind, tearing away that crucifying picture? Was it possible not to die of such pain?

She was so overcome that she barely noticed when two strong hands helped her to her feet and placed a cloak round her shaking shoulders.

'Come, Catherine,' said Jean van Eyck's strong voice. 'Don't stay here. You will catch your death.'

She stared at him wildly.

'Death? … But I am dead, Jan. He has killed me!'

'Don't talk nonsense! Come!'

He led her out, but once she reached the old archway, lit by a single torch bracketed to the wall, she wriggled free of his supporting grasp and leant back against the wall. The wind whipped her hair about her face, but its blustering energy seemed to give her strength.

'Leave me here, Jan … I need to breathe!'

'Breathe, then … but listen to me, Catherine! I know what you must be suffering now, but I forbid you to say that you are dead and that your life is finished! All men do not forget so easily. There are some capable of a greater love than you could dream of!'

'If Arnaud can forget me, who else could I ever trust?'

Without uttering a word, the painter unfastened his doublet, drew forth a folded and sealed parchment and held it out to her.

'Take this, and read it … I think the time has come to fulfil my mission. This torch gives enough light to read by … Read it then. You must! You need to …'

He slipped the parchment into her icy fingers. She twisted it round and round for a moment … It was sealed with a black sealing wax imprinted with a single *fleur-de-lis*.

'Open it,' Jan whispered.

She obeyed, almost automatically, and bent to decipher the few words of the brief message. She spelled them out, like a child.

'My longing for you never leaves me. Come back to me, my sweet love, and it is I who beg for forgiveness … Philippe.'

Catherine looked up and met the painter's anxious eyes. He spoke to her in a low, urgently persuasive voice.

'There is a man who has never forgotten you, Catherine … You spurned him, left him, humiliated him! But he thinks only of being allowed to love you again! Knowing the extent of his mad pride, you can appreciate all that that letter means, can't you? Come back with me, Catherine. Let me take you back to him. He loves you so much he will make you forget all your troubles! Once again you will be queen … and more! Come.'

He tried to lead her away from the place, but she resisted him. She gently shook her head. 'No, Jan. I would be queen, you say, and more! But what about the Duchess?'

'Monseigneur loves you alone. The Duchess has done her duty in presenting him with a son. He expects no more of her.'

'My pride would demand more! Whatever wrong Messire Arnaud may have committed, I still bear his name, and I could never debase it, like a prisoner, at his enemy's court.'

'You have had nothing to do with politics for a long time. Everything sorts itself out, Catherine. It won't be long before King Charles VII and the Duke make peace; everyone knows that!'

'Perhaps. But I have a son. I must bring him up in a manner suited to his rank. He shall never see his mother recognised as the Duke's mistress. I would never inflict such a gilded dishonour upon him!'

'You are still suffering from the shock of such a dreadful piece of news. Go and sleep for a while, Catherine. Tomorrow, by daylight, everything will look different to you. And you will realise that you owe it to yourself to live the brilliant destiny you have rejected. You would have lands of your own, a principality! Your son would be powerful beyond your dreams … Listen! Believe me! The Duke loves you more than ever!'

The young woman placed her hands over her ears and shook her head sorrowfully.

'Hush, Jan! I don't want to hear any more this evening. I am going back … to sleep for a while, if I can. Forgive me … you cannot understand.'

Pushing away his proffered hand once again, she ran back to the great hall. It was nearly dark, but the dying embers cast a fitful glow over the sleeping bodies scattered over the floor. Catherine saw Josse, curled into a ball like a cat, sleeping near the hearth. Only Ermengarde, sitting a little way off, was still awake.

She sat up as Catherine appeared, but the young woman signed to her not to move. She didn't want to get involved with all these people. More than ever she felt a pressing need for solitude. Not to brood about the letter, which she had dropped a little way back, not to lament her own fate. But she wanted to think, to try to see things straight ... Philippe's summons had been some help at least in giving her back some sense of perspective. The cloisters would be empty at this hour ... Despite the thickness of the walls, she could make out the voices of the monks chanting in the chapel. She clutched her cloak tighter, pushed open the low door leading into the cloisters and set out along the pillared walk, which was supported by massive buttresses built to carry the weight of roofs deep in snow. The chalky moonlight etched the severe lines of the building blackly against the bare white wintry garden.

She started walking slowly, a noiseless shadow amid the heavy shadows of the arches. She felt better if she kept moving. She felt herself regaining her self-possession as the searing agony of a little while back gradually gave way to anger ... After a quarter of an hour, Catherine suddenly discovered within herself, hungry, demanding, a furious desire for revenge! Fortunat had thought to destroy her by describing her husband languishing for love at the feet of another woman, and he had thought to inspire fear in her by depicting the fate of Christian women in the country of the Moors. But the poor wretch did not know that in order to achieve the end she had set herself Catherine had long been prepared for anything, the worst dangers, to murder if necessary, even to sell herself if there were no other way!

No, she would not abandon her husband to this woman! It had cost her too much to gain the right to claim him! What could the smiles and kisses of this infidel weigh when balanced against the terrifying weight of her own sufferings and tears? And if Arnaud thought he was rid of her forever, he was wrong! He might believe her married, but was that a reason to leave her still believing that he was a leper? He had thought only of his mother, not even of his own son, and like a traveller stripped of all encumbrances, had allowed himself to be carried off by the first woman who wooed him ...

'Even if it means working as a slave, under the lash, even if I have to undergo torture,' Catherine muttered under her breath, 'I shall go there myself and seek him out! ... I shall tell him that I know no master but him ... that I am still his wife. And then we'll see who prevails over him, me or this vile Moor!'

As her thoughts grew wilder so her steps accelerated. She was soon pacing rapidly up and down the cloister just as though she had not spent the entire day trudging across a mountain. Her cloak billowed out behind her like a black banner.

'I shall go there! I shall go to Granada!' she cried aloud. 'And I'd like to see anyone try to stop me!'

'Hush, Dame Catherine,' a voice came from behind one of the pillars. 'If you want to go there, it would be as well not to announce your plans from the rooftops … and you had better make haste.'

Finger to his lips, the tall thin form of Josse Rallard suddenly materialised beside her. He carried a bundle beneath one arm and kept throwing nervous glances behind him. Catherine gazed at him in astonishment.

'I thought you were asleep,' she said.

'So did some other people! Dame Ermengarde and your friend the lord-painter! They didn't pay any attention to me. And though they spoke in whispers, I heard it all …'

'What were they saying?'

'That presently, when everyone here was asleep, and you had finally decided to take some rest yourself, they would seize you and take you back with them to Burgundy!'

'What?' Catherine echoed, astounded. 'They want to kidnap me? By force? But that's monstrous!'

'No,' Josse said, smiling his odd, closed-lipped smile. 'All in all, it's even a friendly gesture … At first I thought they had evil designs on you … that they wanted to kill you perhaps … and I almost burst upon them there and then. But it isn't that: they want to kidnap you to save you from yourself, despite yourself. They know you well, and they are afraid you might decide to go straight to Granada, where the only thing that awaits you, in their opinion, is a horrible death.'

'They need only accompany me there,' Catherine cut in dryly, 'and the dangers would be halved. Even a Moorish prince would think twice before murdering an ambassador of Burgundy.'

'Who had no business to be there in the first place! I don't really think that your friend would take the risk, unless his master wished it. No, Dame Catherine, if you don't want to return to Dijon, if you want to escape from them, you must flee … and without delay!'

For a moment Catherine contemplated her strange servitor's irregular features. A suspicion crossed her mind. This story was hard to believe. She had known Ermengarde and Jean van Eyck too long to believe that they would constrain her by force. As for this lad, he was after all only a beggar and a scamp, and she knew scarcely anything about him except that he had agile fingers and a highly elastic conscience. She told him so without preamble.

'Why should I believe you? They are friends, old and faithful, whereas …'

'Whereas I am but a thief, a little Parisian beggar without a sou to his name, isn't that so? Listen, Dame Catherine, you have twice saved my life – once involuntarily, I admit, but the second time quite consciously. Were it not for you, I should now be quietly rotting on some gibbet in Figeac. In the Court of Miracles, among the beggars, there are some things we do not forget. We have our own notion of honour, after a fashion.'

Catherine did not reply at first. Josse could not guess at the echoes these words awoke in her, nor that she had once owed her own life and safety to this very Court of Miracles of which he talked … She said at last: 'Is it to pay off this debt that you are offering to accompany me to Granada? You know that I run worse risks than death there.'

'And if you should die,' Josse said calmly, 'I would be dead myself first! Otherwise I should count myself less than a man! … Now, time presses, Dame Catherine. Make up your mind! Either you believe me and we go, or you don't believe me … and you will wait and see. I know Spain a little, I have been there before. I know something of the language, and I could act as your guide.'

'You could equally well accompany me to Burgundy. And I dare say it would be more agreeable there!'

'I doubt it. These people who want to save you from yourself love you in the wrong way. They don't realise that you could never be happy leaving regrets behind you, leaving undone what you ought to have done! Myself, I would rather see you run every risk and share them with you, because you are like me: you never give up. And I believe you capable of overcoming the direst difficulties. I know full well the risks we shall be running, you and I: the lash of slavery, death, torture, and still worse for you, being a woman … but I think the adventure is worth attempting … You might find your husband again, and I might find the fortune that has never smiled upon me yet. They say the Kingdom of Granada is immensely rich … So? … Shall we go? The horses are saddled already, and waiting under the archway.'

A faint hope dawned in Catherine. This boy alone had hit upon the words she longed to hear. He was brave, intelligent, experienced. No! She was not going to wait till she was delivered, like a pretty, gold-ribboned package to Philippe of Burgundy, merely because two well-meaning lunatics thought this was the best way of ensuring her future happiness. She raised sparkling eyes on Josse.

'Let's go, then. I'm ready,' she cried, galvanised.

'One minute,' he said, handing the bundle to her. 'Here are some men's clothes I stole from one of the soldiers. Put them on and tie yours into a bundle. We can take them with us. But hurry up … It will be harder to pursue you like that!'

She snatched the clothes eagerly and, commanding Josse to keep watch, slipped behind a pillar and started to change, quite oblivious of the cold. A wonderful ardour glowed within her … The moment a chance to fight back presented itself, her chagrin was forgotten. There would be plenty of time to feel sorry for herself if she failed … but she didn't even want to consider that possibility for an instant!

And all of a sudden she seemed to hear a high-pitched lisping voice murmuring to her, out of the misty past: 'If one day you should be left without a place to go, or a thing to do, come and join me. In my little house on the banks of the Génil river, lemon and almond trees grow wild, and the rose bushes scent the air half the year round. You would be my sister and I would teach you the wisdom of Islam …'

Oh, the strange and faithful mirror of memory! The impression came back to her so distinctly that Catherine almost seemed to see, standing before her in the white moonlight, the slender shape of a young man dressed in a long blue robe, with a ridiculous white beard and an immense orange turban resembling a pumpkin … His name issued quite spontaneously from her lips:

'Abou! … Abou-al-Khayr! … Abou the doctor!'

Yet it was true, and she must have been deeply immersed in her grief not to have thought of it before! Abou, her old friend, lived in Granada! He was the doctor, the friend, of the Sultan. He would know what she should do, and would help her, she was sure of that!

Suddenly overwhelmed with joy, Catherine finished dressing hurriedly, rolled her clothes into a bundle under her arm and ran to join Josse.

'Let's go,' she cried. 'Let's be off, quick!'

He stared at her, amazed by the change such a short time had wrought in her. 'Egad! Dame Catherine, you look like a little fighting cock!'

'That's because we are going to fight, my friend, with every weapon, every trick at our command. I shall snatch my husband from that woman or die in the attempt! Into the saddle!'

Catherine and Josse slipped like two shadows from the darkness of the cloisters. The one danger was crossing the great hall, but the fire had sunk still lower, and much of the room was in total darkness … Stealing forward, supple as a cat, amid the outstretched forms, Catherine, securely hidden by her costume, chanced a glance at the hearth. Ermengarde sat chatting in a low voice with Jean van Eyck, who stood facing the fire. They must be discussing their plan … Catherine couldn't help smiling, and blowing them an ironical farewell kiss.

Slowly the two fugitives reached the door. Josse opened it cautiously, but the slight creak it made as it swung open was drowned by the snores of the Navarrese who slept nearby … Catherine slipped through it and Josse followed her.

'Saved!' he whispered. 'Now quick!'

He took her by the hand and led her out of the guest-house. Two horses stood waiting under the arch, already saddled and hooves muffled. Josse pointed joyfully to the clouds massing overhead. The moon was almost hidden already, and the too-revealing moonlight was lessening every moment.

'Look! The heavens are on our side! Into the saddle now, but take care –

the way is narrow and dangerous!'

'Less dangerous than men in general and friends in particular,' Catherine retorted.

An instant later, at a cautious trot, Catherine and her companion were heading toward Pamplona. With an almost defiant gesture, the young woman saluted the gigantic rock, which according to legend had been riven by Roland's sword from top to bottom. He had merely split a mountain in twain! She would do better than that! ...

PART II

THE SHADOW OF
THE PAST

5: The Iron Cage

Josse Rallard reined in his horse and pointed.

'There is Burgos,' he said, 'and night is upon us. Shall we stop there?'

Catherine examined the town laid out below, frowning. After the endless wastes of the frost-bound plateau, buffeted by cold winds, and the washed-out tawny plains, the capital of the Kings of Castile was a disappointment: a large grey and yellow city enclosed by walls of the same colour, and dominated by the threatening bulk of the massive fortress. Nothing remarkable there … and yet, perhaps there was: an immense building under construction, still garlanded by scaffolding but as elaborately wrought as lace-work and faceted like a precious jewel, seemed to glow in the dim evening light like reddish amber. It presided over the town like a mother hen over her chicks – Burgos Cathedral. Below the ramparts a slow-moving, muddy river flowed under a double-arched bridge. The whole place was depressingly suggestive of cold and damp. Catherine clutched her heavy riding cloak more tightly round her shoulders, shrugged and sighed.

'We will have to stop somewhere. So let's go.'

The two riders continued on their way in silence, descended the shallow incline and reached the bridge where the Santa Maria gate, between two round crenelated towers, gave entry to the city. It was market day and the bridge was crowded: there were ruddy-faced peasants with black beards, high cheekbones and low foreheads, dressed in sheepskins or goat-skins; women in grey or red woollen dresses, many of them carrying earthenware pitchers or baskets on their head; ragged beggars; urchins with bare feet and burning eyes. All were jumbled together with the sort of traffic most often encountered on the Spanish roads: donkeys, mules, clumsy carts, with an occasional hidalgo whose noble charger was constrained to travel at the same pace as the rest.

Catherine and her companion pushed bravely in among the throng. Catherine did not so much as glance at the picturesque to-ing and fro-ing of this colourful, noisy crowd, any more than she did at the women kneeling by the riverside washing sheepskins from the high plateau in the yellow waters of the Alanzon and punctuating their activity with shouts and splashings … Ever since her midnight flight from the guest-house at Roncesvaux the young woman's only interest in the journey was in the number of leagues remaining before Granada. She wished her horse had wings and was made of steel, and herself likewise, so that they might never need to stop. But she had to reckon with her horse's legs, and every hour that passed was a further torment to her.

The jealousy that Fortunat's tale of Arnaud's betrayal had awakened in her gnawed at her without respite. Catherine alternated between rage and despair, and all this merely added to the crushing fatigue of the journey, and exhausted her. At night, during the few hours of rest she allowed herself, she often woke with a start, running with sweat, seeming to hear the echo of tender words being exchanged a long way away. Then she would get up and go out into the fresh night air and walk and walk till the fury in her blood was somewhat eased. In the morning, dry-eyed and tight-lipped, she would set forth again on her journey, never once turning back …

She had never worried about the people she had left behind, or about the danger of pursuit. What did she care about Jean van Eyck, or Duke Philippe, or even that misguided and rash Ermengarde de Châteuvillain? Her world now was bounded by the seven letters that spelt the name Granada; and Josse Rallard, the odd squire she had acquired, took his cue from his mistress. He had promised to guide her to the kingdom of the Moors, and he intended to carry out his promise without trying to break the shell of silence in which Catherine journeyed.

Once through the Santa Maria gate, the two travellers found themselves in a vast square paved with rounded cobblestones and flanked on three sides by arcaded houses, the fourth being taken up by the cathedral … Here too there was a crowd, especially around the stalls where cross-legged peasants displayed and sold the produce of their smallholdings. A group of monks, chanting a psalm, was following a banner into the cathedral porch, and small knots of soldiers and constables moved here and there through the throng in twos and threes.

'There is not far away a guest-house for pilgrims, dedicated to Saint Lesmes,' Josse remarked, turning to Catherine. 'Would you like to go there?'

'I'm not a pilgrim any longer,' Catherine answered curtly, 'and I see another inn yonder. Let's go there.'

The Inn of the Three Kings stood backed against the city wall, its low door half hidden by a porch of blackened wood. Catherine dismounted and strode toward it, followed by Josse, who led both horses by their reins.

They were about to pass through the inn door when the crowd in the square, which had been relatively passive if noisy until then, suddenly swept like a human wave toward the city gates, crying and shouting ferociously. The explosion of sound was so sudden and savage that it pierced even Catherine's armour of indifference.

'What are they doing?' she asked.

'I don't know. I think they must have gone to meet something or someone, perhaps the King returning to his castle …'

'Oh, is that all …' Catherine murmured, even less interested in royal processions than in everything else. However, she paused before entering the inn. She even allowed herself to be swept along in the general confusion toward the Santa Maria gate, whence a curious procession had just emerged. A crude peasant cart came lurching forward over the uneven cobbles, surrounded by an escort of armed horsemen, lances in hand. The cart was surmounted by a cage built of stout wooden planks secured by iron bolts. And inside the cage was a man in chains.

All that could be seen of him was a more or less shapeless mass. The cage was too small for him to stand up. He was sitting in it with his head hidden between his knees, protected as far as possible by folded arms from the projectiles raining upon him from all sides. The crowd screamed for his death as they pelted him with rotten cabbages, horse dung and stones; but the massive form within never stirred so much as a muscle. He looked as if he were shaped of clay, for his hair and body were so thickly caked with mud and dust that their real colours were invisible. He was covered with dirty grey rags, but the ugly red crater of a recent wound could be seen on his head.

The crowd shrieked louder than ever, and the escort were obliged to push them back at lance-point, because otherwise they would have dragged the cage from the cart. Catherine could not tear herself away from this violent spectacle, and watched fascinated. She began to feel pity welling up inside her for this sorry wretch whom the populace attacked with such fury.

'My God,' she murmured, speaking her thoughts aloud, 'what can the poor wretch have done?'

'Don't waste your pity, young gentleman,' a slow voice with a pronounced German accent remarked close beside her. 'It is merely one of these accursed brigands who infest the Oca mountains, to the east of this city … They are bloodthirsty wolves who steal, loot, burn and put their prisoners to death with appalling cruelty when they cannot pay the ransom demanded of them.'

Catherine turned in astonishment toward the owner of the voice, who proved to be a man of about forty, with a frank but resolute face adorned by a silky blond beard and a pair of remarkably candid blue eyes. The man was tall, powerfully built, and one sensed the presence of solid muscles beneath the tunic of brown homespun veiled in the fine white dust that announced him to be a stonemason.

Catherine was taken by his frank smile. 'How is it that you speak my tongue?' she asked.

'I speak it badly enough in all conscience,' the man said with a laugh, 'but I understand it perfectly. My name is Hans of Cologne, and I am in charge of the building of the cathedral,' he said, pointing to the scaffolding near at hand.

'Of Cologne?' the young woman echoed, astonished. 'And it is this work that has brought you so far from your own country?'

'The Archbishop Alonso of Cartagena, whom I met three years ago at Basel, summoned me here. But you are not from here either ...'

A slight flush rose to Catherine's cheeks. She had not expected to be questioned about herself point-blank, and her answer was not prepared.

'My ... my name is Michel de Montsalvy,' she said hurriedly, so as not to give the lie to her masculine dress. 'I am travelling with my squire to see a bit of the world.'

'They say that travel forms the young. But you must be very innocent or optimistic, for there is nothing very agreeable to see in this country. Nature is wild here, and the people themselves half savage ...'

He stopped speaking. The crowd had suddenly fallen silent, and the hush was so complete that they could hear the faint moans of the chained man inside the cage.

A troop of constables now rode forward behind a severe-faced man, dressed in black from head to foot, mounted upon an Andalusian horse. His features, in the flickering light of the torches, were implacable and as hard as granite. He advanced slowly, amidst the respectful silence of the crowd, toward the cage.

'That is the Criminal Judge, Don Martin Gomez Calvo,' Hans whispered in tones of anxious respect. 'A terrible man. That apparently austere manner of his conceals a ferocity even more savage than that of the bandits of Oca.'

It certainly seemed as though the crowd gave way almost fearfully before him. The constables following behind did not need to use their weapons at all, because the populace seemed anxious to put as much space as possible between themselves and this alarming personage.

Don Martin circled the cage on horseback. Then he drew his sword and pricked the prisoner with its point. The chained man raised his head, revealing a face half hidden by a shaggy beard. Catherine found herself shuddering, without quite knowing why, and then she took a few steps forward as if drawn by a magnet.

In the silence the prisoner could be heard moaning: 'I'm thirsty,' he faltered, in French, 'thirsty ...'

He cried out his last word and this cry was answered by Catherine's, wrenched from her very heart:

'Gauthier!'

She had recognised her lost friend's voice instantly, and now she had no difficulty in discerning the familiar features beneath the shaggy mat of hair.

A crazy joy swept through her, and for a moment she forgot the pitiable state of the chained man. She would have sped forward like an arrow, but Hans' heavy hand descended on her shoulder, nailing her to the spot.

'Keep still, for pity's sake! Are you out of your mind?'

'It isn't a bandit, it's my friend ... Leave me alone!'

'Dame Catherine, I implore you,' came Josse's voice urgently, as he seized her other shoulder.

Hans jumped: 'Dame Catherine?'

'Yes,' Catherine cried angrily, 'I am a woman, the Countess of Montsalvy. But what does that have to do with you?'

'A great deal. That changes everything.'

Without more ado, the master-mason stowed Catherine under one arm, as if she were merely a bundle, clapped a big hand over her mouth and transported her thus as far as a low building standing behind the cathedral cloisters. He pushed the door open with a flying kick.

'Follow me with the horses,' he called to Josse as he pushed through the crowd. No-one paid the slightest attention to them. All eyes were riveted on the Judge and his prisoner. As they crossed the square, Catherine was conscious of the Spaniard giving orders in his imperious voice, but she could not understand a word. She observed the crowd's satisfied murmur, though, and the almost voluptuous sigh that went up from every breast... Mobs react in much the same way all over the world, and Catherine guessed that the Judge must have promised them some particularly choice spectacle ...

'What did he say?' she was about to call out, but Hans' firm hand clapped over her mouth stifled her cries. He did not release her until they were safely inside the wide, dark passage. Then he turned to Josse, who was following behind, and said: 'Shut the door, fast. And come here.'

The passage opened into a covered courtyard piled with great blocks of stone. Under a covered gallery, a row of half-carved statues of saints could be dimly seen. A fire-pot hanging from a wooden pillar cast a feeble glow about the yard, dimly illuminating the worn rim of an ancient Roman well that gaped in the middle. Hans pointed out to Josse where he should make fast the horses, and then finally set Catherine none too gently down on her feet.

'There,' he said, in tones of satisfaction. 'Now you can scream to your heart's content.'

Catherine was scarlet with fury, and half suffocated, and she sprang at him like a wild cat, but Hans caught her by the wrists and mastered her.

'I demand to be set free,' she cried. 'Who do you think you are? Who gave you permission to treat me like this?'

'The fact is that I have taken a liking to you, young gentleman, Dame Catherine or what you will, and if I had let you do as you wanted, you would by now have been marched off by a dozen guards, solidly bound and gagged and thrown into prison to await the Judge's pleasure. And what use would you have been to your friend then?'

Catherine's anger subsided as she listened to the master-mason's wise counsel, but she was not prepared to give up so easily.

'There was no need to shut me up like this. I am a woman, as I said, and no Castilian but a loyal subject of King Charles of France, as well as a lady-in-waiting to Queen Yolande of Aragon … Here, look,' she said, burrowing into her purse and producing the engraved emerald. 'Here is a ring the Queen gave me … Do you believe me now? That Judge would have to hear me out!'

'Were you the Queen Yolande in person you could not be certain of emerging from the Judge's clutches with your life! Particularly since the Aragon family is unpopular in Castile. That man is a wild beast! And all the jewel would do is provoke his envy. Don Martin would simply seize the ring and have you thrown into some dungeon till your friend had been safely executed.'

'He wouldn't dare! I am a noblewoman and a foreigner. I might complain …'

'To whom? King John and his Court are at Toledo, and anyway, they would be no use to you if they were here. The King of Castile is a weakling who dislikes making decisions of any kind. There is but one man who might help you: the one who is the real master of this kingdom, Constable Alvaro de Luna.'

'Then I shall go to him …'

Hans shrugged. He fetched a pitcher of wine and filled three goblets, which he set down near the well.

'What can you do? The Constable is fighting near the borders of Granada; the Judge and the Archbishop are masters of the town.'

'Then I'll speak to the Archbishop … Didn't you say it was he who brought you here?'

'Yes, that's true. Monseigneur Alonso is a good and just man, but there is an implacable hatred between him and the Judge. He would only have to intercede for your friend's life for the Judge to refuse it. You must understand that the Judge has the support of an army, whereas the other has only his monks. Don Martin knows this … and takes advantage of it. Come and see … but first take a drink of wine. You need it.'

His gentleness surprised Catherine. She looked up. Her eyes met those of this quiet man offering her a cup of wine, a stranger, but one who had proved himself a friend. Instinctively, she found herself looking for a reason. A spontaneous liking no doubt, but also the admiration she had grown accustomed to reading in men's eyes. She knew her own power, and it looked as though this man was not immune to it.

Catherine took a sip of wine from the tin cup. It was rough, strong wine and it did her good, warming her. She drained the cup to the last drop and handed it back to Hans.

'There you are! Now what is it I am to see?'

She followed her host into a low-ceilinged chamber without light or a fire, where there were rows of mattresses covered with bed linen and quilts. A tiny window, stoutly barred, opened into the square below. A strong smell of human sweat and acrid dust reached them.

'My workers all sleep here,' Hans explained. 'But they are all out in the square at the moment … Here, look through this window.'

Outside, the din of shouting and laughter seemed to have redoubled its volume. What she saw drew an exclamation of horror from Catherine. The heavy cage containing the prisoner had been raised by means of one of the massive winches used to lift stones on to the cathedral, and was now dangling at the height of a three-storey building. The crowd massed below, staring upwards and still trying to pelt the prisoner with whatever came to hand … Catherine looked away and met Hans' curious gaze.

'Why have they put him up there?'

'To amuse the mob. This way they can enjoy the man's sufferings until the hour of his execution. Because of course they won't give him any food or drink …'

'And … when?'

'Is the execution to be? In a week's time.'

Catherine exclaimed in horror and her eyes filled with tears.

'A week? But he'll be dead long before then …'

'No,' came Josse's grating voice. 'The man in black said that the prisoner was as strong as a bear and would still be alive to endure the punishment meted out to him …'

'And what is this punishment to be?' Catherine whispered, her throat dry.

'Why tell her?' Hans said reproachfully. 'It would be better to let her wait till the day itself.'

'Dame Catherine likes to look facts in the face, comrade,' Josse answered curtly. 'Don't imagine that she would let you hide the truth from her!' Then he turned toward her. 'In a week's time he is to be skinned alive so that the skin of this exceptional figure of a man can be used to make a statue of Christ. The remains will be burned …'

Catherine's hair stood up on her head in sheer horror. She leant against the wall, clutching her stomach, suddenly twisted by nausea. Hans saw her go green and would have supported her, but she pushed him away.

'No. Don't. I'll soon be all right …'

'Did you really have to tell her that?' the German grumbled.

'He was quite right to tell me. Josse knows what I'm like.'

She sank down upon one of the mattresses and held her head in her hands. The merciless times in which she lived, the horrors of war that had always surrounded her, had inured her to much brutality, but what she had just heard passed the bounds of human imagination.

'Are these people mad? Or am I? Could there be anything more barbarous?'

'Still worse things happen under the Moorish kings of Granada,' Josse said sadly. 'But I have to admit that this country loves blood more than most …'

Catherine didn't even hear him. She kept repeating to herself, as if trying to make sense of such a barbarism, the meaning and significance of a statue of Christ. Such an abomination, such a sacrilege seemed unthinkable.

'There already is a statue of the kind in the cathedral,' the master-mason calmly observed. 'Now come. Don't stay here. It's cold and my men will soon be returning …'

He took her gently by the arm and led her across the inner courtyard as far as an immense kitchen that took up the entire width of the house. A fire crackled in there below a blackened cooking-pot that emitted a tolerably appetising smell. An elderly servant woman sat fast asleep on a stool close to a wine barrel, hands clasped in her lap and mouth wide open. Hans nodded toward her as he sat Catherine down on a bench.

'Her name is Urraca. And she is as deaf as a post. We can talk safely here …'

He went over to the old woman and shook her. No sooner were her eyes open than she let loose a stream of incomprehensible words. Without even looking at the two strangers, she unhooked the cooking-pot and set it down on the table. After that she took some wooden bowls from a chest and filled them with soup, moving with astonishing alertness. Then she went back to sleep on her stool. Hans handed one of the bowls to Catherine, served Josse and sat down beside them.

'Eat first,' he advised, lifting Catherine's bowl to her lips, since she seemed too overcome to move. 'Eat. Afterwards you will be able to think more clearly.'

She sipped the thick flour and bacon soup, burnt her lips and grimaced. Then she set the bowl back on the table and looked from one companion to the other.

'I must save Gauthier. My life won't be worth living if I allow him to die in such a terrible way.'

Her remark was met with silence. Hans calmly went on eating, without replying. When he had finished, he pushed away the bowl, wiped his mouth on his sleeve and murmured:

'Lady, I would not offend you for anything. This man was your servant, even your friend, but time changes men's hearts. The bandits of Oca are cruel monsters, and this man was one of them. His soul must be burdened with crimes like theirs. Why risk your own life for a man like that?'

'You don't understand. You don't know a thing about it. How could you? You don't know Gauthier, or the sort of man he is. I will tell you, Master Hans: there isn't a kinder heart, or more loyal soul in the whole Kingdom of France. It is only a few months since he disappeared, and I know very well that neither gold, nor anxiety to save his own skin, could ever have changed him so utterly. Listen to what I am about to tell you first, and then judge for yourself the kind of man he is.'

Simply, and without seeking for eloquent effects, she told the German of the Gauthier she knew, how he had protected her, saved her life on many occasions, how he had set out in search of Arnaud, and how he had finally disappeared into a ravine in the Pyrenees. Hans listened without saying a word.

'Now do you understand,' she said at last. 'Do you understand how impossible it is for me to leave him to die? Particularly such a horrible death as that?'

Hans was silent a moment longer, flexing and unflexing his fingers mechanically. Then he looked up.

'I understand. I will help you.'

'Why should you help us?' Josse interrupted brusquely. 'We are complete strangers to you, and there is no reason why you should endanger your life for strangers. Life is good. You should hang on to it. Unless you have your eye on the Queen's emerald, of course …'

Hans stood up so suddenly that the bench he was sitting on fell over with a crash. He was scarlet, and he shook his fist menacingly under Josse's nose.

'Say that once again, friend, and I'll smash your face in,' he growled. 'Hans of Cologne expects no payment for his services, remember that!'

Catherine flung herself between the two men, and gently pushed Hans' fist away with her small hand. Josse was staring at the German meanwhile with perfect composure.

'Forgive him, Master Hans. It's difficult to trust people in these times, but I believe you. There are some eyes one cannot be mistaken about. And you wouldn't have behaved as you have done so far if you had any ulterior motive. But there is some sense in what Josse says. Why should you endanger yourself to help us?'

As she spoke, Hans' face returned to its normal colour. When she had finished he regarded his opponent with an expression that could almost have passed for a smile. Then he shrugged.

'I really don't know. Perhaps because I like the look of you. Possibly just to please myself. This man is from the north, like me, like you too. And then he interests me. I am reluctant to let these bloodthirsty brutes hack him to pieces like a carcass in a butcher's shop. I don't think I should sleep so soundly afterwards. And finally … I hate the Judge. He had one of my workers' hands cut off on the pretext that he had stolen something. I should be delighted to pay him back …'

He crossed the room, pulled a roll of bedding out of the corner and spread it out close by the hearth.

'Lie down here and try to get some sleep,' he told Catherine. 'After midnight, when the night is blackest, we will climb the tower and see if we can get to the cage.'

'Do you think there is a chance of getting him out?' Catherine asked, eyes sparkling with new hope.

'I doubt we can do anything tonight. We shall have to see how the land lies up there; and besides, we should have to prepare for his escape first. But we might be able to pass him food and drink.'

It was long after the night-watchman called the midnight hour when the door of the master-mason's house opened and three shadowy figures stole out, two tall and one small. Except for the soldiers and guards posted at the foot of the cathedral towers there wasn't a living soul to be seen in the great square. Only a cat, which slipped like a ghost past the three nocturnal wanderers …

Catherine, Josse and Hans slipped into the shadow of the cathedral cloister, making for the Sarmental door, to which Hans had a key. He was engaged in building a chapel close to the door, as it happened. The three of them stole forward, holding their breath and taking care not to stumble against loose stones. Josse carried a pitcher of water under one arm, while Hans carried a chunk of ham and a small loaf. Catherine alone carried nothing. She walked along with her eyes fixed on the ground, not daring to look up in case she caught sight of the sinister silhouette of the cage darkly outlined against the night sky.

'Careful,' Hans warned as they reached the door at the top of a flight of steps. 'Not a sound in the church itself. It's as hollow as a drum, and there are always two monks in there, praying. They take turns throughout the night. Give me your hand, Dame Catherine. I will guide you.'

She slipped her hand into the master-mason's large, callused paw and followed him obediently, with Josse clutching hold of a fold of her cape. The small door let into the immense cathedral door didn't even squeak as Hans cautiously pushed it open. The three companions could see two monks kneeling in prayer in the choir, their shaven heads reflecting back the yellow glow of a single oil lamp. The monotonous murmur of the two voices was clearly audible.

Hans crossed himself hurriedly. Then he led his two companions swiftly across the half-built chapel and into the deep shadow of the pillars. They crept noiselessly as phantoms toward the tower stairway and then as silently up it. Inside it was dark as a grave. Hans closed the door carefully and then slid the bolt. Two torches lay ready on the ground. He lit one and held it above his head to illuminate the stone shaft.

'I'll put it out when we reach the top,' he said. 'Now, make haste!'

One behind the other they crept up the narrow stairs, not stopping once till they reached the top. When Hans ground the torch underfoot, the three of them were breathless and panting from the speed of their climb. The sharp night air blew cool against Catherine's face. The place where they stood was open to the sky, but although it was a clear night, spangled with stars, it took her some time to get sufficiently used to the darkness to distinguish her surroundings.

'Careful not to fall,' Hans whispered. 'There are stones and planks everywhere.'

They were standing on the German's current working platform. He was engaged in raising tall carved spires atop the square towers, embellished with a wealth of detail that did credit to his skill. The huge winch and its dangling wooden cage were clearly outlined against the sky, and Catherine stared at it with the sort of horror she might have accorded an instrument of torture.

Guided by Hans' attentive hand, she reached the balustrade that ran round the tower and looked over it. The cage revolved gently on its chain just below. Through the wooden slats of which it was built she could just glimpse the prisoner. He was staring up, as if looking at the sky, and a ceaseless, soft moaning sound came from his lips. It was so weak that Catherine shivered with distress. She turned imploring eyes to Hans.

'We must raise him up and get him out of that cage at once. He is hurt.'

'I know. But we can't possibly pull him up tonight. The winch makes a dreadful noise; if I tried moving it I would attract the attention of the guards below, and we wouldn't get a step farther.'

'Can't you do something to stop it creaking?'

'Yes, of course. It needs oiling and greasing, but that isn't a task that can be accomplished in pitch darkness. Besides, as I said, we have to prepare for this man's escape first. For the time being all we can do is try to give him something to eat and drink. Call him very softly. We mustn't attract the soldiers' attention.'

With Josse holding her fast about the waist, Catherine leant as far forward as she dared, and called softly:

'Gauthier! ... Gauthier! ... 'Tis I, Catherine!'

The prisoner swung his head slowly round, but without betraying the slightest sign of surprise.

'Ca-the-rine,' he repeated slowly, in a voice that sounded like something in a dream. Then, after a moment during which she could hear her heart hammering, 'I'm thirsty …' he murmured.

Catherine's heart ached in sympathy. Was he so weak already that words meant nothing to him? She tried again.

'Gauthier! Please, answer me! Look at me! It is Catherine de Montsalvy, you know me!'

'Wait a moment,' Hans whispered, pulling her back. 'Let's give him something to drink first. Then we will see.'

He swiftly fastened the narrow handle of the pitcher to a long wooden pole lying nearby and lowered it gently into the cage. He guided it into the chained man's hands, but Gauthier still stared upwards unseeing.

'Here, friend,' he ordered, 'drink this.'

When he felt the cool damp earthenware in his hands, the prisoner underwent a positive transformation. He snatched it with a hoarse cry and drank from it greedily, draining it to the last drop. When it was empty, he let go of it and sank back into his torpor. Catherine's heart was too full to do more than murmur:

'He doesn't recognise me. He seems scarcely to hear what is said to him.'

'That must be fever,' Hans said. 'He has a wound on his head. Now let's try and get him to eat something.'

The solid food was received as avidly as the water had been, but the prisoner remained quite deaf to Catherine's appeals and entreaties. He looked up at her, staring through her as if she were transparent, and then looked away again. A sort of slow monotonous chant came from him, a rambling unconscious lament that Catherine found terrifying.

'My God!' she cried. 'He has gone mad!'

'I don't think so,' Hans said encouragingly. 'But, as I have said, he is probably delirious. Now come, Dame Catherine. There is nothing more we can do for him at the moment. We shall return home now. Tomorrow, during the day, I shall see that the winch is oiled so that it doesn't squeak. And possibly tomorrow night we may be able to get him out of there.'

'But how can we ever get him out of the city? The gates are solid-looking, and well guarded.'

'One thing at a time. I have an idea …'

'With a length of good rope,' Josse whispered, opening his mouth for the first time since they had entered the church, 'it would always be possible to drop down from the ramparts.'

'Yes … if the worst came to the worst. But I think I may have a better solution. A master-mason learns many things simply by keeping his eyes open. Now, we must get down again.'

With one last look at the caged man, Catherine allowed herself to be guided back to the stairs. The monks were still at prayer in the dark cathedral nave, quite unsuspecting of the presence of the three companions. The door closed behind them without a sound. Catherine and the two men found themselves back in the street.

When they reached the master-mason's house, Hans gave his guests a few words of advice.

'As far as everyone here is concerned, you will both be cousins of mine on their way to Compostela. But try not to mingle too much with the workers all the same. Some of them are from my country and they would be surprised to find you did not speak our tongue. Apart from that you can come and go as you please.'

'Thank you,' Catherine replied, 'but I don't really want to go outside much. The sight of that awful cage makes me feel ill. I shall stay in the house.'

'Not I, though,' said Josse. 'When there is an escape to arrange, it's as well to keep one's eyes and ears open.'

The next day was torture for Catherine. She stayed shut up in Hans' house, trying not to look outside, where a heavy rain had been falling since the morning, or to hear the occasional threats and curses shouted at the wretched prisoner in the cage. She spent the day alone with old Urraca as sole company. She did not find her particularly consoling. From time to time the old woman's sunken lips would utter words Catherine did not understand. Urraca went about the kitchen talking to herself as deaf people often do, doing her work almost automatically. At the time of the midday meal she pushed a bowl across the table toward Catherine, accompanied by some half-burnt cakes and a pitcher of water, then returned to her stool, where she sat studying the young woman so intently that it began to prey on her nerves. Catherine finally turned her back on her and went to sit in the inner courtyard to await the men's return.

Josse had gone out at the same time as Hans, saying he wanted to make a tour of the town and get to know it. When he returned, toward the middle of the afternoon, his face was grave. When Catherine questioned him anxiously, he shrugged.

'It won't be easy getting away from here,' he said at last. 'I really think it might spark off a revolt. The people here are like untamed beasts. They hate the bandits so much that they can't contain their joy at the thought of having one in their power. If anyone takes their prey from them they will probably tear the whole place down.'

'Let them,' Catherine cried. 'I don't care! We don't belong to this country. The only thing I care about is Gauthier's life ...'

Josse flashed her a quick, sidelong glance. 'Do you like him as much as all that?' he asked, with a trace of sarcasm that was not lost on Catherine. She turned her violet eyes on his, and declared, with some arrogance:

'Yes, I do love him ... as if he were my own brother, if not more. He is only a peasant, but his great heart, his courage and loyalty, make him worthier of gold spurs than many a noble I can think of. And if you hope to get me to leave this town and abandon him to these savages, you are wasting your time. Even if I should lose my life in the attempt, I must try every means of saving him.'

Josse's mouth curved like a half-moon in a silent smile, while a sparkle danced in his eyes. 'And who said anything to the contrary, Dame Catherine? I merely remarked that it would be difficult and that we ran the danger of sparking off a revolt, that was all. Listen!'

Just then another salvo of jeers and curses, and cries of 'Death to him', was heard outside in the dusk.

'The Judge has doubled the guard at the foot of the tower. There is a great crowd out there, packed into the square, all soaked by the rain but howling like wolves.'

'He has doubled the guard?' Catherine echoed, going pale.

'It isn't the guard that worries me, it's the crowd,' said Hans, who entered just then, dripping water. 'If the rain hasn't driven them away, they are quite capable of spending the whole night there, peering upwards. In which case, it's farewell to our scheme.'

He shook himself like a dog, twisting his shoulders to get the drops off them. The look he gave Catherine was compassionate. Her face was white as chalk, and she was clearly fighting for self-control. She did not speak for a moment, and Hans occupied himself in removing his shoes. which were loaded with mud. Finally she asked:

'What about the winch? Have you been able to see to it?'

'Yes, of course. I pretended that something had gone wrong with it, and slapped enough grease on it to fry it in. But what can you hope to achieve, with all those people down there, staring and shouting? We wouldn't even be able to give the prisoner any food or drink.'

'They must go!' Catherine gritted between clenched teeth. 'They *must!*'

'Yes, but how are we going to make them?' Josse asked. 'If the waters of heaven itself can't arrange it …'

At that precise moment a clap of thunder boomed out, so unexpectedly that it made the three of them jump. And it seemed as though the heavens opened. The rain became a torrent. Great jets of water hurtled down with such violence that in a few minutes the square was deserted. The crowd dispersed, running back to their homes, protecting themselves as best they could against the sudden downpour. The guards shrank up against the cathedral wall in search of shelter. The workers left the towers. The cage alone remained, buffeted by the wind and rain so ferociously that it started swinging like a pendulum.

Catherine, Hans and Josse stood crowding for a view out of the little window overlooking the square.

'If only this would last,' Catherine murmured. 'But it's only a thunderstorm …'

'Some thunderstorms last,' Hans remarked encouragingly.

'In any case, it's growing dark … and it will be an unusually black night tonight. Now come, my men are returning. You must sup, and get some rest. We have a lot to do tonight …'

The evening dragged by even more slowly for Catherine than the day had done. The rain did not abate. Its furious drumming could be heard on the roof. The workmen supped in silence and then, one by one, shoulders bowed with fatigue, crept upstairs to their beds. Only two or three stayed behind to drink beer with Hans from the great barrel near the hearth.

Catherine sat opposite Josse in the chimney-seat, waiting. Josse had his cap pulled down over his eyes and his arms folded, feigning sleep.

Catherine closed her eyes too, but sleep would not come. Too many thoughts crowded into her mind, all of them connected with the man in his wooden cage exposed up there to the fury of the elements. Catherine found herself thinking sadly that the heavens themselves seemed intent on meting out punishment to the unbeliever that Gauthier was. Then she grew both anxious and impatient about the task that awaited them. Would they ever succeed in carrying out their plan? And once Gauthier had been freed from that dreadful cage, how would they smuggle him out of the city? Wouldn't brave Hans suffer terrible consequences for his part in the escape? These and many more were the questions that tormented her, especially since they seemed unanswerable.

At last the men withdrew and the fire sank low. Old Urraca had long since disappeared into some corner. Darkness gradually crept over the smoky kitchen. The house was full of snores, but Catherine still sat, eyes wide open, listening to the heavy beating of her heart. She did not even feel like stretching out, and as soon as Hans' figure appeared she stood up. Josse was on his feet a moment later.

'Come,' Hans said … 'It's now or never …'

The three of them were standing close to the well on the working platform. The rain had stopped but the night was pitch dark. The cage was no more than a darker smudge in a sea of shadows. The roofs of the town and the surrounding countryside were completely swallowed up.

'It's too dark to see a thing,' Catherine whispered. 'What can we do?'

'I can see just enough,' Hans interrupted. 'That's the main thing. Careful, Josse. I am going to winch up the cage …'

The master-mason rolled back his sleeves, spat on the palms of his hands and seized hold of the immense wheel at which Catherine gazed in alarm, finding it hard to believe that a single man would ever succeed in moving it.

'I'm going to help you,' she whispered.

'No … let me be. It would be better for you to help Josse grab hold of the cage when it comes level with the platform. That won't be too easy, either. Don't worry about the winch. I know it of old.'

Hans took a deep breath and began dragging at the huge handle. The cage trembled for a moment and then, very slowly, started to rise. There wasn't a sound to be heard. The greasing must have been very thorough. There was no movement from the cage. The man inside seemed to be lying there in an inert mass.

'Pray God he's not dead,' Catherine whispered, alarmed by this immobility.

'Pray God Hans manages to bring it up here, that's all,' Josse answered, anxiously. 'Raising a cage like that alone is work for a titan.'

And the fantastic strain Hans was undergoing could be guessed at from his laboured breathing. Catherine felt in the innermost particles of her being this terrible struggle between one man's strength and the great weight suspended from the winch. The cage was moving only a fraction now.

'My God, he'll never do it!' she groaned. And she was on the point of springing to Hans' assistance when something cut short her breath – a shadowy figure had just emerged from the dark well of the tower staircase. She didn't even have time to cry out. The newcomer said two or three words in an unknown tongue and then set to work, helping Hans.

'Who is this man?' Catherine asked, dumbfounded.

'Don't be afraid. It's Hatto, my chief assistant. He guessed what we were about, and he has come to help.'

'Why should he?'

'Gottlieb, the man whose hand Don Martin had cut off, is his brother. You can trust him.'

'Anyway, we have no choice … not that a helper isn't rather useful …'

'That is no exaggeration. I thought I was going to have to let go altogether. This cage is so heavy it seems to drag your muscles out of their sockets.'

Without a word, Catherine joined Josse, shuddering a little at the thought of what Gauthier had narrowly escaped. The cage was rising up faster now, and the top of it was level with the platform. Then it rose above it … Josse reached out with a hook and pulled the cage toward him.

'Gently,' Hans whispered, 'gently. We must get it down without making any noise.'

This part of the proceedings was difficult and dangerous. Catherine held her breath. Despite the cold night, she was running with sweat. But as she grasped hold of the rough wooden cage she felt a sharp thrill of triumph. For a moment the cramped little prison revolved gently a few inches above the platform, and then, so slowly that Catherine's heart pounded wildly, came to rest. The men at the winch gave a sigh of relief. Catherine sensed rather than saw them wiping their brows on their sleeves.

'This night is as black as ink,' Hans grumbled. 'We have to grope about … Can you find your way to the door?'

'Yes,' said Josse, 'I have it.'

The heavy iron bolt that secured the door was too crudely fashioned to present much difficulty. Once the door was open Catherine leant inside, feeling impatiently for the inert, soaked human mass within.

'He's not moving at all,' she said anxiously; 'he must be dead …'

'We'll see about that!' Josse replied. 'Out of the way, Dame Catherine. Let me have a look …'

'Be quick,' Hans mumbled, 'look at the sky …'

Just then a faint gleam shone forth from behind a screen of clouds. It was not very bright, but it suddenly made visibility much greater.

'If one of the guards or any other citizen should take it into his head to look up and see that the cage has moved, we shall have the whole town about our ears in a moment. In which case, may the Lord protect us!'

'In all the countries of the world,' Catherine observed dryly, 'churches are a place of refuge.'

'In all the other countries perhaps … but here I'm not so certain.'

Slowly and cautiously the three men drew the prisoner out of the cage. He was quite motionless. They couldn't even hear him breathe. Catherine hurriedly placed her hand over his heart, and withdrew it with a sigh of relief.

'He's alive,' she whispered. 'But I don't know how long he is likely to last.'

'Quick,' Hans commanded. 'Undress him.'

'But why?'

'You will soon see. For the love of God, make haste. The sky grows lighter every minute.'

As if to underline his words, they heard one of the guards below coughing, and then the clink of lance on stone. All four accomplices froze, hearts beating wildly, awaiting the cry that must give them away … But nothing happened. Four sighs of relief escaped simultaneously. Josse, Catherine and Hatto tore off Gauthier's clothes while Hans opened the heavy sack he had been carrying. It contained a massive piece of wood roughly carved into the shape of a man bent double.

'The cage must look as if it is still occupied,' Hans whispered, 'otherwise the town will be searched by dawn and we will never have a chance of getting this man out. With a little luck, no-one will notice the trick for several days.'

Catherine had already guessed what the German had planned to do. It took very little time to remove the rags in which Gauthier was clothed. They wrapped his unconscious body in a cloak while Hans installed the decoy in the cage, covering it as best he could with the prisoner's rags together with a few he had brought with him. A lump of clay, also wrapped in rags, gave the illusion of a head resting on its arms. In the dark the effect was astonishingly convincing.

'This would not take anyone in, standing on the towers in broad daylight,' said Hans, 'but it should pass muster from below.'

It was the chains binding the prisoner that presented the most difficulty. Hans had brought various tools in the bag he gave Josse, but the tricky thing was to file off the chains without wounding Gauthier. The slightest cry from him would have been fatal. Catherine held her breath fearfully as Hans started sawing at the ankle bracelets; in spite of the greasy rags wrapped round all the tools, the noise was fearful. But the master-mason was unusually skilful. The operation was concluded without so much as a sigh from the wounded man.

They hastily arranged the manacles and chains on the crude dummy figure in the cage. Then, after closing up the cage, Hans and Hatto started working the winch, while Catherine and Josse made certain that it descended without bumping or jarring. A few minutes later, the horrific instrument of torture had regained its place alongside the tower. Not a moment too soon!

Almost as if it had been waiting till now to show itself, the moon swam out from behind a belt of clouds and its harsh white light flooded the whole scene. At the same time, they heard the guards exchanging a few words in their guttural language at the foot of the tower.

Catherine saw Hans' teeth flash, and realised that he was smiling.

'Let us go,' he whispered. 'The heavens really are on our side tonight! We shall have to carry our freed man now, and that's not going to be too easy in view of his weight! The tower staircase is steep. It's as well that Hatto has come to our assistance. You go in front, Dame Catherine, and carry the torch to light the way.'

The three men picked Gauthier up, one by the feet and the other two by the shoulders. Meanwhile Catherine hurriedly lit the torch in the shelter of the staircase. Then the little party entered the narrow stone shaft, moving very slowly with their burden.

Although his privations had left Gauthier much thinner, he still weighed a good deal, and it was no easy feat manoeuvring his huge frame down such a narrow stairway. Catherine preceded the group, nervously glancing back at the wounded man from time to time, searching for some slight flicker of life under the layers of filth and straggling beard that almost masked his face. But there was nothing, not the slightest sign of returning consciousness. There was only a sigh of relief as the three men reached the foot of the tower and their task grew correspondingly easier.

Easier, but also more dangerous. It only needed one of the praying monks to turn his head, or one of the guards outside to look inside the church, for the four conspirators to be irrevocably lost.

Holding their breath, Catherine and her companions glided stealthily toward the door. They were almost upon it when suddenly, and quite unexpectedly, Gauthier uttered a moan. In the profound silence of the church, barely disturbed by the monotonous murmurings of the monks, it resounded in Catherine's ears like the Last Trump. The three men only just had time to lift their burden into the shadow of one of the immense pillars, near the screen of one of the small chapels, while Catherine clapped her hand hastily over the wounded man's mouth.

The next few moments were agony for all of them. Catherine felt her heart thumping in terror in her breast. And because they were all squashed together, she could hear Hans' agitated breathing in her ear. The monks had stopped praying in the choir. They looked in the direction from which the sound had come. Catherine could see the profile of one of them silhouetted against a candle flame. The other even made as if to get to his feet, but his companion detained him.

'Es un gato,'* he said. And with that they went back to their prayers. But the little group were not much better off than before. Catherine felt Gauthier stirring beneath her hand. He was trying to shake off this gag. And if he were to start to groan in earnest she would never be able to stifle the noise.

'How are we going to keep him quiet?' Catherine whispered in alarm, pressing her hand down as hard as she dared. A faint sound escaped from underneath, like water running under a stone. Once more, they believed themselves lost. The monks were bound to stop praying again. And this time they would surely come to see …

'If it's necessary to knock him out, we'll knock him out,' Josse remarked imperturbably. 'But we must get out of here.'

Suddenly, in the far depths of the church, they heard a bell tolling, followed almost immediately by the grave and mournful chanting of some fifty men, gradually growing louder. Catherine felt Hans start beside her, and when she turned round he was smiling.

'The monks,' he said. 'They have come to sing the Prime. Now is the moment.'

With one accord, the three men snatched Gauthier up and swung off with him along the side aisle as if he had been as light as a feather. Not a moment too soon. Gauthier's groans came without stopping now. But the holy men's strong voices, which sent plain chant echoing to the lofty vaulted roof of the cathedral, more than engulfed the sick man's complaints. They

---

* 'It's a cat.'

rushed through the door like a whirlwind. Whatever happened, they must not be seen by the approaching procession of monks winding toward them from the direction of the cathedral cloister. Breathless and panting, the four companions and their burden emerged into the porch. The moon was still shining but there was a patch of intense darkness all along the cathedral wall.

'One last effort,' Hans whispered joyfully, 'and we've made it! Quick now, let's take him home …'

A few moments later the low door of the master-mason's house swung silently shut behind them. Catherine was exhausted and deliriously happy all at once, and she collapsed on the wall of the well. Then, unable to control her taut nerves a moment longer, she burst into hysterical sobs.

6: The Death of a Sinner

Wisely, Hans, Josse and Hatto left Catherine to sob away all her accumulated tensions. They carried Gauthier into the shed where the master-mason kept his blocks of marble and sandstone, laid him on a bed of straw that Hatto hastily made ready for him, and set about examining his wounds. Catherine suddenly realised that she was alone. She dried her eyes and went in search of the others. She felt extraordinarily relaxed, relieved even of her physical weariness. Her tears had done her good. The joy of having rescued Gauthier from Don Martin's cruelty was exhilarating, even if the task was only half complete as yet, even if he proved to be dying …

But her joy did not last long when she found herself looking at his long, outstretched form. He was emaciated, appallingly filthy, and although he did open his eyes from time to time, their grey gaze was cloudy, absent. When they fell upon the young woman, there was not the slightest sign of surprise or gratitude to be seen in them. She bent over him and softly spoke his name, but in vain; the Norman looked at her vaguely but with no sign of recognition.

'Has he gone mad?' she asked anxiously. 'He seems to have lost his memory. He must be very ill. Why did you bring him here instead of into the house?'

'Because it will soon be daybreak,' Hans replied. 'Urraca mustn't find him when she gets up.'

'Why not, since she's deaf?'

'She may be deaf, but she isn't blind or dumb, and she may not be as stupid as she looks. We will care for this man now as best we can, wash him and dress him and tend him. By then it will be morning. We have to get him out of the city without delay.'

'But how can we possibly take him in this condition? What shall we do with him on the journey?'

'I will provide you with the means of conveying him,' Hans said solemnly. 'But from then on, this man's safety will be your responsibility, Dame Catherine. I cannot go with you, nor can I keep him here. It would be more than my life is worth, and my men's as well … And while I may have helped you thus far, because I like you and because I hate Don Martin, I am not that weary of life or anxious to abandon my work here. You must know that once outside this city you can no longer count upon my assistance. I am sorry about it, but there it is.'

Catherine heard Hans out attentively. She had been foolish to expect anything more from him, but he had come to her aid so impulsively that she had grown to believe, however subconsciously, that he would continue to do so. However, she was much too sensible not to acknowledge that he had abundant good reason for this decision. She must not ask any more of him. She held out her hand to him, with a warm smile.

'You have already done more than enough, my friend, and I owe you my sincere and undying gratitude for having undergone so many risks on behalf of a complete stranger. Don't worry about me. I have always managed to tackle the problems that presented themselves to me so far. And I shall assuredly dispose of this one likewise.'

'After all, I'm still here, if it comes to that,' Josse murmured casually. 'Now let's be practical. You said you would provide us with the means of transporting him, Master Hans. What is it?'

'A wagon for transporting stone. I have to send a load for repair work to the King's Hospital, which stands close by the monastery of Las Huelgas, a half-league or so from the city. We shall set out as soon as the gates are opened. Your friend will be hidden among the stones. The guards won't be able to poke about with their lances in among them. We will set your horses to draw the wagon. I will procure another cart to take this man on from there and some more horses to bring the wagon back. After that it will be up to you, and the grace of God.'

'I didn't expect as much,' Catherine said, simply. 'I thank you with all my heart, Master Hans!'

'Enough talk for now. We must see to him, and get the wagon ready. It will soon be daybreak.'

The four of them set about their task without another word. Gauthier was stripped of his rags, washed, dressed in coarse but clean and serviceable clothes, though somewhat skimpy as none of the three men came anywhere near his size. It proved almost impossible to clean his head-wound thoroughly, because it was covered by a thick crust of blood and matted hair. But they smeared it as best they could with mutton fat, and then shaved him and cut his hair so as to make him almost unrecognisable. He abandoned himself to their attentions almost like a child, merely uttering soft moans from time to time. But he drank the hot soup avidly, together with a pitcher of wine that Hans offered him. Josse watched him drink thoughtfully.

'The best thing would be to make him drink as much wine as possible. Then he might sleep while he is on the wagon and so prove less of a danger. Imagine what would happen if the guards heard these moans coming from the wagon?'

'There's no need to make him drunk,' Hans said. 'I have some poppy seeds that I use to relieve the suffering of any of my men who get hurt while they are at work. I will give him some a little later on, ground up in some wine. He will sleep like a child after that.'

While they had been occupying themselves with Gauthier, a band of clear sky had appeared along the horizon, and the dark was fast receding. Cocks could be heard crowing hoarsely from all directions. Hans looked anxiously up at the sky.

'We must get the wagon ready now,' he said. 'Urraca will soon be coming down from her garret.'

He hastily prepared the drugged wine and gave it to Gauthier to drink. Then he wrapped him in a blanket and carried him out to the solid-looking wagon that stood in a stable alongside the house. Helped by Josse and Hatto, he started loading the wagon with blocks of stone artfully disposed so that the Norman was well hidden but at the same time in no danger of being crushed. The cracks were stuffed with straw.

They were just in time. For no sooner had Gauthier vanished from sight beneath his improvised defences, than the household came to sudden life. Old Urraca, owlish eyes swollen with sleep, came creaking painfully down the ladder-type construction that led to the floor above, and began clacking about in her clogs between the yard and the kitchen, drawing water from the well, fetching logs and blowing hard on the embers she had carefully buried under a pile of ash before retiring to bed the previous night. Soon there was water bubbling in the pot and the old woman started cutting thick slices of black bread with an alarmingly long knife. These she laid out on the table, together with some onions hanging from the main beam.

The workmen started appearing next, yawning and stretching. After dousing themselves in cold well-water they came in for their food. Catherine, yawning and stretching like the rest, had taken up her accustomed place at the hearth; understandably enough, for it was a freezing morning. As for Josse, pretending to have great difficulty shaking himself awake, he left the building and took a stroll round the square. He wanted to see how the new occupant of the cage looked when seen in broad daylight. Hans watched him go with an air of disquiet, but he was soon reassured. The wink and click of the tongue that Josse addressed to him on his return seemed to suggest that all was well. Then he turned to his workers and started talking to them in their native tongue. Catherine caught a mention of Las Huelgas in passing, and guessed that the master-mason must be telling them that he would be spending that day at the famous monastery. The Germans nodded approvingly. No-one spoke. One after another they filed out of the room, with a faint bow in

Catherine's direction, and set off toward their stone-yard, already stooping at the thought of another day's work to come. Hans smiled at Catherine.

'Eat something quickly, and then we will set off. The gates are opening now —' And even then, the creaking of the Santa Maria gates could be heard nearby, followed by the cries, voices and usual hurly-burly of the square. Hans turned to the door.

'Where is Josse?' he asked. 'Out in the square again?'

'I think so, yes.'

'I'm going to find him.'

Automatically, still hungrily devouring a heel of black bread and an onion, Catherine followed him out. Josse was not far off. His thin figure was standing a few paces from the house, hands on hips. He appeared to be enthralled by something that Hans and Catherine soon found no less absorbing. A troop of horsemen thundered into the square. The young woman recognised the alguacils, and in their midst the Andalusian horse and black plumes of Don Martin Gomez Calvo. Simultaneously, a gang of carpenters came running up, carrying beams, planks, ladders and hammers. An immense man, dressed in deep crimson, appeared to be their leader.

'The executioner,' Hans commented in a colourless voice. '*Donnerwetter!* Does this mean that …?'

He did not finish his sentence. The meaning of the scene unfolding before Catherine's horrified eyes was all too apparent. The carpenters, acting with diabolic speed, were engaged in building a low scaffold, stimulated to even greater efforts by the executioner's vigorous gestures and the cracking whips of three overseers who had suddenly appeared.

'The Moorish slaves,' Hans breathed. 'You must flee, and at once. See what Don Martin is doing.'

Catherine turned to look at the Judge. It did not take a moment to fathom what he was about. He was standing in his stirrups, one bony finger pointing first up and then down, signalling his desire to have the cage lowered at once.

At this, Josse turned on his heels and ran back toward the house. He was white to the lips.

'Be careful!' he cried. 'Don Martin was afraid that the bad weather might have weakened his prisoner too much. So he has given orders for the execution to take place at once. And he looks like a man in a hurry.'

Just then, an identical gang of yellow-turbaned Moorish slaves made an appearance, loaded with logs and faggots of wood for the pyre where the condemned man was to be burned after being skinned alive.

Without a word, Hans took Catherine and Josse by the arm and pulled them hurriedly back into the house. They raced toward the wagon, where Hatto was just yoking up their horses. The three companions sprang on to the vehicle: Catherine next to Hans, who held the reins, while Josse sat at the back, legs dangling and cap pulled down over his eyes in the pose of a conscientious worker setting off for a day's work, regardless of what might be happening elsewhere. Hans cracked the whip and the wagon rumbled out of the shed and headed toward the Santa Maria gate.

But progress was hampered by the vast crowd of townspeople thronging into the square, brought there by news of the imminent execution. They were pushing and thrusting their way from all directions, a solid sea of people, jostling each other for a good vantage point. Shutters flew back at all the windows, and dark-eyed ladies crowded to them to look out. People were even clambering up onto the roofs, despite the slippery frost that covered them. The people of Burgos were eagerly preparing, it seemed, for a choice spectacle.

Catherine's eyes slid nervously round to the scaffold, where the carpenters were putting the last touches to a stake in the shape of a cross and dangling with chains, to the pile of logs that was rising at miraculous speed, and finally up to where the cage was slowly descending. It was already halfway down. And the wagon was moving forward at a snail's pace.

'Paso!' Hans shouted, standing up on the driver's seat and cracking his whip 'Paso!'*

But the crowd was far too absorbed in the preparations for the execution to pay much attention. The only response to his shouts were contemptuous glances. These people seemed determined to keep their places even if it meant being trampled underfoot by the horses. The German lost his temper.

'Careful!' he shouted, allowing his whip to curl round a stubborn shoulder. At the same time he reined his horses in so hard that they reared up and their flailing hooves thrashed just above the heads of the crowd. At this the people fell back with a cry of alarm, and Hans drove his horses full tilt toward the gate.

But just then the cage touched the ground, and it took Don Martin no more than a cursory glance inside to see that his prisoner had escaped. Catherine, watching him anxiously, saw his olive skin turn green. He sprang down from his horse and began shouting orders. The crowd, already furious at being disappointed of their treat, began to roar like a stormy sea. The wagon was just passing through the gate … With a sinister creak the portcullis dropped just in front of the horses. Don Martin had given orders for the gates to be closed and the whole town be searched.

Catherine felt close to fainting. She leant back on her seat and closed her eyes. Hans' voice came to her in a whisper, like a voice in a dream.

'Courage, my beauty. This is not the moment for a fit of the vapours. We must put a bold face on it. It's our one chance.'

And with that he proceeded to hurl abuse at the guards, unleashing

---

* 'Make way! Make way!'

upon them (in impeccable Castilian) a long and furious tirade to the effect that he, for one, had his work to do, and these setbacks had nothing to do with him. With a wealth of angry gestures worthy of Don Martin himself he pointed first to the closed portcullis and then to his wagon, evidently trying to persuade the guards to let him through. But the latter, leaning heavily on their pikes, merely shook their heads and refused to listen. Hans slumped back on his seat, looking discouraged.

'What are we to do?' Catherine asked, almost in tears.

'What do you think? We are going to stay here and wait … with all the risks that entails.'

Catherine's head drooped, and she folded her hands and began to pray silently, ignoring what went on behind her. By now the square was seething like a raging sea. Pushed this way and that by the alguacils, who were trying to force a passage through the crowd to search the nearby houses, and belaboured by a rain of lance blows, the townspeople were squealing like pigs being slaughtered. Pain and rage mingled in their protests. Quarrels and disputes broke out on all sides, and even some laughter. Don Martin's men were by now pushing into all the inns, roughly questioning both inn-keepers and guests. Everyone seemed terrified lest the face of a stranger, or even a face that was merely a little unfamiliar, should turn out to belong to one of those terrible bandits from the forest of Oca who had doubtless come to procure the escape of their comrade-in-villainy. Fear wormed its way into every soul present, and with it, a wild panic.

All of a sudden, from the other side of the closed portcullis, came the faint sound of religious chanting. It was so familiar that Catherine looked up.

'*E ul treir*
'*E sus eia*
'*Deus aia nos!*'

The ancient, secular chant of the pilgrims to Compostela. The one they always took up when weariness threatened to overpower them, the very one that she herself had sung a few weeks earlier on leaving le Puy for the deserted roads of Aubrac. A faint hope awakened in her. She found herself believing that the old chant must be God's answer to her fervent prayer. She jumped off the wagon and ran to press her face to the portcullis and stare through the bars. A troop of ragged, dusty pilgrims was advancing toward the gate across the Roman bridge, standing as upright as tired legs and heavy heads would allow. And in front of them, eyes raised toward heaven and fanatical gaze scanning the clouds, strode Gerbert Bohat, brandishing his long staff in time to the rhythm of the chant …

'Well, well, well,' Josse murmured, slipping next to Catherine, 'so we meet again!'

But Gerbert had not seen his former companions and fellow-pilgrims. He stopped a few feet from the closed portcullis and called up to the ramparts where the soldiers stood on guard.

'Why is this gate shut?' he demanded. 'Open to the Lord's holy wanderers!'

Then he repeated this in Spanish. The man-at-arms made some reply that must have been to the effect that Gerbert could go to hell, so surly was the man's tone. This was too much for Gerbert's fragile veneer of Christian gentleness. He raised his voice and apostrophised his adversary in a thundering blast of invective.

'What's he saying?' Catherine asked.

'That no Christian city, ever, has dared to close its gates to the pilgrims of Compostela, that he and his pilgrims are exhausted, and that many of them are sick and there are some wounded among them in urgent need of care, having fallen into the hands of brigands, and that he expects the gates to be opened instantly.'

'And what are they answering?'

'That Don Martin refuses to let them be opened.'

The discussion continued for a few minutes longer, growing more rapid and more violent with every passing moment. Finally Gerbert Bohat took up an expectant position, leaning on his staff, while the pilgrims collapsed all about him, overcome by fatigue.

'And now?'

'Gerbert demands to see the Archbishop. The soldier told him they would fetch Don Martin.'

The Criminal Judge appeared a moment later, and Catherine caught a glimpse of his tall black silhouette and bow legs climbing the stone stairs leading to the ramparts. Hans, in his turn, had climbed down from his wagon, despite the guards' attempts to make him return home, and he now joined his companions.

'This may be our chance,' he whispered. 'I heard Don Martin saying that the brigands who attacked the pilgrims might be those of Oca, and that it would be as well to question Gerbert and his followers.'

And a moment later Don Martin's sharp voice rang out above Catherine's head. Gerbert saluted him politely but did not abandon his stiff-necked bearing when answering the Judge. A further incomprehensible exchange followed and then, suddenly, the Judge's tone of voice completely changed and became strangely gentle.

'He says he will have the gates opened to admit these holy people —' Hans whispered in astonishment. 'But I don't much like this new gentleness of his. And the art of interrogation tends to mean only one thing with Don Martin. However, the portcullis is to be raised, that is the chief thing, and we must take advantage of this.'

'But they might pursue you,' Catherine protested. 'They might even shoot at you. If you were struck by an arrow I should never forgive myself.'

'Nor I,' Hans smiled half-jestingly, 'but we have no choice in the matter. If they discover who we are transporting, we should share the same fate. We've made our bed, now we must lie on it. Listen to that din back there! They are searching all the houses. If I have to die, I'd rather it was by an arrow than on the scaffold.'

Hans climbed resolutely back into his seat and motioned to Catherine and Josse to follow suit. They were just back in their places when Don Martin Gomez Calvo appeared beneath the arch with a squad of alguacils. He started angrily on perceiving the wagon and came striding toward them. As she watched him approach, his thin face twisted with rage, Catherine almost died of fear. He would order the wagon moved back and searched now. She listened in an agony of apprehension to his shrill voice cursing Hans, convinced that nothing, now, could save her, or Gauthier, or their friends, from that empty scaffold that stood across the square with the expectant air of an animal about to be fed.

But she had underestimated the master-mason. He met the Judge's rage with Olympian calm, explaining (as Josse whispered to Catherine) that he absolutely must transport this load of stones to Las Huelgas, because he was already running late on a job with which the Constable Alvaro de Luna had charged him. The name of the most powerful man in Castile had its expected effect. Don Martin's fury subsided by several degrees. His sharp, mistrustful eyes lighted upon each of the occupants of the wagon in turn. Catherine had difficulty restraining a shudder of disgust under the scrutiny of those cruel eyes. There was a moment of terrible silence, and then, at last, Don Martin's thin lips parted and he uttered a short sentence. Catherine felt Josse start beside her. Hans remained quite impassive but, seeing him gather the reins more firmly into his hands, Catherine realised that they must be about to depart. Just then the portcullis started slowly rising. But there was a troop of armed men standing behind the wagon and all around it too. Don Martin stepped out onto the drawbridge and made a peremptory signal to the pilgrims to come forward. They got to their feet painfully and shuffled forward in some vague sort of order. Gerbert alone remained as haughty as ever.

'Come, let us go,' Hans whispered. 'We are taking up too much room. We can wait on the bridge till all the pilgrims have passed.'

The wagon lumbered slowly forward and passed out of the damp shadow of the gate. Catherine, who had felt till then as though every stone in the city walls was pressing down upon them, suddenly felt her heart lift. Hans drew in his wagon to let the pilgrims pass. They seemed quite overwhelmed with weariness and in a desperate state. The crossing of the mountains must have been a terrible ordeal. Catherine and Josse recognized a few faces, but all of them bore visible signs of the sufferings they had had to undergo. Their clothes were in rags, their bodies bruised, swollen and even in some cases bleeding and wounded. The brigands must have treated them very badly. Not one of them had any spirit for singing.

'Poor folk,' Catherine murmured. 'We might easily have been like this too.'

'But we aren't, praise the Lord!' Josse breathed with a satisfaction that, as it turned out, was to be short-lived. For almost at once the drama occurred. No sooner had the pilgrims reached the Santa Maria gate than the soldiers surrounded the group and took them prisoner.

''Od's blood!' Josse swore, 'but ... they are arresting them!'

Don Martin wants to put a few questions to them,' Hans said sombrely. 'He wants to be sure of them ... temporarily.'

'But this is terrible,' Catherine cried. 'What can he hope to learn from these poor folk? They need care, not guards!'

'Don Martin will want to ask them if the brigands of Oca have reclaimed their comrade, for a start. And then where they have their hideout. It remains to be seen what these poor wretches fear most – Don Martin or the bandits' revenge.'

Catherine did not reply. She turned back toward the town and watched in a torment of anxiety as the drama unfolded. For while some of the pilgrims allowed themselves to be dragged off without resistance, others were struggling with the Alcalde's men; and foremost of these, naturally, was Gerbert Bohat. They heard him cry, 'Treachery! Defend yourselves, my brothers, it is God's will!' And he flung himself courageously into the fray, armed only with a frail staff against the lances and swords of the soldiers. Catherine, Hans and Josse watched fascinated, eyes wide with horror. Blood flowed in dark rivulets that glistened under the hot sun. The Castilians allowed their brutality free rein, and Don Martin, standing a little way off, arms folded, observed the scene, occasionally passing his tongue across his lips.

The mêlée did not last long, because the odds were hopelessly unequal. The pilgrims were soon mastered. Catherine, almost beside herself with indignation, suddenly heard Gerbert's cry as a tremendous lance-blow struck his chest. A brief order was heard, and instantly the unfortunate Clermontois was thrown into the river, the yellow waters of which, still swollen from the heavy rains, bore him first slowly and then ever faster away. The other pilgrims were driven into the city and the portcullis fell once again.

Catherine shook Hans impatiently out of his apparent stupor of astonishment. 'Quick, let's be off. The road is clear now. And we might even be able to fish him out again.'

'Who?' Hans said, gazing at Catherine blankly.

'Him, of course … Gerbert Bohat, the man those wretches threw into the river. He might not be dead …'

Hans obediently set the wagon moving. Fortunately, the road to Las Huelgas followed the river Arlanzon. Josse had left his perch at the back of the wagon to join the other two in front. His face was haggard and his eyes clouded. He stammered:

'Pilgrims! God's wanderers who only claimed the asylum that is their due …'

'I told you the people here were savages,' Hans spat out, with sudden violence. 'And Don Martin is the worst of them all! … I didn't think you would need any proof of that after the business of the cage, but it seems blood had to be shed to convince you! I cannot wait to finish my task here. I shall return joyfully to my own country on the banks of the Rhine … A great river, that one, a real, majestic river … nothing like this dirty little trickle!'

Catherine let him work off his fury. The sculptor's jangled nerves needed some release … She kept watch on the yellow waters, looking for Gerbert's body. All of a sudden she caught sight of it, a long black shape drifting toward the muddy bank. She stood up and pointed.

'Look, there he is! Stop the wagon!'

'He is dead,' Hans said. 'Why stop?'

'Because he may not be quite dead. And even if he is, he has a right to a Christian burial.'

Hans shrugged. 'Dirty water is as good as the ground in this stinking country. But we can stop if you really want to.'

He halted the wagon along the side of the rutted track. Catherine sprang down at once and, with Josse at her heels, raced down toward the river. She headed for a sharp bend toward which the body seemed to be drifting. Josse waded into the water, caught hold of Gerbert and carried him back to the bank. He and Catherine dragged him up and laid him on the pebbled bank. The Clermontois' eyes were closed, his nostrils pinched, his lips white and set, but he still seemed to be breathing faintly. There was a deep wound in his breast, but it had stopped bleeding.

Josse shook his head. 'He hasn't much longer to go, Dame Catherine. There is nothing to be done; he has lost too much blood.'

Without replying, she sat down and took Gerbert's head, with infinite gentleness, onto her lap. Hans had come up and silently passed her a sort of goatskin gourd that he had fastened to his belt before leaving home that morning. It contained wine. Catherine wet the pale lips with it. Gerbert shuddered, opened his eyes, and stared in astonishment at her.

'Catherine!' he stammered. 'Are you … are you dead too …? I have thought so much about you!'

'No, I'm alive, and so are you. Now don't talk.'

'I must. You are right … I can tell by my pain that I am still living – but not for long! I would like a priest so as not to … die with my sin!'

He made a pathetic attempt to sit up, gripping hold of Catherine's arm. Josse knelt behind him and raised him up very cautiously. The wounded man looked at the three faces bending over him, and sighed.

'Not one of you is a priest?'

Catherine shook her head, trying not to cry.

'Then … you will have to hear my confession, Catherine,' he said, trying to smile. 'I drove you away, all three of you, and condemned you to wander without us … because I believed I hated you … as I hated all women. But I realised then … that with you, it was different. I have never stopped thinking about you … and the road became a hell to me … A drink!… A little more wine … It gives me strength …'

Catherine helped him to drink some more. He collapsed for a moment, then recovered himself and opened his eyes again.

'I am going to die, and that is well. I was not worthy to touch the Apostle's tomb, because … I killed my wife, Catherine … I killed her out of jealousy … because she loved another. I would have liked to kill all women with her –'

He fell silent, and jerked backwards, and once more Catherine thought he must have died. But after a moment he opened his eyes, already clouding in death. His voice was weaker now and he spoke stumblingly. His lips gasped for the air that eluded them.

'Forgive me … you must forgive me … I've suffered … oh, so badly … Alysia… I loved her … I could still love in those days …'

His next words were incomprehensible. The feeble flicker of life that the wine had kindled in Gerbert's bloodless body was fast fading. He grew paler than ever, and his features seemed to grow pinched and tight.

'It's the end,' Josse murmured.

Death seemed very near. The white lips moved without uttering a sound. Catherine felt the exhausted body stiffen in her arms in the last spasm of the death agony. Then the dying man managed to breathe one last word.

'God …'

The word was no more than a sigh, and this sigh was the last. The eyes closed, never to open again. Gently Catherine laid the body down, wiped her eyes and looked at Hans. He seemed changed to stone.

'Where shall we bury him?' Catherine asked.

'The monks at the King's Hospital will see to it. We must put him in the cart too.'

Josse and Hans together carried the dripping corpse up to the wagon, wrapping it as best they could in his pilgrim's cape. They laid him on the stones piled on top of Gauthier. The latter, wrapped in his blanket and lying on a heap of straw, had not moved a muscle. He slept heavily, rendered unconscious by the drugged wine Hans had administered to him. Hans cracked his whip.

'Luckily there isn't far to go,' he said in a hoarse voice that betrayed the emotion they all three shared.

It was only a few minutes before the white walls and square tower of a rich Cistercian monastery appeared, two doors offering the only break in its imposing facade.

'Las Huelgas,' Hans muttered. 'The most noble convent in Spain. King Alfonso VIII and Queen Eleanor of England founded it a long time ago for the daughters of the high nobility and also as a burial place for their family, and descendants. But, from what I hear, this high destiny seems to have been somewhat forgotten of latter years.'

Just then, to Catherine's great astonishment, strains of music came wafting from the convent's romanesque windows. These chords of viols, lutes and harp had nothing religious about them. A clear woman's voice could be heard singing a love song, and there were occasional sounds of laughter. The sky, now a warm blue, and the dazzling sunshine combined to give this strange convent an air of great gaiety.

'What does this mean?' Catherine asked in amazement.

'That these days the nuns of Las Huelgas are chosen more for their beauty and aptitude for love than for their piety or ancestry,' Hans replied sarcastically. 'King John, who is an artist, who loves music, and the Constable, who loves women, pass many – and highly agreeable – days here. It is not here that we shall leave our dead man, or our stones, but with the old monks of the King's Hospital, who for their part are ill-at-ease with these perfumed neighbours of theirs.'

The old hospice stood a little way off and was a much less elegant sight than the handsome convent. Its stonework was crumbling and threatened to collapse altogether in one or two spots. The pilgrims to Compostela no longer stopped there, preferring the Hospice of Santolesmes in Burgos itself. The King's Hospital was slowly sinking into oblivion.

'The repairs I am supposed to do here are urgently needed,' said Hans. 'But here we are.'

He had driven the wagon through the gate-tower that led into the inner courtyard, and now an elderly porter monk came forward, a

106

welcoming smile on his parchment face.

'Master Hans,' he cried. 'Truly, the Lord has sent you – the belfry of the chapel threatens to collapse on top of our heads at any minute. You have arrived just in time. I will go and tell the Lord Abbot.'

As he hurried off across the cobbled court with its tufts of weeds, Catherine slid slowly down from her seat.

When Josse and Catherine left the King's Hospital an hour later, their morale was at its lowest point, despite their successful escape. Gerbert's death still weighed heavily on the young woman's mind. She reproached herself with it as if in some way she was to blame. And besides, Gauthier's condition worried her terribly …

Some time earlier when, after a rapid muttered conference between Hans and the Abbot, the long form, wrapped in its coarse covering, had been taken down from the wagon, a strange and terrifying thing had happened. The Norman had woken from the drugged sleep when they laid him out on a bench. But no sooner had he opened his eyes, which were rolling wildly, than a strange sort of fit seemed to seize him. His body went rigid and his jaws clenched so forcibly they could hear his teeth grinding. Then the giant suddenly jerked off the bench and rolled about on the ground with violent movements of his head and body. At last he sank into a deep coma, while a white froth dabbled his lips. Catherine recoiled in horror and flattened herself against the wall as if she would have liked to vanish into it. Hans and Josse did not move: they stood by, watching with knitted brows. Meanwhile the Abbot crossed himself precipitately and ran off across the courtyard. He soon returned, carrying a whole bucket of holy water, which he threw over the wounded man. In his wake there trotted a little monk carrying a huge censer that gave off a thick suffocating smoke.

Hans had no time to foresee the Abbot's move and spare poor Gauthier a douche of cold water. But he set to work at once to calm the good man's anger, the import of which was made quite clear by his furious gestures. In the Abbot's eyes, the stranger was possessed of the devil, and must be taken out of the consecrated ground of the hospice immediately. Hans looked at Catherine in dismay.

'You must leave here at once. They are going to give you a cart to transport him in. The Abbot believes him to be possessed of the devil … and there is not much I can do for you.'

'But is he really … possessed?' Catherine asked in anguish.

It was Josse, quite unexpectedly, who took upon himself the task of informing her. 'The ancient Romans called this illness the sacred illness. They claimed that God inhabited a man taken by convulsions. But I once knew a Moorish doctor who said it was nothing more or less than a sickness originating in the brain.'

'You knew a Moorish doctor?' Hans echoed, surprised. 'But where was that?'

Josse's thin brown face flushed suddenly. 'Oh,' he said casually, 'I've travelled a lot ...'

He did not enlarge on the subject, and Catherine knew why. In an expansive moment, Josse had confided to her that ill-fortune had once sent him to row two years in a slave galley, whence his unexpected scientific knowledge.

'A Moorish doctor ...' Hans murmured thoughtfully.

While they wrapped Gauthier up in his covers again and carried him, now almost calm, to the cart drawn up ready in the courtyard by a monk, Hans told his two new friends what he had heard of the strange Archbishop of Seville, Alonso of Fonseca. A luxurious, greedy man, an avid collector of precious stones and a fervent alchemist, the Archbishop kept a curious court in his stronghold of Coca, where alchemists and astrologers greatly outnumbered the religious fraternity. The great marvel of this court, according to rumour, was a Moorish doctor of great learning and quite unnerving skill.

'When the Constable Alvaro's men are not within earshot, the people of Burgos freely whisper that this doctor works miracles. Why not go to see him? If you go toward Toledo you will pass through Coca without going far out of your way.'

'Why would the Archbishop receive us there?' Catherine asked sceptically.

'Three reasons: his hospitality, which is proverbial, his interest in all the strange things that happen beneath his roof, and finally ... didn't I tell you that he was a passionate collector of precious stones?'

Now Catherine understood. If there were no other way to obtain the care of the magician of Coca, Queen Yolande's emerald would certainly open the fortress gates to her.

She made her decision instantly. She was ready for much greater sacrifices to save Gauthier than a slight detour on her journey and the loss of a jewel, albeit one dear to her heart. She thanked Hans for his unselfish efforts on her behalf with a warmth that made the German's face quite crimson. When she impulsively pressed her lips against Hans' ill-shaven cheek she saw his blue eyes fill with tears.

'Perhaps we shall meet again one day, Dame Catherine?'

'When you have finished your work here, and I am back at Montsalvy, you shall come to us and work miracles of carving!'

'That is a promise.'

A last handshake between the two men and the cart jolted off, with one last wave from Catherine, along the road to the south. Gauthier lay comfortably on a bed of straw in the back. Josse had the reins, and he kept the horses moving at a brisk pace. The two horses were unused to drawing carts, and they demanded constant vigilance and a firm hand on the reins. But Catherine had nothing to do but look at the passing countryside.

Despite the sun that flared in the bright sky, the whole region, treeless, arid and wild, had an air of savage melancholy enhanced by the distant tolling of the death knell for the dead pilgrim.

Catherine's mind dwelt on the mysterious Gerbert, the strange criminal walled in his pride and suffering as if in an armour of forged steel. She had guessed at the distress hidden beneath that inflexible manner of his, and she was sorry now that she had not made a greater effort to understand. With a little friendliness she might have succeeded in opening that locked heart … they might have been friends. Nevertheless, there was a voice that whispered deep inside her, telling her that she was trying to blind herself to the truth. A man like Gerbert knew only two emotions: love and hatred. He had chosen to hate her from fear of loving her; and now the tranquillity of death had come to calm that raging soul for all eternity. Perhaps, instead of grieving, she should be thanking God for His mercy …

Catherine's thoughts moved from Gerbert to Gauthier, but she preferred not to let them dwell there. His condition was a source of such bitter pain to her that there was a danger of her resolve cracking just at the point when she had most need of it. It was a great thing to have succeeded in snatching him from a terrible death, especially when she had so long believed him quite lost to her. Why should the Archbishop's Moor not succeed in restoring him to sanity so that they could then ride on, with all their forces intact, into the fabulous kingdom of the Moorish King to rescue Arnaud?

Arnaud … Catherine discovered, with astonishment, that for many days past she had scarcely thought of her husband, so absorbed had she been with her attempts to rescue Gauthier. But now that she had leisure to think about him, she discovered that her fury had not diminished in the least. In fact, it burnt all the more fiercely now that she had found Gauthier again. It seemed cruelly unjust that so much suffering had been endured on behalf of an erring husband, who might even now be languishing, quite unsuspicious of the fact, in the arms of an infidel, in the ravishing dream setting of a Saracen palace; while his wife watched the yellow mournful wastes of old Castile unfold around her with a heart full of bitterness. These thoughts produced their usual effect. She threw a resentful glance round her.

'What a dreadful place!' she cried. 'Is it like this all the way to Granada?'

'Fortunately not,' said Josse, with a curious smile twisting his lips. 'But I have to admit that we are not out of the desert yet.'

'Where shall we be spending the night?'

'I don't know. As you see, there are not many villages. And the majority of the ones there are, are ruined and deserted. The great Black Death, in the last century, ravaged the cities and depopulated the countryside.'

'But there are still some survivors,' Catherine grumbled. 'And you would have thought they might have found time to grow some wheat here over a hundred years.'

'You have forgotten the Mesta.'

'What's that?'

'The corporation of sheep farmers. They are one of the few productive powers of this region. Their immense flocks travel from region to region with the seasons, and nothing is allowed to stand in their way. How do you expect people to grow anything at all under such conditions? Here, look!'

Josse pointed with his whip-handle toward the horizon, where a large dark brown patch seemed to undulate against the pale sky. 'There are a few hundred head of sheep there, and as you can see, they are well guarded.'

Indeed, the usual pastoral figures of shepherds, in their long clothes, were accompanied by several men riding on mules. Their clothes were equally rustic but each of them wore a large cutlass at his waist. Josse shrugged.

'Those animals are a source of wealth to a few men. The rest of the country folk live in dire poverty. But, with a little luck, we may find a château or even some little inn where we can spend the night ...'

'All I ask is that there should be some stream, or river, or even a small pond somewhere nearby. I haven't felt so dirty for a long time ...'

Josse cast a mocking glance at her, and then shrugged once more. 'How simple that sounds! But water is even harder to come by in these regions than food, Dame Catherine!'

The young woman gave a sigh of discouragement and slumped down in her seat. 'Really life doesn't seem to be worth living!' she sighed. 'How long do you think it will take to get to Coca?'

'Five days or so, if these two beasts will agree to go at the same speed instead of each going their separate ways!'

In the forlorn hope of charming the horses into submission, Josse struck up a drinking song, in such a cracked voice that Catherine made a face.

'What are you hoping for?' she asked slyly. 'That it's going to rain or that these animals will suddenly take the bit between their teeth?'

But her bad temper had passed. She even joined in Josse's singing, and like this, the journey seemed a little less monotonous.

7: The Alchemist of Coca

Despite the refractory behaviour of the horses, Josse was as good as his word. The journey lasted only five days. Five days in which scarcely anything happened, and which proved less uncomfortable than Catherine had feared. They were able to buy cheese, black bread and milk for a few coins in the occasional villages, small towns or shepherds' huts they passed. Catherine even found the river she dreamt of near the little town of Lerma, where hundreds of goatskin bottles hung drying in the sun, fastened in great bundles to the eaves of houses. The water was still icy cold, but the weather had suddenly and unexpectedly become quite summery. The chill winds and rains had been succeeded by an intense heat that made the young woman all the more unpleasantly aware of the lack of water and other refinements. The sight of the river went to her head. She could barely wait for Josse to drive a little way out of the town before tearing off her clothes, with a hurried command to Josse to turn round, and plunging into the water head first. All this so rapidly that her slender body flashed only briefly in the sun before vanishing under water.

Of all the baths she had ever taken, this one struck Catherine as the most delicious, even though the water was not crystal clear. She swam about luxuriously for several minutes, moving from side to side of the river before eventually settling on a rock to hide behind while she scoured away at every inch of her body. She would have given a great deal just then to have a piece of the scented soap that Burgundian women used to make in Flanders, expressly for the use of the beautiful mistress of the Great Duke of the West; this was really the one thing she missed of her past. But it didn't prevent her from making the most of her bath. From time to time she glanced in the direction of Josse and the cart. But the former seemed changed to stone. Sitting stiffly upright in his seat, he stared fixedly at the horses' ears, while they took the opportunity of munching up a few sparse blades of grass.

When she felt clean again, Catherine stepped out of the water and clambered hurriedly into her petticoat. But she didn't put back her men's clothes again. The sudden heat made their thick woollen stuff unendurably uncomfortable; and besides, they were stiff with dirt. After the springtime freshness of the river water, the smell of sweat they gave off was unbearable. She took a fine grey wool dress from her bundle of clothes, a clean petticoat and some stockings without holes in them, which she proposed to put on a little farther along the road.

When she returned a moment later, dry, her hair newly arranged, she observed that Josse had not budged by so much as a hairsbreadth. She couldn't resist remarking, maliciously: 'Well, Josse? Doesn't the cool water tempt you after all that driving and all that dust?'

'I don't like water,' Josse answered, in such a dismal voice that she burst out laughing.

'I don't like drinking it either! But it feels good to wash in. Why didn't you come and join me, Josse?'

She put the question to him in perfect innocence but, to her great surprise, Josse went scarlet with embarrassment. He cleared his throat, but his voice was still suspiciously hoarse when he declared:

'Many thanks, Dame Catherine … but that river didn't appeal to me at all.'

'But why not?'

'Because …' He paused for a moment and then, taking a deep breath like a man who has come to a decision, he added, 'Because I think it might be dangerous.'

'Dangerous? And you let me swim there?' Catherine said, delighted by the youth's embarrassment.

'It wasn't dangerous for you.'

'I just don't understand.'

Josse was visibly in torments, shifting uncomfortably about on his seat as if it were red hot. He was still staring obstinately ahead, but all of a sudden he looked round and met Catherine's laughing eyes, and declared with great dignity: 'Dame Catherine, I have always been a sensible man, which is why I have lived as long as this, and why, I hope, I shall be permitted to live to a ripe old age. I spent a long time dragging my worn-out shoe leather and starving belly over the streets of Paris, and I took good care in those days to keep away from the kitchens where strings of fat capons hung gilding over a hot fire – food I could never hope to eat. I don't know if I make myself clear?'

'Quite clear,' Catherine said, climbing into the seat beside him. She wasn't smiling now, and the glance she bestowed on her companion held something approaching respect, as well as friendliness. Then she added, in a perfectly neutral voice: 'I'm sorry, Josse. I suddenly felt a wild urge to tease you.'

'Tease me, or test me?'

'Both, perhaps,' Catherine admitted frankly. 'But you passed the test with flying colours. Now shall we go?'

The rest of the voyage passed without further skirmishes. Gauthier was still more or less unconscious in his bed of straw. From time to time he succumbed to one of the terrible fits so alarming to Catherine. In the intervals, he relapsed into a comatose state, which was particularly frightening because he no longer seemed to have the strength to feed himself. He had to be fed like a baby. The last evening, Catherine turned to Josse with tears in her eyes.

'If the journey lasts much longer we won't even get him as far as that Moorish doctor.'

'At sunset tomorrow,' Josse promised, 'we should see the towers of Coca.'

And so it came about. The next evening, as the sun sank toward the horizon in a glory of crimson and gold, Catherine had her first glimpse of the fabulous castle of the Archbishop of Seville. For a moment, it took her breath away: soaring from the red earth, from its very bowels so it seemed, the fortress built of crimsoned stone had the air of a palace of a Thousand and One Nights. Coca was a fantastic jewel of Mudéjar art, concocted in the early years of the century by the nostalgic mind of an imprisoned Moorish architect. A forest of slender organ-pipe turrets stood out against the pale sea-green sky, flanking massive brick towers, and the high Saracen crenellations were like lace festooned about the summit of its double walls and immense square keep. It looked more like the palace of an emir than the dwelling of a Christian bishop, but the splendour of its design in no way diminished the brooding threat that its great bulk, poised at the head of a narrow ravine, seemed to impose. On the opposite side of the ravine it had access to a plateau from which it was separated by a deep gully.

Silently, Catherine and Josse contemplated the crimson jewel that was to be – at least for a while – a stopping-place on this long journey. Catherine's heart ached for a moment. God knows why, but she suddenly saw herself staring at another fortress, under another sky, in another place; one less fantastic, perhaps, but more threatening still, with its smooth black walls and precipitous towers. Was it Alonso of Fonseca's reputation for eccentricity that made her think, as she stood gazing at Coca, of Bluebeard's castle, the luxurious and terrible Champtocé where she had suffered so much? But here she had nothing to fear. She had come only to ask for succour for a wounded man; and yet she found herself hesitating before entering this castle as if it contained some veiled threat ... Josse turned toward her with a look of inquiry.

'Well then? Shall we go in?'

She shrugged her shoulders as if shaking off an unwelcome burden. 'We have no choice, no alternative, have we?'

'That's true.'

Without further comment, Josse headed the horses toward the flattened arch over the narrow gate, which looked so slender in the Moorish ogival frame. Motionless guards stood posted on either side, looking as fixed in time as in their strange setting. They fitted so well into the silence of the deserted plateau that they merely deepened the dreamlike impression made by this silent fortress. Only the banner gently flapping above the keep in the soft evening breeze seemed alive. To the great astonishment of Catherine and Josse, the soldiers did not stir as the cart approached. And when Josse informed them, in his best Spanish, that the noble lady Catherine de Montsalvy wished to see his Eminence the Archbishop of Seville, they contented themselves with a nod in the direction of the main courtyard, the astonishingly colourful decor of which could be glimpsed from where they stood.

'What a badly defended fortress!' Josse muttered.

'I don't know,' Catherine said. 'Remember the terror of that peasant from whom you asked the way an hour ago . . . Listen to that silence of this place, and that village, which seems almost dead! I think myself that its evil reputation is as good a protection as an army ... I can't help wondering if we really are going to visit a man of God ... or the Devil incarnate!'

The sombre atmosphere preyed on Catherine more than she cared to admit, but apparently Josse was above fears of that kind.

'In the position we're in,' he grumbled, 'I don't really see what is to be lost by going in and finding out.'

Archbishop Alonso of Fonseca was quite as bizarre as his castle but a great deal uglier. He was small, thin and bent, like a plant no gardener would ever trouble to water. His pale face and red-rimmed eyes indicated that he did not often see the light of sun, preferring nocturnal vigils. His hair was black but sparse, like his beard, and he was further afflicted by a nervous tic that made him keep nodding his head, a habit that became somewhat trying for those who spoke to him. After ten minutes' conversation, Catherine found herself dying to do likewise. But he had the most beautiful hands in the world, and his voice, low and soft as dark velvet, was quite bewitching.

He welcomed this travelling noblewoman without the least trace of astonishment, although her appearance and equipage were scarcely usual for a lady of high degree. His courtesy was impeccable. It was quite usual during a long, arduous journey, to ask for shelter at castles and monasteries along the way. The Archbishop of Seville's hospitality was legendary. But his curiosity seemed aroused when Catherine spoke of Gauthier and the treatment she hoped to be able to find for him at Coca. His curiosity, and at the same time his mistrust.

'Who told you, my daughter, that an infidel doctor was to be found among my servitors? And how could you suppose that an Archbishop would keep such a man under his roof?'

'I saw nothing strange in that, Your Eminence,' Catherine interrupted. 'In Burgundy once I too had a celebrated doctor from Cordoba among my suite, though he was indeed more of a friend than a servant. As for the man who suggested that I should come hither, it was the master-mason of the Cathedral of Burgos.'

'Ah, Master Hans of Cologne! A great artist, and a good man! But tell me something of this Moorish doctor of yours. What was his name?

'They called him Abou-al-Khayr.'

Fonseca let out a sharp breath, which told Catherine a great deal about her friend's fame within these walls.

'Do you know him?' she asked.

'All men of enlightenment have heard tell of Abou-al- Khayr, personal physician, friend and counsellor to the Caliph of Granada. I fear that my own doctor, skilled as he may be, is not his equal, and I cannot help wondering why you came here, my child, instead of taking your servant straight to him.'

'It is a long way to Granada, and my servant is very ill, Monseigneur. And I don't even know how to enter the Caliph's kingdom!'

'Your reasoning is sound, my child.'

He got up from the high-backed chair where he had been sitting when he received his visitor and clapped his hands softly. The tall, thin silhouette of a page stepped out from the shadows.

'Thomas,' he told him, 'there is a cart in the courtyard with a sick man in it. I want you to have him brought, as gently and carefully as possible, to Hamza and ask him to examine him. I shall go to inquire presently what the doctor's diagnosis is. Then you will see that the Dame de Montsalvy and her page are suitably accommodated. Come, noble lady, we will sup meanwhile.'

With a gallantry that would not have disgraced a secular prince, Don Alonso offered Catherine his hand to take her to the table. She could not help blushing at the contrast between her own shabby, dusty garments and the crimson and azure brocades in which the Archbishop was magnificently arrayed.

'I am not worthy to sit beside you,' she said apologetically.

'With eyes like yours, my dear, you would grace an emperor's table. Besides, you will find clothes more suitable to your rank in your room. But I cannot help feeling that, after having travelled so far over our terrible roads, you must be dying of hunger and longing for something to eat?' the Archbishop concluded with a smile.

Catherine smiled back and finally accepted his beautiful outstretched hand. Almost unconsciously, too, she was happy to have a chance of turning her back on the page Thomas, whose presence made her feel strangely uneasy. Not that he was ugly; he was a boy of 14 or 15, with noble, regular features. But there was something famished, cruel about the matt pallor of his complexion and his long skinny body. As for his eyes, Catherine told herself privately, they were intolerable – a strange thing in such a young boy. Icy blue, unblinking, they blazed with a fanatical brilliance that made one shudder. And his funereal garb struck a sinister note amid the sumptuous splendour of the Archbishop's apartments. As Catherine walked at Don Alonso's side along a narrow gallery of fretted marble overlooking the great courtyard, she could not help remarking on the boy.

'Dare I say that Your Eminence's page strikes a strange note amid these beautiful surroundings?' she said, pointing to the sparkling marble traceries that surrounded the courtyard and the colourfully-tiled walls.

'I wish I were not obliged to keep him with me,' the Archbishop sighed. 'Thomas is an exceptional boy: a hard, inflexible soul given over entirely to God. I fear that he judges somewhat harshly me and my entourage, and our way of life here. Science and beauty do not interest him, whereas they are my whole reason for living. He hates the Moors more than Lord Satan himself, I believe. Whereas I admire their wisdom.'

'But why take him into your service then?'

'His father is an old friend. He hoped that young Thomas would adopt a more amiable approach to religion under my auspices, but I fear I have failed in that respect. He dare not ask me to dismiss him. But I know that he ardently desires to enter a Dominican order in Segovia, and I certainly do not intend to stand in his way. He has been here only three months. After six months I propose to send him there. He really is too lugubrious.'

Catherine caught a glimpse of the page's black figure in the courtyard below, giving orders to a crowd of varlets, before she went into the room where supper was laid out. She shivered again, recalling the icy stare, heavy with contempt, almost revulsion, with which the unknown boy had favoured her.

'What is his name?' she found herself asking.

'Thomas de Torquemada; his family came from Valladolid. But think no more of him, my dear, and let us go to the table.'

It had been a long time since Catherine had eaten a meal like this one. The Archbishop's larder appeared to be well supplied, and his cooks were versed in all the mysteries of Western cuisine together with some more exotic imports from the East. Hot, spiced wines from the prelate's episcopal lands – where he never set foot – were there to wash down a feast of various fish and meats, rounded off with sweetmeats dripping in honey. The meal was served by an army of servants in red silk turbans, and by the time she finally got up from the table Catherine's weariness had magically disappeared.

'It is time to go and see Hamza now,' Alonso said as they left the table.

She hurried after him through immense, richly-furnished apartments, along long, cool corridors and across the courtyards till they came to the central keep. The rich meal she had just eaten, and the heady wines, made the ascent of the staircase leading to the Moorish doctor's room, high in the tower, something of an ordeal.

'Hamza also studies the stars,' Alonso told her. 'I thought it best to accommodate him as high up as possible so that he would be nearer to them.'

The room into which Alonso now led Catherine had cut into its ceiling a large hole through which they could see the night sky embroidered with stars. Some curious instruments were laid out upon an ebony coffer. But Catherine paid no heed to these, or to the improbable collection of pots, jars, phials, horns, crumbling parchments, bundles of herbs or curious instruments. She had eyes for one thing only: the long marble table to which Gauthier had been strapped by stout leather thongs. A man in white robes and turban stood beside him, shaving his head with a slender blade that glittered in the light of a hundred or more thick wax candles. The heat the candles gave off was overpowering, and the smell of hot wax quite nauseating, but Catherine was interested only in the doctor. She barely noticed Josse standing at the other end of the table. The Moor Hamza was an impressive-looking man. He was tall and stout, with the same silky white beard Catherine had often admired in her friend, Abou-al-Khayr. His snowy garments and piercing eyes gave him something of the air of a prophet, but the hands that were busy around Gauthier's head were amazingly small and delicate, like bird's claws attached unexpectedly to the body of some grizzled bear. There was something hypnotic about their skilful movements.

When Catherine and her host entered, Hamza did not pause in his work but greeted his master with a curt nod and the young woman with a fleeting glance. Catherine herself was gazing anxiously at the rows of instruments polished to silvery brightness laid out beside a small brazier full of hot coals. Meanwhile Alonso and Hamza had a rapid conversation, the gist of which the Archbishop then translated.

'This man's condition stems from the wound in his head. Look for yourself: just here his skull has been fractured, and the bone is pressing on his brain.'

He pointed at the wound now clearly visible on the shaved, bruised skull. The damaged part was all too obvious.

'Is it hopeless, then?' Catherine stammered.

'Hamza is very skilful,' Alonso murmured with a smile. 'He has operated before now on men whose skulls had been cracked by battle-axes and bludgeons.'

'What is he going to do to him?'

To Catherine's great surprise, it was the doctor himself who answered her question, in almost perfect French:

'With the help of this trepan,' he explained, pointing to a curious instrument, one end of which terminated in a sort of arrow, 'I propose to incise the cranial wall around the depression, so as to be able to remove the damaged part like a little cap. I shall then be able to see if there is any damage to the brain itself, and possibly straighten out any fractured bone. Otherwise we shall simply have to put ourselves at the mercy of the All-Powerful … But in any event there will be a lot of blood, and this is not the sort of spectacle for a woman to see. It would be better if you were to withdraw,' he said, with a rapid glance at Catherine. She stiffened, and clenched her fists stubbornly.

'And suppose I prefer to stay?'

'There is a good chance that you would faint … and my task is quite complicated enough already. I would rather you left,' he repeated, quietly but firmly.

'This man is my friend, and he is going to suffer torments under your knife. I might be able to help him.'

'Suffer? Do you really think so? See how he sleeps.'

And indeed Gauthier slept like a child in the bonds that held him fast, moving not so much as a finger.

'He will awake when he feels the knife.'

'Sleep like his ignores the knife as it does the flame. He is not sleeping because I drugged him … but because I told him to sleep. And he will not awake till I order him to.'

Catherine felt her hair standing on end. She threw a look of such horror at the Moor, and crossed herself so fervently, that he could not help laughing.

'No, I am not this devil you Christians seem so afraid of. I merely studied at Samarkand and Bokhara. The wise men there make use of a force that they call hypnotism and that stems from the human will and can be induced by light. But it is a difficult thing to explain, especially to a woman. Now, I am about to begin … Off you go.'

As he spoke, he fastened Gauthier's head down with a leather strap, seized a glittering scalpel and drew a rapid circular incision on the scalp. Drops of blood appeared; Catherine went pale. Don Alonso led her gently to the door.

'Go to your rooms, my child. Thomas will escort you there. You will be able to see the sick man when Hamza has finished.'

Catherine felt suddenly weary. Her head was heavy. She followed the page's thin figure, which had somewhat mysteriously appeared on the staircase of the keep. Thomas walked in front of her without making a sound or speaking a word. It was like walking with a ghost. He stopped in front of a door of carved, painted cypress wood and pushed it open, stepping aside as he did so.

'Here you are,' was all he said.

She did not go in at once but stopped in front of the boy.

'Come and tell me … when it is all over,' she said, smiling. But the boy's eyes were like ice.

'No,' he said harshly. 'I shall not go back to the Moor's room again. It is the devil's lair, and this medicine he practises is sacrilege. The Church forbids the letting of blood.'

'Yet your master does not object.'

'My master?' The boy's lip curled with a look of inexpressible scorn. 'My only master is God. Soon I shall be able to serve Him truly, may the Lord be thanked. I shall forget this house of Satan.'

Catherine was irritated by the solemn tone and fanatical pride, ridiculous enough in such a young boy, but before she could speak sharply to him, reminding him of the respect owed to Don Alonso, her eye was caught by a tall figure advancing slowly toward her down the gallery. It was a monk, dressed in black, reading intently. The cord around his waist hung loose on a bony body, and his grey hair was close-cropped around a large tonsure. At first sight there was nothing surprising about this monk; unless perhaps it was the black eye-patch over one of his eyes. He was a monk like any other. But as he came forward, Catherine felt the blood run cold in her veins, while her mind raced feverishly. All of a sudden she gave a cry of terror and, under Thomas's astonished eyes, ran into her room and slammed the door behind her. She leant against it panting, and then tore at the collar of her dress, which seemed suddenly to be strangling her. The face she had seen coming toward her in the gallery, beneath the monk's tonsure and eye-patch, was that of Garin de Brazey!

For a moment Catherine thought she must be going mad. Nothing seemed real: the time, the place were all ghostly, insubstantial. There was only this terrifying face before her eyes, this forgotten face that had vanished so many long years ago, only to suddenly reappear.

Her knees were weak as water. She slid to the ground, leaning against the door, and took her head in both hands as if trying to quieten the storm inside it. Old, tormenting memories swam up out of the depths of the past; images bitter as bile. She saw Garin again in prison, in chains, his legs in irons. She heard him begging her for the poison that would spare him the shame of being dragged through the town. She heard the voice of Abou-al-Khayr too, murmuring, as he handed her the poisoned wine, 'He will sleep … and never wake up.'

Then she saw herself, the following day, nose pressed to the window as she stared out through the grey misty morning. The rest of the picture was clear now, as sharp as an etching: the angry mob, the massive white-grey horses that were to drag the condemned man to the scaffold, the puddles of steely water, and finally the red-garbed, athletic figure of the executioner carrying the white, motionless form of a naked man over his shoulder. 'He is quite dead,' Sara had said. And what reason could there have been to doubt it? Catherine could almost see the long, white shape now against the red-tiled floor of this unknown room ... How could it have been so rigid if he was not dead? Yes, of course it had been Garin's body she had watched being dragged away, jolting and jerking over the uneven cobblestones. Well then, who was the other man ... the one who had just appeared to her in the gallery, the one with Garin's face and black eye-patch? Was it possible that the Lord Treasurer of Burgundy was not dead, that by some unlikely miracle he had eluded the death reserved for him? No, it wasn't possible! Even if Abou-al-Khayr had merely drugged the wine instead of poisoning it, the condemned man's body had still been hanged upon a gibbet. Garin, dead or alive, had been hanged. Sara, Ermengarde, the whole city of Dijon had seen the grisly carcass hanging from the gallows ... They had all seen it, except Catherine herself. She was in a state of such agitation now that she was beginning to disbelieve the evidence of her own memory. Perhaps it had not been Garin's body she had seen dragged off to execution? She had been so distressed that day. Perhaps her eyes had not seen truly through the mist of tears that had dimmed them? But then, why would her friends and servants have lied to her, if they had noticed something amiss? Could the deception have been so perfect that it had fooled a whole city?

Then, all of a sudden, a terrible thought crossed her mind. If Garin was still alive, if it really was him she had seen in a monk's robes, then her marriage to Arnaud was null and void, she had committed bigamy, and Michel, her little Michel, was a bastard!

Her whole being rose in revolt against this monstrous idea, and she rejected it with all her strength. She refused to accept such a thing. It wasn't possible! God, fate could not treat her so cruelly! She had known nothing but suffering and despair with Garin. He had given her a life of riches and splendour, but a life of shame, and she did not want to go back to that for anything in the world!

'I'm going mad!'

At that, the threatening storm of madness broke, and at once a dreadful reaction set in. Catherine stood up. She wanted to flee, to leave this castle with its ghosts and return to the sun-baked roads that led toward Arnaud. Dead or alive, ghost or flesh and blood, Garin was not going to ruin her life! He was dead and he must stay dead. But she must run away before there was the chance of being recognised. She turned to the door and would have opened it.

'*Dama*,' came a soft voice from somewhere behind her.

She whirled round. Two young servants were kneeling beside a great gilded and painted leather chest at the far end of the room, close to a window set with slender columns, pulling sparkling jewelled silks and satins out and heaping them on the red-tiled floor. Such was her panic that Catherine had not even noticed them before. She rubbed her eyes, restored to reality once more. No … she couldn't possibly run away. There was her friend Gauthier; she could never abandon him! A sob rose in her throat, and she moaned softly. Was she always to be the prisoner of her own heart, bound and tied by bonds she had woven herself?

Embarrassed at having been surprised in a state of such agitation and weakness, she responded mechanically to the timid smiles of the little maid-servants who were offering her the choice of gold or silver brocades, gleaming satin or softest velvet – three dresses that had belonged to the Archbishop's dead sister. The two girls came toward her and led her by the hand to a low stool, where they made her sit down and then, without more ado, set about undressing her. Catherine let them carry on without protest. It was easy to slip into the ways of former days, when she would surrender herself for hours at a time to the attentions of a team of maids under Sara's watchful eye.

As she thought of her old friend she suddenly felt more alone than ever. What would she not have given to have had Sara with her that evening? How would the gypsy-woman have reacted to that terrifying apparition? Catherine asked herself. And the reply came at once, clear and positive. Without wasting a moment, Sara would have followed on the tracks of the disquieting ghost; she would have pursued him and made him talk. She would have dragged the truth out of him!

'And so must I,' Catherine said, like a voice in a dream. 'I have to know the truth!'

That was obvious. She would never have rest or respite till she penetrated right to the heart of the mystery. The monk whom she had seen had been so absorbed in his reading that he had not noticed her. He must have a chance of seeing her quite clearly, in broad daylight. She would know from his reaction … and then …

Catherine refused to let herself think of what would happen next. But she knew now that she was ready for the fray again. Nothing, and no-one, not even a phantom returned from the land of the dead, was going to keep her away from Arnaud. Garin must be dead, quite dead, so that her love could live. Anyway, even if he had escaped from death, it was unlikely that he would want to resume his former life. Why otherwise would he be wearing a monk's habit, living buried away in the heart of a fortress in Old Castile? He was a monk, dedicated to God, bound to God by bonds as tight as those that bound her to Arnaud. And God never gave up His servants. But still she wanted to know …

The chill night air entering through the open window made her shiver. The two maids had washed her almost without her realising it, and they were now rubbing her bare skin with delicate oil and costly perfumes. She pointed absentmindedly at one of the billowing dresses proffered to her. A wave of yellow silk was passed over her head, to fall about her body in a mass of tiny rippling folds, but her heart was too heavy to appreciate the caress of the delicate material against her skin. She used once to love rich dresses and magnificent materials, but that was a long time ago. What was the point of a flattering dress that would not be seen by the man you loved?

At the far end of the great room the two maid-servants were drawing back the embroidered curtains of a tall bed of ebony inlaid with ivory, and preparing to turn back the coverlets, but she signed to them that she was not yet ready for bed. She would never be able to sleep with all these unanswered questions spinning round her mind. She walked swiftly toward the door, her hissing silken train trailing behind her, and opened it. Josse stood on the threshold. His eyes widened in astonishment for a moment at finding her dressed like that; but then he smiled his slow, familiar smile.

'It's all over,' he said. 'The Moor's slaves have taken our patient to bed. Do you want to see him before you retire?'

She nodded, and shut the door behind her. Then she took Josse's arm and walked along the gallery where the phantom had vanished a little while earlier. The place was lit by torches set here and there. Catherine walked swiftly, head held high, eyes fixed before her.

But Josse was meanwhile observing her closely. 'You seem to have something on your mind, Dame Catherine.' It was a statement rather than a question.

'I am worried about Gauthier, naturally.'

'No. Earlier on, when you left the tower, your face wasn't so strained, and your eyes were not haunted. Something must have happened. What is it?'

'I might have known that you can see in the dark,' she said, with the shadow of a smile. Then she made up her mind. Josse was intelligent, discreet, full of cunning. While he could never quite replace Sara, Catherine knew she could trust him.

'You are right,' she admitted. 'I came across someone a little while ago in this gallery: a monk. He was tall and thin, with grey hair, a face that might have been carved in granite, and he wore a black eye-patch. I want to know who this monk is. He looks alarmingly like … like someone I used to know very well, and believed dead.'

Josse smiled. 'It shall be done. I will take you to Gauthier's room, and then set about finding out what you want to know.'

He left her at the door of a room situated several floors below the Moor's in the same keep, and then vanished round a bend in the stairs, as swift and silent as a current of air. Catherine pushed the door gently and went in.

The room was much smaller than her own, barely large enough to take two stools and the bed on which the Norman's gigantic frame lay. Catherine went forward on tiptoe. Gauthier lay sleeping on his back, with a huge bandage wrapped round his head. In the light of a flickering candle placed on the stool beside the bed his face looked calm, but unusually flushed. She thought he might perhaps be feverish, and bent forward to touch his hand, which lay on the coverlet. But someone stopped her. Hamza emerged from the shadow of the curtains, a finger to his lips.

'I have given him a powerful drug to make him sleep,' he whispered. 'Otherwise his pain might affect his recovery adversely. Leave him now. His fever is rising.'

'Will he be cured?'

'I hope so. There were no lesions on the brain, and this man has an exceptional constitution. But one can never be certain that there will be no ill-effects.'

They both left the room. Hamza advised Catherine to go and get some rest, assuring her that Don Alonso himself had already been asleep for many hours. Then he bowed to her and returned to his laboratory, leaving Catherine to retrace her steps alone. She walked slowly across the courtyard, breathing in the scents of the slumbering countryside. All the wild plants that the sun had warmed during the day were exhaling their perfumes. The air was redolent of thyme and marjoram. Her recent emotional reaction had left Catherine with a deep longing for peace and silence. The massive red walls of the castle were swallowed up in the night. There wasn't a sound to be heard except for the occasional tread of a sentry or cry of a night bird. She paused for a moment beneath the arches where brilliant tiles glowed like a garden by moonlight, and sought to quieten the beating of her heart. Then, remembering that Josse might now be waiting for her in her room, she walked toward the stairs that led up to the gallery. But just then the page, Thomas de Torquemada, stepped out from behind a pillar. The young woman started – this habit of his, of appearing soundlessly where one least expected to see him, was disagreeable. He was like a sombre ghost haunting this princely dwelling. But this time the surprise was on both sides. Confronted by Catherine in her shimmering silk dress, haloed by golden tresses casually flung back from her brow, the sinister boy seemed petrified in his tracks.

They stayed like that for a moment, face to face. Catherine saw a look of disbelief enter the pale ice of that unblinking stare, together with a sort of superstitious terror. His mouth opened, but no sound came. Thomas passed his tongue over his thin lips, and his eyes sparkled suddenly as they slid down the young woman's neck, followed the outline of her low-slashed gown, lingered on the soft valley between her breasts, the perfect contours of which were clearly defined by the soft silken material, caught in by a gold sash underneath. The boy had evidently never seen such a sight before. As he stood there, apparently rooted to the spot, Catherine gave him a cold smile, while her hand instinctively drew the folds of her dress more closely about her.

'Would you mind letting me pass?' she asked.

At the sound of this voice, Thomas jumped as if awakened from a dream. A look close to terror spread across his face, which, from scarlet, now reverted to its usual ghastly pallor. He crossed himself hurriedly several times, flung his arms out before him as if to drive away this too seductive vision, and cried hoarsely: '*Vade retro Satanas!*' Then he turned on his heels and fled. The darkness of the courtyard swallowed him up in an instant.

Catherine shrugged and went on her way. She found Josse waiting for her back in the gallery, leaning against the door-frame with folded arms.

'Well?' she asked eagerly. 'Have you found out who this monk is?'

'He is called Father Ignacio, but it isn't easy to persuade the Archbishop's servants to talk about the man. They all seem scared stiff of him. I really think they are more frightened of him than they are of the Moor, or of the black-clad page with the face of a fallen angel.'

'But where does he come from? What is he doing here? I How long has he been living in this fortress?'

'Dame Catherine,' Josse observed calmly, 'I am sure that Don Alonso, who appears to take great pleasure in your company, will be able to tell you more about this strange person than I can, for he is the only person here who has any dealings with him. Father Ignacio is an alchemist, concerned with transmuting metals, and he seeks, like so many others, the celebrated Philosopher's Stone. But his chief duty here seems to be to look after the Archbishop's treasure, the extraordinary collection of jewels he keeps here. Someone told me that Father Ignacio is an expert in these matters, and that … Dame Catherine, are you sure you feel all right?'

Catherine leant against the wall, ghastly pale. The blood drained from her face and the ground seemed to shift under her feet. Josse could scarcely be expected to know how hard this news of the mysterious monk's knowledge of precious stones would strike her. Garin himself had been an avid collector of jewels.

'No …' she said faintly. 'I am very tired, that is all. I can hardly stand up …'

'Well, go straight to bed, then,' Josse said, with a kindly smile. 'Besides, I have nothing more to tell you. I might add that it is rare to meet Father Ignacio here, because he hardly ever leaves Don Alonso's private apartments, where he has his alchemist's laboratory and where the treasure is kept.'

He pushed open the painted door as he spoke, and revealed her room softly lit by clusters of tall red candles. She went in, shoulders bowed, stricken by misery. Josse watched her go in without a word. He had no idea why this Father Ignacio should have such a disturbing effect on the young woman, but something like pity awoke in him for this ideally beautiful creature whose life, instead of being full of gentleness and pleasure, seemed to be an unbroken series of pitiless struggles and difficulties that would have dismayed a strong man. He had a vague feeling that in taking some part in her fate he was in some way performing the best action of his entire life. Almost without knowing what he was doing, the one-time beggar, his eyes fixed on the slight figure standing forlornly in the middle of the room, murmured:

'Have courage, Dame Catherine. One day, I know, you will be happy … happy enough to forget all these bad times.'

Catherine turned slowly toward him. He had spoken the words she needed to hear, and they corresponded so perfectly with her own pathetic craving for relief and respite that she heard them without surprise, without wondering why he should suddenly have felt impelled to say them … Their eyes met. In Josse's glance she saw real, sincere friendship, unclouded by desire. The sort of friendship one man offers another. In a sense this was what destiny had made of them: brothers-in-arms. And this gave her a feeling of such security, a good warm feeling, that Catherine even managed a smile.

'Thank you, Josse,' she said simply.

8: One Night in Spring

The emerald in Don Alonso's long, elegant fingers took on unexpected brilliance in the torchlight. It sparkled and flashed so breathtakingly that the Archbishop's eyes lit up with real passion. He could not stop toying with the jewel, and from time to time the blue-green sparks it threw off brought almost rapturous exclamations from him. He spoke to the jewel as if it were a woman. He murmured words of love to it, to which Catherine listened in astonishment.

'Splendour of the deep, marvel of distant lands whose gods have eyes that flash as mysteriously! What jewel is as beautiful, as alluring, or as dangerous and inscrutable as thyself, incomparable emerald! For they call thee the jewel of bad luck ...'

Then, abruptly, the Archbishop broke off his amorous litany and turned to Catherine, pressing the ring back into her hands.

'Keep it, hide it! You mustn't tempt me with such an exquisite jewel, because it makes me too covetous!'

'I had hoped Your Eminence would accept it,' she murmured, 'in return for the care you have lavished on my servant and the generous hospitality you have shown to me.'

'I should count myself vile and unworthy of my name, my dear, if I were not generous with both toward a woman of my own rank. I cannot accept repayment, for my honour would feel slighted by doing so. And besides, such a jewel, carrying the arms of the Queen, would be over-lavish repayment for my slight services.'

Catherine slowly slipped the ring back on her finger, and Don Alonso's enamoured glances followed it. She could not repress a small sigh of disappointment. For she had hoped, in offering this precious ring to her host, to be asked to view his own collection of jewels, which Father Ignacio kept. As it happened, in the ten days since she had arrived at Coca, she had never once seen that alarming apparition again; the apparition she both longed for and dreaded. Father Ignacio had vanished as completely as if the castle's red walls had swallowed him up. And Catherine's tormenting curiosity seemed to grow apace. She must know the truth. At whatever price. But how could she ask Don Alonso to grant her such a favour without good reason?

Then an idea struck her, somewhat hypocritical no doubt, but she had no scruples in adopting it. She must penetrate those secret rooms where the alchemist lived. She twisted the ring dreamily round her finger, and murmured, with her eyes on the emerald:

'Of course, this stone may be imperfect … no doubt it is unworthy to figure among the other gems in your collection … which they say is without equal anywhere.'

A flush of pride crimsoned the Archbishop's features. He smiled at the young woman with genuine good will, and shook his head vigorously.

'My collection is beautiful, I admit … but scarcely unrivalled. There are princes with collections as fine, and finer. But, all the same, my modest little treasure is worth seeing. I assure you, my dear, that I would not scorn that emerald – on the contrary. The reasons I gave for refusing it are the real ones. And as proof, I'll tell you that I would gladly buy the stone from you, if you would consider selling it.'

'It was given to me,' Catherine sighed, seeing her hopes dwindle. 'I would not like to sell it.'

'That is quite natural. But as for my collection, I should be delighted to show it to you … so that you can compare your jewel and mine and see for yourself that your emerald would scarcely have disgraced my collection.'

Catherine almost jumped for joy. She had won! She followed her host eagerly through the labyrinth of passages and rooms, and then down several flights of stairs. Instead of climbing to the roof of his dwelling, they seemed this time to be heading down toward the cellars. A narrow door hidden among the blue tiles in one of the audience rooms revealed a spiral staircase that seemed to plunge toward the bowels of the earth. It appeared to be in frequent use and was well lit by many torches. The steps were low, broad and comfortable to walk down and there was a thick silken rope to hold on to. The walls themselves were hung with tapestries. As for the splendour of the room into which the staircase led, this was truly stupefying. One needed only to glance round the magnificent tapestries, the brocade cushions, the gilded tables laden with jewelled goblets and pitchers, the silken carpets from far-off Cathay, scattered about the red marble floor, and the golden candelabra with their forest of white tapers, to realise that Don Alonso made frequent and lengthy visits to this chamber. Here he would fondle the contents of one or other of the great coffers of scented cedarwood, gold-studded sandalwood and painted and gilded leather, which were provided with massive bronze locks making them all but impregnable.

At the far end of the room, which was long and narrow, Catherine beheld a sort of cell, furnished with much greater austerity, where a long funnel containing some green liquid stood on a great brick furnace, bubbling gently. A long glass tube led from it to an immense copper basin where something gave off a faint steam. This, doubtless, was the alchemist's laboratory. But she did not linger over the details of the decor. Her heart missed a beat, and her lips grew dry: she had just caught sight of Father Ignacio's austere silhouette standing close to one of the slender green marble pillars that supported the vaulted ceiling. The mysterious monk stood before one of the coffers, examining with minute care a topaz of unusual colour and size. So absorbed was he in this task that he did not even turn his head when Don Alonso and Catherine entered the treasure-chamber. He did not turn till his master laid one hand upon his shoulder. Catherine stiffened as the brilliant light of a nearby candelabrum revealed the features identical to those of her first husband. She felt the sweat standing out on her brow and the blood draining back into her heart. She felt she would suffocate for a moment, and she clasped her hands nervously, trying to control her emotion. Quite unaware of the storm raging within his visitor's breast, Don Alonso addressed a few rapid words of Spanish to Father Ignacio, who nodded in agreement. Then he turned toward her.

'This is Father Ignacio, Dame Catherine. He is an extraordinary man as well as a truly saintly soul. However, his researches into alchemy and the composition of precious stones have made him suspected by his fellow-monks of being some sort of sorcerer. Under my roof he has found the peace and tranquillity necessary for his work, as well as the means to pursue it. I know no-one more expert in the matter of gems. Show him your ring ...'

Till then Catherine had been standing in the shadow of a pillar, but now she stepped forward into the light and boldly threw back her head and looked the monk straight in the eyes. She felt a tremor of fear as Father Ignacio's single eye contemplated her, but she did not let it show. She examined this face that seemed to have surged out of oblivion to confront her, searching almost fiercely for signs of astonishment, incredulity, even uneasiness ... but there was nothing. Father Ignacio bowed correctly toward the young woman, who was wearing a violet velvet dress that matched her eyes, clasped below the bosom with a gold belt and then falling open over a white satin petticoat. There was nothing in that inscrutable face to suggest that he had recognised her.

'Well,' said Don Alonso impatiently, 'aren't you going to show him your emerald?'

She held up her little hand, half covered by the gold-embroidered white satin sleeve, so that the emerald caught the light. But her eyes were still glued to the monk's face. He took her hand in his, without the least trace of emotion, better to examine the stone. His fingers were warm and dry. When they touched hers, Catherine began to tremble. Father Ignacio glanced at her inquiringly, but then returned to his inspection of the jewel. He seemed to be impressed, for he finally looked up with an admiring gleam in his eye, which Catherine found positively exasperating. Was the man dumb? She wanted to hear his voice.

'It appears that this emerald, which you thought might be flawed, strikes Father Ignacio as entirely satisfactory,' the Archbishop said, smiling.

'Can't he speak?' the young woman asked. 'Or is the saintly monk dumb?'

'By no means. But he doesn't speak your language.'

When his master questioned him in Spanish, Father Ignacio answered in a slow, grave voice ... a voice that could easily be Garin's, transformed by the foreign tongue or deliberately disguised ... or the voice of a complete stranger.

'I shall show you my own emeralds,' the Archbishop went on. 'Almost all of them come from Djebel Sikait, and they are very fine ...'

As he went to open a coffer standing in the middle of the room Catherine, left standing face to face with the monk, could no longer contain the question which burned on her lips.

'Garin,' she whispered, 'is it really you? Speak to me, for Heaven's sake. You do recognise me, don't you?'

The monk looked at her in surprise. A vague, melancholy smile curved his thin lips for a fleeting moment. Then slowly he shook his head ... 'No comprendo,' he murmured; and then he bent over his topaz again.

Catherine went closer, as if she too wanted to examine the huge gem more closely. Her velvet dress brushed against the monk's homespun. She was beginning to feel angry. The resemblance, even close up, was quite startling. She could have sworn this man was Garin, and yet ... there was a slowness about his gestures, a hoarseness about his voice, that baffled her.

'Look at me,' she begged. 'Don't pretend you don't recognise me. I haven't changed that much. You know perfectly well that it is I, Catherine.'

But once again the enigmatic monk shook his head, and moved a little way off. Behind her, Catherine heard Don Alonso's beautiful deep voice calling to her to come and admire the stones he had brought out for her to see. She hesitated for a second, and glanced rapidly at Father Ignacio. His hands were perfectly steady as he calmly laid the topaz on the velvet lining of a little casket that contained several others. He seemed to have forgotten her presence.

The hour she spent in the subterranean chamber left Catherine with the feeling of having lived through a waking dream. She gazed unseeingly at all the jewels her host displayed to her. They were of many hues, but all of them of rare beauty, and yet her eyes kept returning to the monk's austere black silhouette in the hope of surprising a gesture, expression or glance that would give her the key to this living enigma. Father Ignacio was as absorbed in his work as if he were absolutely alone. When Catherine and Don Alonso left the room, he gave them the same brief salutation as before. They climbed in silence toward the upper apartments.

'I will see you back to your room,' the Archbishop suggested pleasantly.

'No ... please don't bother. Your Eminence is kind, but I want to see how my servant is before going to bed. I will go to see him now.' She paused, on the point of departure, and finally said: 'But there is one thing I would like to know: this Father Ignacio seems a remarkable man. Has he been looking after your magnificent collection for very long?'

'Seven or eight years, I think,' Don Alonso replied, quite unsuspectingly. 'My people found him one day weak and starving on the high road. On account of his strange practices, he had been expelled from the monastery in Navarre where he had taken his vows. I believe I told you – they took him for some sort of sorcerer. And yet ... perhaps there is something a little strange about him, wouldn't you say? He was on his way then to Toledo, where he hoped to be initiated into the mysteries of the Kabbala. But none of this can possibly interest you, Dame Catherine. I will leave you now to go and get some rest. Really, I feel quite exhausted.'

The contemplation of his treasures seemed to have increased his habitual nervousness. As Don Alonso departed, Catherine observed that the tics she had noticed before were more pronounced than usual.

The prelate's last words kept echoing in her mind. She passed a shaking hand across her damp forehead. 'Seven or eight years ...' It was ten years since Garin had been hanged. Could he then, by some miracle, have transported himself to the Navarrese monastery, whence he had been expelled for sorcery? Or had there never really been a monastery in Navarre? However, this business of sorcery perplexed her. Garin was passionately fond of precious stones – he was like the monk in that respect. But Catherine had never seen him take any interest in alchemy. He was interested in most things, certainly, but there was nothing remotely resembling a laboratory in the house in the Rue de la Parcheminerie, or at Brazey either. Was one to conclude that he had conducted his esoteric experiments in secret? Or had the taste for such things come to him later, when he had lost his fortune? Finding the fabulous Philosopher's Stone; now that was a project to tempt a ruined man!

Catherine shook off her thoughts abruptly. She had had enough of them. She was walking toward the keep, pretending not to notice Thomas, who had suddenly materialised in the courtyard. She was always encountering the sinister page these days. He would habitually appear at some point along the way, whether she was on her way to chapel, to the keep or to some quite different part of the castle. She never knew when she would see him next. He never spoke to her, but stared at her from a safe distance, with a look of mingled anger and lust. Catherine felt uneasy in the presence of this tall black figure, and she made a point of ignoring him. She paid no attention to him on this particular occasion but went straight up to Gauthier's room.

The Norman was fast recovering from the operation Hamza had performed on him. His extraordinary constitution, together with the scrupulous cleanliness that Hamza maintained all about him and the good food provided at the castle, had helped him surmount all the dangers that frequently made operations of this kind fatal. But unfortunately the giant appeared to have lost his memory.

He had regained his sanity, certainly, and he was perfectly aware of what went on around him, but he remembered absolutely nothing of what had happened before he opened his eyes in that little room after the operation. Not even his own name. Catherine was beginning to despair of his recovery. When the Moorish doctor had first told her that Gauthier had returned to consciousness, she had rushed to his bedside, but when she had bent over him, she had been cruelly disappointed. The giant had gazed at her with eyes full of admiration, as if she had been some fairy-like apparition, but without the slightest hint of recognition. She had spoken to him then, repeating her name, telling him over and over again that it was Catherine, and that he must recognise her ... but Gauthier had merely shaken his head.

'Forgive me, lady,' he murmured. 'Truly you are as beautiful as the dawn ... but I don't know who you are. I don't even know who I am,' he added sorrowfully.

'Your name is Gauthier Strongitharm, and you are both my servant and my friend ... Have you forgotten everything we went through together, all our adventures? Have you forgotten Montsalvy, Michel, Sara, Messire Arnaud?'

Her voice broke as she uttered her husband's name, but there was no kindling of recollection in the giant's lacklustre gaze. He shook his head once more.

'No ... I don't remember a thing.'

At this she turned to Hamza, who stood watching her quietly from one corner of the room, his hands folded over his white robe. Her stricken eyes implored him, and she murmured piteously: 'Is there ... nothing to be done?'

He signed to her to join him and then led her out of the room. 'No, there is nothing more I can do. Nature alone has the power to restore his memory to him.'

'But how?'

'An emotional shock perhaps. I must admit I had hoped that your appearance might do the trick, but I was disappointed.'

'And yet, he was deeply attached to me.I might even say that he loved me, without daring to show it.'

'In that case, try to reawaken that love of his. Then perhaps the miracle will occur. But again, it might never happen. And then you will have to act as his memory and teach him all about his own past.'

Catherine repeated these words to herself as she entered the little room with its single candle. Gauthier sat in the narrow window embrasure staring out into the night. With his long legs folded under him, and wearing a sort of striped kaftan held in at the waist by a long scarf, he looked taller than ever. He turned as Catherine entered and revealed a face that pain had scoured and hollowed, but grey eyes as steady as they had ever been. Thin as he was, the Norman's powerful physique was still striking. Catherine used once to tell him, jokingly, that he looked like a siege engine. Something of this still clung to him, but his illness had endowed the rough features with a touching youthfulness and a sort of pale distinction. Even his huge white hands seemed more delicate. Now that he was not lying down, the little room looked too small to hold him.

He was about to stand up as the young woman entered, but she stopped him, and laid her hand on his bony shoulder.

'No … don't move. Why haven't you gone to bed yet?'

'I don't feel like sleep. I feel stifled in this room! It's so small!'

'You won't have to stay here much longer. As soon as you are well enough to ride, we will leave this castle.'

'We? Are you going to take me with you?'

'You have always travelled with me,' Catherine said sadly. 'It used to strike you as quite normal … Don't you want to come with me now?'

He did not answer at once, and Catherine's heart tightened painfully. What if he refused? What if he decided to seek some other fate? She was no more to him than a pretty woman, now that his memory was gone. And yet she had never, never needed him so badly as she did now: she needed the strength, the impregnable refuge he had always been for her. Gauthier's broad chest had stood between herself and suffering for so many years past – had she found him and delivered him from a horrible death only to lose him again, more surely? She felt tears stinging her eyes.

'You don't answer,' she murmured.

'I just don't know. I would like to follow you, because you are so beautiful … like a star. But if I am to rediscover my past, it might be better if I left on my own. Something inside me tells me that I ought to go alone, that I have always been alone …'

'No, that's not true! You have hardly ever left my side these three years past! We have suffered and struggled, and defended our lives together. You have saved my life so many times! How shall I go on if you abandon me?'

She collapsed onto the foot of the bed, overcome by this fresh blow. She hid her face in trembling hands, and murmured sorrowfully:

'I beg you, Gauthier! Don't leave me … I am lost without you, lost!'

Bitter tears rolled between her fingers. She felt dreadfully lonely, abandoned by everyone. There was this monk, this living nightmare who haunted the castle walls; there was homesickness for her own country, her son; and, worst of all, there was this lacerating stab of jealousy every time she allowed herself to think of her husband. That Gauthier should turn away from her now, that he should forget the past, was more than she could bear ... She heard him faltering:

'Do not cry, lady. If it grieves you so much, I will certainly go with you.'

He bent toward her, examining her sweet, beseeching, tear-wet face.

'I wish I could remember,' he said sadly. 'It cannot be difficult to love you. You are so beautiful. You look as if you were made of sunlight. Your eyes are softer than the night ...'

Timidly, he put his hand under her chin and tipped her face toward him so as to get a better look at the velvety irises, now sparkling with tears. The Norman's agitated face was now close to hers, and Catherine lost her self-control. She seemed still to hear Hamza's voice murmuring, 'You must try to reawaken that love of his ...' She whispered:

'Kiss me.'

She saw him hesitate. Then she arched up against him and sought his lips with her own, slipped her arms around his massive neck and clung to him. His mouth was unresponsive for a moment under hers, as if it paused on the brink of sexual excitement. Then, suddenly, Catherine felt it come to life, warm and hungry, and the giant's arms tightened around her. Entwined together, the two of them rolled onto the bed.

As his mouth fastened on hers impatiently, Catherine felt her body, chaste for too long, quickening to a storm of passion. She had always felt a deep tenderness for Gauthier, but when she had offered him her lips a moment before, she had thought only to supply the sudden shock that might restore his memory. But now desire swept through her to match the passion in the body pressed against her own ...

The thought of her husband flashed through her mind, but she rejected it angrily. No, even his memory should not stop her giving herself to her friend. Their love had not stopped him giving his kisses and caresses to another woman! She felt a hunger for revenge that only redoubled her expectation of pleasure to come. She saw that Gauthier was fumbling inexpertly with the laces on her bodice. She pushed him gently away.

'Wait! Don't be in such a hurry ...'

With a supple movement of the hips she was on her feet. The faint candlelight struck her as inadequate.

She did not want to give herself to him furtively, in the dark. She wanted as much light as possible to shine on her face and her body when he made love to her ... She took the candle and lit the two candelabra standing on a chest against the wall. He sat on the foot of the bed watching her, uncomprehendingly.

'Why all this? Come to me ...' he begged, reaching for her impatiently, eager to hold her. But she stopped him with a look.

'Wait, I tell you ...'

She moved a little way off. Then she picked a knife off the table and cut the laces of her dress with a single stroke. She flung it aside with joyful alacrity, then stepped out of her white satin petticoat and fine chemise. Avidly, the grey eyes followed each of her movements, sliding over her body as she unveiled it to him. Catherine felt his eyes on her breasts, on her belly, her flanks, and she rejoiced in the sensation as if it were a caress. When the last item of clothing had fallen to the floor, she stretched herself like a cat in the warm candlelight, then slipped onto the bed and, at long last, held out her arms.

'Now come to me!'

He sprang upon her ...

'Catherine!'

At the height of their love-making he had cried out her name, as if he were calling her, and now he gazed in bewilderment at the tender face clasped in his hands.

'Catherine! Dame Catherine. Am I still dreaming?'

Joy surged through the young woman. Hamza had been right after all. Love had awoken him, had worked a miracle upon him! ... The man she held in her arms was no longer a stranger, a body whose spirit was elsewhere. He was himself again ... and she felt happier than she had for a long time. He was trying to push her away, but she wound her arms more tightly round him and drew him to her again.

'Don't move ... Yes, it is me ... you aren't dreaming – but don't go now. I'll explain it all to you later. Stay with me. Make love to me ... Tonight I belong to you.'

The lips beneath his were too soft, the body he clasped too yielding ... It was such an old dream of his, to one day possess the body of this woman he adored! A dream resolutely and harshly banished from his mind for so many years! It was almost like waking from a long slumber, but this soft warm skin and intoxicating perfume were unmistakably real. He yielded to their spell with wild passion, slaking himself with her like a man suddenly offered wine after interminable long days of thirst. Catherine allowed herself to be possessed joyfully, abandoning her body with all its pent-up animal sensuality to this hurricane of love.

Yet she was conscious, around midnight, of something strange happening. She was certain she heard the door of the room creaking. She sat up and listened for a moment, motioning Gauthier to keep silent. The candles were guttering low by now, but there was enough light for her to see clearly that the door was not moving. There wasn't a sound to be heard. Then Catherine told herself that she must have been mistaken. She forgot the door and went back to her lover …

It was near dawn when Gauthier at last fell asleep. He seemed to crash into a deep sleep, like a falling tree, and the keep was soon reverberating to a mighty snoring that made Catherine smile. Those were the real trumpet calls of victory! She watched him sleeping for a moment. He looked peaceful, relaxed, lips softly parted. There was something childlike about that gigantic frame outstretched across the turbulent bedclothes. She felt a great tenderness for him. The love he had given her was, she knew, a precious thing. Gauthier loved her for herself, unselfishly, and this love warmed her sore heart.

She bent over him and softly kissed his closed eyelids. Then she hurriedly pulled on her clothes so that she could be back in her own room before daybreak. Dressing herself again was not a simple matter; the cut laces of her bodice were a hindrance, but she finally succeeded in doing it up after a fashion. Then she slipped out of the room and crept down the stairs on stockinged feet so as not to make too much noise. The sky was beginning to grow light above the battlements. The torches along the passages were smokily burning themselves out. Here and there throughout the building the castle guards slept at their posts, leaning on their pikes. Catherine managed to get back to her room without encountering a living soul. She flung off the dress she had held clutched around herself and slid between her cool linen sheets with a sigh of contentment. She felt weary, shaken to the marrow by the night of passion she had just passed with Gauthier, and yet in some way she seemed strangely freed of her phantoms, almost happy again. Of course it was not the intoxicating, marvellous oblivion that only Arnaud had ever succeeded in giving her.

In the arms of the one man she had ever really loved, Catherine forgot herself, melted into greater and still greater joy, abandoned her own personality and will to become one flesh, one heart, with him. But this past night her own deep attachment to Gauthier, her ardent desire to snatch his spirit from the perilous shadowy land of madness, and her own painful sensual hunger, had stood her instead of passion. She had discovered the peace of body and mind that can be found in the love of a sincere and passionate man … Even the irritating problem represented by Father Ignacio seemed to have dwindled somehow, and lost some of its mystery …

As for the immediate future, and the possible consequences of her new relationship with Gauthier, this was something Catherine refused to think about. Not now, anyway … Later … Tomorrow … Just now she was weary, so weary! She was dying for sleep. Her eyelids closed and she sank into happy oblivion.

The soft caress of a hand travelling over her belly and thighs woke her with a start. It was still very early. The window of her room showed only faintly blue. Catherine's sleep-clouded eyes suddenly lighted on a figure sitting on the bed beside her, but at first she did not recognise her visitor through the mists of sleep. Then the cool morning air and the renewed attentions of this exploring hand woke her abruptly. All her sheets and coverlets had been thrown aside so that she lay there shivering and stark naked. Just then the shape moved and bent over her. Catherine's eyes widened in terror as she recognised Thomas de Torquemada. But she scarcely knew him, his face was so diabolically contorted. His eyes were starting out of his head, and he kept grinding his jaws so that a trickle of saliva appeared at the corner of his mouth ... She was about to cry out for help, but a brutal hand fastened abruptly over her mouth. She struggled to free herself, but in vain. A sharp nail tore her breast, and a violent blow from his knee forced her legs apart, while a naked body, covered with cold acrid sweat, flattened itself on top of her.

Almost beside herself with revulsion, she writhed and twisted beneath the youth. He struck her so savagely across the face that she moaned. He sneered, speaking in a half- whisper.

'Enough of that, bawd! ... I saw you tonight, in the tower, with your servant ... Ah, you really put your heart into it, didn't you, slut? You know how to please men, don't you, you whore? Come on then, show me your tricks! ... It's my turn now. Kiss me, woman!'

He interspersed his insults with damp kisses, which made Catherine's gorge rise, and little whimpering noises that were almost equally disgusting. He held her down with one powerful thin hand, but for all his frantic efforts, he was unable to enter his victim. Catherine could scarcely breathe under the bony hand that was clapped over her lips when Thomas was not tearing at them with his own. She was beyond coherent thought, solely intent on throwing off this damp and slippery horror, this loathsome nightmare of a man. The demon of lust that inhabited this boy was more terrifying by far than anything she had known before. Even Gilles de Rais had not been quite so repulsive!

For a second the hand over her mouth relaxed its pressure. She took advantage of this and bit it so savagely that Thomas cried out and instinctively drew back his hand. At this she screamed with all her might, with the despairing strength of a trapped animal ... He hurled himself upon her, striking her over and over again in an effort to silence her, though he was now shouting almost as loudly as she was, carried away by a positive frenzy of hatred. Half-unconscious by now, Catherine barely heard the banging on her door. Then there was the crash of splintering wood, followed by the clatter of bolts and locks hitting the tiled floor. In the first ray of morning sunshine, she caught a glimpse of Josse, tossing aside the beam he had used to batter down the door, which Thomas must have locked behind him. The one-time beggar flung himself on to the bed and grabbed Thomas, beating him with professional thoroughness. Catherine hid herself as best she could under the tumbled pillows and closed her eyes so as not to see what followed, but she could not help hearing the dull thud as Josse's fists struck home against the page's body or the flood of extraordinary Parisian oaths and insults that he heaped upon him at the same time.

One last blow, a final kick on the young satyr's thin buttocks, and Thomas, naked as the day he was born, found himself flung into the passage like a mere package. He did not tarry a second, however, but took to his heels, while Josse, muttering and swearing, went across to a cupboard whence he flushed the two little maid-servants who had come running up on hearing the din and then taken refuge from the ensuing violence. He indicated Catherine, huddled in her bed, covers pulled up to her chin, only her eyes showing.

'Now see to Dame Catherine, you two! I'm going to see the Lord Archbishop and tell him what I think of his precious page! Have you ever seen a more repulsive little creature? I hope you are all right, Dame Catherine? He was knocking you about like a madman when I came in.'

The Parisian's calm tones reassured Catherine. She forced a smile. 'I must be covered with bruises, but I don't think it's at all serious. Thank you, Josse. If you hadn't come … God, what a monster! And such a young boy! I won't forget that nightmare in a hurry,' she added, close to tears.

'Youth is nothing to do with the matter. My own theory is that young Thomas is possessed of the devil. You don't need to look at him twice to see that cruelty is in his blood … and the germ of quite a few vices! I feel sorry for the monastery where he is going, and I feel a bit sorry for God Himself! He will have a terrible servant in this boy!'

Josse stood thoughtfully in the middle of the room, frowning. He stared unseeingly at the sun, which now burst through the window in an aureole of flame. Then, abruptly, he muttered:

'The boy has had a good hiding, Dame Catherine. But if you ask me, it would be best not to tarry here too long. As soon as Gauthier can travel …'

'I think he can now. His memory has returned …'

Josse Rallard raised his eyebrows and darted a look of genuine astonishment at her.

'He has recovered, then? But yesterday when I went to see him, just before the curfew, he was still in the same state.'

Catherine, whose scratches and bruises were being examined by the maid-servants, felt herself blushing. She looked away, in embarrassment.

'The miracle took place during the night,' she said.

There was a short silence, which increased Catherine's embarrassment still further.

'Good,' Josse said at last. 'In that case we shall be able to set off without delay.'

And he strode calmly from the room, leaving Catherine to the attentions of her maids.

An hour later, Don Alonso presented himself at Catherine's door in a state of extreme agitation. He seemed more nervous and febrile than ever. His beautifully-shaped hands fluttered restlessly and his splendid deep voice rose perilously close to a squeak. He offered profuse and almost unintelligible apologies to the young woman, the gist of which seemed to be that he was going to get rid of Thomas.

'This painful incident has made up my mind, my dear. Tomorrow the little monster leaves for the Dominican monastery in Segovia, since he seems so set upon going there, and good luck to the worthy monks! I wish them well of him!'

'I too plan to leave tomorrow, your Grace, if it please you.'

'What? So soon? But what about your servant?'

'He is now quite well enough to continue his journey with us. I am eternally grateful to you, your Eminence. Your kindness, your generosity ...'

'Come, come ... enough of that ...'

He looked at Catherine for a moment. She sat in a high-backed chair, dressed in a black velvet dress that covered her neck to the chin and her hands as far as the fingers, and she looked the picture of grace and dignity. He smiled at her, paternally.

'Ah well, fly off, my pretty bird! But I shall miss you! Yes, I shall miss you. Your presence brought a little sunshine into this austere place ... Ah well. That's life. I shall see to the preparations for your departure.'

'Your Eminence,' Catherine said, faltering, 'you are too kind ...'

'Kindness has nothing to do with it,' said Don Alonso, laughing. 'You know quite well that I am an elderly aesthete in love with beauty and harmony. When I think that a woman like you had to travel in an old cart piled with hay I get gooseflesh all over. You don't want to condemn me to a lifetime's remorse and bad dreams?'

Catherine slid to her knees, by way of reply, and respectfully kissed the Archbishop's ring.

A wave of emotion swept over Alonso's tanned face. He sketched a rapid blessing in the air, then laid his hand on her bowed head.

'I don't know exactly where you are bound for, my child, and I am not going to ask you. But something tells me that you are heading for danger. Remember, if things become too difficult for you, that you have a friend here, and a home. Both will be ready to receive you like a father any time you want.' And he blew his nose violently to disguise his emotion.

With that, his Grace the Archbishop of Seville departed in a great flurry of crimson brocade, announcing as he went that he was going to see to the preparations for her departure personally and that Catherine was not to have anything to do with them whatsoever ... He would see her two hours later for luncheon.

The moment he had left, Catherine rushed to the keep. She was eager to see Gauthier again, although she felt slightly disappointed that he had not yet come in search of her. Perhaps he was still asleep? She lifted up her skirts in both hands, tore up the steep staircase and pushed open the door, to find herself face to face with her friend. He sat at the foot of the bed, with his face buried in his hands, so that it was impossible to tell whether he was thinking, sleeping, or even weeping. His whole attitude bespoke such despondency that Catherine felt quite disconcerted. She had expected to find Gauthier happy, quite himself again, and still glowing with the joy they had found together the previous night. But it seemed that this was far from being the case. She had expected anything but this ...

She knelt down beside the giant and took his great hands in her own. They were damp.

'Gauthier,' she cried sorrowfully, 'what is wrong?'

He turned toward her a face ravaged by weeping, and in his grey eyes there was a look of incredulity and despair. He looked at her as if he had never really believed in her existence.

'My God,' she murmured, close to tears herself, 'you are making me afraid!'

'So,' he said slowly, 'it wasn't a dream ... It really is you. I wasn't dreaming?'

'What?'

'Last night ... that incredible night. I wasn't delirious, then? My head has been full of such strange things, for such a long time now ... strange blurred dreams ... that it's got to the point where I hardly know what is real and what is daydream.'

Catherine gave a faint sigh of relief. She had feared that his illness might have returned. Now she said, calmly and gently, with great sweetness: 'No ... you were really cured last night. And ... you also became my lover,' she added candidly.

He took her by the shoulders and scanned her lovely upturned face hungrily. 'But why? Why all of a sudden did you come to me? What happened? How did we get to that point? The last time I remember seeing you is at Montsalvy, and now I find you again ... where are we now, come to that?'

'At Coca, in Castile. In the castle of the Archbishop of Seville, Don Alonso of Fonseca.'

He echoed her dreamily. 'At Coca ... In Castile. But how did we get

139

here? I have no idea.'

'What exactly do you remember?'

'The last thing I clearly remember was a battle. The bandits of the forest of Oca, who were holding me prisoner, were attacked by the alguacils. The soldiers took me for a brigand too. I had to fight in self-defence. I was wounded. It was a terrible blow. I thought my head was smashed to bits. And then … nothing … No, not quite … I remember being thirsty, and cold … The only other thing I remember was this ceaseless tearing wind …'

'The cage,' Catherine thought to herself, taking care not to mention that appalling instrument of torture. Nevertheless she would have to help Gauthier recover his memory as completely as possible.

'But how did you fall into the hands of the bandits of Oca?' she asked. 'A Florentine minstrel whom you met on the road to Roncesvaux told me he had seen you fall victim to an ambush by Navarrese mountain-folk. He saw them fling your body into a deep chasm … After that … there's no use pretending … I thought you must be dead.'

'I thought so too. I was wounded. They attacked me like a swarm of wasps. Then they tore my clothes off and threw me into the ravine. By rights I should have had my back broken, but the gods were watching over me. A sapling broke my fall, and when the cold brought me round again I found myself caught up in its branches. My position was serious enough though. I was shivering with cold, night was falling, and I was stark naked. I felt as weak as a newborn child, and yet I was determined to survive. Although I had lost a great deal of blood I was able to think clearly. What should I do? Return to the road? That would be dangerous, partly because I was too weak to manage the climb, and partly because my attackers might still be lurking around. There was no way of telling whether they were not waiting somewhere in the hope of waylaying some traveller in the approaching darkness. The second time, they would certainly have made certain that I did not live to tell the tale …

'I was thinking this when I suddenly noticed fires kindling in the valley below me. This gave me new courage. I assumed they must mean shepherds or woodcutters, and I began slowly climbing down toward them, clinging to the bushes and rocks all the way. I can't tell you how long this descent lasted. Soon I had only the red flames in the darkness to guide me. How I got to the bottom without breaking every bone in my body is still a mystery to me …'

'And the shepherds took you in then, and looked after you?' Catherine said.

'They took me in, yes, and looked after me, and more … but they weren't shepherds.'

'What were they then?'

'The followers of a certain robber-baron of the region – Vivien d'Aigremont.'

Catherine frowned. She remembered hearing the name spoken in varying degrees of terror by the monks of Roncesvaux, as well as by the peasants of St Jean Pied-de-Port.

'How did you escape?'

'I didn't escape, that's just the point. That Vivien d'Aigremont is a wild beast, one of the man-eating kind whose claws are forever bloody. He took me in only because he thought I might have some commercial value. They looked after me, it is true, but they loaded me with chains as soon as I could walk, and took me like that to Pamplona, where the swine sold me as a slave, and got a fair price too, believe me. I am worth a goodly sum in gold coin,' Gauthier added with bitter irony. 'It was the Bishop of Pamplona who bought me, to look after his kennels. The hounds he kept there were fearsome beasts, but their master outstripped them in ferocity. The day when a small boy was thrown to them alive, as a meal, I managed to escape. Fear lent me wings – I knew quite well what my fate would be if I were caught: the same as befell that unfortunate child. But I didn't know the country, or its accursed language. When I finally met a man who understood what I was saying, it proved my undoing … for he was one of the bandits of Oca. He took me back to his companions, and I found I had merely exchanged one lot of chains for another. I was just planning my escape once more when the alguacils turned up. Being so tall, I seem to have been mistaken for the leader of the band. In any case, there wasn't a hope of my making myself understood in their tongue. I was knocked unconscious and captured. And you know the rest better than I do, no doubt …'

'Yes, I do …' Catherine stroked the Norman's rough cheek gently. 'You have suffered terribly, Gauthier, I know, but I have always been convinced that death was powerless against you. You are indestructible … like the earth itself!'

'The earth can be torn by earthquakes, and swallowed up by floods, and I am only a man like any other.'

But, as Catherine's hand lingered on his cheek, he gently removed it and said:

'Now it's your turn, Dame Catherine. If you want me to understand, you must tell me everything … everything, you understand?'

She fell back, looking at him with eyes full of pain. Then she stood up and went to sit on a bench by the window. Not that she had ever expected to avoid giving Gauthier a frank explanation of the facts – hadn't she promised him, that night, at the height of their sensual madness: 'Tomorrow I'll explain everything.'

'You shall know everything. I had no intention of hiding anything from you. Well then, when the Florentine minstrel came to tell us that he had seen you perish ...'

The story took a long time to tell. Catherine spoke slowly, thinking carefully, so as not to forget a single detail. She spared him nothing. It was all there: the flight from Montsalvy, the pilgrimage to the Virgin of Puy, the departure with the pilgrims, the meeting with Ermengarde de Chateuvillain and Josse Rallard, the theft of the Sainte-Foy rubies, the arrival of Jean van Eyck and the letter from Duke Philippe, Fortunat's spiteful revelations, the flight with Josse from Roncesvaux, and finally the rescue of Gauthier himself in a Burgos lusting for blood, and their arrival together at the Archbishop's rose-red fortress.

Gauthier did not interrupt her once. And his eyes did not leave her face for a second. It was as though he wanted to make sure that she was not hiding anything from him. When she came to the end of her recital he sighed deeply, strode across to the window embrasure and stood with one foot resting on the window-seat.

'So, Messire Arnaud is a prisoner of the Moors?' he said slowly.

Instantly Catherine's jealous anger swept over her like a flood of bile. 'A willing prisoner! Didn't I tell you that he went with this woman of his own free will? Didn't I tell you what Fortunat told me? The infidel is more beautiful than the rising sun, he said, and my husband fell in love with her at first sight.'

'And you believed that? An intelligent woman like you? Remember Fortunat's fanatical attachment to his master, remember all those visits he paid to the leper-house at Calves, in all weathers. What you cannot know, since you were not there at the time, is the rage and fury he felt when the Seigneur de Brézé came to Montsalvy and everyone there was convinced that you were going to marry again! I have never heard such screams of anger, such vicious promises to make you pay for that treachery. Fortunat hated you, Dame Catherine. He would have said anything at all to hurt and humiliate you.'

'He would not have lied to that extent. After all, he did swear – he swore, do you hear? – on the salvation of his soul, that at that very minute Arnaud was enjoying love in the Princess's palace. Now, would anyone risk their eternal salvation merely to gratify a simple case of hatred?'

'More people than you realise, perhaps. In any case, Messire Arnaud may well be receiving love in this palace, but who knows whether he reciprocates it? Besides ...' And Gauthier wheeled round and faced Catherine so that he towered above her with all his great height. 'You would never have set out on this mad journey, Dame Catherine, if you hadn't expected more. You would have returned to Montsalvy, possibly to the King's Court where Seigneur de Brézé would have been waiting with open arms ... Or you might even have been reminded of the love of the

Great Duke of the West. A woman like you never admits defeat; I know that better than anyone. As for this story of Messire Arnaud being lost to you – tell that to someone else, Dame Catherine. You will never get me to swallow a tale like that.'

'Suppose I wanted only to bring his treachery home to him? Perhaps I want to see him writhe when he is discovered, a Christian and a King's captain, languishing at the feet of some dusky Mooress …'

Gauthier went suddenly crimson with anger. 'Don't make a fool of me, Dame Catherine. Are you telling me that you would travel all that distance simply to make a scene in front of your husband?'

'Well, why not?'

Standing on tiptoe, arms folded and small head thrown back, she looked like an angry little fighting cock. For the first time since the night before, when they had made love so ardently, the two were face to face.

'Because it isn't true. Because he is the only man you have ever loved. Because you are eaten up with anger at the thought of him in another woman's arms, and you will know neither rest nor respite, even if it means braving the worst dangers, till you have rejoined him … and reconquered him!'

'To pay him back for his treachery!'

'By what right? Whose was the first betrayal? Shall we talk about the Sire de Brézé? To make use of such glowing terms to describe your beauty he must have had some intimate knowledge of it. Surely he would never have expected to wed you if you had given him no encouragement? And how must he have felt, the leper, the outcast of Calves, on learning that fine piece of news? What torments must he have suffered! For Fortunat hid nothing from him, you know. If I had been in his place I should have escaped and torn you bodily from your handsome knight's arms, and then killed you with my own hands before giving myself up to justice!'

'Perhaps that's because you love me,' Catherine said bitterly. 'He didn't think like you …'

'Because he loves you even more! More than himself, since he sold his own sufferings cheap so that you might enjoy a new happiness. Believe me, the jealous fires that consume you are nothing to those that must have tormented him in his appalling loneliness. Do you suppose I can ever forget my last picture of him? That tortured man walking away in the sunlight, amid the tolling death-knell and wailing bagpipes, carrying that other sunshine in both hands?'

At this harsh reminder of the most dreadful day of her life, Catherine closed her tear-dimmed eyes, tottering a little.

'Enough,' she begged. 'Be silent, have pity on me.'

'In that case,' he said more gently, 'stop trying to fool me, and yourself. Why try to lie to us both? Because of last night?'

She suddenly opened flashing eyes. 'Perhaps it is because of last night then! Perhaps I don't want to go to Granada any more!'

'I suppose you must have been struggling with yourself for many days now,' Gauthier said wearily. 'Torn one way by jealousy, to the town where your husband lives; torn another by the longing to give it all up, to go back to your child, to the calm and safety of a normal life. What happened last night has not made any difference.'

'Why do you say that?'

'Because I know it is true. Last night you made me a wonderful present … an unexpected gift, but you did so for two reasons. Firstly, from pity …'

'Gauthier!' Catherine protested.

'Yes, yes, from pity first of all, because you wanted to cure me at all costs; but also out of spite. It was a sort of revenge you were exercising, and a way of taking some of the sting out of the images that haunt your slumbers.'

'No,' Catherine protested tearfully, 'it wasn't that, it wasn't only that. Last night I was happy too, I swear to you!'

A sweet smile lit up the Norman's frowning face. 'Thank you for those words. I do believe that you love me, Dame Catherine, after a fashion, but …' and he pointed at the massive gold and pearl crucifix presented to Catherine by the Archbishop, which she wore sparkling against her severe velvet gown, 'dare you swear by this God you worship that it is not he whom you truly love? He, your lord and husband? You know very well that you will go on loving him as long as there is any breath left in your body!'

This time the young woman said nothing. She bowed her head and her tears flowed freely over her velvet gown.

'You see now,' Gauthier said softly. 'And as for that marvellous night, which I shall always remember but which I beg you to forget, we shall never speak of it again …'

'Don't you love me anymore, then?' Catherine asked in a small voice.

There was a heavy silence. Then the Norman muttered in a voice that sounded hoarse: 'The gods of my people are witness that I have never loved you as much as I do now! But it is by virtue of this love that I must now beg you to forget. If you don't, my life will be hell … and I would have to leave you. We are going to leave this place and continue this journey that takes us to the Kingdom of Granada. I will help you find Messire Arnaud again.'

'There are some other things you don't know. It is possible that I no longer have the right to claim Arnaud de Montsalvy as my husband.'

'What do you mean?'

'That I may not have been free to love him … because I fear that my first husband may still be alive.'

Gauthier said nothing, but his raised eyebrows and his very silence seemed to question her. Hurriedly then, like someone shaking off an intolerable burden, she told him of her amazement at seeing the one-eyed monk, her terror when so many strange coincidences seemed to hang thereby, and lastly of her visit to the treasure-chamber the previous day and the unbearable uncertainty in which this had left her. She was about to continue, describing her fears and scruples, when Gauthier suddenly took her by the shoulders and began shaking her as if to wake her from a nightmare. He was deathly pale.

'Silence, Dame Catherine … and listen to me! We are going to leave this castle immediately, do you hear, and you are never coming back. Otherwise, by Odin, I swear you will lose your reason! All this has been too much for you! Now stop this wakeful dreaming, leave this country of nightmares and bad luck! Continue your journey and just remember this: before God and before man you are the wife of Arnaud of Montsalvy; you bear his name and you have a son by him. There is nothing to add to this. Forget everything else.'

'But supposing this monk were Garin de Brazey?'

'There is no reason why you should ferret out the truth. As far as the whole world is concerned, himself included no doubt, he has been hanged. If he managed to escape, he has doubtless shaped himself the sort of life he wants. If he wished to change it he would not have left you in this state of uncertainty. His attitude dictates what yours should be. Garin de Brazey is dead, do you hear? Dead! Only Father Ignacio, who has nothing in common with him, is still living! Now go and get ready and let us leave this castle of bad omen as soon as possible.'

Just then, the sound of trumpets shattering the sunny silence of this immense landscape brought Catherine sharply back to earth. She went to the door, smiling sweetly at her friend.

'You are always right, Gauthier, but that is the sound of the trumpet calling me to eat. Don Alonso is waiting and I don't want to be late.'

'Tell him you are leaving.'

'I have already done so. But I told him we would be leaving tomorrow, and I think you must restrain your impatience till then. One more night, Gauthier, just one more night. It isn't much …'

'Not much? I can't agree with you there. One can live a whole lifetime in one night. Many things can be done or undone in the space of one night! But you are right – we owe the Archbishop too much to act rudely toward him. Tomorrow at daybreak, then!'

Catherine ran down the stairs. As she passed through the low door into the keep, she had the impression of a shadow retreating swiftly into the gloom, a shadow that closely resembled Thomas de Torquemada. She gave a shudder of recollection, but by now she had entered the great courtyard, which was full of soldiers, monks and servants chatting to each other during a break in their duties or looking for a shady corner to stretch out. This was the time of day when heat felt like lead and apathy seized everyone. Catherine walked toward them. The golden sunlight was warm and reassuring. It seemed to dispel the phantoms and sinister shadows. With a light step she hastened toward the banqueting-room.

Catherine was woken in the middle of the night by a searing heat, and an unconscious awareness of a violent, lurid light. The flames lit up her room as brightly as day, and for a moment the young woman thought she must be in the grip of a nightmare. But in a moment she realised that this was no dream but a blazing reality. The door of her room was burning fiercely, and bundles of straw and sticks scattered about on the floor of her room were blazing away, giving off a thick cloud of smoke. Panicking, Catherine leapt out of bed and ran naked to the window, where she flung back the shutters and gulped in the night air … But the draught from the window only served to fan the blaze within. It roared and sparkled, and tongues of flame came licking toward the wooden chests and chairs standing near the fireplace. One of the wall hangings near her bed caught fire …

'Help!' Catherine shrieked. 'Help, fire, fire!'

She could hear noises beyond the flames, but the wall of fire was so dense she could not believe anyone would hear her.

'Help, help,' she shrieked at the top of her lungs. She whirled round to the window. It was fifty feet to the ground below, and the darkness made it a terrifying abyss. All the same … if no-one came to her assistance, it would be better to jump! The fire was spreading at dizzy speed. Catherine detected an unknown smell amid the suffocating smoke, an acrid smell, caused no doubt by whatever it was that had helped to create such an inferno so swiftly and efficiently.

She leant out of the window, gasping for air, but already thick black smoke was billowing out of the opening. Her lungs were burning so much that she couldn't cry out, her eyes were scorched by the heat. Catherine felt her strength failing. She was suffocating. In a moment she would lack the necessary strength to climb out of the window and jump … She was too weak for that now. Her legs buckled under her.

She was going to collapse under the black coil of smoke that came twisting toward her like a greedy snake. She began to cough, and each time it felt as if she were breathing in fire. At the moment of losing consciousness she suddenly saw all the faces that had peopled her life, friends and enemies alike, pass before her in a weird cavalcade … She saw Sara's fond eyes, the Duke's sarcastic face, Garin's enigmatic expression, Gauthier's grey eyes and Arnaud's mocking smile. Then she knew that she was about to die, and sought wildly for a scrap of prayer …

When she regained consciousness, Catherine felt as if she were lying in a stream. She was soaking, wet through, and her teeth were chattering. Her tear-wet eyes saw nothing but a red fog, but she was aware that hands were rubbing her none too gently. Then she was wrapped in something rough-textured but warm. The same strong hands wiped her face, and at last she was able to recognise the irregular features of the figure bent over her. It was Josse. He gave his curious tight-lipped smile when he saw that she had opened her eyes.

'About time,' he muttered. 'I thought I was never going to get through that curtain of flames. But luckily a part of the wall crumbled and left me a gap to go through. I caught sight of you, and I just had time to pull you out …'

When she sat up, Catherine realised that she was lying on the tiled floor of the covered gallery. Flames were pouring out of the far end, where the door of her room used to be, but there wasn't a living soul to be seen.

'But there's no-one here,' she said. 'How is it that the fire has not awoken everyone in the castle?'

'Because the Archbishop's quarters are also in flames. All the servants are busy trying to put out the fire so as to save Don Alonso. Besides, the doors into this gallery were barricaded from the outside.'

'How did you get in, then?'

'Because I decided to spend the night in here under one of these stone seats. After what happened this morning, I felt uneasy. No-one could see me like that, and I planned to keep watch on your room like this. But I must have slept too heavily. That's my trouble – when I'm tired I sleep like a log. The fire-raiser didn't see me, but on the other hand he made so little noise that I didn't wake up when he was stacking up his bundles of sticks.

'The fire-raiser?'

'You don't imagine that a fire like this started all by itself? Any more than the one in the Archbishop's quarters. I have a pretty shrewd idea who is responsible; moreover …'

As though to add weight to his words, the low door at the still undamaged end of the gallery opened, and a long white shape stepped through it carrying a torch. Catherine was horrified to recognise Thomas. He wore a monk's robe, his eyes were strangely dilated and he walked almost automatically toward the fire, apparently oblivious of the clouds of thick smoke billowing into the gallery.

'Look,' Josse whispered. 'He doesn't even see us.'

It was true. The youth walked like a somnambulist. Torch in hand, like the fallen angel of vengeance and hatred, he seemed to be in the grip of a trance. His lips moved from time to time. Catherine caught one word: *fuego*. Thomas passed close by her without even noticing. She coughed; he heard

147

nothing, but went on walking toward the fire, engulfed in thick coils of smoke.

'What is he saying?' Catherine whispered.

'That fire is beautiful, sacred. That it purifies. That the lord of fire will be raised to God's side … That this dwelling of the Evil One must burn so that the souls of its inhabitants may be freed and return to God … He is quite mad, a pyromaniac,' Josse said, adding: 'He has left the gallery door open behind him. This is the moment to escape through it and sound the alert.'

Catherine followed Josse, but at the threshold she suddenly stopped and turned back. The smoke had almost swallowed up the tall, thin white shape.

'But,' she faltered, 'he will be burned alive!'

'The best thing that could happen to him, and to a lot of other people too, I dare say,' Josse declared, grasping Catherine firmly and dragging her out. She kept up with him as best she could, but kept stumbling over the folds of the coverlet that was all she had over her. As she ran on, dragged by Josse's wiry hand, she suddenly tripped over something. The pain was intense, and she gave a cry and collapsed moaning on the ground. Josse swore under his breath, but then, seeing there were tears in her eyes, he put one arm round her to help her cover the last few metres between themselves and the fresh night air. Till then they had encountered not a living soul, but once in the courtyard they found the place in a turmoil of activity. A mass of attendants, soldiers, monks and serving-women were running about in all directions, giving sharp cries like a flock of frightened birds. A long chain of slaves kept passing buckets between the great well in the courtyard and the entrance to the Archbishop's apartments, in an attempt to put out the flames that leapt through every window. This was being done to an accompaniment of cries, lamentations and prayers from all sides of this voluble crowd.

The excitement in the courtyard was caused by the fact that the second fire had just been discovered and the inhabitants of the castle were beginning to panic, imagining that all four corners of the great building were aflame.

The great courtyard, the red shining walls of which reflected the leaping flames and the human agitation within, gave a good impression of hell itself. Catherine, who was still shivering more from shock than from anything else, since the night was warm and the fires made it hotter still, wrapped her coverlet more tightly around herself and sought refuge beneath the pillared arcades, fixing anxious eyes on the keep, which seemed to stand aloof from all the commotion in its massive silence.

'Gauthier?' she murmured. 'Where is Gauthier? He must have heard this din …'

'The walls of the keep are immensely thick,' Josse observed, 'and then I dare say he sleeps heavily …'

But just then, as if to give the lie to his words, the chain of slaves that had formed up to fight the fire blazing in Catherine's former wing of the castle, were knocked flying as if they had been a pack of cards ... The Moors crashed into each other with a great clattering of buckets and splashing of water ... They were swept back toward the centre of the courtyard as if by a hurricane and Gauthier suddenly emerged from the door. With the bandages round his head and the long white kaftan, he looked much like the infidels he was scattering about; but he was a giant amid dwarfs. He marched a skinny white shape in front of him, gripped by one enormous fist. This strange pair advanced, stumbling, and finally the smaller one collapsed on the ground, almost at Catherine's feet. It was, of course, Thomas ...

He stared at the young woman, and a glimmer of returning consciousness was in those sleepwalker's eyes. A lightning flash of rage crossed them as he recognised his enemy. His thin mouth twisted in a vicious grin.

'Still alive,' he hissed. 'Satan himself protects you, she- devil! The fire is powerless over you ... but you won't always escape punishment!'

Josse snatched his dagger from his belt and leapt on the youth with a growl of anger, pointing the blade at his throat. 'You won't escape it a minute longer, in any case!' he cried. And he would have struck home before Catherine, too frozen with horror at this exhibition of implacable hatred, could have lifted a finger to stop him; but Gauthier's massive hand fell on the Parisian's wrist, arresting it in mid-air.

'No, leave him alone! I wanted to strangle him myself a little while ago, when I found him standing outside Dame Catherine's door brandishing a torch, but then I realised that he was mad, a sick boy ... You don't kill people like him, you leave them to the being who inhabits heaven – whoever that may be – to take care of. Now, let's be off!'

Catherine pointed at her coverlet and shrugged. 'Like this? Barefoot and dressed in a blanket? You must be a little deranged too!'

Gauthier silently tossed her the bundle he was carrying under one arm, smiled, and said at last:

'Here are your clothes, and your purse. I found them in your room ... instead of the corpse I expected, which happily turns out to be alive. Now get dressed!'

Catherine didn't need to be told twice. She crept into a dark corner of the courtyard and hurriedly slipped on her travelling clothes, buckling her purse round her waist and making certain as she did so that the dagger and the Queen's emerald were still there. When she got back to her companions she saw that Thomas had gone, and Josse likewise. She questioned Gauthier, who stood with folded arms watching the servants at their fire-fighting. The fire, which had been discovered in the nick of time, was coming under control at last.

'Where is Josse?'

149

'In the stables. He is getting our horses ready. Don Alonso gave orders about them last night.'

Just then, the one-time beggar returned, leading three horses and a pack-mule carrying sacks that must contain food and clothing. The Archbishop had thought of everything

When Gauthier tried to hoist Catherine into the saddle she protested sharply:

'What do you think? That I would creep off like a thief without even making sure that our host is safe?'

'He wouldn't be angry if you did. In any case, you certainly aren't safe here. I know all about the attempt on your life,' Gauthier said, but Catherine cut in fiercely, violet eyes kindling with anger. She looked first at one man and then at the other.

'So, the two of you think you can get together and tell me what to do, do you? And yet it's only a little while since you met for the first time!'

'Men like us recognise each other at once,' Josse said smoothly. 'We were made to get on with each other.'

'In any case, where your safety is concerned,' Gauthier added, 'we should always be in complete agreement. You are not very prudent, Dame Catherine.'

Gauthier's words seemed to conceal a veiled reproach. And his eyes too were reproachful. Catherine had to look away, seized by a pang of remorse. Yes, he was reproaching her for setting memories between them both that should never have been more than a dream; things were different now, however much she might try to go back to the old way. Kisses and caresses can leave scars as cruel and sensitive on a man's soul as a red-hot brand on his flesh.

'Have you the right to reproach me with that?' she said bitterly. Then, with an abrupt change of tone, she declared, 'However that may be, I don't intend to leave this place without first bidding farewell to Don Alonso.'

Ignoring the two men, she turned and walked swiftly toward the arched doorway that led to the Archbishop's wing. The slaves had departed now, because the fire was completely extinguished. Only a few wisps of black smoke curled out of the windows, and an unpleasant smell of burning filled the morning air.

Day was breaking rapidly, as it always does in southern climates. Night was vanishing with every minute, like a dark dustsheet suddenly snatched off the earth by some mysterious celestial housewife. The sky glowed with pink and gold, and the castle shone like a giant ruby in this pearly-pink dawn. Cries and hurrying footsteps could still be heard in the apartments, and Catherine paused on the now unguarded threshold. How was she to make herself understood by all these people whose language she could not speak? She was on the point of calling Josse to follow her into Don Alonso's quarters when a tall black silhouette materialised in front of her. For all her self-control, Catherine could not help staggering back a little, gripped by the superstitious terror that always took hold of her when she found herself face to face with Father Ignacio.

The one-eyed monk looked at her without astonishment, and bowed slightly. 'I am glad to meet you here, noble lady. I was about to visit you myself, at his Eminence's request.'

A sudden anguish tore at Catherine's throat. She stared at the monk with eyes where despair and fear were mingled. 'You … you speak our language?'

'When necessary, when I have to … yes, I speak your language, as I also speak English, German and Italian.'

Catherine felt all her old fears and doubts returning. Garin, too, spoke many languages. Oh, this unbearable uncertainty! It took the form, this time, of a sudden rush of anger. 'Why then did you pretend not to understand me the other day, in the treasure-chamber?'

'Because there was no need, and I didn't understand what you were trying to say …'

'Are you so sure?'

Oh, if only she could decipher the enigma of this closed face, that one eye that refused to meet hers and stared distantly at the far end of the courtyard past her shoulder. If she could but wrest the real truth from this ghost! … Hearing him speaking French, Catherine had tried to recognise Garin's intonations, Garin's voice… and yet it was impossible to say whether this was indeed his voice, or another's. Now she heard this same voice explaining that Don Alonso had been slightly injured by a cedar-wood column felled by the fire, and that his Moorish doctor had given him a powerful sleeping-draught to make him rest peacefully. However, before falling asleep he had charged Father Ignacio to make certain that Catherine was safe and sound, to see to the details of her departure, as if Don Alonso were there in person, and make sure that it was not delayed by the fire.

'Don Alonso begs you to treasure his memory in your heart, noble lady, as he does yours … and to pray for him as he will pray for you.'

A sudden gust of pride swept through Catherine. If this man really were Garin, he played his part to perfection. She was not going to fall short.

'Tell his Eminence that I shall not fail to do so, and that I shall never forget his great kindness toward me. Tell him too how grateful I am for the help he has given me, and that I shall be grateful for his prayers, for in the lands where I am bound, I shall be in constant danger! …'

She stopped for a moment and looked hard at the black-clad monk. Nothing! Not a quiver! He might have been made of stone, impervious to all feeling, even to simple pity. Once again he merely bowed respectfully.

'As for you …' Catherine began, in a voice trembling with anger. But that was as far as she got. Just as he had intervened earlier between Thomas and Josse's dagger, Gauthier stepped in now and laid a restraining hand on her shoulder.

'Say no more, Dame Catherine. Remember what I told you. Come. It is time to leave.'

This time she submitted to his authority. She turned away docilely and joined Josse and the horses. She allowed herself to be helped into the saddle without a word, and set off towards the gatehouse. As they passed under the raised portcullis, she turned back for a last look, only to find her view blocked by the Norman's broad shoulders immediately behind her.

'Don't turn back,' he commanded harshly. 'You have your own road to travel, straight ahead … and you must never turn back! Remember what I told you. Before God and before man, you are the wife of Arnaud of Montsalvy. You must forget everything else.'

Once again, she obeyed, and stared out to where, beyond the red archway, stretched the magnificent arid profile of the high plateau. All the same, she had caught one last glimpse of the monk's' tall black form, standing where she had left him, hands in his sleeves. Motionless, enigmatic, he stood watching them leave. Catherine felt this image taking root in her heart, in her flesh, like a thorn that would always lacerate her love … supposing she ever found it again.

She rode along in silence, letting the reins dangle across her horse's neck. Josse took the lead, planning their route. She followed mechanically, oblivious of the countryside already scorching beneath the pitiless Castilian sun. After a hard climb, they gained a panoramic view of red ochre plains and mountains, speckled here and there by straggling villages crouched round their meagre hemp fields. Occasionally they came across the squat silhouette of some little Roman church, or the towering wall of some monastery, sometimes too a skinny castle perched on a rock like a nostalgic heron dreaming on one leg … but Catherine saw none of this. She saw within herself only the menacing shape of the black monk, whose silence seemed to condemn her. At the feet of the Virgin of Puy she had begged God to give her back her husband! Could God have played such a cruel trick on her heart, her love? Could God have arranged for the husband she believed dead to cross her path while she was still desperately searching for the living one? What should she do now? Gauthier had said she ought to carry on, at all costs, never looking back … But Gauthier did not know her God. And who could tell what God expected of her?

The images of Father Ignacio and Garin were superimposed on each other in her mind. All her recollections of her first husband clustered round the rigid figure of the monk. Garin on the eve of their marriage; Garin with his face contorted by hate in the keep of Mâlain; Garin finally in prison, irons on his ankles, his empty eye-socket exposed for the first time. Hot sun notwithstanding, Catherine seemed to feel the damp dungeon air again, the smell of mould and corruption in her nostrils. She saw, yes, she saw Garin turning his mutilated face toward her as she entered the prison. And suddenly she started.

'My God,' she murmured. 'Why, of course … How is it I didn't think of that before?'

She stopped her horse in the middle of the overgrown track and looked at first one then the other of her companions, both of whom had halted too. And all of a sudden, quite unexpectedly, she burst out laughing. A clear, young, happy laugh … a laugh of relief that unknotted her stomach, relaxed her throat, brought tears to her eyes, an uncontrollable laughter that soon had her bent double over her saddle …

God, how funny! … How could she have been so stupid as not to notice at once and save herself all this ridiculous misery? … No, it really was the most ridiculous, grotesque thing that had ever happened to her … She laughed and laughed till she was breathless … She heard Josse exclaim anxiously:

'But she must be going out of her mind!'

And that great idiot Gauthier answering, in the most solemn tones in the world: 'Perhaps it's the sun. She isn't used to it.'

But when they tried to make her dismount, so as to rest awhile in the shade, she stopped laughing as abruptly as she had begun. She was red from so much laughing, and her eyes were streaming with tears, but the look she gave the Norman was clear, happy.

'I've just remembered, Gauthier! Father Ignacio is missing his right eye … and it is the left eye that my late husband, the Lord Treasurer of Burgundy, lost in the battle of Nicopolis! I am still free, do you hear, free to reclaim Arnaud from the Moorish infidel!'

'Won't you rest for a minute,' Josse asked nervously, only to be met with a fresh burst of laughter.

'Rest? You must be going mad! On the contrary, I want to proceed at full gallop! To Granada! To Granada with all speed! Here I come, Arnaud of Montsalvy!'

PART III

AL HAMRAH

9: The House of Abou-al-Khayr

Two weeks later, three dusty, ragged beggars entered the horseshoe arch of Bab-el-Ajuar, the Mountain Gate, in the midst of a great throng of people on their way to the market. No-one paid any attention to them, for there were innumerable beggars in Granada. The tallest of the three, a veritable giant of a man, walked in front without uttering a sound. A mute doubtless. Then came the woman, but apart from dirty feet in worn slippers there was nothing to be seen of her under the shabby length of black cotton enveloping her, save a pair of dark, glowing eyes. The third, who must have been blind, to judge from his hesitant steps and the way he clung to the two others, was a little swarthy man who as he stumbled along kept trying to appeal to the charity of passers-by by chanting lines from the Koran in a lamentable cracked voice. Certainly no-one could have recognised the three dashing cavaliers who had left Coca a fortnight earlier in this pitiful little group. The disguise was Josse's idea.

'We are doomed if anyone recognises us as Christians,' he had told the other two.' Our heads would soon be used to decorate the walls of Granada, the Red City, and our bodies would be thrown to the dogs. The only way to get through unnoticed is to pass ourselves off as beggars.'

The former beggar had shown himself a true artist in the matter of transformations. The Court of Miracles, of which he had long been one of the principal ornaments, had given him an excellent training.

He knew to perfection how to roll his eyes so that only the whites showed, and he looked just like a blind man.

'The blind are treated with some respect in Islam,' he explained. 'Like this we will not be molested.'

As for Catherine, since entering the Kingdom of Granada she felt she needed another pair of eyes to take in everything around her. She had already forgotten the trials and difficulties of the latter part of the voyage. She, Gauthier and Josse had been obliged to flee from plague-stricken Toledo, where the Jews as usual were having to bear the brunt of the people's fear and dissatisfaction. They were persecuted, their holy books burned in the public squares, their goods confiscated, and they themselves murdered on the slightest pretext. The ancient city of the Visigoths, so old that it claimed Adam as its first king, was turning into a bloodbath from which the three travellers fled in disgust.

Only to encounter new dangers. The army of the Constable of Castile, Alvaro de Luna, was returning north after fruitless skirmishing on the frontiers of Granada, and the country through which they passed was being made to pay for an inglorious and unprofitable campaign. Luna's men looted and pillaged their way across the countryside as though it was a conquered land. The mountain-folk, so poverty-stricken that they often lived off the scanty plants growing on their infertile plateaux, scattered at the approach of the army like a flock of sparrows before a hawk. The three French had followed their example. They had been stopped near Jaen by some members of the advance guard, but thanks to Gauthier's strength and Josse's cunning they had managed to escape, thankful to emerge with only the loss of their horses. In any case, as Josse pointed out, they were approaching the frontiers of the Moorish kingdom, where they would have had to abandon their mounts, since beggars were rarely in a position to travel on horseback.

'We could have sold them,' Gauthier remarked, in true Norman spirit.

'To whom? There isn't a soul in this smiling land with money enough to buy so much as a donkey. The land is fertile, but with the incessant fighting thath has gone on here for so many years not even the grass will grow. Either it's the Saracens making sorties toward the north, or the Castilians marching south in the hope of reconquering their lands; but one way or another the result for the people of Jaen has always been the same – devastation!'

The three companions had pursued their journey on foot, walking all night over the rough tracks of the Betic mountains, hiding throughout the day, guiding themselves by the stars, which seemed to have no secrets from the Parisian beggar or the giant from the forests of Normandy. This last part of the journey was gruelling, but Catherine bore up gamely. This unknown sky, which turned so blue at night, these stars so much bigger and more brilliant than any she had hitherto seen; all these signs told her that they were fast approaching the strange, fascinating, dangerous country where Arnaud dwelt.

Their road took them through scenes that spoke of war, suffering and death. Often in the dark they would stumble on some corpse quietly rotting under a bush, or during the day's rest the sinister cry of vultures would fill the indigo sky. The huge black birds circled slowly above them before dropping like a stone on some spot in the landscape. But when Catherine caught her first glimpse of Granada in all its splendour, set like a jewel on the verge of a valley of green and gold, framed by mountains sculpted like a pearly shell still iridescent from the sea, their peaks crowned with snow, she was rapt in admiration.

Countless streams gushed down the mountainside, converging in the swift, clear, rushing waters of two rivers, the waters of which refreshed this magnificent landscape that seemed to proffer to the heavens, like a stupendous jewel, the rosiest, the most glittering of all Moorish palaces. A high wall, set with square towers all along its length, tenderly enclosed a delectable garden of flowers, trees and flesh-coloured pavilions. Here and there fountains glittered, the liquid mirror of a lake or pool shone amid the green. Even the rough brickwork of the outer walls seemed to acquire a velvet softness, as if reluctant to break the harmony of this radiant valley, its smiling fertility outspread before them like a silken carpet.

The town lay all about this enchanted palace, perched on hills and hemmed about by walls. Slender red and white minarets soared into the sky next to the green and gold domes of the mosques. Palaces towered above houses, but highest of all rose the imposing mass of the Islamic University, the Medessa, rivalled only by the immense Maristan Hospital, at this date the best equipped in Europe.

The sun was shining, and from every minaret rose the piercing wail of the muezzins calling the believers to prayer.

At this point the mountain road formed a sort of terrace from where the whole prodigious landscape could be seen. Catherine sat down on a stone near the verge, and the other two, sensing that she had much on her mind, left her to meditate in peace while they rested a bit farther along, at a bend in the road.

Catherine couldn't take her eyes off the astonishing landscape at her feet. This then was the object of her crazy journey, undertaken against all better judgement, and she was moved to tears to find it so beautiful. Surely this must be the land of dreams and of love? Could one possibly live here other than happily and delightedly?

She had suffered, endured, trembled, shed blood and tears, but now she had arrived! *Arrived!* No more interminable roads and endless horizons. No more sleepless nights wondering if she would ever arrive, reach the place that in her worst moments she had begun to think imaginary. Granada lay before her, outstretched at her feet like an affectionate beast, and her joy in discovering it so was so great that at first she forgot the dangers that awaited her there.

Arnaud was only a little way off now, and he must live in that fabulous, well-guarded palace!

Well-guarded! ... Too well-guarded? The thought suddenly struck her, and snuffed out her joy. Those dream gardens grew within a fortress. Those green palms, green bowers and roses hid soldiers and arms! And this woman, this woman she hated without having even seen, would surely have every means to defend herself and hold her prey captive. How was she to find the palace gates, much less enter them? How to find Arnaud in that intricate network of streets and alleys, small as it was?

It would need an army to conquer that city, and Catherine knew that the forces of the ferocious Constable of Castile had been besieging the place unsuccessfully for years. No-one could boast of having unlawfully crossed the frontiers of Granada and have lived long enough to tell the tale.

Sensing a powerful need to stave off the discouragement that had followed hard on the heels of triumph, Catherine fell on her knees in the dust, folded her hands and closed her eyes. She knelt there for minutes on end, praying, beseeching heaven as fervently as she had at the feet of the strange little Black Madonna of Puy, to take pity on her at long last, to give her back the man who, with her child, made up her only treasure upon Earth. 'You would not allow me to reach this distant shore, O Lord, only to cast me back upon the waters. You would not make my labours vain and bring me here only to lose my heart and my love forever, because you are justice itself. And though I have oftentimes deserved your wrath, you will not punish me further, because you are mercy itself, and I am beseeching your grace.'

A hand gently touching her shoulder made her open her eyes again. She saw Josse bending over to help her to her feet.

'Praying out in the open, Dame Catherine, this is rashness indeed! Have you forgotten that we are in an infidel country here? As you see, there is not a single church or chapel to be seen, nothing but mosques where these miscreants pray to their own god. Get up quickly! If anyone were to see you!'

He pulled her back to her feet. She smiled at him behind her black veil.

'Forgive me. I believe I had really forgotten. It is all so lovely here. It is hard to believe this is not Paradise itself. And this is what terrifies me, my friend. Surely, living amidst such beauty, everything else must seem insignificant! It must seem hard to breathe away from these mountains, these clear streams and scented gardens. How can I be angry with my husband for refusing to leave such a place, when he had known only the horrors of a leper-house before leaving our own country?'

'Messire Arnaud is not the man for a soft life and flowering gardens,' Gauthier cut in curtly. 'I find it hard to imagine him playing the lute or inhaling the scent of roses at dawn and dusk. The sword, the coat-of-mail, that is what he loves, and more than that even, the rough life of camps and the open road. As for this so-called paradise …'

'Funny paradise,' Josse interrupted slyly. 'This palace, or rather palatial-town – which they call the Al Hamra, "the red one" – is like a rose; there are sharp thorns beneath the scented petals. Look there.'

The Parisian's thin hand pointed first toward the mountain crests bristling with forts, the walls of which had nothing gentle about them. No flowers there, no trees to be stirred by the blossom-scented winds, no whispering palms. Only the sinister glitter of steel, the gleaming points of the Moorish helmets above their white turbans. Then Josse's hand descended toward the city's double-fortified walls, pointing at the merlons surmounted by curious ball-shaped objects.

'Decapitated heads, how welcoming!' he said briefly. And Catherine shuddered; but her courage refused to be weakened. The snare was delicious, flowery, but she would tear her way through its enchantments with her bare hands, with her love alone to aid her.

The rags she wore, like those of the other two, had been stolen by Josse from corpses discovered in the mountains. She had been disgusted by their filthiness, but at least she felt safe under this black cotton covering. This country, where women were allowed to show only their eyes, had its practical side for anyone who wanted to conceal themselves.

Catherine allowed herself to be led toward the leafy mass of greenery that contrasted so effectively with the warm-toned walls of Al Hamra, her heart beating with a mixture of hope and fear. The Crusaders of earlier times must have felt something analogous to this at their first glimpse of Jerusalem … In the midst of a noisy, gesticulating crowd, smelling of jasmine and rancid oil, Catherine crossed the first, somewhat dilapidated outer fortifications. The second seemed far away, across a space empty of all trees and buildings but almost as densely-thronged as a fairground on market day. That was where they held the market for grain, forage and hay. Donkeys, mules, sheep, even a few nonchalant camels, wandered about among the sacks piled on the ground, next to which Muslims squatted in their dusty djellabas, calling out to attract customers. A bit farther off they were selling firewood, coal, and farther still it was straw, clover, green fodder. The second wall, which was much higher, opened into the town itself through the horseshoe gate of the Alcazaba, and it provided a red backdrop to this multi-coloured crowd, whose skin-tones ranged through every shade on Earth, from red to black, passing through the browns, greys, yellows and ochres.

Once through the second gate, all was green. Great heaps of myrtle, basil, tarragon and bay, scenting the blue air, stood next to sacks of olives, lemons, almonds and capers, and other goatskin sacks filled with butter and honey … This red city, the white heart of which, with its flat-roofed whitewashed dwellings, Catherine was now entering, was like a great horn of plenty flowing with wealth. It was like the outstretched claw of that immense, secret, fertile Africa that stretched beyond to the farthermost heavens, a claw fastened on this tip of Europe. Of all the conquests made by the fearsome Almoravid and Almohad sultans, black-veiled men come from the great

Atlas and fabulous Marrakesh, little remained: only this kingdom of Granada, as small, red and sweet as the fruit it shared a name with, containing the whole essence of the East and of Africa within its walls.

'What a fabulous country!' Catherine breathed in wonderment. 'Such wealth ...'

'Better not to speak French,' Josse whispered in her ear. 'It's a language not much used among the Moors. Now here we are in Granada. Have you any idea where your friend the doctor lives?'

'He told me his house stood on the bank of a river ...'

She broke off, wide-eyed, staring at a procession coming toward them up the street that wound between whitewashed, windowless houses. Ahead came runners armed with sticks, who pushed aside the street vendors and pedlars with their cries and ringing bells; then came riders wearing white burnouses. Finally a golden litter appeared, carried on the shoulders of six ebony-black slaves stripped to the waist. It floated along above the sea of turbaned heads like a caravel over the waves. Catherine and her companions just managed to flatten themselves against a wall in time to escape being whacked by the sticks carried by the shouting runners. As the litter passed in front of Catherine, a breeze parted the blue silk curtains just enough for her to see inside, where a slender, supple creature dressed all in blue veils lay back against golden cushions. Her long black hair was interwoven with gold sequins. She hastily drew a veil of blue silk across her face, but not before Catherine had time to notice the woman's beauty, her haughty profile and great black eyes, together with the jewels about her throat.

'Who is this woman?' she asked in a choked voice. 'She must be a princess at least ...'

Without answering, Josse in his assumed whining voice inquired of a water-carrier nearby who the lady in the litter was. The answer shattered Catherine. Josse did not need to translate it for her, because since crossing the frontier into the Moorish kingdom the young woman had employed the time learning what little Arabic he could teach her. She knew enough to follow a simple conversation, and she had perfectly understood what the water-carrier was saying.

'That is the precious pearl of the Al Hamra, the Princess Zobeïda, sister of the Caliph.'

The Caliph's sister! The woman who had stolen Arnaud from her! Why was it that no sooner than entering the Moorish city she should have to clap eyes on her rival? And what a rival! ... In one fell swoop all the hope and confidence that had upheld Catherine throughout this interminable journey from Puy to this foreign city, crumbled to nothing ... That fleeting glimpse of the enemy, in all her beauty, had given a bitter searing to her jealousy that seemed to take all the colour out of this warm, sunny morning. Catherine sank back against the sun-warmed wall. She felt overpowered by an immense weariness, born of all the accumulated fatigue of her long journey together with this shock she had just received. Great tears welled from her eyes … Arnaud was lost to her. How could she believe otherwise after seeing that dazzling vision in blue and gold? The battle was foredoomed …

'To die,' she murmured to herself. 'To die at once …'

She spoke to herself, almost inaudibly, but Gauthier heard her. While Josse, embarrassed by this sudden display of grief, moved off tapping his stick, toward a pedlar selling 'ripe almonds and juicy pomegranates', Gauthier stepped in front of the swooning Catherine and shook her roughly.

'Well, what difference does this make?' he asked. 'Why do you want to die all of a sudden? Because you have seen this woman? It is she you are fighting against, isn't it?'

'Fighting?' She gave a tragic laugh. 'Fighting with what? It isn't even possible to fight! Fool that I was to think I could win him back. You saw her, the infidel Princess? Fortunat was right … She is more beautiful than the rising sun! I haven't a chance against her.'

'Not a chance? Why ever not?'

'Just remember that dazzling vision … and then look at me.'

He stopped her just as she was about to make the fatal gesture of tearing off the black veil that seemed to be smothering her and uncovering her face and golden hair.

'You have had a bad shock but you must take hold of yourself. People are looking at us … This weakness of yours is endangering all of us. Our unaccustomed language …'

He did not have to say more. With a colossal effort of will Catherine managed to pull herself together. Gauthier had said the one thing that could have helped her: reminding her that her behaviour was endangering the other two as well as herself. And now Josse was returning. Groping along the wall, the pseudo-blind man whispered:

'I know where the doctor lives. It isn't far from here. Between the Alcazaba hill and the walls of the Al Hamra, on the river banks. The almond-seller told me that there is a great house surrounded by palm-trees, between the Cadi bridge and the Hammam.'

Without another word they set off again, hand in hand. The feel of her companions' rough palms reassured Catherine a little, and so did the thought of finding Abou-al-Khayr again. The little Moorish doctor knew how to say the right, comforting words. Time and again his strange philosophical maxims had saved her from despair, from a torment she thought would end by killing her.

All of a sudden she was impatient to be with him, and blind to this city that had captivated her only a few short minutes before. Her companions were now leading her into a strange little street, overhung with climbing roses that filtered the sun's rays into thin shafts of light. On either side were little shops without doors, where the metal-workers plied their trade. The sound of their hundreds of hammers beating away filled the street with a joyous din, and in the shadowy interiors rows of basins, pitchers and cooking-pots of red and yellow copper gleamed softly, turning them into a sort of treasure-cave.

'The metal-workers' stalls,' Josse explained. But Catherine neither saw nor heard. She kept seeing that haughty ivory profile, the long dark eyes glowing between thick lashes, the slender, graceful body coiled amid piles of cushions.

'She is too beautiful,' she kept repeating to herself. 'Too beautiful …'

She repeated this cruel little remark to herself over and over again like an obsessive leitmotiv. She was still saying it when Abou's house confronted her, amidst the tufted palms that seemed to spring right out of its heart, on the banks of a clear river that was lost to view behind the walls.

'Here we are,' Gauthier said. 'The journey's end.'

But Catherine shook her head as she stared up at the pink palace towering high up above them on its rocky scarp. That was the journey's end, up there … and she no longer had the strength or courage to undertake the climb.

Yet when the handsome, brass-studded double doors swung open before them, time seemed to melt away. Catherine suddenly felt ten years younger as she recognised the tall Negro, dressed and turbaned in white, who stood there. It was one of Abou-al-Khayr's two mutes.

The slave frowned and looked disapprovingly at the three beggars, and was just about to close the door again when Gauthier swiftly put his foot in it, preventing him, while Josse spoke to him peremptorily.

'Go and tell your master that one of his oldest friends wishes to speak to him. A friend from the country of …'

'He cannot speak,' Catherine interrupted. 'This man is dumb.'

She spoke in French, and the Negro looked at her with astonishment and curiosity. She saw a spark of recognition kindling in the large protuberant eyes, and hastily pulled off her veil.

'Look,' she said again, in Arabic. 'Do you remember me now?'

By way of reply the slave knelt, seized the hem of her gown and kissed it. Then he leapt to his feet and ran off into the inner garden that could be seen beyond the square hall with its brick-paved floor and slender columns, which gave on to a courtyard filled with flowering shrubs and the three famous palms. A big scallop of translucent alabaster let fall a trickle of fresh water that cooled the whole place.

The plants and, above all, the festoons of roses and orange-trees laden with white, superbly-scented blossom made up the whole decoration of this house. It was a beautiful house, certainly, but its elegance lay in the pure line of the colonnade, the transparent alabaster of the carving around the first-floor gallery, the clear water flowing through the garden. Abou-al-Khayr liked simplicity in his day-to-day life, though without any sacrifice of comfort.

Just then they heard a pair of slippers slap-slapping across the tiled courtyard, and in an instant Abou-al-Khayr appeared, so exactly like the mental picture Catherine kept of him that she could not help giving a cry of surprise. The little doctor's face, still decorated with its absurd ritual white silk beard, was as smooth and clear-featured as ever, and he was dressed exactly as he had been on the day of their first encounter: the same gown of thick blue silk, the same immense red silk turban draped in the Persian style, the same crimson Moroccan slippers over blue silk socks. He appeared not to have aged by a year, by a day even! His black eyes still sparkled with their customary ironical flame; his smile was so familiar that Catherine suddenly longed to weep, for as she saw it she suddenly had the paradoxical sensation that she was coming home.

Abou-al-Khayr ignored Gauthier and Josse, who were bowing ceremoniously. He stopped in front of Catherine, looked her up and down for a moment and then said simply:

'I was expecting you. But you have been slow in coming.'

'Me?'

'Yes, yes. You will never change. O woman of a single love! Like a moth you prefer to die in the flame than to live in the dark, am I not right? Half your heart is here. Who can live with only half a heart?'

Catherine's cheeks flushed scarlet. Abou-al-Khayr had lost none of his wonderful gift for reading her innermost heart. Anyway, what was the point of standing on formality? She went straight to the heart of the matter.

'Have you seen him? Do you know where he is? What is he doing? How does he live? Is …?'

'There, there … Calm yourself.' The doctor's soothing hands folded round her own, which were trembling, and held them still. 'Woman of little patience,' he said gently, 'wherefore so much haste?'

'Because my patience is running out, that is why… I can't go on, friend Abou. I am weary … desperate,' she almost shouted the last phrases, so overwrought were her nerves.

'No, you are not desperate. Otherwise you would not be here, I know. The poet wrote: "When, O when, O Lord, will my heart's desire be granted? When shall I be at peace next to his tumbled locks?" And you feel like the poet; that is only to be expected.'

'Not now. I suddenly feel old all of a sudden …'

Abou-al-Khayr's youthful laugh rang out so clear and spontaneous that

Catherine felt suddenly a bit ashamed of her weakness. 'Who are you trying to convince? Naturally you are tired, dusty from your long journey ... so dusty that your soul itself feels soiled, isn't that so? You feel dirty and dingy to the core. But that will pass. You are still beautiful, even in your beggar's rags. Come, you need rest, care and food. Then we will talk. Not before ...'

'I saw this woman ... She is so lovely ...'

'We shall talk of her anon, and you will feel comforted. Now, you must think of this house as your own, and Allah alone knows how glad I am to receive you here, O my sister. Come, follow me. Now that I think of it, who are these men? Your servants?'

'More than that: my friends.'

'Then they shall be mine too. Now come, all of you.'

Catherine let herself be led to the narrow stone stairs that led up to the gallery above. Josse and Gauthier, still somewhat bemused by their first encounter with the strange little doctor in his eccentric clothes, followed hard on her heels. Josse had stopped playing a blind man and trotted along happily.

'Brother,' he whispered to Gauthier, 'I think Dame Catherine's battle is already half won. This little man seems to know the meaning of true friendship.'

'I think you are right about that. About the victory I am not so certain ... You don't know Messire Arnaud. He is as proud as a lion, as stubborn as a mule, and as brave as an eagle ... but he can be cruel too. He is one of those men who would rather tear out their heart than weaken when they feel they have cause for offence.'

'Didn't he love his wife?'

'He adored her. I have never seen a couple more passionately in love. But he believed she had given herself to another and he fled. How can I tell what he thinks now?'

Josse did not answer. Ever since meeting Catherine he had been impatient to see the man who had so solidly bound to himself the heart of such a woman. And now they were almost there, his curiosity was devouring him.

'We shall have to wait and see,' he murmured to himself.

He said no more, because Abou-al-Khayr was just then opening a little painted door that led into an immense room, informing them that his servants would soon be arriving to see to their needs. Then he clapped his hands together three times before opening a similar door for Catherine. This, doubtless, was the finest room in the house: the ceiling was of red and gold cedar-wood, intricate as a carpet; the walls were embellished with gold mosaic; the marble-flagged floors were spread with soft silky rugs. Ogival niches in the walls held mirrors, candelabra and washing things, a copper basin and jug. In each corner of the room, four chests of gilded leather stood ready to take clothes, but of course there was no bed to be seen. It must have been rolled up and stacked away in a hidden corner of the room, as was the Moorish custom, while a round divan standing in a mirrored recess at the far end of the room welcomed its occupant with a heap of colourful silken cushions. The windows all opened on to the inner courtyard.

Abou-al-Khayr allowed Catherine to take in every detail of this pleasant room, where nothing had been neglected that could please a woman's taste. Then he slowly opened one of the chests and drew out an armful of coloured silks and gauzes, which he spread out on the divan with an almost feminine care.

'You see,' he said simply. 'I really was waiting for you. I bought all this at the silk stalls the day after I learned that your husband was here.'

Catherine and her friend stood face to face for a moment, and then, before he could stop her, she snatched up his hand and kissed it, while the tears flowed freely from her eyes. He gently withdrew his hand.

'The god-sent guest is always especially welcome among us,' he said gently. 'But when this guest is one close to our hearts, then there can be no greater, purer joy for the true believer. It is I who should thank you.'

An hour later, with all the dust of the journey washed away, comfortably attired in the clothes presented by their host – for the two men, ample gowns of finely-striped black and white wool girdled by a wide silk sash, for Catherine, a silk gandourah cut low over the bosom, and for all three fine leather slippers embroidered in silver – the travellers installed themselves round the massive silver table surrounded by heaps of cushions in Abou-al-Khayr's rooms. The table was spread with a veritable feast – slices of roast mutton, little pies stuffed with a mixture of pigeon meat, eggs and almonds, and above all, every variety of fruit and vegetable, many of them unknown to these travellers from the far north.

'I love the fruits of the earth most of all,' Abou said, smiling as he bit into a huge piece of scented melon, after offering slices to the assembled company. 'They enclose the sun.' There were oranges, lemons, apples, pumpkins and fresh beans arranged on platters and appropriately seasoned, as well as aubergines, chick peas, bananas, grapes, almonds and of course pomegranates. The effect of these piles of variously coloured fruits was pleasing and refreshing. Josse and Gauthier, enlivened by the contents of a tall, slim pitcher of wine their host had thoughtfully placed beside them, fell upon everything hungrily and curiously. They devoured it all greedily, with a relish that brought a smile to Abou's lips, for he was frugal enough in his own eating habits.

'Do you always eat like this in your house, seigneur?' Josse asked, with frank greed.

'Don't call me seigneur, call me Abou. I am only a simple believer. Yes, I always eat like this. You see, we do not know the meaning of famine here. Sun, water and rich soil are given to us in abundance. All we have to do is thank Allah. I realise that you cannot even conceive of a country like this in your own cold northern climate. I dare say that is why,' he added with sudden melancholy, 'the Castilians dream of chasing us out of here, as they have already expelled us from Valencia, Cordoba, the Holy City, and other parts of this peninsula that we have made rich and prosperous. They do not realise that a great part of our wealth comes from the East and Africa, the ships of which ply freely along our coastline … and that things will never be the same the day that the Kingdom of Granada falls into their hands.'

As he spoke, he was watching Catherine out of the corner of his eye. Despite her long journey, the young woman was scarcely eating a thing. She had nibbled at a slice of watermelon, a few almonds and pistachios and now she was toying with a little gold spoon at a rose-petal ice that one of the mutes had just placed before her. She sat gazing into the leafy depths of the beyond, not even listening to the others talking. She seemed a long way from this cool, pleasant room with its a carved stucco ceiling, visiting in spirit the palace-fortress that stood so close and yet so inaccessible behind its pink walls, where Arnaud's heart beat for another woman.

Abou-al-Khayr divined that tears were not far from her eyes. He signalled to one of his slaves and murmured a few words in his ear. The Negro made a sign that he had understood and left the room. A few minutes later a shrill but powerful voice screamed from the doorway.

'Glorrrrry to the Duke! Glorrrry to the Duke!'

Catherine emerged from her unhappy reverie, starting up as if she had been stung by a wasp. She stared in amazement at the great Negro, who was grinning from ear to ear as he set down beside her a silver perch upon which the most enormous, superb parrot sat preening its long crimson-tinted feathers.

'Gedeon!' she murmured incredulously. 'I don't believe it!'

'Why not? Didn't you give him to me when you left Dijon? It has always been both a souvenir of you, and a precious friend. You can see that I have taken good care of him.'

Catherine was stroking the bird's feathers with a look of childlike joy. The parrot preened and strutted on its perch, cooing like a dove and watching her with its great round eyes. It opened its big red beak and screamed again:

'Allah is Allah, and Mahomet is his Prophet!'

'He seems to have made great strides,' Catherine said, bursting out laughing. 'And he is more handsome than ever!' She bent over the parrot as once she had done in Uncle Mathieu's shop, and it gently pecked at her lips.

'What a lot of memories he brings back to me,' she murmured, suddenly prey to melancholy again. For Gedeon had been the Duke's first gift after he had fallen in love with her. He had been the faithful companion of a whole part of her life, almost from the moment when she had snared the Great Duke of the West while at the same time losing her heart irretrievably to Arnaud of Montsalvy. A whole host of faces and figures seemed to rise up beyond the parrot's feathers. But Abou-al-Khayr had no intention of letting her slip into despondency once again.

'I didn't have him brought here to make you feel sad again,' he observed softly, 'but to show you that neither time, nor men, change as much as you suppose. Time can sometimes return.'

'The Duke's time is quite dead.'

'I was not alluding to that, but to the wonderful moments that love has given to you.'

'Love has not given me so many.'

'Enough to fill your whole life with their memory, however … and enough for your husband to have difficulty in forgetting too.'

'How do you know?'

'Who could have talked to me about your life together … except him?'

Catherine's eyes suddenly kindled, and her cheeks flushed. 'Have you … have you seen him?'

'Well, of course,' Abou said, smiling. 'You haven't forgotten what great friends we used to be? He remembered me too, and that I lived in this town. He sent for me almost as soon as he arrived in Al Hamra.'

'And you managed to see him?'

'I am the doctor as well as the humble friend of the Caliph, who always treats me well. I must admit though that the Princess Zobeïda, whose prisoner your husband is, does not like me at all since I saved the life of the Sultana Amina, whom she hates. In fact I would go as far as to say that she hates me too, and that it was only her great desire to please the "Frankish Lord" that moved her to consent to my visit. However, I was able to talk to Messire Arnaud for at least an hour.'

'You said he was this woman's prisoner,' Catherine exclaimed, her face suddenly darkened by jealousy. 'Why do you lie? Why not use the right word, a man who knows the value of words as well as you do? Why didn't you say her lover?'

'Well … because I know nothing about that,' Abou confessed quite simply. 'That must be the secret of the Al Hamra nights … and most of the servants there are mutes.'

Catherine hesitated for a moment, then plunged in. 'But … is he really cured of leprosy?'

'He never had leprosy. There are illnesses that resemble that accursed disease … but that your Western doctors cannot recognise. The Princess Hadji Rahim's doctor is a saintly man who has made the Great Pilgrimage; a fact that does not prevent him being, in my view, a colossal fool. But he was nevertheless able to see at first glance that your husband was not a leper. To make certain, he merely held your husband's arm over a flame … and he screamed; proof that the limb has not grown insensible.'

'But what could that strange disease have been, then? I saw the white blotches on his arm with my own eyes.'

'At the school of Salerno, the celebrated Trotula called this ailment vitiligo, or white blotch. And I am persuaded that there are a great number of unfortunates afflicted with this disease in your leper-houses, whom your ignorant physicians have wrongly diagnosed as lepers.'

There was a long silence. Gauthier and Josse sat still as statues, not uttering a word. They merely listened closely, waiting to speak until their opinions might be required. Catherine made use of this silence to marshal her thoughts. The questions she still had to put to Abou were more painful still. The first came tumbling out.

'Why did Arnaud go with this woman?' she asked hoarsely. 'Did he tell you?'

'Why does a captive go with his captor?'

'But what holds him captive? Is it force … or love?'

'Force, I'm quite certain, because he explained to me how Zobeïda's Nubians captured him near Toledo. As for love, it's just possible that this is one of the bonds that hold him there. But I rather doubt it.'

'Why?'

'I wish you hadn't asked me that. The answer is bound to upset you. The fact is that Arnaud of Montsalvy no longer believes in true love. He says that since another man made you forget the passion that united you both, no other woman can ever give him a pure and sincere love.'

Catherine took the blow bravely. She could be honest with herself, and she was unlikely to forget her flirtation with Pierre de Brézé for a long time. She had so often reproached herself with it … especially that unfortunate night in the orchard at Chinon when Bernard d'Armagnac had found her, already half seduced in the arms of the handsome knight.

'I deserve that,' she said simply. 'But the strength of love is powerful – and this woman loves him, doesn't she?'

'Passionately, with an abandon that astonishes and alarms her entourage. The power of the "Frankish Lord" over Zobeïda is absolute. He can do no wrong … other than to glance at another woman. Woe betide any woman who wins a smile or pleasant word from him! She is executed immediately. Some ten among them have met their death in this fashion. So that none of Zobeïda's servants dares even so much as to look at the man whom she loves in this savage manner. They serve him on their knees, muffled up as closely as if they were out in the street. For, contrary to custom that dictates that men and women should live separately from each other, the pavilion where Messire Arnaud is lodged stands in Zobeïda's own garden.'

'And the Caliph accepts this?'

Abou-al-Khayr shrugged. 'Why not? So far as he is concerned, your husband, unless he were to become converted to Islam, is only a Christian slave among many. He looks upon him as his wild sister's favourite toy, nothing more. Besides, the Sultan Muhammad knows his sister's terrible rages too well to attempt to cross her in anything. The Nasrides are a strange family ... where death is easily come by, as you will learn. Keeping oneself upon the throne is an exhausting task in itself, and when you hear that Muhammad VIII has had to recapture his own twice already, you will understand the position better. That pink palace hides a viper's nest. It is dangerous to set foot there ...'

'That's why I want to do so. I want to get in there.'

Abou was too shocked to breathe for a moment, while Gauthier and Josse made the first sounds of protest that had escaped from them for quite a while.

'You want to get into the Al Hamra?' Abou finally repeated. 'You must be out of your mind. That's not what you should do. Although Zobeïda hates me, I will go there personally under one pretext or another and tell your husband that you are here in my house. I have already warned him that you would be coming in any case.'

'What did he say?'

'He smiled and shook his head. "Why would she come?" he said. "She has everything she ever wanted – love, honour, riches – and the man she has chosen is one of those who know how to hold a woman. No, she will never come."'

'How little he knows me,' Catherine sighed. 'You were right.'

'I am glad ... I will go to see him then, and ...'

He got no further, because Catherine laid her hand on his arm to stop him. 'No. That's not what I want. For two reasons: the first is that either, when he knows I am here, he will tell you that I no longer mean anything to him ... which would kill me, or he might try to join me here, thus putting his life in danger.'

'That is one reason. What is the other?'

'The second is that I want to see, do you hear, see with my own eyes what his relationship is with this woman. I want to know if he loves her, do you understand? I must know if she really has managed to drive me out of his heart. I want to count their kisses and spy on their embraces. I have no illusions, believe me. I see myself as I am. I am no blushing maiden any longer. As for this Zobeïda, she was beautiful enough to throw me into despair a little while ago ... Why shouldn't she have succeeded in winning his heart?'

'Suppose she had?' Gauthier threw in boldly. 'Suppose this woman had won over Messire Arnaud, what would you do then?'

The blood slowly drained from Catherine's face and she closed her eyes, trying to shut out the picture of Arnaud in the Princess's arms; a picture that was all too horribly vivid now that she had seen Zobeïda.

'I don't know,' she said at last. 'I really don't know … but I must find out first. And the only way I can find out is to go there.'

'Let me go, then, Dame Catherine. I would be able to find out if your husband was in love with this other woman, believe me. And that way at least you would be in no danger.'

This time it was Abou-al-Khayr who replied. 'And how would you get in, man of the North? Zobeïda's apartments are part of the harem, though they may stand a little way off from it, and the Caliph's guards are stationed at all the doors. The only men who ever enter there are eunuchs.'

'Is Messire Arnaud?'

'His case is different. He is a prisoner, and Zobeïda keeps her treasure well guarded. You would lose your head in the attempt, and all to no purpose …'

Gauthier would have protested, but the doctor silenced him with a gesture. He turned to Catherine. 'And how were you planning to enter Zobeïda's apartments?'

'I don't know. As a servant, perhaps. Is that impossible? I speak your tongue, thanks to Josse, and I am a good actress.'

By way of proof, Catherine described her stay with the gypsies, and the way she had kept up a difficult and dangerous role for several weeks. 'Then I was intent only on avenging Arnaud and myself. Just think what I shall be prepared to do when it is a case of finding and getting back my one reason for living! I beg you, Abou, help me … help me to get into the Al Hamra. I must see him … I must know …'

She held forth imploring hands, and Abou looked away, distressed at finding himself so powerless before a woman's tears. He was silent for a moment.

'It's pure madness,' he sighed at last. 'But I've known for a long time that when you set your heart on something you always get it. I promise I will give the matter serious thought. But it will take time … An adventure like this has to be prepared for carefully and secretly. Leave this to me, will you? And meanwhile avail yourself of this house and garden. You will find it very restful here … Take care of yourself; sleep and live in peace while you wait –'

'Wait?' Catherine protested. 'Wait? What are you saying to me? Do you think I'm in any state to rest and live comfortably while … while I'm eaten up with jealousy?' she declared frankly. 'While I'm consumed with the longing to see him again?'

Abou-al-Khayr stood up, slid his hands into his wide sleeves and looked severely at Catherine. 'Very well then, let jealousy devour you and desire consume you a few days longer. You were thrown into a panic a few hours ago by Zobeïda's beauty. Were you thinking of going to meet the man you love with lacklustre hair, a face all covered with freckles, hands roughened by holding the reins, and a body as thin as a starving alley cat's?'

Catherine hung her head in bewilderment, and her cheeks grew as red as the pomegranates on the table. 'Have I become so ugly?' she faltered.

'You know quite well you haven't,' Abou intervened curtly. 'But in our country a woman lives and breathes only to give pleasure to a man. Her body must be the repository of the delicate scents he loves to smell, the harp he loves to make vibrate beneath his touch, the garden of roses and orange-trees where he is pleased to gratify his desire. These are the weapons of Zobeïda ... and you must obtain them too ... or rather rediscover them. Then you will be able to fight your rival on equal terms. Remember the lady of the black diamond who conquered the heart of a prince? Tomorrow I will take you myself to the neighbouring hammam and place you in the care of Fatima, who takes care of the women's quarter. She is the ugliest old woman I have ever seen, and the queen of procuresses, but she is more skilful than anyone at changing a work-worn mule into a sprightly mare with a gleaming coat. And she owes me many favours: she will do wonders with you. Now, I will leave you. I have some patients to see. We shall meet again tonight.'

He went out of the room with his customary dignity, leaving Catherine wondering if 'the work-worn mule' was meant to be applied to herself. She was asking herself this so visibly that both Gauthier and Josse burst into a great roar of laughter. Josse laughed till he cried.

'I've never met anyone as amusing as this little man,' he cried, slapping his thighs. 'Oh ... oh ... oh ... oh. No, it's too funny!'

Catherine watched the two men rolling about with mirth for a moment, wondering if this time she was really going to lose her temper. But laughter is infectious, and she could not hold out for long. She decided to join in.

Seeing her laugh so heartily, Gedeon thought it only polite to follow suit.

'Ha ... ha ... ha ... ha!' he shrieked. 'Insupporrrrrtable ... Catherine! Glory to the Duke!'

A cushion flung by Gauthier's accurate hand cut him off in mid speech.

10: Fatima the Bath Attendant

Catherine lay stretched out on a marble slab covered with a red cotton bath sheet, trying to empty her mind of everything, as she had been told to do. She gave herself up to the attentions old Fatima and her assistants were bestowing upon her, keeping her eyes closed so as to avoid meeting Fatima's rolling white eyes. The old woman was even uglier than Abou-al-Khayr had led her to expect.

She was an enormous Ethiopian, black as ink, and apparently as strong as a bear. Her thick, crinkly black hair, scarcely touched by grey, was cut as short as a man's, and her big eyes rolled in their sockets, the pupils almost drowned in the yellowish whites streaked with fine red veins. Like her two assistants she was stripped to the waist, her black sweat-streaked skin shone and her huge breasts, the size of water-melons, swung heavily as she moved. From time to time she rolled back her thick red lips, disclosing a gleam of white teeth, before setting to work massaging the young woman's body with hands the size of washboards.

When Catherine had arrived at the hammam, wrapped in a large green veil, riding a donkey and solemnly escorted by Abou in person, with the two mutes walking three paces behind, Fatima had bowed deeply and then struck up such a rapid conversation with the little doctor that Catherine would not have known what they were talking about if Abou had not forewarned her what he was going to say, to explain the presence of a blonde woman in his house.

His idea was a simple one, if a little surprising in view of the doctor's deep distrust of womenfolk; he had just bought this beautiful blonde slave off a barbarian ship anchored off Alineria, and he destined her to be the comfort of his declining years once Fatima had worked her magic on her and rendered her fit for the bed of a fastidious believer. But he had requested the fat Ethiopian to attend to Catherine separately from the other clients, because he feared that the news of his magnificent acquisition might start tongues wagging. Her friend's bashful expression, lowered eyes and delighted air were almost too much for Catherine, who nearly burst out laughing; but Fatima took all this for passion. Or rather, when a considerable sum in gold dinars had changed hands, she concluded that the virtuous Abou-al-Khayr must be passionately in love, and that one should never put too much faith in appearances. For all the little man's dignity and disdainful airs, he was, when all was said and done, no different from any other man; and a beautiful girl could always work her will on him …

She set to work at once. Two Mooresses, as skinny as their mistress was stout, removed her clothes in a twinkling, and she found herself sitting on a wooden stool in a tiled room full of steam. She was left there to sweat for a good half-hour, after which the two attendants led her, gasping for air, to the massage slab where Fatima stood waiting, hands on hips, like the executioner awaiting a victim.

Catherine was stretched out on the slab like a piece of dough. Then, without wasting a second, Fatima put a coarse woollen glove on her right hand, snatched up a pot full of some sort of ochre-coloured paste with her left, and began daubing it on her client with dizzying speed. In a flash the young woman found herself transformed into a sort of mud statue with holes for her eyes and mouth. Then Fatima's powerful hands massaged her with the earth and washed her down with clear water, after which she was wrapped in a large woollen cloth and led to another table with a neck rest that left the hair hanging down free.

Catherine's hair was soaped repeatedly, rinsed, rinsed again, then swept up and finally rubbed with jasmine essence. During the whole time of these various operations she had not heard a single word from stout Fatima. The woman did not decide to speak till after her client, turbaned in a white towel and wrapped in a loose white woollen robe, had been installed on a sort of day-bed scattered with a multitude of cushions. Then Fatima clapped her hands and a eunuch appeared, carrying a large copper tray covered with a mass of little plates, which he set down on a low table beside the bed. Fatima, who had not even troubled to cover her nakedness when the eunuch appeared, pointed to the tray.

'You must eat everything on there.'

'Everything?' the young woman cried out in dismay. For she could see several different types of meatballs steaming on the tray, two different soups, one of them also containing meatballs, cucumbers pickled in vinegar, roast aubergines, a sort of ragout with a strongly perfumed sauce, and finally several types of cake and sweetmeat dripping with honey and bristling with almonds. Enough to feed Gauthier himself! 'I can never get through all that!' she exclaimed timidly, awed by Fatima's impressive bulk. But the masseuse was unmoved.

'You can take as long as you like over it, but you must eat everything. Mark my words, Light of Dawn: your master Abou-al-Khayr gave you to me so that I might make you the most beautiful creature in all Islam. And I have my reputation to think of. You are not going to leave here till your body is as smooth and suave as a rose-petal cream.'

'How do you mean, I won't leave here?' Catherine asked.

'You are not going to leave this house until you are fit for your master's bed,' the Negress stated calmly. 'Till then, this room will be your home. You will be tended, cared for, watched over like ...'

'Like a goose that needs fattening,' Catherine exclaimed angrily. 'But I don't want to stay here. I shall be bored to death.'

'You won't have time to be bored. You are beautiful, but dreadfully thin. Your skin is dry. There is a great deal to be done. And besides, you will be able to walk in the garden, and take the evening air on the terrace, and finally, properly veiled and guarded, you will be allowed to walk in the town. Believe me, you will not have time to get bored. Besides, the length of your stay depends upon you, and your cooperation. The sooner you are ready, the sooner you can leave ... although I must say I cannot understand your eagerness to receive the little doctor's caresses. He must have a big brain, but not much muscle. I should judge him an unsatisfactory lover. Now eat!'

And with this parting injunction Fatima went out, leaving Catherine torn between rage and laughter. How dared Abou imprison her with this woman? He had taken good care not to reveal to her that she would not be allowed out till she was in full possession of all her charms again, because he had known very well what reaction to expect. Besides, it was not hard to guess that in confiding her to the care of this black mastodon, he had intended to shield her from her own impulses and procure her time for reflection. Perhaps he had acted wisely after all. The best thing was to obey.

Obediently, therefore, she devoured the contents of the tray and drank, suspiciously at first, then with growing pleasure, the strong hot sweet mint tea ... and thereupon fell asleep. When she awoke, she found Fatima standing at the foot of her bed, grinning with all her strong white teeth in evidence.

'You slept almost two hours, and you ate everything. Good. We understand each other. Now we can carry on.'

Carried from her divan by two maids as carefully as if she had been a crystal vase, Catherine was taken to an epilation room where a specialist removed every trace of superfluous down with a thick paste compounded of chalk and yellow arsenic. Meanwhile a hairdresser covered her hair with a light henna rinse that, when it had been washed away, left superb red-gold gleams in it. The masseuse rubbed her client's body with a scented oil and began massaging her. This time Catherine abandoned herself to the treatment with real pleasure. Fatima's hands were capable of immense strength or astonishing gentleness. No doubt to encourage her, as she worked away on her stomach muscles, the fat Ethiopian declared:

'When I have finished with you, you will even be able to compete with Princess Zobeïda, the pearl of the harem.'

The name made Catherine start. She was instantly all ears, and questioned Fatima further, with apparent casualness.

'I have heard talk of her. They say she is very beautiful. Do you know her?'

'Certainly I know her. She was even brought to me once for treatment, after an illness. She is the most beautiful panther in the East. Cruel, savage, passionate, but beautiful! Oh yes, admirably fair! And she knows it, too. Zobeïda is proud of her body, and its perfection, and of her breasts, on which one could mould faultless drinking cups … and she likes to show them off. In the privacy of her apartments and her private garden she wears nothing but transparent gauzes and superb jewels, all the better to rejoice her lover's eyes.'

Catherine's throat went dry.

'Her lover?'

Fatima rolled Catherine over like a pancake and began massaging her back. Then she sniggered.

'I should say her lovers, for they whisper in the bazaar that more than one handsome warrior has entered her apartment by night through a secret door in order to satisfy her sexual appetite. They even say Zobeïda has found pleasure with well-muscled slaves … whose corpses were found later on in the moats of the Al Hamra.'

Catherine hovered between anxiety and relief. If, on the one hand, Zobeïda were really such a Messalina, it might well be easier to snatch away her prey … but on the other hand, how to be sure that a similar fate did not await Arnaud? And why did Fatima have to add:

'But for some months past, the old gossips have had a new tale to tell around the fountains and the caravanserais. Zobeïda has but one lover now, a Frankish captive, whom she is mad about. Now no-one else enters the secret door into her garden.'

'Have you seen this man?' Catherine inquired.

'Once. He is handsome, virile, haughty and silent. In a certain measure, he resembles Zobeïda; like her he is a beast of prey, a wild animal … Ah, their love-making must not lack for violence and passion, and their caresses …'

This was more than Catherine could stand.

'Enough,' she cried. 'I order you to be silent!'

Fatima stopped, astonished by this sudden display of violence in her client, and stood gazing at her in perplexity while she automatically wiped her hands on her cotton loincloth. The young woman had buried her face in her arms to hide the onrushing tears. Suddenly a slow grin spread over the

Negress's moon face. It seemed to her that she understood the reason for her client's sudden despair … She bent over the outstretched form, taking care that no-one else should overhear her.

'I know why you are unhappy, Light of Dawn. It is painful to you to hear speak of Zobeïda's handsome lover when you are destined for the caresses of only a weakly, ageing man. And in my view you are right, because your beauty deserves something better than the doctor … But comfort yourself, my beauty; we may find something better for you …'

Catherine lifted up a face all red and blotched with tears. 'What do you mean?'

'Nothing. I know what I am saying; but it is too soon to speak of this. Look at the state your face is in, silly little fool. Now let me see to it.'

As night came on, the terraces of houses in Granada took on the appearance of strange, misty gardens. All the women, dressed in their soft dark veils, sparkling with gold sequins, or relying less on jewellery when their fresh complexions were sufficient adornment, assembled beneath their respective roofs to breathe in the soft evening air, nibble sweetmeats and exchange gossip from one terrace to another. Even the humblest maid-servant was permitted to take the air. The men for their part preferred to gather together in the town squares to talk, listen to the storytellers or admire the feats of the tumblers; or, if it were permitted by the particular Muslim sect to which they belonged, they would attend the open-air cabarets, most of them situated in gardens, where they could amuse themselves, drink wine and watch the dancers.

That evening, when Fatima installed her amidst a heap of silken cushions, beneath the night sky, Catherine had the curious feeling of having changed her skin. First because she felt quite extraordinarily well, relaxed, almost weightless, and then because the new face Fatima had given her struck her as both unfamiliar and attractive. She had lingered for almost an hour in a great bath full of warm water eating the fruit that a slave, kneeling on the brim, peeled and handed to her. Then they had painted her face before dressing her up in strange new clothes. Her teeth had been rubbed with special paste, her lips tinted a ripe red while her eyes had been elongated with kohl till they almost reached her hairline. Her nails were painted and shone like pink pearls and she felt wonderfully at ease in her new costume: billowing pink muslin trousers secured by a heavy gilt belt at the hips, leaving waist and stomach bare, with a brief, short-sleeved bolero of pink satin on top. A tiny round cap on her head anchored the immense pink veil in which she was expected to swathe herself before stepping out on to the roof.

Fatima and her one client (Catherine had learnt that the hammam was to be closed to all others while she was under treatment – a ridiculously extravagant gesture on Abou's part, which had vastly impressed the stout masseuse) remained there for a long time in silence. The night was unusually tender, scented with jasmine and orange blossom. The view from the terrace over the town, with all its little alleys and still-open bazaar glittering with a host of tiny oil lamps, was novel and fairy-like to a woman accustomed to the darkened cities of the West, where the curfew transformed the streets into the haunt of cut-throats. Catherine stared at it for a long time, fascinated. A strange, frail, piercing music arose from some distant cabaret, competing with the soft thundering of a nearby waterfall.

But soon Catherine's eyes left the town to dwell on the great mass of the palace, which towered above Fatima's house. The house stood on the bank of the Darro, at the mouth of the deep ravine that the river cut between the Al Hamra, poised on its rocky promontory on the one side, and the Albaicin hill and the Alcazaba Kadima fortress on the other. Some two hundred yards above it, the deep crenellations of the palace walls stood out sharply against a velvet sky. There was no light there, and not a sign of life other than the metallic footsteps of unseen sentries. Catherine seemed to read a threat in those silent walls. They seemed to be defying her to free their prisoner …

The young woman's eyes remained fixed on this disquieting silhouette for such a long time that after a while Fatima noticed it.

'It seems that the palace fascinates you, Light of Dawn. What do you think of when you look at it?'

Catherine replied boldly. 'Of the Princess's lover, the handsome Frankish prisoner! I come from the same country, as you know. I can't help being interested in him.'

Fatima's fat hand descended over her mouth, effectively sealing it. In the darkness, Catherine saw the Ethiopian woman's eyes rolling in terror.

'Are you so weary of life already?' she whispered. 'If that's the case, it would be wiser for me to send you straight back to your master. The nearby terraces are within hearing distance, and I seem to see the saffron veil of Aïcha, the wife of the rich spice merchant, and one of the town's worst gossips. I am old and ugly now, but I still enjoy the scent of roses and eating black nougat.'

'Why is it dangerous to speak as I did?'

'Because the man you have mentioned is the only one throughout Granada of which no woman is allowed to think, even in dreams if she dreams aloud. Zobeïda's executioners are Mongol prisoners sent to her as a mark of homage by the Ottoman Sultan Mourad. They know how to prolong agony for days and days on end without causing death, and it is better to incur the Caliph's wrath than Zobeïda's jealousy. The favourite Sultana herself, Amina, the Dazzling One, would not take such a risk.

Zobeïda hates her quite enough as it is. That is why she rarely resides in the Al Hamra itself.'

'Where does she live, then?'

Fatima's fat finger indicated the delicate pavilions and gilded roofs of a great isolated building standing outside the city walls to the south. It appeared to spring from the bosom of a huge garden, the overhanging terraces of which were mirrored in a sparkling stream.

'The Alcazar Génil, the private palace of the Sultans. It is easy to guard, and Amina feels safer there. The Sultans have rarely lived in it, but Amina is all too conscious of the force of her sister-in-law's hatred. Certainly Muhammad loves her, but he is a poet at the same time as a warrior, and he always had a weakness for Zobeïda that the Sultana mistrusts.

'If the Princess got her way,' Catherine observed, 'I have the impression that that palace would not keep her safe for long.'

'Longer than you might think. Because there is this too ...'

Fatima pointed out a sort of fortress not far from the Medersa, bristling with crenellations and illuminated by a host of fire-pots. It appeared to be guarding the southern gate to the town and gave an impression of formidable strength.

'That is the dwelling of Mansour-ben-Zegris. He is Amina's cousin. He has always loved her, and he is certainly the richest man in the town. The Zegris and the Banu Siradj are the two most powerful families in the city, and of course, they are rivals. Amina is a Zegris, which is one more reason why Zobeïda, who protects the Banu Siradj should hate her. You cannot imagine the upheavals caused to the city by the quarrels between these two families. If the Caliph Muhammad has already lost his throne twice, you can safely assume it was the work of the Zegris.'

'And he returned to power for the third time without punishing them?'

'How could he? The Merinid Sultan who rules at Fez over the immense territories of the Mahgreb is the friend of the Zegris He would have unleashed his great anger against us, and the savage warriors of the desert would have soon been besieging our walls. No, Muhammad preferred to come to terms with his enemy. Amina's sweetness and gentleness, for she is devoted to her family as well as passionately in love with her husband, had a great deal of influence over the treaty that was drawn up between the two. That is why Muhammad continues to allow Mansour-ben-Zegris to stay there, crouched outside his gates like a mastiff about to spring.'

Fatima's voice stopped speaking and there was silence between the two women for a moment. Catherine thought over what she had just heard. All this information, apparently harmless enough, might well prove highly valuable to someone on the brink of a rash and dangerous venture. She made a careful note of all these new names she had just learned: Amina, the Sultana whom Abou-al-Khayr had saved from death; Mansour-ben-Zegris, the cousin who loved Amina; and the rival family in Zobeïda's protection, the Banu Siradj. She repeated them over and over to herself slowly so as to be certain of not forgetting them.

She opened her mouth to ask Fatima another question, but a mighty snore arrested her. The fat Ethiopian, tired from her day's work, had slipped down among the cushions on the ground and lay with her mouth open, and her hands clasped round her huge belly, loudly heralding the night. Catherine smiled silently, then nestled back among her cushions and resumed her daydreaming.

A week later, Catherine found herself transformed. The calm, indolent, comfortable life at Fatima's establishment, the rich food, the long, lazy hours in warm, hot and cold baths, and above all the dexterous and incredibly complicated attentions that the Ethiopian had bestowed upon her, had worked wonders. Her body had lost its pathetic skinniness, her flesh had recovered its magnificent bloom, and her skin had become as soft and fine-textured as a flower petal. She had at last grown accustomed to the strange costumes of the country and now took pleasure in wearing them.

Abou-al-Khayr had made her several visits during the week to check on her progress, but neither Gauthier nor Josse had been able to accompany him. His visits were rapid and somewhat, formal for he took care to maintain the detached attitude of a dilettante who has come to examine the repair work being done on some rare treasure he has unearthed.

He had managed to whisper to her that he had not yet stumbled upon a way of introducing her to the palace, though he was formulating plans; but this scarcely satisfied the impatient Catherine. She felt quite ready for action now. The long mirrors of polished silver in the massage-rooms reflected a vision of exquisite loveliness whose power she was eager to exploit. But it seemed Fatima was still not satisfied.

'Patience,' she counselled, painting her face with the care of an illuminator. 'You still have not achieved the perfection I could wish for.'

She took care to hide her beautiful client, and only the servants and eunuchs were permitted to go near her when she was receiving visitors. However, one morning, as Catherine stepped streaming wet from the pool, she caught sight of Fatima in conversation with an old woman, sumptuously dressed in green brocade, whose weasel eyes had insolently appraised the finer points of her anatomy. The two women seemed to be having some sort of dispute, and Catherine could have sworn that she herself was the subject of this discussion. But, after an approving nod, the old woman disappeared with a clatter of slippered feet. When Catherine interrogated Fatima about her, the Ethiopian merely shrugged.

'An old friend of mine. But if she returns, you must take care to be pleasant and nice to her ... because she could do a lot to help you if you really want a more ... more virile master than the little doctor.'

Fatima refused to say more, and 'Light of Dawn' had to be content with these few mysterious words, the meaning of which she could merely guess at. But had Abou not said that Fatima was the queen of procuresses? She contented herself with observing gently:

'A more virile master, yes ... but I should be completely happy if I were able to discover the beauties of the Al Hamra thanks to this master.'

'That is not impossible,' Fatima answered slyly, and Catherine did not persist this time.

The day after the old woman's visit, Catherine was given permission by Fatima to visit the stalls in the bazaar. She enjoyed idling in the warm, dusty, splendid atmosphere of these interminable streets roofed over with reeds, where every sort of marvel seemed to spill in profusion from the tiny stalls. Fatima had allowed her to visit them two or three times, heavily veiled of course, and attended by two maids who never stirred from her side, plus a tall eunuch carrying a long whip of plaited hippopotamus hide.

She had set out as usual this particular morning, with her escort, veiled in a length of honey-coloured satin that left only her kohl-blackened eyes showing. She walked slowly toward the big silk stall situated close to the foot of the ramp leading into the Al Hamra palace. The town was veiled in a blue mist, which promised that the day would be unusually hot. Here and there the townspeople were spraying water about the alleyways to try to preserve a little coolness and lay the dust. It was very early still, only two hours after dawn, but this and the cool twilight hour were the only times when it was at all pleasant to leave the shade of the houses. Nevertheless, the usual market-day hubbub spread throughout the town.

Catherine had just left the shade of a mosque and was going toward the entrance to the stalls, crossing the sun-filled space in front of Bab-el-Ajuar – the great red arch, guarded by gigantic Nubians, that formed the first portal to the Al Hamra – when the sound of strident, warlike music fell upon her ears. A party of men on horseback, playing a sort of bagpipe and beating small round drums, appeared through the gate, followed by a powerful troop of armed men. Swarthy- complexioned soldiers with fierce eyes, lances at their sides, mounted on swift Andalusian ponies, escorted a group of sumptuously-dressed knights, each of whom carried a falcon or hawk perched on their left wrist, which was protected by a thick leather glove. The hoods over the birds' eyes were of crimson silk embroidered with gems, while the cavaliers themselves wore tunics of rich silk and carried weapons studded with enormous stones. Great noblemen, without doubt. They all had fine-cut, haughty faces, short black beards and dark, glowing eyes. Only one of them, however, rode bareheaded, with nothing over his face. He went a little in front of the rest, silent, arrogant, one hand negligently grasping the reins of his superb mount, a beast of dazzling snow-white that caught Catherine's eye. At once she glanced up from the horse to the rider. She stifled a cry. The mount was Morgane, and the rider was Arnaud ...

He sat very upright on his embroidered saddle, at least a head taller than his companions, and he was dressed in the oriental fashion, but in a gold-embroidered black silk that contrasted strongly with the bright colours worn by the rest of the party. He also wore, thrown carelessly back over his shoulders, a great burnous of fine white wool ... His handsome face, with its strong features and imperious profile, was as lean and fine-drawn, and almost as tanned, as those of the Moors. His black eyes glowed darkly, but there were streaks of silver in the thick black hair at his temples.

Catherine stood rooted to the spot, shattered to the core of her being, devouring him with her eyes as he spurred his temperamental steed forward, indifferent, distant, oblivious of everything save the great falcon perched on his wrist, which he brought close to his face now and then as if speaking to it. Catherine stood motionless, thunderstruck, incapable of uttering a sound. She had always known that he lived only a short distance away, but to find herself suddenly face to face with him, to see him like this, so near and yet so inaccessible ... No, she had not been prepared for that.

Unaware of the drama being played out only a few feet away, the riders moved on their way. They were about to vanish round the corner of a red brick palace, the slender windows of which were heavily screened ... A sudden impulse threw Catherine on the trail of that tall black and white silhouette now vanishing down a narrow alley. But strong hands gripped her arms, holding her fast, while the eunuch, eyes rolling wildly, came and stood in front of her, barring her way.

'Let me go,' she commanded angrily. 'What are you doing? I'm not a prisoner ...'

'Fatima's orders are clear,' one of the women explained apologetically. 'We are to prevent you doing anything that might place you in danger. You were trying to follow the riders ... isn't that so?'

'Is it forbidden to take a closer look at them?'

'Indeed it is. The soldiers' scimitars strike swiftly, especially when they are escorting the Princess's Frankish prisoner. Your head might have fallen even before you realised it ... and Fatima's whip would not have spared us either ...'

Catherine realised it was this, rather than the thought of her own death, that frightened the servants ... but still, they were right. What folly might she not have committed if they had allowed her free rein? She would surely have cried out, torn the veil from her face so that the man she loved might recognisee her ... and when the news of the public scandal reached Zobeïda it would have meant her death ... and his too, perhaps. No ... it was better like this. But it had been a painful moment.

Still trembling all over from shock, Catherine turned on her heel. 'Let us return,' she sighed. 'I don't want to walk among the stalls now. It is too hot.'

However, she paused for a moment by the wall of the little green-domed mosque ... Two beggars, one immensely tall and thin, arms crossed beneath his rags, and the other, a little twisted figure sitting on his one leg, were watching the glittering cortege of riders disappearing afar off. Some of their words reached the young woman.

'The Princess's captive must be bored by the wonders of the Al Hamra. Did you see how gloomy he looked?'

'What man would not be, who had lost the precious gift of freedom? The man is a warrior. That can be seen by his carriage ... and his scars. And war is the headiest of all drinks. He has only has love now ... It's not much ...'

Catherine pretended to have a thorn in her foot, the better to listen, and while her two maids knelt and examined her foot, she drank in every word the men were saying. The least word about Arnaud was precious to her. But what followed was even more important, because the tall beggar went on casually:

'They say that Zobeïda is thinking of sending him across the blue sea. The great lands of the old Mahgreb would be softer under his courser's hooves, and there are many rebel tribes over there to subdue. The Sultan would doubtless accept the services of so perfect a knight, even if an infidel – and he would not be the first to embrace the true faith.'

'But would our Caliph allow his sister to leave?'

'Who has ever succeeded in thwarting Zobeïda's will? Did you see who was guarding her precious hostage? The Vizier Aben-Ahmed Banu Siradj himself ... She will leave when she wants to, and the Merinid Sultan will give her warm welcome.'

Now a group of richly-dressed women were approaching, and the two beggars abandoned their conversation to launch into a whining complaint in the hope of getting a few alms. Catherine had heard enough in any case. She slipped on her sandals hastily, wrapped her great veil closely round her, and before her maids could restrain her, she was running full tilt toward Fatima's house.

The gossip exchanged by the two beggars had thrown her into considerable panic. For these street-beggars to discuss him so curiously, for the whole town to buzz with rumours about him, the Frankish prisoner must indeed be a figure of the greatest interest and curiosity. Zobeïda's prisoner was all but a legendary figure ... and one who must need to be closely guarded. If that damned Princess took Arnaud to Africa she would have to pursue him there, set off on her travels again, risk new dangers, almost impossible ones this time, because there would be no little doctor to help her in the mysterious cities of this country called Mahgreb. She must prevent this happening at all costs; find Arnaud first, flee with him ...For a moment she was tempted to rush straight round to the little doctor's, but she knew that he would be tending his patients at this hour. And the guards from the hammam would have no trouble in recapturing her before she got there. So she went into Fatima's house and ran straight into the inner courtyard, which was planted with lemon-trees, pomegranate-trees and vines. Then she stopped on the threshold of the narrow gallery that ran round the court. Fatima was there, but she was not alone. The stout Ethiopian was walking along dressed in an astonishing garment striped in all the colours of the rainbow, with a turban draped round her head after the masculine style. Beside her, Catherine recognised the old woman of the previous day, strolling about the little alleys encircling the central fountain. This time the silk gown she wore was of a twilight violet embroidered with large green flowers.

When she caught sight of Catherine standing breathless at the entrance to the garden, Fatima instantly realised that something must have happened, and she left her visitor with a word of apology and hastened over to the young woman.

'What is the matter? What happened? Where are your guards?'

'They are following behind. I came to say farewell, Fatima, farewell and thank you. I must return to … my master.'

'He has not come to claim you, so far as I know. Did you meet him in the street?' the Negress asked in a tone full of suspicion.

'No. But I must go back to his house as soon as possible …'

'You seem in a great hurry all of a sudden. Especially since Abou the doctor is not at home. He has been summoned to the Alcazar Génil. The Sultana has hurt herself in the bath …'

'Very well … he will find me when he returns, that is all! It will be a nice surprise for him …'

'And for you? Will the night that awaits you be a nice surprise too, do you think?'

The Negress's large eyes probed Catherine's vacillating glance, examining her face, which was growing pink with embarrassment.

'Sooner or later,' the young woman murmured.

'I thought you were anxious above all things to enter the Al Hamra?' Fatima said slowly.

At this word Catherine's heart missed a beat, but she forced herself to remain casual.

'What is the use of dreaming? Whose dreams ever come true?'

'Do what I say and this dream of yours will come true, and that speedily. Come with me.'

She took Catherine's hand and tried to pull her along, but she resisted, seized by a sudden mistrust.

'Where are you taking me?'

'To that woman over there, beside the fountain ... and to the Al Hamra itself, if you still want to go there. That old woman is Morayma. Everyone here knows her and makes a fuss of her, because she is in charge of the master's harem. She noticed you the other day ... and she has come back for you. Go with her, and instead of the little doctor, you will belong to the Caliph.'

'To the Caliph?' Catherine repeated in a pale voice. 'You suggest that I should enter the harem?'

Her instinct was to reject the proposition with horror, but then a remark of Abou-al-Khayr's came to mind: 'Zobeïda's apartments are part of the harem'. And another: 'It is in Zobeïda's own garden, in a separate pavilion, that Messire Arnaud lives ...' Entering the harem was a way of getting closer to Arnaud. And she could hardly find a better opportunity. She banished the little voice of fear from her mind: if she merely went up to Zobeïda's captive and spoke to him, she would be handed over to the Princess's Mongol executioners. She had so often defied torture and death. The executioners of Granada could not be much worse than those at Amboise. Besides, once Arnaud recognised her, the two of them would be able to fight together ... and die together if necessary. Catherine was quite prepared to die with him if that were the price of being reunited with him again forever. It would be a hundred times better to die with him than to leave him in that woman's clutches ...

She made up her mind. She threw back her head, meeting Fatima's anxious eyes, and smiled.

'I will go with you,' she said. 'And I thank you for what you have done. The only thing I ask is that you will have a letter delivered to the doctor. He has been kind to me.'

'I understand that. Abou the doctor shall have his letter. But come now; Morayma is getting impatient.'

And the old woman did indeed show signs of agitation. She had left the pink fountain and was now hurrying forward with the air of a woman who has no time to lose. Fatima whipped off Catherine's veil with the rapid gesture of a conjurer, so that her hair, interwoven with gold threads, glittered in the sunshine, and her slender body was revealed in its wide muslin trousers and short gold embroidered bolero, the deep-cut neckline of which barely covered her bosom ... Catherine saw the old woman's eyes gleam in the shadow of her green and lilac veil. With an impatient gesture, the old woman threw off her veil, exposing wrinkled yellowish skin and the fierce profile of a bejewelled elderly Jewess: her toothless mouth was sunken and her smile was a twisted grimace. The only beautiful things were her hands, which were covered with sparkling rings. Morayma must have taken great care of them and anointed them daily with oils and creams, because they gave off a strong perfume whenever they moved, and their skin was

186

soft.

Nevertheless, Catherine could not help shuddering slightly when these same hands felt her hip to judge the softness of her own skin.

'You need not fear,' Fatima remarked boldly. 'The texture is smooth and fine and unblemished.'

'So I see,' said the old woman. She calmly unfastened Catherine's bolero and uncovered her breasts, which she pinched between finger and thumb to test their firmness.

'The most beautiful fruits of love,' Fatima added, making an inventory of her wares as coolly as a carpet-seller. 'What man would not prefer these to his right mind? You may search the world over, Morayma – from the icy countries of the North to the burning desert sands, and even as far as the Great Khan's lands – without finding a more perfect flower to offer to the All Powerful Commander of the Faithful.'

Morayma merely nodded approvingly before asking Catherine: 'Open your mouth.'

'Why?' the young woman protested, forgetting her good resolutions at finding herself treated like a mare on market day.

'To make sure that your breath is sweet,' the old woman replied sharply. 'I hope your character is obedient and adaptable, my girl. I would not care to offer the Caliph a rebellious or capricious woman.'

'Forgive me,' Catherine said, flushing. She opened her mouth obediently, revealing a pink palate and sparkling white teeth. The old woman inserted her nose cautiously. The young woman had to fight back a sudden desire to laugh as Morayma gave an amused glance at Fatima.

'What do you give her to chew, you old witch? Her breath is exquisite.'

'Jasmine flowers and cloves,' Fatima answered grudgingly, for she hated giving away her secrets. But she knew that the keeper of the harem was not a person to trifle with. 'Well, have you made up your mind?'

'I am taking her. Go and get ready, woman, and make haste. I have to go …'

Catherine raced to her room and collected up her clothes, leaving the two women to discuss what, for Fatima, was the most important point at issue – the price, which must certainly be high.

'I shall have to give something to the doctor,' she heard the fat Ethiopian protesting.

'The Caliph has always had the right to claim a slave girl. It is an honour for any of his subjects to offer him one …' The bedroom door banging shut prevented Catherine hearing the rest of the conversation, but this haggling was a matter of little interest to her. She knew quite well that Fatima would pocket the larger part of the gold she would receive, making great play, for her client Abou-al-Khayr, of the Caliph's incontrovertible rights and the use of *force majeure*.

Catherine rapidly snatched up a scrap of paper and a pen and scribbled a short note to Abou, telling him of her departure for the harem. 'I am glad,' she wrote, 'because I shall be able to see my husband at last. Don't worry yourself about me, but try to stop Gauthier and Josse doing anything foolish. I shall try to get news to you, possibly via Fatima ... unless you can find a way of entering the harem ...'

A cry from below made her jump. Old Morayma was growing impatient. Hastily she snatched up a bundle of clothes at random and stuffed them under her arm, picked up the veil she had been wearing earlier and entered the gallery just in time to catch Fatima counting out a respectable pile of gold dinars with a look of absurd glee. As soon as Catherine appeared, the harem keeper's hand seized her arm, snatched away the clothes and flung them contemptuously on the ground.

'You don't need this rubbish. At the palace I shall dress you according to the Master's tastes. Now, come ...'

'One moment,' Catherine begged. 'Let me say farewell to Fatima.'

'You will be seeing her again. I often summon her to the harem, for she knows many of the secrets of beauty and love.'

But Fatima had heard, and she poured the gold into a little goatskin bag and came to join the other two women. She arranged Catherine's veil in an almost motherly fashion, and Catherine made use of the opportunity to slip her the little note to Abou. Then Fatima smiled at her encouragingly.

'You go to meet your destiny, Light of Dawn. But when you are the beloved, the precious jewel of the Caliph, remember old Fatima ...'

'Don't worry,' Catherine replied, taking the game to its logical lengths, 'I shall never forget you.'

She meant what she said. It would be impossible to forget the curious but nevertheless amusing days she had spent with the massive Ethiopian. And Fatima had been kind to her, when all was said and done, even if she had been acting out of self- interest.

Two white mules, harnessed with red leather and tinkling with little bells, were brought up for Catherine and her new mentor to ride. Then Morayma clapped once, and four skinny Nubians, swathed in white up to their eyes, stepped out of a nearby alleyway. They drew their scimitars with their long curved blades and, as they took up their positions on either side of the two women, the little procession set off.

It was stiflingly hot by now. The air vibrated with heat, and the pitiless sun shone down from an almost colourless sky onto the roofs of the town. But Catherine did not even notice the temperature. All she could think of, in her excitement, was the palace, the threshold of which she was at long last about to cross. The distance between herself and Arnaud was shrinking with every minute. She had seen him a little while ago. Now she would be able to try to speak to him, and take him back with her on the road to France.

188

How she was going to get back was a problem she dismissed from her mind. And yet it would be difficult enough. Even assuming that they managed to escape from the palace, they would still have to reach the frontiers of the kingdom somehow or other. Even over the frontiers there was no knowing if they would be safe from Zobeïda's vengeance. It seemed unlikely. They would first have to place many leagues between themselves and their pursuers. Muhammad's fiery horsemen were too accustomed to ignore the frontiers of their kingdom to consider them a barrier in that pursuit.

Afterwards they would have to retrace the whole dangerous journey across Castile, with the risk of encountering worse ambushes than the ones they had met on the way there … Then the Pyrenees, and their robber bands, then … No. None of that mattered; only one thing mattered: regaining Arnaud's love. Catherine did not care what happened after that.

As she entered the red arch of Bab-el-Ajuar behind Morayma, Catherine could not help giving an inward shiver of triumph. The Nubians on guard had paid no attention to them …

They followed a path that wound through a vale laced with streams and shaded with silvery olive-trees, and climbed a steep hill toward a tall gate, the overhanging archway of which was cut through the middle of a great square tower with no crenellations. This impressive portal in the inner wall of the palace was the real entrance to the Al Hamra. As they drew near, Catherine noticed a white marble hand pointing heavenwards carved on the keystone of the brick horseshoe arch.

'That is the Gate of Justice. That hand symbolises the five precepts of the Koran,' Morayma commented. 'And those towers you see not far from here are those of the prison.'

She said no more. But Catherine grasped the meaning behind what she said. It was obviously intended as a warning, if not a threat. Equally threatening was the massive double gate with its iron bars and immense nail-heads looming up before them in the gloom of the great arch. It was guarded by knights wearing shining mail beneath crimson burnous, their helmets pulled down as far as their fierce eyes. When their master gave the order to close the gates it would be quite impossible to find a way through these massive walls. The pink palace, as well as the little town enclosed within its ramparts (houses, windmills and the seven garden cupolas of a towering minaret and immense mosque could now be seen) must close like a trap that refuses to yield up its prey. Unless, perhaps, they were able to find the mysterious door through which Zobeïda's lovers of a single night entered the palace? But there might be no more to that story than idle gossip. The corpses in the moat might easily have been thrown from the ramparts. In which case they would have had to use the legendary lovers' staircase.

Catherine's sharp eyes were already peering about, proof that she felt less confident than she would have liked to admit, looking for a secret exit from this magnificent and sinister palace, which struck her as being as alluring and dangerous as a poisoned flower. She looked away hastily so as not to see the bloody heads, some of them quite fresh, hanging from hooks along the walls. At the moment of crossing the threshold into this unknown world, Catherine felt an icy hand clutch her heart. She took a deep breath, gritted her teeth, staring hard at Morayma's bent back beneath the ridiculous green and violet flowers. She must not weaken at this point ... not now, and especially not on account of anything so feeble as a moment of animal fear. She had looked forward to this for far too long ...

And then, by a miracle, somewhere in the scented depths of the as-yet-invisible gardens, a nightingale sang, sending up notes as clear as a mountain stream toward the incandescent sky. A nightingale at this time of day, in this crushing heat ...? Catherine's heavy heart grew lighter. She saw this as a good omen, and pressed her mule forward on Morayma's heels.

The sudden cool of a tunnel, a sharp bend, a steep path deluged in sunshine, and then at last, round the corner, the oriental grace of two tall, slender doors at right angles.

Morayma, who had been waiting for Catherine at the top of the path, pointed out to her the one in front of them. 'The Royal Gate, which opens into the Caliph's seraglio. But we will take this one, the Wine Gate, which will take us directly to the harem through the upper town, the administrative city of the Al Hamra.'

As Catherine's eyes lingered on the massive wall running between three crimson keeps, which towered up on their left, the old woman smiled thinly.

'You will never enter this part of the Al Hamra. This is the Alcazaba, the fortress that makes the Al Hamra impregnable. Do you see that huge tower that stands guard over the ravine, over there? Admire the power of your future master. That is the Ghafar, the key to our defences. At night you will often hear the bell ringing in the tower, but don't let that alarm you, Light of Dawn. That does not mean danger but merely the irrigation times in the valley, which the bell regulates throughout the night ... Now let us hurry. The heat is unbearable and I want you to look cool when the master sees you.'

Catherine shivered. Apparently she would not be allowed much of a breathing space before being presented to the Caliph. However, in this as in everything else, she was resolved to let events take their own course, and to make the best use of them for her own ends.

11: The Poet-King

The long harem bathing-pool, decorated with gold and blue mosaic, was enveloped in warm, scented steam when Catherine entered it, hustled forward by Morayma. Her eyes were still heavy with sleep. The old Jewess had ordered her to sleep for two hours after her meal, and her ears were still buzzing. A stupefying din greeted her in this room where some fifty women were all chattering at once. A group of slaves, most of them black, stood around the pool full of blue scented water where a whole troop of pretty girls frolicked about, laughing, shouting, splashing each other. The pool looked as if a miniature storm had struck it, but the water was so clear that it scarcely veiled the bathers' bodies, if at all. Every shade of skin was represented in this charming and luxurious setting. The deep bronze of African girls with slender hips, pointed breasts; the soft ivory of Asiatics; and the rosy alabaster of a few Western women mingled with the amber skin of Moorish girls. Catherine saw every shade of hair; black, chestnut, red, and even a blonde so fair as to be almost white. She saw eyes of every colour, and heard voices of every timbre. But her appearance under the auspices of the mistress of the harem silenced everyone and left the pool quite calm for a moment. All the women froze, every pair of eyes turned toward the newcomer whom Morayma was undressing swiftly on the glittering mosaic floor, and Catherine observed with a shiver of foreboding that the expression on all the women's faces was identical: one of total hostility.

Catherine realised this at once, and it made her uneasy. It was horrible to stand there while all those hostile eyes examined her, for those of the slaves were no less venomous than their mistress's, and she felt as if she were being pelted with hot coals. Morayma gauged the atmosphere equally rapidly. Her harsh voice rang through the room.

'This one is called Light of Dawn. She is a slave purchased at Almeria. Take care that nothing unpleasant happens to her, otherwise the whips will be busy! I shall not accept that the verge of the pool was slippery, or that she felt sick in the bath, or got indigestion from eating too many sweets, or that the wall crumbled under her feet, or that she met with a stray viper in the gardens, nor any other accident. Remember that, now! Now you, go and take a bath.'

A murmur of protest greeted this little speech, which Catherine heard with a shudder, but no-one dared to answer back. Still, as she dipped her toe in the scented water, Catherine had the unpleasant sensation that she was stepping into a nest of serpents. All these slender gleaming bodies seemed as supple as snakes, and all these fresh rosy lips looked as though they would gladly have spat out venom.

She swam about for a few minutes without much pleasure. Everyone avoided her mistrustfully, and she had no wish to prolong this disagreeable bath a moment longer than necessary. She was already swimming up to the edge of the pool to place herself at the disposal of the two slaves who had been allocated to her and who stood waiting with thick cotton towels to dry her, but she suddenly noticed a pretty blonde girl reclining on a heap of cushions nearby. She had a pretty fresh, plump body, all rosy and dimpled, and she was smiling at her in the friendliest way. She approached her, and the girl's smile deepened. She even abandoned her negligent pose and held out a somewhat oversized hand.

'Come and lie down here with me and don't take any notice of the others. They are always like this when a new one arrives. You understand, a new companion is also the threat of a dangerous new favourite.'

'Why dangerous? Are all these women in love with the Caliph, then?'

'Heavens no, though he is not without charm!'

The girl fell silent. She had spoken without thinking in French instead of Arabic, and this had made Catherine jump.

'You are from France?' she replied, also in French.

'Yes … from the Saône countryside. I was born at Auxonne,' she added, with a shadow of sadness. 'I was called Marie Vermeil, but here they call me Aïcha. But are you French too, then?'

'As French as they come,' Catherine said, smiling. 'I was born in Paris, but I was raised at Dijon where my uncle, Mathieu Gautherin, had a draper's shop in the street of the Griffon, at the sign of the Great Saint Bonaventure …'

'Mathieu Gautherin?' the other replied thoughtfully. 'I seem to know that name … It's funny, but I seem to have seen you before somewhere. Where could that be?'

She stopped. The golden shape of a beautiful Moorish girl was swimming toward them through the blue water, and her tigerish green and gold eyes flashed over them both a look of unmistakable hatred. Marie whispered hurriedly:

'Watch out for her. That is Zorah, the current favourite. The vultures circling round the Execution Tower are more tender-hearted than that viper.

She is even more wicked than Princess Zobeïda, because the Princess scorns the perfidious tricks in which Zorah is so practised. If you please the master you will have everything to fear from that Egyptian.'

Catherine had no time to put any further questions. Morayma was approaching with the two black slaves, no doubt considering that she had spent long enough chatting to Marie-Aïcha.

'We can talk again later,' Marie murmured, before falling gracefully into the pool in such a way that Zorah had to dive aside so as not to have her land on her back.

Though she was almost dry, Catherine allowed the two women to towel her carefully all over and then cover her whole body with a light scented oil that gave her skin the soft patina of pale gold. She was about to slip on her striped silk robe when Morayma spoke up.

'No. You are not to get dressed at once. Come with me.'

Catherine followed the Jewess through various bathrooms – some hot, some cold – till she came to a chamber with slender colonnades entirely covered with blue, pink and gold filigree decoration. A gallery screened by gilded jalousies ran right round it, at first-floor level. There were beds piled high with coloured cushions set back in alcoves between the columns, and there were five or six very beautiful girls lying nonchalantly, stark naked, on these beds. Morayma pointed out the one empty bed.

'Lie down there.'

'What for?'

'You will soon see. It won't take long ...'

Women's voices were heard, singing a gentle monotonous song, but no-one in the room spoke. When she had made Catherine lie down in a seductive pose, Morayma stationed herself in the centre of the room close to a fountain that trickled into a marble pool. She looked up toward the closed gallery as if waiting for something. Catherine curiously followed the direction of her glance.

She seemed to see a shadow behind the thin gilded latticework, but a shadow so utterly motionless that she felt at first that she must be suffering from a delusion. All this – the waiting, the bath, the slow tempo of this life – exacerbated her impatience to be finished with it, to find her husband again. What was she doing on this divan amid all these other naked women ...? The reply was not long in coming. A hand raised one of the shutters and threw something that rolled onto Catherine's divan. Catherine sat up and saw that it was merely a fig, and was about to pick it up when Morayma ran forward and took the fruit. Catherine saw that she was flushed with excitement and her little eyes gleamed.

'The master has chosen you,' the mistress of the harem cried. 'And you have barely arrived. This very night you will be admitted to share the royal couch. Now, come. We have only just enough time to make you ready. The master is in a hurry.'

Without giving Catherine time to dress, she rushed her through rooms and galleries till they reached the pavilion, one of the most modest in the whole harem, where she had lodged her new acquisition.

Once there, Catherine had no time to ask questions. The Caliph's choice had given rise to a flurry of activity that left no time for reflection. Finding herself handed over to a positive army of masseuses, perfumers, pedicurists, hairdressers and dressers, the young woman thought it best to abandon herself quite passively to their attentions. In any case, it might be useful to approach the Caliph – from near to. Who knew if she might not gain a certain influence over him? As for the … contingencies that intimacy with the King of Granada implied, Catherine was not unduly alarmed by the thought. In any case, she would scarcely be allowed much choice in the matter. Any resistance on her part would risk the destruction of her plans and endanger her own life, Arnaud's, and those of their friends. Besides, when one makes war, one makes it wholeheartedly, and one is not too concerned about the means to the end.

He sat cross-legged on a divan spread with silk rugs. She stood a few paces away, radiant in a cloud of rose-pink veiling: the Caliph Muhammad VIII and Catherine gazed at each other. He with unmistakable admiration, she with a mistrust tinged with astonishment. Heaven knew why – perhaps because of the alarming portrait she had been given of Zobeïda – but Catherine had been certain that the latter's older brother would turn out to be an arrogant, cynical, brutal man, a sort of Gilles de Rais doubled with La Trémoille …

But this prince who sat looking at her was not a bit as she had imagined him. He must have been between 35 and 40 years old but, strangely enough in a Moor, his un-turbaned head was covered with a thick crop of dark gold hair like the short beard on his tanned face. His eyes, grey or blue, were a strong contrast to that dark skin, and when he smiled, his teeth were white and powerful. With a swift gesture, Muhammad pushed aside the roll of paper on which he had been writing with a stylus when the young woman and Morayma had entered the room.

He had watched her approaching in silence as she walked beside the cypress-shaded stream that led up to his abode. It had been a long route, through arches and along a covered way before crossing the gardens around the rose-covered palace on top of the little hill next to the Al Hamra. This was the Djenan-el-Arif, the Architect's Garden, where, in summer, the Caliph liked to pass his time. Even more than the seraglio itself, this was a paradise of roses and jasmine. Roses as dark as crimson velvet or white with a rosy heart like snow at sunrise; and they clambered all over the hill, mirrored in pools, trailing about the white columns of the porticos. They scented the blue, star-spangled night. As she and Morayma had approached the palace, this heady fragrance had made Catherine's eyelids droop and her temples throb, while the blood had flowed more slowly in her veins.

Muhammad said nothing while Morayma prostrated herself and told him of the joy of this new odalisque at finding herself singled out her very first night, and he remained silent while she praised the beauty and sweetness of Light of Dawn, Pearl of France, the amethyst depths of her eyes, the grace of her body … But when she stood up and tried to remove the muslin veils that made the young woman into a cloudy pink statue, he stopped her with a peremptory gesture and ordered her to leave.

'Go now, Morayma. I will send for you later …'

And so they were left alone. The Caliph rose to his feet. He was less tall than Catherine had expected; his legs seemed too short for his powerful torso, arrayed in a green silk gandourah that was slit to the waist and gathered into a wide belt of chased gold, studded with huge square emeralds. He went up to her and smiled.

'Don't tremble so. I won't hurt you.'

He spoke French, and Catherine gazed at him in astonishment. 'I am not trembling. Why should I? But how do you come to speak my language?'

His smile deepened. Muhammad was standing close beside her now, and she could smell the faint scent of leather and verbena given off by his clothes.

'I have always liked learning things, and travellers from your country have always been warmly welcomed here. A monarch needs to be able to understand ambassadors from foreign parts whenever possible. Interpreters are all too often disloyal … or treacherous! A prisoner, a saintly man from your own country, taught me the language when I was a child … and you are not the first woman who has come from beyond the tall mountains to this place.'

Catherine recalled Marie and decided this was sufficient explanation. She did not answer. By now Muhammad's long slender fingers were busy detaching the veil that covered her head and the lower half of her face. He did so slowly, gently, with the care of an aesthete unwrapping a precious object on which he has long set his heart. Her soft face crowned by red-gold hair, capped in a little lattice-work of fine pearls, appeared; then her long slender neck. Another veil fell aside, then another. Morayma, a consummate artist in this respect, for whom the secrets of kindling a man's desire were as familiar as her own face, had swathed her in veil after veil, knowing the pleasure her master would find in removing them. Beneath these many layers of diaphanous material Catherine wore nothing but wide pleated trousers of the same transparent stuff, caught in round her ankles and at her hips by plaits of pearls. She yielded herself to these supple hands that grew more caressing as the veils fell away one by one. She wanted to please this man, who was charming enough in all conscience, who was gentle with her and wanted only an hour of pleasure with her when all was said and done … the pleasure that Gilles de Rais had taken by force, that Fero the gypsy had obtained by means of a love philtre, that she had almost given to Pierre de Brézé, and that she had offered so spontaneously to Gauthier. So many men had already passed through her life. This one certainly would not be the worst.

Soon the veils were heaped on the lapis-lazuli tiles like gigantic fallen rose petals. The Sultan's hands now caressed bare skin and lingered in long stroking movements, but still he had come no nearer. He gazed at her … stepping back a few paces the better to contemplate her under the soft light emanating from the gold lamps hanging from the arches.

They remained like that for a long time, Catherine standing there in all the splendour of her proffered beauty, Muhammad half kneeling a little way off. In the depths of the tall cypress-trees, a nightingale let fall a liquid cascade of clear notes, and Catherine remembered the bird that had sung as she crossed the tall red gate to the Al Hamra. Perhaps it was the same little songster?

But now Muhammad's voice rose in soft counterpoint in the darkness:

'I picked the dawn rose in my garden,
'And the nightingale sang to me,
'For he, like me, suffers from loving a rose,
'And fills the morning air with his lament.
'I wandered the sorrowful paths unceasingly,
'Prisoner of this rose and this nightingale …'

The verse was moving, and the Caliph's warm voice made it more melodious still, but that was where the poem ended. For Muhammad was drawing closer to Catherine as he sang, and the last word finished on her lips as he swept her up in his arms and carried her off into the garden.

'The place for a rose is among her sisters,' he murmured against his captive's lips. 'I want to pluck you in the garden.'

There were velvet pillows and cushions heaped on the marble rim of a pool in which the stars were reflected. Muhammad put Catherine down there and then tore off his robe impatiently and flung it aside; the heavy emerald-studded belt splashed into the pool without his heeding it. He flung himself down on the cushions and drew the young woman into his arms. She shivered a little, but she too was carried away by the strange attractions of this man, the magic of a night drenched in perfumes and calmed by the singing of nightingales and the soft chirruping of crickets. Muhammad knew how to make love, and Catherine yielded herself docilely to the tender sport, only just aware beneath the waves of pleasure of a faint sense of guilt tinged with revenge that was not without its charms.

And the great watery mirror in which the slender silver crescent moon was now rising grew suddenly still, the better to reflect the double image of the two joined bodies.

'I shall give the wind a blossom picked from your own flowering face, and I shall breathe the scent of the paths where you walk,' the Sultan murmured in Catherine's ear. 'You are the essence of all the flowers in this garden, Light of Dawn, and your eyes are as clear as limpid water. Who taught you love, O most scented rose?'

Catherine blessed the shade of the jasmine curtain above them, which hid her sudden blushes. It was true, she liked to make love, and while her heart was given to another, her body enjoyed the skilful caresses of a masterly lover. And this was what she told him, though with a shade of hypocrisy.

'What pupil would not respond with so skilful a teacher? I am your slave, my lord, and I do but obey you.'

'Really? I own that I hoped for more ... but, for a woman like you, I am patience itself. I will teach you to love, with your heart as well as your body. Here you will have nothing to do but afford me each night a greater joy than the one before.'

'Each night? But what about your other women, my lord?'

'Who, having once savoured the divine hashish, could ever be content with ordinary spices?'

Catherine could not help smiling, but her smile faded swiftly. She remembered the fierce eyes and green pupils of Zorah, the Egyptian. Eyes recalling those of the unfortunate, wicked Marie de Comborn, who had tried to murder her and whom Arnaud had stabbed to death like the venomous animal that she was. Muhammad was offering her the role of declared favourite, and Catherine guessed that not even Morayma's threats would stop the Egyptian from murder if for her sake the Caliph were to forget all his other women, and Zorah in particular.

'You do me a great honour, my lord,' she began; but just then a party of torch-bearers appeared beneath the portico, lighting up the night with ruddy, flickering reflections.

Muhammad was propped on an elbow and watched them approach, frowning.

'Who is it dares to disturb me at this hour of night?'

The torch-bearers were escorting a tall, thin young man with a short black beard and a crimson silk turban. His arrogant bearing and sumptuous clothes all denoted a personage of high rank, and Catherine suddenly recognised one of the huntsmen who had accompanied Arnaud that very morning.

'Who is it?' she asked.

'Haben-Ahmed Banu Siradj … our Grand Vizier,' Muhammad replied. 'Something serious must be afoot to bring him hither at this hour.'

All at once the man who had shown himself to Catherine under such a human light became the all-powerful Caliph, Commander of all Believers, before whom all persons, of whatever rank, were obliged to bend the knee. While Catherine took refuge beneath the cushions in the darkest corner of the arbour, hiding the white body that these men's eyes must not see, Muhammad put on his striped robe once more and stepped out to greet them. The torch-bearers knelt on seeing him, while the Grand Vizier prostrated his proud, silk-clad body on the sandy path. The flames dancing around him gave him the air of a huge, sombre ruby, but Catherine did not like the gleam in his eyes. This man was false, cruel, dangerous.

'What do you want, Haben-Ahmed? Why have you come here at this time of night?'

'Only fear for your safety, O Commander of True Believers, could impel me to disturb you at this hour, and trouble your infrequent moments of rest. Your father, the valorous Yusuf, has left Djebel-al-Tarik at the head of a tribe of Berber horsemen and is riding toward Granada. I thought I should warn you of this without delay …'

'You did well. But does anyone know why my father should have left his retreat?'

'No, All Powerful, we do not know. But if you will permit your servant's suggestion, it might be prudent for you to send someone to discover his intentions.'

'No-one but I can discover his intentions. He is my father, and my throne was his. If anyone is to go to meet him, it must be me; that is what the ties of blood dictate … and the more so if Yusuf comes here with warlike intentions.'

'But in that case, would it not be better to remain here in safety?'

'Do you take me for a woman? Go and give the necessary orders. The horses must be saddled, and the Moors are to prepare. I want fifty men to accompany me.'

'No more, Lord? This is madness.'

'Not one man more. Go, I say. I shall return to the Al Ham-ra in a few moments.'

Bent almost double, Haben-Ahmed retreated with small backward steps, apparently quite overcome with respect and awe; but Catherine had seen the gleam of wicked joy that flashed in those black eyes when Muhammad announced his intention to depart. The Caliph waited for the man to leave before returning to his new favourite. He knelt beside her and stroked her tumbled hair.

'I must leave you, my wonderful rose, and my heart grieves. But I shall make haste so that not too many nights elapse before my return.'

'Are you not venturing into great danger, my lord?'

'What is danger? To rule is to meet a new danger every single day. It lurks everywhere: in the flowers of my garden, in the cup of mead handed to you by an innocent child, in the softness of a perfume … Perhaps you yourself are the most intoxicating … and the most fatal of all these dangers!'

'Is that what you really believe?'

'No, not where you are concerned. Your eyes are too soft, and too pure. It is cruel to have to leave you …'

He kissed her long and passionately, then stood up and clapped his hands. As if by magic, Morayma's figure stepped out of the shadow of the black cypress-tree. The Caliph pointed to the young woman still covered by a pile of cushions.

'Take her back to the harem … and take great care of her. You will see that she lacks for nothing during my absence, which will not be long. Where have you installed her?'

'In the little courtyard off the baths. I did not know where to put her as yet.'

'Lodge her in Amina's old apartments, those in the Ladies' Tower. Give her as many servants as you see fit, and above all, watch over her. Your head will answer for her safety.'

Catherine saw the troubled look in Morayma's eyes. Clearly the results had surpassed her expectations. The old Jewess had not been expecting such a dazzling, such an alarming mark of esteem. The manner in which she spoke to the young woman while Muhammad strode back toward his dwelling made this quite clear. There was a new note of respect in it, which amused Catherine.

'You will have to find my veils,' Catherine told her. 'I can't dress myself in cushions …'

'I will go to find them, Light of Dawn. You must not move. The Precious Pearl of the Caliph must not exert herself at all. I will go and see to everything. Then I will have a litter brought to conduct you to your new apartments …'

She was about to leave when Catherine detained her with a gesture.

'No. I want to return as I came, on foot. I like these gardens, and the night is sweet. But … tell me, aren't these new apartments a long way from those where the Princess Zobeïda lives?'

Morayma gave a startled jump and began to tremble.

'Alas no. They are very near, and that is what alarms me. The Sultana Amina fled from there as far as the Alcazar Génil so as to put as much distance as possible between herself and her enemy. But our master refuses to believe that his favourite sister is not like himself. You will have to take great care not to anger her, Light of Dawn, otherwise your life will hang by a thread … and my own head will soon fall to the executioner's axe. Above all, avoid Zobeïda's private gardens. And if you should ever encounter the Frankish Lord whom she loves, then turn aside, veil yourself closely and run away as fast as you can.'

She herself began running at this, as if Zobeïda's Mongols were already at her heels. Catherine could not help laughing at the spectacle of the short legs scurrying along in their immense pointed slippers beneath the draperies of her veils. She looked a bit like a frightened duck. The new favourite was not afraid. In one fell swoop she had won the position of favourite and would soon be taking up her quarters in her enemy's immediate vicinity … close to Arnaud! She would be able to see him, she was certain, and this thought made the blood race through her veins. She even forgot all about the hours, pleasant as they were, that she had just passed in these dream gardens. The night of love with Muhammad was the price she had had to pay to come within touching distance of the man she had been so long seeking. And, when all was said and done, it was a small price –

A few moments later, Catherine, wrapped in her pastel veils again, set out with Morayma trotting happily along in front of her. And so she left the Architect's Garden.

It was well past midnight when Catherine and Morayma entered the harem, where the armed eunuchs stood guard. A labyrinth of flowered arches, latticed galleries and arched corridors finally led them into a huge patio where narrow alleys intersected a veritable profusion of plants and flowers. On one side of the garden all the buildings were brightly lit by innumerable oil lamps, but the far end was almost in darkness, illuminated only by a single lamp swinging above a graceful archway toward which Morayma now bent her steps. A moment later the two women heard the most appalling din from within the harem, the hubbub of a hundred shouting voices! There was the sound of oaths, insults, even groans. The sound of revolution itself! Morayma threw back her head like an old warhorse at the sound of the trumpet, frowned and muttered angrily:

'It's started again! Zorah must be up to her tricks once more!'

'What tricks?'

'That Egyptian's lunatic games! When the master chooses any other woman but herself for the night, she goes mad. She has to vent her fury on something, or someone. Usually another woman, just so that she can have the pleasure of scratching, biting, insulting. Blood has to flow before Zorah's rages are appeased.'

'And you let her behave like that?' Catherine cried indignantly.

'Let her? You don't know me. Go to your rooms; this is the door, in front of you. There are servants waiting there for you. I will come shortly to see how you are … Now follow me.'

The last part of this remark was addressed to the two eunuchs, black as ebony in their scarlet robes, who stood guard at the entrance to the patio. They followed without a word, drawing the hippopotamus-hide whips from their belts as they did so, with the automatic gestures of servants long accustomed to this sort of intervention. Catherine watched the trio hurrying off along the scented pathways with the alacrity of destiny eager to strike. Soon she found herself alone amid the gleaming, juicy foliage of the orange-trees. She felt wildly happy at finding herself alone for a moment and was in no hurry to retire for the night. The air was so sweet with its drowsy scents, and the soft echoes of a distant lute could be heard from the lighted buildings beyond.

That was the place that drew Catherine like a magnet. She stood in the shadow of the trees, unable to tear her eyes away. Those were Zobeïda's apartments, she was quite certain! One had only to see the guard of some ten black eunuchs standing by the entrance to realise that. They carried at their belts not whips but long gleaming scimitars that augured ill for anyone rash enough to approach too close.

And yet Catherine burned to know what was going on in those softly-lit rooms, the light from which glimmered through the starry jasmine fronds and lingered on the red sandy floor of the garden. An almost animal instinct told her that Arnaud was in there, behind that wall of marble and flowers, so near that had he spoken she would almost certainly have heard his voice. She sensed it perhaps from the way her heart thumped painfully, from the black bitter wave of jealousy that swept over her. The Sultan's caresses were far from her mind now, reduced to the common level of mere formalities by this sudden, brutal, devastating rage that tore at her. It had been only a poor revenge after all, a sordid piece of calculation aided and abetted by the clamour of her unsatisfied senses. Catherine was appalled to rediscover, whole, intact and tormenting, the savage bite of a jealousy, as ancient and primitive as love itself …

Then a woman's voice was heard in the night, dominating the soft chords of the music; a warm, grave voice, trembling with passion. It spoke with such powerful emotion that Catherine stood rooted to the spot, listening intently. She did not understand the words uttered by this magnificent dark velvet voice, but her whole feminine instinct told her that this was the voice of a passionate woman asking for love

She was so entranced by the mystery voice as she listened that she did not notice almost all the lights going off in Zobeïda's pavilion. The garden grew blacker and the brightness of such windows as remained lit grew softer and rosier. The singing had grown softer, not much louder than a hum … Catherine was unable to hold out another minute against her consuming curiosity, and she went closer to the Princess's pavilion.

She was beyond thinking logically. The mortal danger she was incurring did not enter her mind. Her instinct for self- preservation went no further than removing her slippers and gliding forward across the soft sand barefoot, crouching behind the bushes so as not to be seen by the guards. Thorns drove painfully into her feet, but she did not utter a sound or try to pull them out. At last, she reached the window …

Carefully, carefully, she stood up. Her eyes glanced past the green-tiled window embrasure. She had to bite her hand to stop herself crying out. Arnaud was there, just in front of her.

He sat cross-legged amid the cushions of a huge pink silk divan that took up almost half of the ravishing little room. The walls were entirely covered with green glass, and the effect was like being inside some glowing gem. His tanned skin, black hair and the wide gold-embroidered pantaloons he wore contrasted strangely with this softly feminine setting. His broad shoulders and strong muscles looked as out of place there as a battle-axe in the midst of laces and furbelows. A closely-veiled slave stood nearby, constantly refilling the large golden goblet that he held in one hand. He was handsomer than ever, but Catherine was astounded to see that his gaze was clouded and abstracted, and she realised that he was quite drunk! This shocked her. She had never seen her husband under the influence of wine. Like this, with his flushed cheeks and glittering eyes, he looked as ferocious as Gilles de Rais. The man Catherine was looking at was a stranger to her.

But she instantly recognised the woman sitting a little way off, half reclining amid the silver cushions. It was she who was singing, her long supple fingers nonchalantly plucking the strings of a little round guitar. This was Zobeïda herself … and she was lovely enough to take one's breath away.

A mass of large milky pearls covered her neck and shoulders, wound about her slender arms and ankles and scattered in the black cloud of her loosened hair. The rest of her was veiled in a jade green cloud of diaphanous material that concealed none of the charms of a perfect body. Catherine felt her rage growing as she discovered that her rival was even more ravishing than her brief glimpse earlier had led her to believe. She saw too that Zobeïda's eyes never left her prisoner, whereas he scarcely even glanced at her. He was staring into the distance, into the oblivion that drunkenness brings. But it was a joyless drunkenness, and Catherine sensed that he had brought it on deliberately.

All of a sudden Arnaud's stubborn indifference proved too much for the Moorish woman's patience. She flung her guitar aside impatiently, motioned to the slave girl to leave, and then moved closer to Arnaud, stretching out beside him and laying her head on his lap.

Catherine shivered in the dark, but Arnaud did not move. He went on deliberately, methodically draining his cup. Then Zobeïda began forcing him to notice her. Catherine saw her ring-bedecked hands slide over

Arnaud's body in a lingering caress, then creep toward his shoulders and slip around his neck. She pulled him down toward her upturned face. The goblet was empty now, and Arnaud flung it aside with a contemptuous gesture. Catherine had to close her eyes as Zobeïda lifted herself up and fastened her lips on his in a passionate kiss.

But almost at once the couple drew apart again. Arnaud got to his feet, wiping the blood away from lips that Zobeïda had bitten ... The Princess rolled onto the carpeted floor.

'Bitch!' he exclaimed angrily. 'I shall have to punish you ...'

He snatched up a hunting-crop from a low table and struck Zobeïda with it across the back and shoulders. Catherine stifled a scream, her jealousy quite forgotten in fear for Arnaud's safety. The haughty Princess would never endure such treatment! She was surely going to call for help, strike the bronze gong next to the divan to bring her eunuchs and executioners running ...

Not a bit of it ...! Moaning softly, the proud Zobeïda dragged herself across the carpet till she reached Arnaud's bare feet. She kissed them, wound her pearl-decked arms round his legs and gazed up at him with the swimming eyes of a tamed animal. She was murmuring words Catherine could not catch, but little by little their magic seemed to be working its spell on the man. Catherine saw him drop the whip. He seized Zobeïda's hair and dragged her face up to his lips, while his free hand tore off the fragile and encumbering veils. Their bodies fell, entwined, to the floor, and outside the sky, the trees and the walls began slowly circling round Catherine in a terrifying saraband.

She flattened herself, panting, against the palace wall, struggling not to swoon. She felt as if her life were oozing out of her, as if she might die right there in the darkness, only two paces from this shameless pair whose groans of pleasure resounded in her ears ... She felt convulsively for her familiar dagger, at her hip, but encountered nothing but soft muslin. Then she began groping blindly about her, in the grip of a primitive desire to kill, to be revenged. Oh, if she could but find a weapon, confront her faithless husband, like some avenging goddess, strike down this creature who loved him so abjectly, with the debased passion of a slave girl! ... But instead of the weapon she was looking for, Catherine's hand seized a creeper, the thorns of which pierced her hand so painfully that she had to smother a scream. But the pain miraculously brought her to her senses again. Just then, the sound of voices, of people running to and fro, brought her sharply back to reality. She recognised Morayma's nasal voice and slipped furtively away from her hiding-place, stealing forward under cover of the shrubs and trees, until she reached the central alley again, just as Morayma herself appeared.

The old Jewess cast a suspicious glance over Catherine.

'Where have you been? I was looking for you ...'

'It was so … lovely in the garden … I didn't want to go inside yet,' Catherine stammered, with some effort.

Morayma took her by the wrist without a word and led her toward the Ladies' Tower. When they reached the lighted colonnade she turned and scrutinised her prisoner frowning. '

'You look deathly pale! You aren't sickening, are you?'

'No. A little tired perhaps.'

'In that case, I can't think why you are not already in bed. Now, come!'

Catherine followed obediently till they came to a suite of rooms. She did not even see them. All she could see in her mind's eye was the love scene she had just witnessed, and her heart bled inwardly. Morayma, who had been expecting cries of joy at the luxury the Caliph's love had conferred upon this slave-girl, was quite mystified when Catherine sank down upon a silken mattress, almost the moment she entered the room, and wept as though her heart would break.

The mistress of the harem was wise enough not to ask too many questions. She merely dismissed the cloud of hovering servants with a peremptory sweep of the hand and then sat patiently at the foot of the bed to wait till the tears were finished.

She attributed Catherine's behaviour, philosophically, to the strong and conflicting emotions of a crowded day. But Catherine wept for a long time; she wept till weariness itself put an end to her sorrows. No sooner did her sobbing cease than she drifted into the heavy sleep of an exhausted animal … Morayma herself had fallen asleep a moment or two before, and sat nodding at the foot of the bed. The summer's night, punctuated by the soft tolling of the irrigation bell, spread its dark mantle more securely about the town of Granada.

Catherine's room was so crowded with people when she first opened her tear-swollen lids that she instantly closed them again, convinced that this was all a part of her feverish dreams. But then the feel of cool, damp compresses on her eyes convinced her that it was all real. She was awake. A purring voice spoke up close beside her.

'Now, wake up, Light of Dawn, my precious pearl! Wake and see the glory that is yours!'

Catherine opened her eyes mistrustfully. The glory in question turned out to consist of an army of slaves kneeling, arms laden with objects of one kind or another, all over the floor of the room. They were offering her silks, muslins of every hue, heavy gold jewellery set with stones of barbaric size and splendour, coffers of perfumes and rare oils and essences, birds with long trailing coloured feathers that looked like great dazzling clusters of gems. But what most caught the new favourite's eye was the massive shape of Fatima, the stout Ethiopian herself.

Fatima sat cross-legged upon a huge cushion, hands clasped across her red-silk-draped belly, black face split by a great moon smile. She watched Catherine awaken with a look of triumphant joy. A young, coffee-coloured slave girl was bending over Catherine, bathing her eyes. When the Ethiopian noticed Catherine staring at her, she stood up and bowed with astonishing suppleness, so that the absurd peacock's feathers in her hair swept the ground.

'What are you doing there?' Catherine asked coldly.

'I have come to salute the rising star, O splendid one! The talk in the bazaars is of nothing but the Caliph's new beloved, of the rare pearl that it was my privilege to discover ...'

'And I suppose you came here at dawn to claim your reward?' Catherine asked.

But her contemptuous tone did not wipe the smile from Fatima's face. Evidently the Negress was carried away by such complete, overwhelming happiness that she could think of nothing else.

'Heavens no! I came to bring you a gift!'

'A gift? From you?'

'Not exactly. A gift from Abou-the-doctor! You know, Light of Dawn, we seriously underestimated the beauty and simplicity of that man's soul!'

The mention of her friend's name dispelled Catherine's indifference as if by magic. There was something comforting about the thought of Abou in this mire of rage, pain and disgust where she was plunged. She raised herself on one elbow, dismissing the slave-girl who knelt a little way off.

'What do you mean?'

Fatima's black hand indicated a huge pannier of golden straw on which was piled the most magnificent mountain of fruits Catherine had ever seen, most of them quite unknown to her.

'He came round at daybreak to bring me this and beg me to take it to you at the Al Hamra at the earliest opportunity.'

'Asked *you*? But there is no reason why he should feel grateful toward you, surely? You tricked him!'

'That is why I say that Abou-al-Khayr has a noble soul. Not merely did he come to see me, but he showed himself full of gratitude for what I have done. "You have made it possible for me to assure my Caliph's happiness without even having thought of such a thing," he told me, quite tearfully, "and henceforth the Commander of the Faithful will remember Abou in his prayers, the man who sacrificed him a priceless jewel."' Fatima turned toward her, her voice rising in excitement. 'As for yourself, he begs you to accept these fruits and honour each of them with the contact of your lips. Thus they may serve to strengthen your heart, which may be agitated by your good fortune, ease your fatigue and help give you the radiant beauty that will make your happiness last. He assures me that these fruits have magic powers for you alone!'

Fatima would have cheerfully gone on pronouncing well-turned phrases of flattery, but Catherine had suddenly realised that this dawn offering must contain more than just fruit, however magnificent. She forced herself to smile, suddenly longing to be rid of all these people, starting with Fatima herself.

'Thank my former master for his kindness. Tell him I never doubted his generosity, and that I shall do everything possible to conquer the heart of the man I love forever. If I do not succeed, I shall not be afraid to die,' she said, boldly playing on the double meaning of her words.

Seeing that her visitor showed no signs of leaving, and that the slaves all appeared frozen in their gift-bearing attitudes, Catherine called Morayma, who had just entered the room, and whispered in her ear.

'I am still tired, Morayma. I would like to sleep longer so as to get my strength back and look beautiful when my master returns. Is that possible?'

'Nothing is impossible now, O rose amid the roses! You have only to give the word. You will be left to rest as long as you like. I like to see you so sensible, so anxious to please! You will go far!'

Her henna-stained hand pointed to Catherine's eyes, still swollen with weeping.

'It is well the Master is absent! You will have all the time you need to get back the radiance of happiness! Leave the room, all you others!'

'Come and see me again soon, Fatima,' Catherine said to the fat Negress, who was withdrawing with the rest, looking much crestfallen. 'I shall doubtless be needing your skills, and I shall always be pleased to see you.'

It needed only this to make the drooped peacock plumes recover their former bouncing glory. Swelling with pride, already seeing herself as the new favourite's chosen confidante, perhaps even the new Sultana's if Catherine succeeded in giving the Caliph a son, Fatima withdrew majestically, the bearers of royal gifts in a troupe behind her.

'Now sleep,' said Morayma, pulling the sweeping pink curtains around Catherine's bed. 'And don't eat too many fruits,' she warned, as Catherine pulled the basket toward her. 'They can make you swell up if you eat too many of them. And as for figs ...'

But the sentence was cut short as Morayma suddenly flung herself face down on the floor, palms and face hidden. For the Princess Zobeïda had suddenly appeared on the threshold, framed in the graceful curves of a Moorish arch.

Her hair hung loose to her hips and she wore nothing but a simple green-blue silk robe belted in gold. But despite her casual attire she was the image of aristocratic arrogance. Catherine's blood seethed when Morayma whispered:

'Get up and kneel! The Princess is here! …'

Nothing on Earth would have induced the young woman to do as she was bid. Was she to prostrate herself on the ground before this heathen woman who had dared to take her own husband away from her? Not even to save her life! The hate she felt for this woman seared her to the heart. She stayed as she was, flinging back her delicate head proudly, and watched the other woman approach, her eyes narrowing angrily.

'For pity's sake … for my sake as well as yours, kneel …!' Morayma whispered. But Catherine merely shrugged.

Meanwhile Zobeïda had reached the bed. Her large dark eyes examined the occupant with more curiosity than anger.

'Don't you hear what she says? You should kneel in front of me!'

'Why should I? I don't even know who you are!'

'I am your master's sister, woman, and as such I am your ruler. In my presence you are not permitted to raise yourself above the dust that you are! Get up and kneel!'

'No,' Catherine said distinctly. 'I am quite comfortable as I am, and I have no wish to get up. But I am not stopping you from sitting down.'

She saw a gust of anger darken the beautiful smooth face, and for a second she trembled for her safety. But no … Zobeïda controlled herself. Her red lips curled in a scornful smile and she shrugged.

'Your good fortune has gone to your head, woman; and this time I am prepared to be indulgent. But you will soon discover that I reign here in my brother's absence. And furthermore, kneeling or lying down, you are still no more than the dust beneath my feet! In future I warn you to be more respectful. Another time, I might be less patient. I am in a good humour today.'

Now it was Catherine's turn to struggle with the anger raging within her. In a good humour? And she knew only too well what was the reason for this good humour. One had only to look at the Princess's negligent dress, her loosened hair, the loose garment slipped over her naked body and the blue shadows under her eyes … How long was it since she had left Arnaud's arms?

Abruptly the Princess's laughter shattered the threatening silence.

'If you could only see yourself! You look like a cat about to scratch! Truly, if you were not a complete stranger to me, I would suppose that you hated me. Where are you from, yellow-haired woman?'

'I was captured by barbarian pirates and sold into slavery in Almeria,' Catherine recited.

'That does not tell me where you come from. Are you French?'

'Yes, indeed. I was born in Paris.'

'Paris! … The travellers whom my brother pleases to entertain here say that Paris was once a city without equal for its wisdom and wealth, but that war and poverty are destroying it more each day. Is that why its inhabitants are sold into slavery?'

'I fear you are somewhat ignorant of my country's affairs,' Catherine said curtly, 'and I should find it difficult to explain them to you.'

'What does it matter? I am not in the least interested! In fact, with a few exceptions, you strike me as fit for little else but slavery. I shall never understand the masculine taste for your white skins and yellow locks. I find it all so insipid!'

Zobeïda stretched and yawned, with a movement supple as a cat's, and turned her back on Catherine. She was almost at the door when she turned.

'Ah, one thing more. Listen to what I have to say, woman, and understand it well if you value your life; my brother's whim – which will not last for long, you may be quite certain – has installed you in a sultana's palace, close to my own apartments. But if you hope to please the Sultan for many nights to dome, take care not to come near them. Only the slaves in my employment, or those I may invite, have the right to enter them. I shall not tolerate a foreigner, a heathen, wandering about there. If you are seen near my pavilion, you die!'

Catherine did not reply. She understood that this severity was born of fear of a woman from the same country as Arnaud. For a moment she was tempted to tell her rival what she thought of her, but she restrained herself. Why bother to arouse this girl's dangerous wrath? A duel of words with Zobeïda would not give her back Arnaud. But she could not resist murmuring: 'Have you a treasure hidden in your dwelling?'

'You are too talkative and too inquisitive, yellow-haired woman! And you are trying my patience. Thank Allah that I have no desire to distress my brother by breaking a toy of his before he has had time to get weary of it! But you had better hold your tongue and keep your eyes veiled if you want to keep both the one and the others! Blind and dumb, you would be fit only for the stray dogs in the market-place. Remember: don't come near my dwellings! Not that you will be my neighbour for long, anyway ...'

'And why not?'

'Because you disappoint me. They are all talking about you in that palace, and I was curious to contemplate such an extraordinary beauty, but ...'

As she spoke, Zobeïda returned to Catherine's side. Her nonchalant walk and feline movements were irresistibly reminiscent of a black panther. She leant forward now, and Catherine's heart missed a beat, for the Princess had selected an enormous pink juicy peach from the basket. Her sharp white teeth bit into it greedily. Catherine was not certain what the basket contained, and she shuddered to think that the Princess might discover it first. Was there something buried under the fruit ... or inside the fruit? One could never tell, with Abou-al-Khayr. She watched wide-eyed as Zobeïda ate the peach, juice streaming down her fingers. When she had finished, the Princess threw the stone at Catherine as if she were a rubbish bin and finished her sentence:

'But you are not as beautiful as I expected! No, really, I know many lovelier women than you!'

She leant forward again, chose a black fig with purple gleams and slowly, languidly, strolled away again. Wild with rage, Catherine snatched up a large melon and prepared to hurl it after her. But the sea-green silk had vanished, and Catherine let fall the melon as Morayma finally struggled back to her feet, moaning pitiably. She had stayed prostrate on the floor throughout the whole conversation, because Zobeïda had forgotten to order her to get up again. She had been so appalled by Catherine's audacity that she had chosen to make herself as small as possible, flattening herself into the silk rug. Her joints ached, however, after kneeling for so long.

'Allah!' she groaned. 'My bones are crackling like dry tinder! Now whatever possessed you, Light of Dawn, to stand up to the formidable Zobeïda like that? Truly, I am amazed that you are alive! The previous night must have been kind to the Princess for her to act so graciously!'

These evocative words were more than Catherine could bear.

'Go,' she hissed between clenched teeth. 'Get out! Vanish from my eyes, unless you want me to complain to the Caliph about you on his return …'

'What's the matter with you?' the old Jewess protested. 'I did not say anything offensive.'

'I want peace, do you hear? Peace! Now go, and don't come back till I call you. I have already said that I wanted to sleep. To *sleep*. Is that clear?'

'Yes, good, good. I am going …'

Morayma was impressed by the new favourite's angry tones, and she judged it prudent to get out of range. Left alone with her rage, Catherine wasted no time expressing it further. She pulled the basket across and began emptying it, piling all the fruits up on the bed. They were many and various, and she had to go right down to the bottom to find what she was looking for, without quite knowing the form it would take.

Catherine found three things fastened to the golden basket, one of which at least made her exclaim with joy: her beloved sparrow-hawk dagger, faithful companion of her darkest moments. Two other things came with it: a little glass phial in a silver case and a letter, which she hurriedly read.

'When the traveller enters the deep forest where the wild beasts prowl he needs a weapon to defend himself. You did a rash thing in running off without letting me know, because I would have chosen a rather different fate for you … less dazzling but safer. But he who seeks to combat the will of Allah is a fool, and you have but followed your destiny. Your servants watch over you from afar. Josse has joined the Vizier's guard and now dwells in the Alcazaba, near the palace. But Gauthier finds it hard to play the role of dumb servitor that I have assigned him. He follows me everywhere, and I am thinking of paying many visits to the Commander of the Faithful when he returns. Till then, venture nothing. Patience, too, is a weapon.

'As for the phial, it contains a swift-acting poison. A wise man must foresee failure ... and the Princess's Mongol torturers are all too skilful at playing symphonies of suffering on poor human harps –'

There was, naturally, no signature. Catherine hurriedly burned the note in the large bronze perfume-burner in the centre of the room. The note was written in French, but the palace held too many surprises to risk keeping it ... Catherine watched the scrap of paper twist, blacken and shrivel to a fine ash. She felt infinitely better, her heart was lighter and her mind cooler. Now that she was armed, her own position seemed much improved. She had the means to strike that accursed Zobeïda and wrench her from Arnaud's arms forever, so long as she was prepared to follow her into death.

Catherine clutched the cold steel of the dagger to her heart and slipped down among her cushions again. She needed to think calmly about her next move.

12: The Panther and the Serpent

Marie, the young French odalisque, sat on a huge embroidered leather cushion eating a rose-petal sherbet with the grace of a young cat. She was silently observing Catherine, who lay on her stomach, chin in her palms, reflecting sombrely on her fate. At this siesta hour the whole palace was sunk in silence and peace. Only the slaves, whose function was to wave their immense feathered fans over the sleeping beauties, seemed to move at all. The plants themselves stood petrified in the blazing heat outside.

Zobeïda's visit, now three days past, had shattered all Catherine's plans. The Princess, not content to forbid her new neighbour access to her apartments, had taken special precautions against her.

When Catherine had tried to leave her apartment to walk in the garden with her servants she had found two lances crossed, barring her path, while a guttural voice commanded her to return to her room. But when she had protested against this forced imprisonment, the eunuch who had been charged with her protection informed her that during the Caliph's absence his most precious favourite was to be guarded night and day lest any harm should befall her.

'Harm? In this garden?'

'The sun burns, water drowns, insects sting and the viper brings death!' the Negro answered, unmoved. 'My orders are precise. You must stay in your own rooms.'

'Till when?'

'Till the Master returns.'

Catherine did not press the point. Zobeïda's strange solicitude was alarming, for she had no illusions about the Princess's feelings for her: Zobeïda instinctively hated her quite as much as she hated the Princess. What other explanation could there be for this close guard, these severe restrictions? Zobeïda could have no inkling of the bonds between herself and Arnaud. As far as the proud Princess was concerned, she was just another slave, even if the Prince's whim had raised her temporarily above the rest. Was she afraid that her captive would become too interested in the favourite if he caught sight of her? Perhaps it was the fact that Catherine belonged to the same race that prompted these precautions. Plain fear of the executioners would normally have been sufficient to keep the favourite far from the Princess's apartments … Catherine had been striving for an answer to all these questions for three days now, but in vain. When Morayma was questioned she seemed strangely discreet. She bent almost double, as if searching for something almost too small to see, and when she looked at Catherine, her eyes were full of fear. Her visits too were remarkably brief. She came to see if there was anything Catherine wanted and then vanished with evident haste. Catherine did not understand what was going on at all. Her constant fear of learning that Zobeïda, and Arnaud with her, had left for the distant lands of the Mahgreb, was slowly but surely breaking down her resistance. The nights were the worst time. Then, her wild imagination fed her jealousy to such a pitch that there were moments when Catherine was on the point of flinging herself into the first rash enterprise that entered her head. Then, on the fourth morning, Marie-Aïcha had arrived, closely veiled according to tradition, but smiling.

'I thought you might be bored,' the young woman said, pushing back her veil, 'and Morayma did not object to my coming here!'

'And the eunuchs let you through?'

'Why not? Their orders are to stop you going out, but you can receive visitors.'

Marie's presence had done Catherine good. She was a friendly creature, and besides, she came from the same part of France: Burgundy. Catherine had been astonished to find, as Marie told her own story, that it had more than one similarity to her own. It seemed this pretty daughter of a Beaune winegrower had had the misfortune to catch the eye of one of the Duke's sergeants. This man enjoyed the Duke's favour, and he had asked that Marie Vermeil be given to him in marriage. Thus an order had reached the little home in Beaune that she should prepare for her wedding. Marie might have accepted the situation philosophically, for the sergeant, Colas Laigneau, was a fine lad, but she had long been in love with her own cousin, Jehan Goriot, to whom she had plighted her troth.

Jehan was something of a rascal, short of money but never of girls, and always dreaming of fabulous adventures. He had an agile tongue and a fertile imagination, and when she was with him Marie felt she was dreaming wide awake. She adored him just as he was, despite his innumerable infidelities, and when the Duke's order came to say that she must wed Colas, she had lost her head, begged Jehan to take her away and flee with her to those southern lands of sunshine and flowers about which he had never stopped prattling since a wandering minstrel had first spoken of them to him.

Jehan loved Marie, after his own fashion. She was beautiful and good. He desired her ardently, and the idea of running away with her, especially if it meant taking her from someone else, attracted him. But he had no money. It was then that they had committed their crime: Marie had borrowed half her father's savings, naturally without telling him, whereas Jehan had pilfered the house of the bailiff, who had gone to Meursault for the day to inspect his lands there. That very night, a dark night, the two lovers had fled toward the Saône, never to return. But Marie, who had believed she was escaping to happiness, was soon disenchanted.

It was true that Jehan had taught her about love, and Marie had formed a taste for it, but in giving herself to him, she had gradually lost all value in her lover's eyes. Moreover, she had loved him too much, and he had finally grown bored with her. Eventually the fine black eyes of the beauties of the Midi had cast their spell over the youth, who now had only one idea in his mind: to get rid of Marie, who kept talking to him of marriage. And he had found the most abject of means to achieve his end: aware of the appeal of his fiancée's rounded beauty, he had sold her to a Greek merchant in Marseilles. The merchant had abducted the girl at night and taken her on his ship to the slave market at Alexandria, where she had been purchased by the Saracen purveyor to the Caliph of Granada.

'And that is how I came to be here,' Marie concluded frankly. 'I have often regretted that Burgundian marriage; that Colas might not have been a bad man after all, and I could have been happy!'

'And Jehan?' Catherine asked, fascinated.

There was a murderous gleam in the girl's eyes as she replied: 'If I ever find him again, I shall kill him!' And she said this in such a quiet voice that Catherine did not doubt that she meant every word. After this, encouraged by Marie's confidences, she told this new friend her own story.

It took a long time to tell, but Marie listened from start to finish without interrupting once. It wasn't till Catherine had finished her recital that Marie sighed:

'What a fabulous story! So the mysterious Frankish prisoner is your husband! And here was I ... believing you were just a poor ordinary girl like me! I remember now where I saw you before: it was at Dijon, when my father took me there to the fair. I was still little more than a child, but I took away this dazzling vision of a lady as beautiful and as brilliant as the sun.'

'You must find me greatly changed!' Catherine remarked, a shade bitterly.

'Changed?' the girl said gravely. 'Certainly you have changed, but in those days your fine clothes and jewels almost detracted from your beauty. Now, it shows more! You are different now, that is all.'

'Now, please,' Catherine said gently, 'don't treat me like a great lady! Just as a friend; for that is what I need.'

With this, the ice between them was broken, and the two young women found themselves allies, as close as if bound by blood ties. Marie, who had come to see Catherine partly out of curiosity, partly out of boredom, now found herself devoted to her body and soul, for better or for worse.

'Promise me, if you escape, that you will take me with you, and I will do everything in my power to help! You must suffer dreadfully on account of Zobeïda!'

'If I leave this palace and this town, you will come with me, I swear it.'

Then the girl gave her new friend some highly interesting information.

'You are in danger,' she said. 'If the Caliph does not return, your life will be worthless.'

'Why hasn't he returned already?'

'Because Haben-Ahmed Banu Siradj, the Grand Vizier, hates him almost as much as he desires Zobeïda, who was his lover before the arrival of the Frankish knight. He wants to seize the throne and share it with the Princess … and this so-called expedition that Yusuf, the former Caliph, is said to have mounted against his son sounds not quite credible to me. The two men do not like each other, but Yusuf is weary of power. Only someone as credulous as Muhammad would believe that his father wanted to win back the throne he freely gave up. He is credulous and Banu Siradj is cunning. I fear that the master may have gone out to meet a well-armed ambush.'

'In that case,' Catherine said, going pale, 'I am lost.'

'Not quite. Muhammad may be credulous but he is brave. He is a great warrior, and he may yet win the encounter. Which is why Zobeïda has done no more than put you under constant guard. If her brother returns, she will appear to have done no more than keep a strict watch, a trifle too strict perhaps, over her beloved brother's favourite. And should the news of the Caliph's death be brought, you would not live an hour!'

'Why? What have I done to her?'

'You have done nothing. But Zorah the Egyptian has taken care of that. She is popular with the Princess, toward whom she always behaves in the most nauseatingly servile manner. And since Zorah wants your death at any price, she has showed some imagination … one might almost say genius, since she seems unwittingly to have stumbled on a vital truth!'

'What truth?'

'Only one person dares oppose the Caliph: Zobeïda. And the one way to achieve this is to play on her jealousy regarding the Frankish captain. Zorah has made use of the fact that you come from the same country and hinted to the Princess that you are in love with her prisoner and want to speak to him!'

Catherine gave a cry of terror, hastily stifled by a shaking hand.

'She said that? My God! I am lost! How is it that I have not been handed over to the executioners already?'

'That is certainly what Zorah was hoping for, knowing Zobeïda's temperament. But the Princess is not mad. To kill you after the Caliph has fallen passionately in love with you, in his absence, would be to admit her implication in the Banu Siradj plot and her hope that she would not see him return alive. If he returns he will find you safe; but be certain that you will not live long to enjoy his caresses. It is not the executioners you will have to fear. Zobeïda will contrive some well-organised accident so that suspicion cannot fall on her. She knows her brother well enough to realise that beneath his poetic gentleness he hides a streak of savagery quite worthy of his own sister! His rages are rare but dangerous; and his passion for you is boundless … if I am to judge by all this!'

Marie pointed at a roll of paper covered with a velvet sleeve studded with sapphires, which Muhammad had sent his beloved. During the past few days Catherine had received a white plume fastened by a buckle of immense pink pearls, a gold cage full of blue parakeets and an extraordinary work of art: a gold peacock with an outspread tail encrusted with gems of every size and colour.

'All this is reassuring,' said Marie. 'It proves that the Commander of the Faithful is still with us … and may Allah preserve him!'

Just then, the arrival of the slaves bringing their meal interrupted the exchange of confidences. But while Marie fell upon the dishes with every appearance of satisfaction, Catherine sank into a deep reverie that the other girl was careful not to disturb. Catherine realised that her situation was even worse than she had supposed. The news of Muhammad's death might arrive any minute … and what then? God alone knew how many minutes more she had to live. She would not even have the chance to let Arnaud know, and she might die a few feet away from him without his even suspecting the fact. And how would she call upon her friends' help in such circumstances? Josse was at the Alcazaba, among the Caliph's troops, but how could she ever get a message to him? Could she summon Fatima to her and give her a letter for Abou-al-Khayr? Would it reach him? In any case, would there be time?

Marie had finished her sherbet and now started nibbling at some fat dates encrusted with sugar. She was determined not to disturb Catherine. But just then Catherine turned round abruptly and looked the girl straight in the eyes.

'Since that's the case,' she said calmly, 'there isn't a moment to lose. I must act today.'

'What are you going to do?'

Catherine did not answer at once. She allowed herself a moment's hesitation before confiding her plans – because, after all, it was her own life that would be at stake, and this girl had been a virtual stranger to her only three hours earlier. But little Marie looked at her with such clear, candid eyes that Catherine's slight twinge of mistrust vanished. If she could not trust this child, then she would never be able to trust anyone again. And time was pressing. She made up her mind.

'I must get out of here and see my husband …'

'Obviously. But how? Unless …'

'Unless?'

'Unless we changed clothes and you left instead of me. There is one good thing about this costume: one would need second sight to see just what is hidden beneath all these veils. Especially as our skin is the same colour, and if we keep our eyes down, no-one can see their colour.'

Catherine's heart beat faster, but less erratically. Marie had quite spontaneously suggested doing the one thing she had been a little nervous of asking of her. She took the girl's hand in her own.

'Do you realise you would be risking your life in all this, Marie? If anyone came while I was out …'

'I should say that I had been attacked and tied up. It is not difficult to tie someone up here; there is plenty of fine, strong cloth around. If someone comes, I shall be in the clear … almost. And if no-one comes, you can untie me when you get back, and when you have seen your husband!'

'How could you explain my absence if Morayma suddenly appeared?'

'I would say that you were stifling in here and absolutely had to get some fresh air.'

'Even to the point of tying you up and borrowing your clothes?'

'Why not? If you only knew the ridiculous ideas that the boredom of this harem life puts into women's heads, you would know that nothing much astonishes Morayma any more! But be careful all the same. What you want to do is extremely dangerous. Anyone who tries to speak to the Frankish knight is risking death. If Zobeïda catches you, nothing, not even the thought of her brother's anger, would save you from her fury. In moments like those she is deaf and blind to everything save her own hatred.'

'Too bad. He who nothing ventures, nothing wins! What is bothering me is how I am to get past the guards. Zobeïda's private garden is the other side of this building, isn't it? And I have heard that my husband lives in a separate pavilion there …'

'That's right. It is known as the Prince's Pavilion, because it was built for one of Sultan Muhammad V's brothers. Its walls stand beside a pool of blue water … and the Frankish lord leaves it only to hunt, under heavy guard. Zobeïda fears that the attractions of his own country might prove stronger than her own, and she has appointed the Grand Vizier his guard in chief.'

'But I thought he loved her?'

'A typical touch of cruelty on Zobeïda's part. Banu Siradj hates his rival and doubtless hopes, once he is Sultan, that he will be able to get rid of him. But for the moment the most important thing to him is to please the Princess. She could not have chosen a better guard, and she knows it. But to get back to our plan. It is not so difficult to get into Zobeïda's garden. There is near my room a little door that is always kept locked but can be opened with a steel blade and a little skill. It opens into the gardens. There is a wall between Zobeïda's gardens, but it is not very high and a supple person could easily climb it with the help of the overhanging cypress-tree. You should find that perfectly simple after all the things you have done.'

'Yes, that would be easy enough. But if the wall is so easy to climb, why doesn't my husband climb over it too?'

'Because the Prince's Palace is closely guarded by Zobeïda's most faithful eunuchs. There are many of them, blindly faithful, and their scimitars are sharp.'

This was not encouraging. Catherine chose to ignore this unpleasant detail, however, and made Marie repeat over and over again how to reach her room without attracting attention, and then how to find the famous little door that the young odalisque described in minute detail.

'You seem to know it very well,' Catherine remarked.

'There are some superb plums growing in the Caliph's garden, reserved for his table alone ... which I adore!' Marie explained.

Catherine could not help laughing. The two friends went on chatting away, waiting for dusk to fall.

The plan they had worked out could not be executed in broad daylight. But the intervening hours seemed long to Catherine, who, at the thought of the agonies of jealousy that each night brought her, was all the more eager to approach her husband.

She knew all too well how Zobeïda whiled away the night.

She watched the day fading with a feeling of real relief. When her slaves brought the dinner, she ordered them to put it down and leave her.

'We will return to help you retire for the night, mistress,' said the principal servant.

'No. I will go to sleep by myself tonight. My friend will stay here for a little while longer. We want to be left in peace. Tell Morayma that she need not pay me her evening visit. I need nothing at all, except peace and quiet. You may put out some of the lamps. The bright light upsets me.'

'As you wish, mistress. I wish you a good night.'

As soon as the slaves had gone, leaving the two women in soothing semi-darkness, Catherine and Marie nibbled a few minced balls of mutton and some honey cakes, then they set about putting their plan into execution. Marie took off all her clothes and handed them to Catherine, who gave her her own. She was much the same height as Catherine but somewhat plumper. She had to tie the belt of the midnight blue pantaloons somewhat tighter about her hips. Then, with the help of some long strips of torn veil, the two friends made the bonds that were to keep Marie bound and helpless in Catherine's bed.

'Don't forget to gag me,' Marie said. 'Otherwise, it won't be convincing!'

A silk scarf was found, but Marie made one last recommendation before her mouth was gagged.

'Whatever you do, stay veiled, even if the veil is somewhat hindering in climbing walls. If you don't show your face your position will be less serious if you are caught. Not much less, but it's worth raising the odds as far as possible on your side. And now may God go with you!'

'And with you too, Marie. And don't worry, I shan't forget my promise to you, unless I die.'

After making sure that her prisoner was not too uncomfortable, for her captivity might last for several hours, Catherine bent over and kissed her on the forehead and saw Marie's eyes glow in the gloom. Then she carefully drew the rose-coloured curtains round the bed and stood back to examine the effect. The light silk coverlet came as high as Marie's nose, and in the shadowy room the illusion was perfect ...

Catherine wrapped her friend's blue veil around herself. All she wore beneath were pantaloons and a brief short-sleeved jacket that covered her breasts, but nothing more. Despite the veil she could move quite freely. After a whispered farewell she walked toward the door.

The guards put up their lances automatically, but she murmured to them in as close an imitation of the girl's voice as she could manage:

'I am returning to my room. Let me pass. I am Aïcha.'

One of the eunuchs turned his large black face and flat nose toward her and sneered:

'You are returning very late, Aïcha! What is the favourite doing?'

'Sleeping,' Catherine said, disturbed by these questions.

'I have to make certain that you are not carrying anything away with you,' he said, resting his lance against the wall. 'The favourite has received some magnificent gifts ...'

The black hands began feeling her over with a persistence and insolence that began to raise serious doubts in Catherine's mind as to his total lack of virility. She already knew that there were cases where these repulsive creatures had been incompletely castrated, which left them with strange appetites. He must belong to this category. As he started undoing her belt to continue his investigations further she lost her temper.

'Let me go,' she said. 'Or I'll call out.'

'Who will come? My comrade is deaf and dumb and hates women.'

'The favourite!' Catherine said boldly. 'She is my friend. She will come if I call, and then it will be too bad for you! She would be sure to ask the Caliph for your head, and I am sure he would not refuse her such a modest gift.'

She had the satisfaction of seeing the black face go grey with terror. The eunuch's hands fell, he seized his lance and shrugged.

'So, one can't even joke a bit … Get along with you, then, and be quick about it … We shall meet again …'

She did not need to be told twice. She drew her veil more closely round her and stepped into the darkened patio. She crossed it confidently, passed through a latticed mirador and found herself in the heart of the harem itself, in the hall of the Two Sisters, thus named after the two huge twin tiles that formed the central ornament. This was when things began to get dangerous, because there were several women in this dazzling room, diapered in red, blue and gold, sparkling with iridescent stalactites like a marine grotto beneath the ethereal cupolas worked in honeycomb carvings. The women lay on cushions, rugs or divans, and chatted, ate sweets or dozed. Some of them spent the night there, because they had no specific room to themselves. The whole scene made a sumptuous, warm, vivid picture.

To Catherine's great relief, none of the women paid any heed to her. Except when one of them was summoned to the Caliph, the harem women were not in the least concerned with their companions' activities. Their lives were all identical, all founded on the same pattern of indolence and tedium.

Catherine crossed the room, mentally repeating Marie's directions over to herself, not only to avoid losing her way but also to give the impression of being perfectly at home. She just had to follow the little pillars. Beyond stood the jewel of the Al Hamra in general and the harem in particular; the Court of Lions, a dream in white-sculpted marble around a fountain guarded by twelve marble lions with mouths spouting sparkling streams of water into intersecting canals that ran along at the level of the red-tiled floor enamelled in green and gold. Huge orange-trees scented the patio where the silence was troubled only by the singing fountains, the gentle sliding of water from the marble pool. The place was so beautiful that, for all her haste, Catherine stopped for a moment, enchanted. She imagined herself for a moment alone with Arnaud in such a place … How wonderful it must be to be in love in such surroundings: to listen to the murmur of the fountains and go to sleep at last under the velvet sky with immense stars streaming a faint silver light onto the shining, multi-coloured tiles roofing the galleries.

But Catherine was not there to dream. She shook off the magic of the place, and slowly, silently walked round the arcades. There was not a soul about in the court where the lions, crouched on their rigid paws, mounted their silent, pouting guard. Marie's room was somewhere here. She found it easily enough but did not enter. Instead she hastened down an almost hidden passage where at last she discovered the little garden door.

The place was dark. One oil lamp hanging some way off threw only a flickering light, and Catherine had some difficulty in finding the lock. She groped about, panicked at not finding it at once. How was she to force the lock in this semi-darkness? But gradually her eyes grew accustomed to it. She could see the outline of the lock more clearly. She pulled back the wrought-iron latch and then inserted the point of her dagger, which she had kept hidden in her gold belt, into the rudimentary lock. At last she felt it yield. The cedar door swung open soundlessly, revealing the huge gardens muffled in darkness.

Catherine slipped through hastily. The place was deserted, and she enjoyed slipping across the soft-sanded paths. Soon the barrier of cypresses appeared, and the low wall that enclosed Zobeïda's private domain. It appeared to be of recent construction, due no doubt to the presence of the Frankish knight. Climbing it was child's play to Catherine. She was still as supple and agile as when, still adolescent, she had run about the quays of Paris with her friend, Landry Pigasse, and climbed up to join the stonemasons building the church towers.

She stopped on top of the wall to take stock of her whereabouts. Beyond a pool of water she saw an elegant portico flanked by a square tower that was known as the Ladies' Tower and that formed part of Zobeïda's private suite. Beyond stretched the vague outlines of the hills of Granada, for this tower was part of the ramparts. There were lights shining beneath the portico, where various slaves stood idly. Catherine looked away, and some distance off, on the right, she recognised with a pounding heart the little pavilion described by Marie and known as the Prince's Pavilion. It stood surrounded by lemon-trees and cypresses and gazed at its reflection in a calm pool silvered by moonlight. It had slender columns and an elegant porch. Lights there revealed the threatening silhouettes of the eunuch guard and their gleaming scimitars. They were pacing to and fro in front of the building, with slow, measured, almost mechanical steps, their yellow turbans and billowing embroidered costumes reflected in the gleaming pool with its scattering of water lilies.

Catherine stared at the pavilion for a moment, hoping to distinguish a familiar silhouette within. How was she to know if Arnaud was really there, and if he was alone? How was she to enter the little palace if its occupant was not leaving it all that night? Questions that were difficult to answer ...

But Catherine had long ago acquired the habit of leaving the thorniest problems unanswered and plunging into adventures with no thought for the consequences. She climbed down from the wall without a sound. She hesitated for a second as to which direction to follow. The threatening appearance of the guard of eunuchs prevented her approaching too close from that quarter. But she could hear soft music issuing from the Ladies' Tower. How to find out where Arnaud was?

As she reached the skirt of a tall row of cypresses that ran almost along the edge of the pool she suppressed an exclamation of joy: destiny had answered her yet again. Arnaud had just appeared beneath the entrance to the tower. He was alone. He wore an ample white robe, belted in gold, and walked slowly forward to the pool and sat down on the marble rim. This time he was not drunk, but Catherine's heart smote her as she observed how lonely and bored he looked. She had never seen him look so sullen, and the light of an oil lamp hanging close by lit up his face, feature by feature ... But he was alone, truly alone. What better chance could she have? Dropping her slippers, which impeded her running, she raced toward him.

But brutal hands seized her at precisely the moment when she was about to appear in the lighted area near the pool. The shock caused her to cry out, and Arnaud turned round. She was trying hard to escape from the vice of the black arms seizing her, but she was not strong enough. The two eunuchs who had seized her were a pair of gigantic Sudanese. One of them alone would have been able to master her with a single hand. But in her terror she was still aware of only one thing: her husband! He was there, quite near. He stood up; he was coming forward. Beneath the veil that was choking her now, because the Sudanese had pulled it tight about her neck, Catherine tried to utter his name, but no sound came. Just then the glittering shape of Zobeïda appeared, next to Arnaud.

At the sight of the Princess, the Sudanese stood motionless with their prisoner, who was powerless to move. Zobeïda addressed the group.

'What is it? Why the noise?'

'We have captured a woman who was hiding in the garden, O Light of Allah! She climbed over the wall. We followed her here.'

'Bring her to me.'

Catherine was dragged as far as Zobeïda's feet and forced to kneel, held down in the position. Arnaud stood a few paces away, frowning, watching the scene with an expression of disgust. Catherine's heart pounded at finding herself so close to him. Oh, if she could only call out his name, take refuge in his arms ... But the danger that threatened her, and him too, was mortal. She heard him murmur:

'Some inquisitive woman, no doubt, or a beggar-woman from the upper town. Let her go!'

'No-one has the right to enter my gardens,' Zobeïda answered curtly.

'This woman will pay for her folly.'

'She cannot simply be an inquisitive woman,' one of the Sudanese interrupted. 'A peeping-tom does not go about armed. We found this upon her.'

An exclamation of rage burst from Catherine; she had not noticed the men taking her dagger from her while she was struggling with them. Now the silver and gold sparrow-hawk gleamed in the eunuch's black hand as he held it out to the Princess. She was leaning forward to examine it when Arnaud joined her and snatched the weapon away. He stood examining the dagger, his face contorted with emotion. Then he looked at Catherine.

'Where did you get this dagger?' he asked hoarsely.

She could not answer, because emotion seemed to be strangling her, but her wide violet eyes implored and devoured him all at once. She had forgotten Zobeïda, whose flashing black eyes were murderous as she spoke harshly to her prisoner:

'You know this weapon?' she asked. 'Where does it come from?'

Arnaud did not reply. He was still gazing at the dark veiled figure kneeling on the sand, staring up at him with starry eyes. Suddenly Catherine saw him pale. Before she could stop him, he stepped forward and snatched away her veil. He stopped, thunderstruck, gazing at the face before him.

'Catherine!' he breathed. 'You … you, here!'

'Yes Arnaud …' she said softly. 'It's really me.'

There was a brief, very brief and marvellous moment in which both of them forgot everything save the immense joy of finding each other again after so much suffering, and so many tears. They were oblivious of these Moors surrounding them, the growing rage of this woman who stood watching them, all the danger hanging over them. All this vanished, no longer existed. They were alone in the midst of a dead world where nothing mattered except their eyes meeting, devouring each other as if they were about to embrace, and the beating of their hearts that kept the same rhythm once again.

Slipping the dagger automatically into his belt, Arnaud held out his hands to help his wife to her feet.

'Catherine,' he murmured, with inexpressible tenderness. 'My sweetheart!'

The endearment she loved above all others, the word she had never forgotten and that he alone knew how to say! Her heart swooned. But the moment of respite was ended. Zobeïda sprang between them, lithe as a panther.

'What is this talk?' she cried, speaking French, to the astonishment of Catherine. 'Her name is Light of Dawn, and she is a slave bought from the pirates. She is my brother's newest concubine, his favourite!'

All the tenderness that had softened Arnaud's hard features for a moment, suddenly vanished. A flash of anger shone in his black eyes briefly, and he thundered:

'Her name is Catherine of Montsalvy! And she is … my sister!' The pause had been slight, almost imperceptible: the space of a heartbeat. But it had been long enough to restore Arnaud's awareness of danger. To admit Catherine as his wife was to condemn her to the worst, most lingering death on the spot. He knew Zobeïda's furious jealousy all too well! At the same time, his eyes sought Catherine's, at once imperious and exhorting her not to contradict him. But Arnaud need not have feared. Although Catherine would have found a savage joy in declaring herself to be his wife, throwing her claim like a stone in her rival's face, she had no wish to lose her life for the sake of a single word.

Besides, had Zobeïda even believed the pious falsehood? Her narrowed eyes went from one to the other of them without even attempting to conceal her surprise and mistrust.

'Your sister! She does not look at all like you!'

Arnaud shrugged. 'The Caliph Muhammad has blond hair and pale eyes. Does that mean he is not your brother?'

'We didn't have the same mother.'

'Nor did we. My father married twice. Is there anything else you would like to know?'

Arnaud's tone was cutting and haughty. He seemed bent on regaining the advantage that the sensual, almost servile, love of this dangerous mistress gave him. But the presence of the other woman, whom she instinctively hated, close to the man she had shed so much blood to possess, seemed to infuriate Zobeïda. She replied coldly:

'Indeed, there are certain things I would like to know. For example, are the noblewomen of France in the habit of crossing seas and populating the slave markets? How is it that your sister found her way here?'

This time it was Catherine who took it upon herself to answer, trusting that Arnaud had not let out any rash confidences.

'My … brother … left some time ago to seek at the tomb of a great saint a cure for the disease that afflicted him. But perhaps you don't know what a saint is?'

'Guard your sharp tongue if you wish me to hear you out patiently,' Zobeïda retorted. 'All the Moors know of Boanerges, Son of Thunder, whose thunderbolt struck them down once upon a time.'

'Well, then,' Catherine went on calmly, 'my brother set off, and for many months we heard no news of him at Montsalvy. We kept hoping he would return, but he never did. So then I decided to go myself and pray at the tomb of the one you call the Son of Thunder. I hoped to hear news of my brother along the way. And in fact I did: a servant, who had escaped when you took Arnaud prisoner, told me what had happened to him. I came here to seek the brother whom we were already mourning at home ...'

'I thought you were captured by pirates and sold at Almeria?'

'I was sold, in fact,' Catherine lied smoothly, not wanting to get Abou-al-Khayr into trouble, 'but I was captured not by pirates but on crossing the frontiers of this kingdom. I let people believe the other story so as not to have to make elaborate explanations to the man who purchased me.'

'What a touching tale!' Zobeïda exclaimed sarcastically. 'A loving sister takes to the highways in search of her beloved brother. And in order to reach him, she is ready to sacrifice herself to the extent of entering the Caliph of Granada's bed! I might add that she has been so successful in this role that she is the favourite, the master's well-beloved, the precious pearl of the harem ...'

'Silence!' Arnaud interrupted brutally, going pale. When the Moorish girl had first mentioned the Caliph's choice, a little while earlier, Arnaud had been too overwhelmed by surprise and delight to take in the meaning of what she was saying. But this time he realised the full significance of her words, and Catherine watched in dismay as anger took the place of happiness on her husband's face. Now he turned toward her.

'Is this true?' he thundered, so harshly that Catherine trembled. She knew Arnaud's inflexible jealousy too well not to quake at the sight of his clenched teeth and flaming eyes. But Zobeïda's sly grin restored her aplomb completely. It was really too much for him to start interrogating her in this lordly fashion in front of the girl who had been his mistress these many months! She threw back her head, raised her little chin, and answered defiantly:

'Quite true,' she said calmly. 'I had to get here somehow. All the means are equal, in such a case ...'

'Really? You seem to forget ...'

'I would have said it was you who forgot! Might I inquire what you are doing here?'

'I was captured. You must know that if you met Fortunat.'

'A captive usually seeks to recover his liberty. What have you done to regain yours?'

'This is neither the time nor the place to discuss such a matter.'

'That seems like a nice easy way out of a difficult situation ...'

'Silence!' Zobeïda remarked impatiently. 'I must admit I am not entertained by your family disputes. Where do you think you are?'

Her interruption was badly timed. Arnaud directed all his fury against her.

'And who do you think you are to meddle in our affairs? In your country, as in ours, the man has complete power over all the women in his family. This woman belongs to me ... since she is of my blood ... and I have the right to demand an explanation of her conduct. Her honour is mine, and if she has sullied it ...'

He accompanied these words with a gesture so threatening that Catherine instinctively drew back. Arnaud's enraged face, with the flaring nostrils white with anger, and murder in his eyes, was a terrifying sight. And she suddenly felt weary before this display of selfish anger on the part of the frustrated male. How could he ignore everything she had been through, all her sufferings and fears, her tears and griefs, to get where she was now? No! None of that interested him: the only thing he cared about was the gift of her body to this poet- prince ...

The threatening quality of Arnaud's behaviour struck Zobeïda too. No-one could feign a rage like that, and if she had had her suspicions earlier about this too beautiful sister suddenly fallen as it were from heaven, she was now beginning to think she should add fuel to his rage so as to get rid of Catherine. If he should kill her in a fit of murderous anger all would be well! The Caliph could only bow before this display of wounded family honour. Her crimson lips parted in a thin smile as she turned to Arnaud.

'You are right, my lord. Your family honour concerns yourself alone. I shall leave you to decide what to do with her. If you punish her, you need not fear the Caliph's anger. He would understand such an action ... and I should plead for you!'

She ordered the two Sudanese to leave, and was just about to depart herself when Morayma came running up, panting and out of breath. The old Jewess flung herself face down on the ground, with an indignant look at Catherine. Then she waited to be questioned. Zobeïda did not leave her waiting long.

'What do you want, Morayma? Why are you in such a state? Get up!'

As soon as she was on her feet, the mistress of the harem pointed an accusing finger at Catherine.

'This woman escaped from her room after overpowering and tying up one of her companions, and stealing her clothes. I see that she has had the audacity to enter your apartments, O Splendid One! Hand her over to me so that I may punish her as she deserves: with the whip!'

The Princess's lip curled in a wicked smile. 'The whip? You must be out of your mind, Morayma! And have the Caliph see the marks on her body when he returns impatient to enjoy her? No, leave her with me ... Henceforth she will not leave these pavilions except to gratify my brother's desires. She is a French noblewoman, you see, the sister of my own beloved lord. And for this reason she is dear and precious to me too now. My own servants shall take care of her in future, bathing and scenting her when her master sends for her, so that her body may be the perfect poem for him to intoxicate himself with beneath the rose arbours of the

Architect's Garden ...'

Zobeïda was undeniably skilful at throwing fuel on the fire. Every word she uttered was calculated to provoke Arnaud's fury to greater heights ... a fury she fondly hoped might prove fatal. As it was, Catherine's husband was trembling all over, fists clenched, body taut as a bow-string ... Zobeïda flashed him an enchanting smile.

'I will leave you alone with her now. Do whatever you feel must be done, but above all I beg you not to leave me languishing too long in your absence! Every minute without you is an eternity of tedium ...' And then, with a brusque change of tone, 'As for you, Morayma, you may retire too, but do not go too far away. You are to see to installing this woman when her brother has finished with her ... according to her needs, and her rank!'

Catherine bit her lips angrily. What did this bloodthirsty she-cat want? Arnaud to kill her? No doubt the accommodation she meant Morayma to find her was some deep, secret tomb well out of sight of the vultures. Catherine had no illusions about her enemy's sudden solicitude. Now that Zobeïda believed her to be Arnaud's sister, she would almost certainly hate her twice as much as before, because of all the shared memories in which she had no part. This woman was even jealous of the past! As the Moorish woman strolled past Catherine nonchalantly on her way back to her room, she could not resist addressing her maliciously:

'Don't count your chickens too soon, Zobeïda ... I am not dead yet. It is not the custom among us for brothers to kill their sisters, or husbands their wives.'

'All the sons of fate are in the hands of Allah! What do I care whether you live or die! If I were you, however, I would prefer to die. It is the only way you can escape your fate, which is to be a slave among slaves, adorned and caressed as long as you are found pleasing, abandoned and miserable when your hour is past!'

'Enough chattering, Zobeïda,' Arnaud cut in impatiently. 'I am the only one who knows what I should do. Now leave me!'

With a mocking laugh barely concealed behind one hand, and a silky shuffling of slippers over the marble floor, the Princess vanished. Arnaud and Catherine found themselves alone, face to face.

They stayed like that for a moment, not speaking, standing a few feet away from each other, listening to the sounds from the alien enemy palace. Catherine thought bitterly that she had never imaged their reunion would be like this. Perhaps the moment like a few minutes ago when he had torn off her veil and seemed about to take her into his arms. Like that, yes! But now Zobeïda's poisoned darts had struck Arnaud in the quick of his being. Now they would simply set about destroying each other as ferociously as mortal enemies ... Was it for this that they had sought and loved each other in spite of men, wars, princes and all the worst calamities that can befall human beings! What a tragedy!

Catherine scarcely dared look up at her husband, who stood watching her, his arms folded across his chest. She did not want him to see the tears in her eyes. A battle was coming, and she allowed herself a moment of respite before it began. Perhaps he would speak first. But he said nothing, trusting no doubt that this heavy silence would prey on her nerves. Indeed, it was she who attacked first.

She threw her head back defiantly and pointed to the dagger in Arnaud's hand.

'What are you waiting for? Haven't you had clear enough instructions? Draw the dagger and kill me, Arnaud! I plead guilty: I did indeed give myself to Muhammed, because it was the only way I could get into this palace, and because I had no choice!'

'And Brézé? Did you have no choice then?'

Catherine drew a deep breath. If he was going to bring up grudges as old as these, the battle would indeed be fierce! But she forced herself to keep calm, and spoke in a controlled voice:

'Whatever you may have heard to the contrary, Brézé has never been my lover! He wanted to marry me. And for a moment I was tempted to accept. That was after La Trémoille's fall, and I felt too tired to carry on. I felt a desperate need for peace, gentleness and protection. You cannot imagine what spring last year was like, or what our triumph cost me! Had it not been for Brézé, all that would have been left of me was a morsel of bleeding flesh in the hands of the Dame de La Trémoille's executioners ...' She was silent for a moment, waiting for the emotion that the memory of that terrifying hour still evoked in her to pass. Then she went on, dully: 'Brézé saved me, protected me and helped me accomplish my revenge. He fought for your memory, and then, believing you dead, he saw no wrong in offering to marry me. He is a good, loyal man ...'

'How staunchly you defend him!' Arnaud interrupted bitterly. 'I wonder you didn't succumb to this tender inclination ...'

'I didn't because I wasn't allowed to!' said Catherine, who was beginning to lose her temper again. She added, frankly admitting her mistakes: 'Had it not been for Cadet Bernard, I might perhaps have agreed to marry him. But I swear before God that at the time he went to Montsalvy to bring back the decree of banishment, Pierre de Brézé had no reason to believe I would marry him. It was when I learnt of this ... unwarrantable behaviour of his that I broke off relations with him.'

'A fine and touching tale,' the knight remarked drily. 'And what did you do after this parting?'

Catherine had to summon all her patience to stop herself bursting out in a fury. Arnaud's inquisitorial, aggressive manner angered her beyond belief. He was playing a little too well the role of a brother whose honour has been besmirched, demanding explanations without the slightest trace of tenderness, as though there were not years of shared love behind them both. Even the letter he had sent her on leaving Montsalvy had not displayed so much bitterness and wounded pride ... In fact, it had been a loving, gentle letter. Perhaps, believing his life finished, or about to be finished, in the awful degradation of leprosy, he had found the strength in his noble and courageous character to write those understanding and forgiving words. In rediscovering life and health, Arnaud had simultaneously regained all his old violence and inflexibility, and the terrifying fury that had already caused her to suffer so much.

She struggled with herself, and managed a smile, a weary and infinitely sad smile, but one full of gentleness. She held out her hand to him.

'Come with me. Don't stay here where everyone can hear us! Let's go ... look, to the far end of the pool, where that infinitely wise-looking stone lion is standing ...'

The darkness hid the faint smile that crossed Arnaud's face and softened his expression.

'Do you need wisdom so much, then?' he asked, and at the sound of his voice Catherine knew his anger was ebbing. He let her lead him away without protest, and this gave her new hope. They walked along the shining marble rim in silence for a moment. Then Catherine sat with her back resting against the lion, while Arnaud stayed standing. Opposite them the tower and portico shone soft pink against the blue night sky, unreal as a mirage and evanescent as a dream. Nearly all the sounds of the palace were stilled by now, and the only things that seemed alive were the night birds and the fountains. A faint breeze ruffled the delicate rosy reflection of the palace in the pool, and Catherine felt the beauty of the Al Hamra taking hold of her heart again, as it had done a little while earlier in the Court of Lions.

'This place seems made for love and happiness ... why must we persist in destroying ourselves? I didn't come all this way to hurt you and let you hurt me ...'

But Arnaud was not ready to be touched as yet. He rested one foot on the marble verge of the pool and, staring into the distance, said to Catherine: 'Don't try to distract my mind along the flowery paths of poetry, Catherine! I want an exact account of what you have been doing since you left Carlat.'

'It's a long story,' she sighed. 'I hoped you would let me wait and tell it to you later. You seem to forget that we are in danger here. Or I am, at least, if you are not!'

'Why should you be? Aren't you the Caliph's beloved favourite?' he answered sarcastically. 'If Zobeïda continues to love me, no-one will dare lay a finger on you, I imagine.'

Catherine turned away to hide a grimace of pain. 'You always know how to say the things that hurt, don't you?' she murmured sorrowfully. 'Very well, then, listen to me – I will tell you now, since you are no longer the man I once knew and you no longer trust me …'

Arnaud's hand gripped Catherine's shoulder so hard that it ached. 'Stop being so evasive, Catherine. Try to see that I have to know. I *have* to know! I must know why my wife, the person I loved most in the whole world, sought consolation first in the arms of a brother-at-arms, and then came here to sell her body to an infidel!'

'And what have you been doing?' Catherine cried angrily. 'What do you call the thing you have been doing in Zobeïda's bed all these months? … I saw you, do you hear? I saw you with my own eyes, the other night, through the window of the courtyard …'

'What did you see?' he asked haughtily.

'I saw you, you and her, rolling about on the floor together. I saw you whip her and then make love to her … I heard her groans, and I counted your caresses: like two animals on heat! It was disgusting! You were drunk anyway … but I thought I would die of sorrow!'

'Enough! I didn't know you were there!' he retorted with admirable logic. 'But you, Catherine? What else were you doing in the Architect's Garden? And knowing all the while that I was here, close to you …'

'Close to me?' Catherine spat furiously. 'Close to me, in Zobeïda's bed! You thought of me, and me alone …?'

'You have a point there. I had to do something to quench the fury I felt each time I thought of you, imagined you in Brézé's arms, living beside him, talking to him, smiling at him, kissing him … and all the rest! A woman's body is like a flagon of wine; it brings a moment's forgetfulness …'

'A long moment in your case! There might have been other, worthier ways of finding forgetfulness for yourself!' Catherine abandoned all caution. 'Why didn't you try to escape? To come back to Montsalvy, to your own family and home?'

'So that you might be condemned to the block for bigamy? I should have been less eaten up with jealousy if I had loved you less … but I had no wish to see you die!'

'But,' Catherine persisted, ignoring the mention of love, 'you preferred to find "forgetfulness" in the beauties of this palace and your mistress's arms, forgetting that you were a Christian knight making love to an infidel, spending your time hunting, drinking and making love … That wasn't what you told me you were going to do in your letter. If I had not met Fortunat I would have gone to seek you in the Holy Land, because I believed that, cured or not, you wanted to meet death in the service of God, if not of the King!'

'So now you are reproaching me with being still alive! Now that is really beyond bearing!'

'Why didn't you try to escape?'

'I have tried a thousand times … but you cannot escape from the Al Hamra! This palace buried under its roses and orange-trees is better guarded than the strongest royal fortress … Every flower hides an eye or an ear, every bush a spy. Besides, if you met Fortunat, you must know of the mission I charged him with, when I helped him escape as we left Toledo …'

'Yes, he told me that you had sent him to tell your mother of your fortunate recovery!'

'And of my imprisonment in Granada. I asked him to tell her the truth, discreetly, since I believed you to have remarried, and to ask her to see the Constable Richemont and tell him the whole story. He was to be sworn to secrecy, a vow he would certainly have kept, but he would have arranged for a delegation to be sent to the Sultan asking for me to be set at ransom and freed. Then I would have travelled to the Holy Land or the Papal States under a false name, and no-one would ever have heard of me again … but I would at least have been able to pursue a destiny more worthy of myself, and of my name!'

'Fortunat didn't tell me any of that. All he did was spit his hatred for me in my face and gleefully describe how you were happy at last in the arms of an infidel Princess whom you passionately loved.'

'The idiot! And you carried on, even after that?'

'You belong to me, as I belong to you, whatever you might suppose. I renounced everything for you. I wasn't going to renounce you for the benefit of another woman …'

'Which must have given your embraces with the Caliph a pleasant tinge of vengeance, I suppose?' Arnaud inquired harshly.

'Perhaps my scruples were not quite as strong as they might have been,' Catherine admitted, 'but I beg you to remember that it is a long journey from Roncesvaux, where I met Fortunat, and this accursed city! I had plenty of time to imagine all that my evil star was finally to set before my very eyes!'

'Stop harping on that! I would like to remind you that I am still waiting for an explanation.'

'What is the point now? You won't listen, or admit to anything. The chief thing is that I should be guilty to lessen your own remorse, isn't it? You have stopped loving me, Arnaud, and you love this girl so much that you forget I am your wife … and that we have a son!'

'I have forgotten nothing!' Arnaud cried, trying to recapture the violent mood that the mention of their little boy had considerably deflated. 'How could I forget my son? He is flesh of my flesh, as I am flesh of my mother's.'

Catherine stood up, and the two were face to face, like fighting cocks, each looking for weakness in the other's armour so as to wound the more surely. But just as the mention of Michel had softened Arnaud, so the mention of Isabelle de Montsalvy cooled Catherine's rage. She was still angry with her husband for his betrayal, but she loved him too much not to suffer in advance from the blow she was about to strike him. She bowed her head, and murmured ...

'She is no longer with us, Arnaud ... The day after the last feast of St Michael, she died peacefully. She had had the great joy of seeing our little Michel proclaimed Lord of Montsalvy by all the vassals the day before ... She loved you and prayed for you with her dying breath ...'

God, how heavy the silence was for the next few minutes! It was broken only by Arnaud's rapid, staccato breathing ... He said nothing. Catherine looked at him. His handsome face seemed carved in stone. His expression was fixed, his eyes betrayed no emotion, neither surprise nor grief ... but there were great tears rolling down his smooth cheeks. They cut Catherine to the heart. Timidly, she put out a hand and squeezed Arnaud's arm, but received not even a tremor of response.

'Arnaud,' she faltered, 'if you only knew ...'

He interrupted her, not harshly, but curtly. 'Who is looking after Michel ... while you wander the highways?' he asked, in the most colourless voice, as if this were a piece of unimportant information.

'Sara and the Abbot of Montsalvy, Bernard de Calmont d'Olt ... And Donatienne and Saturnin too ... and all the people of Montsalvy, who are gradually recovering their pleasure in living and being your vassals. The countryside is recovering from the ravages of war at last ... and the Abbey monks are building a new castle, close to the southern gate so that the castle and village can assist each other in case of future danger ...'

As Catherine spoke, the strangely enchanting scene before their eyes seemed to fade. It was not the pink palace, the prolific vegetation and silvery waters of the Al Hamra that they saw, but the old country of Auvergne, its wild, turbulent streams; its deep, black forests; its harsh soil mysteriously yielding precious fruit like gold and silver and jewels; its ruddy cattle and stubborn, proud peasantry; its flaming sunsets and fresh dawns; the lilac softness of its twilights and the long sleeves of mist wrapped about the ancient extinct volcanoes ...

Arnaud's arm trembled in Catherine's grip. Their fingers groped for each other like blind things seeking the light, and closed round each other. The feel of Arnaud's warm, hard palm sent a shudder of joy right through Catherine.

'Don't you want to see it all again? There is no prison one cannot escape from, except the grave,' she murmured. 'Let's go home, Arnaud, I beg you ...'

He had no time to reply. Abruptly the mirage vanished and the magic went up in smoke. Zobeïda, preceded by a cohort of eunuch torch-bearers, with Morayma at her side, appeared under the brightly-lit portico and came forward beside the pool. The water seemed to catch fire, the night drew back, the hands that had been clasped a moment earlier fell apart.

Zobeïda's dark eyes fell on Catherine before returning, questioningly, to Arnaud. By the way the Moorish woman frowned, Catherine knew she was astonished to find her still alive. As she soon made clear.

'So, you have forgiven your sister, my lord? Doubtless you had your reasons. Anyway,' she added, with calculated malice, 'I am glad because my brother will be grateful to you. His return has just been announced. The Commander of the Faithful returns to the Al Hamra either tonight or tomorrow! I am sure his first thought will be for his beloved …'

As Zobeïda spoke, Catherine saw all her good work undone. Arnaud was no longer holding her hand, and his eyes blazed with anger once more. Reality had taken over again, with its larger-than-life characters: the Caliph and his sister! But Catherine was not prepared to give up so easily.

'Arnaud,' she beseeched him, 'I have still so many things to tell you …'

'You can tell them to him another time. Morayma, take her to her rooms now and see that she is ready in case my brother returns!'

'Where are you taking her?' Arnaud asked dryly. 'I want to know.'

'Near here. Her room opens onto this very garden. You see how kind I am to her! I am keeping your sister near me so that you can see her. If she stayed within the harem, where you are not allowed, this would be impossible … Now let her go. It is late and the night is long, and we cannot stay here talking till dawn.'

Oh, how purring and persuasive and soothing that voice of hers was! Who could have guessed, for a moment, what a weight of hatred and treachery it concealed? But Arnaud was beginning to understand Zobeïda.

'You seem very amiable all of a sudden. That isn't like you.'

The Princess shrugged and answered suavely: 'She is your sister, and you are my lord. That is enough.'

There are few normal men who are not won over by flattery, and as Catherine watched Arnaud's reaction to this speech she could not help deploring the fact that he was so normal, and had kept such a large streak of naïveté in his make-up. He seemed delighted to hear Zobeïda talking so moderately.

But Catherine was not duped. If the Moorish girl started offering the velvet glove it meant that she must redouble her vigilance; and this sudden show of amiability meant nothing at all. The smile and caressing voice could not cancel out the hard, calculating expression of her eyes. Catherine's dangerous life had at least taught her to read people's eyes and see through the enemy's plots. Arnaud, for all his terrible brush with leprosy and the physical and moral shock caused by such a fearful experience, had never had to hold his own against a swarm of more powerful foes, as Catherine had. A chivalrous and honest man, he found it hard to grasp the guile behind a soft smile or fond word, especially when they came from a woman ...

Still, Catherine allowed Morayma to take her away without protest. Enough had been said, for one night. Before she vanished from sight, however, she turned for one last look, and was somewhat consoled to see that Arnaud was still following her with his eyes.

'A man must choose his own destiny, Arnaud ... and if he is a man of honour he will let no one – no one, do you hear – come between him and his conscience ...'

Her room opened on to the garden as Zobeïda had said. From die narrow but comfortable couch where Morayma had placed her, Catherine could still glimpse the pool gleaming between two slender pillars. Morayma had pointed out the elegance of the little room to her as she arranged her cushions. The walls were of crystal, mauve and almond green, framed in gilded cedar-wood.

'It may be less sumptuous than your former room,' she remarked, 'but it is more elegant I think. Zobeïda does not like big rooms. You will have everything you need here, and you will feel as if you were living in the garden itself!'

The old Jewess was taking great pains to praise Catherine's new lodgings. Was she trying to reassure her and herself at the same time, perhaps? Of the two, she seemed to need reassurance most, for beneath the yellow-embroidered blue robes, Morayma was trembling like a leaf. Catherine tried to force her to speak out.

'Why are you so frightened, Morayma? What are you afraid of?'

'Me?' cried the other disingenuously. 'I'm not frightened, I'm just cold!'

'How can you be cold in this weather? The breeze has gone, and the leaves in the garden aren't even stirring.'

'I'm cold all the same ... I'm always cold!'

While she spoke, she placed a pitcher of milk on the ground by the head of Catherine's bed. Catherine glanced at it in some astonishment.

'Why this milk?'

'In case you feel thirsty. You should drink a great deal of milk to keep your skin bright and supple!'

As Morayma scuttled off as fast as her short legs would carry her, Catherine tried to analyse her present situation. She was not frightened by the proximity of Zobeïda. Surely the Princess would think twice before persecuting the woman she believed to be her lover's sister? It was not the thought of her that tormented Catherine. It was Arnaud ...! How strange and disconcerting he was! When he had first recognised her she had been utterly convinced of his joy in seeing her again, and his love for her. Some expressions cannot lie! But with her venomous insinuations Zobeïda had snuffed out his delight like a candle flame. Arnaud had forgotten that sudden rush of happiness and given himself over to jealousy, the anger of a betrayed husband. And there were still things he did not know about, Catherine thought sadly; episodes like the gypsy camp and the unfortunate Fero, and the keep at Coca … and he must learn about them, otherwise he would never trust her again, and she would never know a moment's peace. He would reject her once and for all if he knew …

At last the weariness caused by a day of such conflicting emotions overcame her and she fell asleep. But her sleep was not the peaceful sort that can restore a person's energy and powers in a few hours. She slept badly, nervously, waking with a start from time to time. Her subconscious was unusually active. Even in the midst of slumber she seemed to be intuitively aware of approaching danger. She could not know what shape it would take, but something seemed to warn her to stay alert.

A sudden suffocating sensation woke her with a jump, and she sat up in bed, covered in sweat, her heart beating wildly. The moonlight streamed over the marble-paved floor of her room. She stifled a scream of horror: there … gliding over the long moonlit patch of floor … was a long, slender, gleaming shape … a snake! It was moving towards her bed!

This was no accident, as Catherine realised in a flash. That pitcher of milk Morayma had placed by the bed! … Milk was the favourite food of snakes! Now Catherine understood Morayma's eagerness to be off that evening, the reason for her trembling. It had all been planned between them! This hideous creature sliding toward her was the work of Zobeïda; death in its most inhuman shape!

Eyes starting with terror, Catherine clutched the silk coverlet against her bare bosom and watched the snake approach with unpleasant trickles of cold sweat running down her back. She had never been so frightened. She felt as if she were completely paralysed. She stared, fascinated, at the long black shape that slowly coiled and uncoiled as it crossed the marble floor toward her, coming nearer and nearer … It was like a nightmare with no awakening, because she did not dare cry out. The snake was not very big but she could see a large, flat, triangular head, and she was terrified that if she screamed the hideous thing would strike all the sooner. Besides, to whom could she call out for help? Catherine had no illusions about the fiendish intention behind this loathsome messenger of death. No-one would come if she called … and she was all alone, as exposed as if she stood on the scaffold, protected only by a few layers of flimsy silk … She couldn't even close her eyes so as not to see the horrible creature.

In her terror her thoughts turned to her husband. She was going to die right there, a few feet away from him, and when her cold corpse was discovered the next morning, Zobeïda would doubtless find an infinity of hypocritical regrets and consoling words. All the rooms opened onto the garden. How could she guess that a snake, attracted by the cool water no doubt, would choose to enter that particular one? And Arnaud would probably believe her ... Then, because the snake was almost beside the bed, because she was too frightened, and because she needed him so desperately, she moaned:

'Arnaud ... Arnaud, my love ...'

And the miracle happened. Catherine thought her terror must have driven her quite mad when she saw him, his tall figure eclipsing the moonlight, summoned from the shadowy garden outside like the good genie of oriental fables. At one glance he took in Catherine's terrified position, huddled in the farthest corner of her bed, and the reptile, already weaving its sinister flat head to and fro. He drew his dagger with one hand, snatched up a robe trailing over a stool as a shield and flung himself bodily on the cobra.

The snake was killed instantly. Wielded with skill and precision, the dagger struck it at the base of the head, almost severing it from the body, which lay inert on the floor. Arnaud raised himself on one knee and looked at his wife. The moonlight fell upon her face, making it even more deathly pale. Her hands still clutched the coverlets against her, but now she was shaking like a leaf. He murmured gently, to reassure her:

'Don't be frightened. It's over ... I have killed it!'

But she could scarcely hear him. The excruciating terror of the last few minutes seemed to have eaten into the deepest crannies of her being, and she lay there, eyes starting, teeth chattering, too weak to answer. Arnaud slid down beside her on the bed.

'Catherine ... answer me, I implore you ... are you all right?'

She opened her mouth, but her lips were trembling too much for her to speak. She wanted to cry, but the tears would not come, and the eyes she raised to Arnaud were still wild with terror; the look in them was so touching that Arnaud could not resist doing the thing that seemed most natural: to take her in his arms.

He felt a surge of deep compassion as he saw how she huddled against his breast, trying, like a child, to make herself as small as possible. He held her more tightly, trying to communicate some of his male warmth to her to still this hysterical trembling. Gently, he stroked the blonde head buried in his neck.

'Poor little one! You were so frightened ... so frightened! That evil woman! I knew she was capable of anything ... and that was why I stayed outside, watching ... but something as vile as that! Now calm yourself, I am here ... I will look after you! ... We shall flee together, and return home ... I love you ...'

The words slipped out quite naturally, and Arnaud did not try to check them. All at once his jealousy and rancour seemed to have cracked; it had happened a little while before, when he was roaming the garden because some dull uneasiness kept drawing him back toward this part of the palace, and he had heard Catherine's faint moan, his own name pronounced with such anguish, and seen the long black glistening shape gliding across to his wife's bed. And now that he held her in his arms, trembling like a sick bird, he realised that nothing and no-one would ever really be able to come between the two of them, that a love like theirs could survive many things and endure many torments, save those of a total rupture. They had but one heart in two bodies, and Arnaud knew he would never be strong enough to reject Catherine completely. The caprice, born of solitude and also of the deep relief he had experienced when he had found he was not a leper after all, had pushed him toward Zobeïda, and it had become a sort of habit necessary to his physical well-being; but it seemed a poor sort of emotion compared with the joy he felt just holding Catherine in his arms.

She clung to him now with both hands, convulsively, murmuring a string of disconnected words into his neck, and for a moment he was afraid that terror might have sent her mad.

'Listen,' he begged. 'Speak to me! Look at me. You know me, don't you?' She nodded, and his anxiety lessened. He started stroking her hair again. 'My sweetheart!' he murmured. 'It's all right, don't be frightened … What can I do to comfort you?'

He felt helpless and clumsy, confronted with this agonised human being who clutched him so despairingly … but then, suddenly, Catherine burst into tears. He realised that she was safe now, that the spectre of madness was drawing away from her, and he began rocking her to and fro as tenderly as a child.

'Weep,' he said gently. 'Weep as much as you want; it will make you feel better …'

The black clouds of fear burst in a veritable deluge of tears. Catherine had never wept as she did now. Whole months of suffering, anxiety and despair were washed away in her tears. She sobbed out her happiness, her relief, her joy, her hope, her love, and even her gratitude at having regained this dear refuge. Everything, past and present, was abolished at one stroke. The only thing left was the gentle warmth of this man she adored, stealing over her and giving back the wonderful sense of security he alone could bring. Her sobs gave way little by little to a delicious feeling of well-being. Slowly, slowly, Catherine calmed down.

13: The Sentence

Catherine's sobs became less frequent, and at last she fell silent. Her breathing returned to its normal rhythm. The tears dried on her cheeks and she stayed motionless for a long while, savouring the exquisite happiness of lying in her husband's arms, hearing his heartbeats, looking out at the moonlit garden. The only thing she was aware of was his hand, gently stroking her head as she had so often done his, in the past. It was so lovely to feel Arnaud there beside her, to breathe in his healthy masculine smell after having believed for so many months that he was lost to her forever.

She began to feel slightly light-headed. She felt so replete with happiness that it had to overflow somehow. She raised her head and pressed her tear-damp lips against Arnaud's neck. He started at this kiss, uneasy at the sudden awakening of his desire. Catherine sensed this instinctively and lingered over her caress, gradually moving nearer his face, and then his lips. But he didn't let her get that far.

Avidly, like a man starving, he crushed his lips over her proffered mouth, and the kiss that began then went on and on till both of them were aflame. And then Arnaud's hands moved down to her shoulders and back, and he realised that she was naked. Gently he pulled away the silken wraps between them. She did not stop him. She helped him, rather; eager to offer herself to him more completely. She kicked the last wrap away impatiently and it fell to the ground, hiding the dead snake that had almost killed her. But Catherine had forgotten it. Life surged up anew in her, the warmth of love shook her to the core. She slipped away from him, lying on her back in the cold moonlight so that he could see her better.

'Tell me if I am still beautiful,' she murmured, sure of his answer beforehand. 'Tell me that you still love me.'

'You are more beautiful than ever, you she-devil … and you know it. As for loving you …'

'Tell me! I know you love me, I can see you do … I'm not ashamed to say I adore you! I love my handsome lord. I love you more than anything else in the world!'

'Catherine!'

She came close to him again, bent on conquering the last shreds of resistance in him, wound her soft arms around him, dizzied him with the touch of her body. She was a living spell, and he was only a man. Without trying to work out how the pitiful creature of a few minutes before had been transformed into this triumphant siren, he acknowledged defeat, took her into his arms again.

'My love,' he murmured against her mouth, 'my sweet Catherine ... My wife!'

The sequel was inevitable. They had both waited too long for this moment, the moment when they would rediscover the gestures of love! If the rose-coloured palace had fallen in on them it would not have stopped Catherine from giving herself to her husband. For endless minutes they made love to each other, with savage passion, forgetful of the danger posed by these shimmering walls, oblivious of everything but this incomparable joy they found in each other.

They might have continued making love for hours on end if a sudden light had not inundated the room, while a strident voice, trembling with fury, shouted:

'And is incest a Frankish custom too? Strange postures for a brother and sister to adopt!'

Instantly the couple separated. Arnaud leapt to his feet. Catherine watched in sudden terror as Zobeïda stepped forward into the middle of the room, her face convulsed with rage, followed by two servants carrying torches. The Princess was unrecognisable. Her face was contorted by hatred, and her golden skin was ashen grey. Her large eyes were bloodshot and her little fists were clenched with an all too evident hunger for revenge. She was grinding her teeth together so violently that her words came out distortedly. She turned her back on Catherine and addressed Arnaud furiously:

'You have deceived me ... but not as much as you thought! I sensed that there was more between this woman and you than the ties of blood. I sensed it ... because of my hatred! I might have loved your sister, but I hated her from the first moment I saw her! That is why I kept watch on her ...'

Arnaud kicked aside the silk coverlet, revealing the black snake.

'Kept watch? What is the meaning of this, then? Had it not been for me, she would have died!'

'I wanted her to die, because I knew there was something between you, do you hear? I was sure ... I came here to take her body away, and I saw you ... I saw you, do you understand?'

'Stop screaming,' Arnaud said disdainfully. 'One might suppose that I belonged to you. You stand there shrieking and shouting abuse like some vulgar bazaar-woman whose husband has been chasing girls. You mean nothing to me ... nothing. You are merely an infidel, and I am your prisoner.'

'Arnaud,' Catherine whispered, alarmed by her enemy's livid face. 'Be careful!'

But Zobeïda still ignored her. 'And this white-skinned woman means a lot to you, I suppose?'

'She is my wife,' the knight answered simply. 'My wife in the sight of God and of men. And if you want to know everything, we have a son, in our own country! Now, try to understand that!'

A wave of joy swept over Catherine in spite of the danger of their situation. She was happy that he had hurled her wifehood as an insult in her rival's face.

'Understand?' A deadly smile twisted the Princess's distorted features, and her voice lost its shrillness and became dangerously soft. 'It is you who are going to understand, my lord. You said it yourself: you are my prisoner, and so you shall remain as long as I want you! What did you imagine, when you triumphantly announced that this woman was your wife? That I would be moved to tears and place your hands in hers, open the gates of the Al Hamra to you and give you an escort to the frontiers while wishing you all the happiness in the world?'

'If you were worthy of your ancestry, daughter of the warriors of Atlas, you would do that very thing!'

'My mother was a slave, a Turkoman princess sold to the Great Khan and given by him as a present to the Caliph, my father. She was a wild beast of the steppes, and they had to put her in chains to possess her. She knew nothing but violence, and she finally killed herself after my birth. I resemble her: I know the language of blood! This woman may be your wife; so much the worse for her!'

'What are you going to do with her?'

'I will tell you.' A disturbing gleam appeared in Zobeïda's eyes. She gave a little dry, nervous laugh, on the verge of hysteria. 'I will have her chained, naked, in the slaves' courtyard so that they can enjoy her for a whole night and day. Then I will have her hung on a cross on the ramparts so that the sun can burn and shrivel this skin that pleases you so much. And then Yuan and Kong will take care of her. But, don't worry, you won't miss any of the fun. That will be your punishment. I don't think that you will feel the need to make any comparisons between her and me after that. My executioners know their task too well! Seize this woman, you there!'

Catherine's heart missed a beat. She held out her arms to her husband, instinctively seeking his protection.

The eunuchs had no time to move. Arnaud snatched up the dagger beside the bed and threw himself between Catherine and the slaves. His face was flushed with anger, but his voice was icy calm as he replied: 'You won't touch her! The first person who moves here will die instantly ...'

The eunuchs froze, but Zobeïda burst out laughing. 'You must be mad! I will call … the guards will come. There are a hundred, two hundred, three hundred of them, as many as I need. You had better admit defeat. Accept your fate. I know how to make you forget. I will have you made king …'

'Do you really think you can appeal to me with arguments like those?' Arnaud sneered. 'And you say I must be mad. It is you who are mad …'

Before anyone could stop him, he seized Zobeïda, held her fast by both wrists and pointed the dagger at her throat.

'Now call your guards, Zobeïda! Call them if you dare, and you draw your last breath … Catherine, dress yourself … We are going to escape!'

'But … how?'

'You will soon see! Do as I say. And you, Princess, you are going to take us quietly to the secret way into this palace you know so well. If you make a sign or a sound, you are dead …'

'You won't get far,' Zobeïda murmured. 'You will be recaptured the moment you set foot in the town.'

'That is my affair. Now, start moving.'

Slowly, followed by the terrified Catherine, they left the room, a curious double silhouette before which the eunuchs fled in terror. They advanced through the garden.

The enterprise struck Catherine as quite mad, and doomed to failure. She had not been really afraid for her own skin when Zobeïda, with sadistic glee, had described the tortures she had in mind for her. Had not Morayma announced that the Caliph's return was imminent? Zobeïda must have forgotten this in her rage … Oddly enough, Arnaud seemed to read her thoughts.

'You are wrong to imagine, Catherine, that fear of her brother would stop this madwoman from having you put to death. She is past all reasoning, past all fear when she is possessed of her devils.'

At this, despite the dagger at her throat, Zobeïda managed to hiss:

'You won't escape … you will die, both of you …'

And suddenly, losing her head completely, she started to scream:

'Help … help me,' and she wriggled like an eel to escape from Arnaud's grasp. She would have screamed again, but this time the scream was strangled, choked by an appalling gurgling sound. The dagger struck home. Zobeïda sank, without a whimper, from Arnaud's hold onto the sanded path, eyes open wide in immense astonishment. She lay outstretched there like a sliver of pale moonlight, under Catherine's horrified eyes.

'You have killed her?' she whispered.

'She killed herself … I didn't really try to strike. The dagger went in of its own accord.'

They stood for a moment looking at each other, with the corpse between them. Arnaud held his hand out to Catherine.

'Come! … We must try to escape! The eunuchs must have given the alarm. Our only chance is to find the secret passage before we are found.'

She slipped her hand into his without hesitation, and let him lead her between the shrubs and bushes. But it was already too late. Arnaud had spoken the truth: their one chance had been to force Zobeïda to show them the secret passage. By now the moment had gone. Day was breaking and the garden was coming to life. There were cries and footsteps all around them. The trapped pair paused for a moment, wondering which direction to take.

'It is too late,' Arnaud murmured. 'We don't have time to flee to the upper town. Look!'

Eunuchs were advancing from all sides, with their sinister curved sabres, the blades of which gleamed in the rising sun. Beyond the screen of shrubs where the Montsalvys had left Zobeïda, shrill screams were heard, the 'You! You!' of mourning expected of slaves and servants.

'We are done for,' Arnaud remarked calmly. 'All that remains for us is to die bravely.'

'I think I will know how to die well if I am with you.' Catherine clasped her husband's hand more tightly. 'It won't be the first time that we have faced death together. Remember Rouen …'

'I haven't forgotten,' said Arnaud, with a fleeting smile. 'But there is no Jean Son to come to our aid here!'

'There is Abou-al-Khayr … and Gauthier and Josse, my squire, who has entered the Caliph's army so as to be able to get into the Al Hamra … We are not alone.'

Arnaud looked at Catherine with admiration. 'Josse … who is that then?'

'A Parisian beggar who was making the pilgrimage to ask pardon for his sins. He is very devoted to me.'

Despite their imminent danger, despite the menacing circle of armed men closing in upon them moment by moment, Arnaud could not help laughing. 'You are a constant surprise to me, Catherine! If you met Satan himself, sweetheart, you would be quite capable of putting a cord round his neck and turning him into the most obedient little lapdog! And I am pleased to hear that you have succeeded in dragging that mountain of muscle and Norman stubbornness called Gauthier all the way here. Now try your powers on these people here!' he added, in a different tone, pointing to the people drawing in upon them. These formed two separate groups. At the head of one, Catherine and Arnaud recognised the torch-carrying eunuchs of a little while earlier, and behind them ten of the Princess's women carrying her body. Catherine recognised the man leading the other group by his crimson brocade turban: it was the Grand Vizier, Haben-Ahmed Banu Siradj …

'You are right,' she murmured. 'We are lost. That man hates you and has no cause to love me …'

The two groups met before coming forward to intercept them. Banu Siradj took a long look at the corpse that the women laid before him, wrapped in its azure veils. Then, calmly, he came forward to the young couple. Catherine instinctively pressed closer to Arnaud, whose arm encircled her shoulder. The death that approached them now in the guise of this young, elegant man struck her as even more horrible than that with which the cobra had threatened her; possibly because death is so much more painful when one has rediscovered love and happiness again after so much suffering. The garden was beautiful in the gilded morning light. The flowers seemed brighter after the cool night, and the water sparkled clear and blue.

Banu Siradj let his heavy, strangely expressionless gaze, fall first on Arnaud.

'It is you who killed the Princess?'

'Yes. She wanted to torture my wife, so I killed her.'

'Your wife?'

'This is my wife, Catherine of Montsalvy, come to find me through the most grievous dangers …'

The Grand Vizier's black eyes slid to Catherine, full of an irony that made her flush. For this man had found her in the Caliph's arms, and the mention of these dangers must inevitably amuse him. She was ashamed, and blamed herself for his half-smile, because it was Arnaud who must suffer for it.

'Doubtless this was your right,' Banu Siradj commented, 'but you have spilled the blood of the Commander of the Faithful, and for this you must die …'

'Very well, take my life, but let my wife go. She is innocent.'

'No,' Catherine protested fiercely, clinging to her husband. 'Do not separate us, Vizier. If he dies, I want to die too!'

'It will not be I who decides your fate,' Banu Siradj explained. 'The Caliph is approaching the town. He will be here in an hour. You forget too soon that you belong to him, woman. As for this man …'

He made an imperious sign. Some of the guards came up and, despite her screams and desperate struggling, Catherine was torn from Arnaud and his hands were tied behind his back, while the young woman was given into the hands of the harem servants.

'Take her to her room,' the Vizier said in bored tones, 'and keep her under close guard. But above all, keep her quiet!'

'I shall not be silent,' Catherine shouted, enraged to see her husband bound and tied and encircled by guards, 'unless you leave me with him, and chain me up too!'

'Be brave, Catherine,' Montsalvy pleaded, 'I need your support.'

'Gag her,' Banu Siradj commanded. 'These screams are unbearable.'

The women fell on her like a swarm of wasps. A scarf was bound round her mouth, another secured her hands, and yet another her feet. And then Catherine found herself being carried off like a bundle by the servants, toward the very room that at the beginning of the night she had left with such high hopes in her heart. The anger that consumed her was so fierce that she could not even weep! Would God permit such an injustice? Would Arnaud have to die for having struck down that bloodthirsty madwoman who had wanted to submit her to the direst of tortures? No … it wasn't possible … it couldn't happen …

Twisting her head painfully, she managed to get a last look at her husband. He was walking off toward the prisons, surrounded by gleaming scimitars, walking very straight and tall despite his bonds, a noble figure in the morning sunlight. Bitter, scalding tears sprang from Catherine's eyes, and they were tears of despair.

'I will save you,' she promised to herself. 'Even if I have to crawl to the Caliph's feet and kiss the ground beneath them, I will make him pardon you …'

Once again she was ready for any rash act, but she knew that there was one price that Arnaud would never permit her to pay, even for his life … He had taken her back … now she belonged to him alone. As they carried her off, she heard the sharp wailing of fifes and drums accompanying the long-drawn-out acclamations of the crowds. Muhammad had reached Granada …

When they came to fetch Catherine, toward evening, to take her to the Caliph, she felt hope stirring within her again. All the same, the events of the day had not been encouraging.

The guard at the doors to her room had been doubled, but the usual swarm of servants and slaves had been reduced to one dumb eunuch, who brought her a meal on a tray at midday. Not one woman had been to see her. Not even Morayma. And this isolation made Catherine uneasy, not so much on her own behalf as on Arnaud's. The severity of this treatment did not augur well for her husband. It might be harder to win his pardon than she had hitherto supposed …

The usual commotion had greeted the Caliph's return, and then the palace had been plunged in silence again. From time to time the wails of the women mourning Zobeïda reached Catherine's ears, piercing and exasperating because they were artificial. Who could genuinely mourn that cruel, bloodthirsty woman? And what would Arnaud's punishment be for having rid the world of her?

Catherine was annoyed not to see Morayma. What was the old fool afraid of? She desperately needed to see her. Abou-al-Khayr must be warned at all costs of the danger hanging over Arnaud. What if the Caliph, in his anger, ordered his immediate execution? Even now, as she fretted about him, Arnaud might have breathed his last! But the young woman rejected this idea vigorously. No, he couldn't possibly be dead. If he were, she would have felt it, her very body would have warned her.

However, with all this anxiety and waiting, Catherine had reached a state of high nervous excitement by the time Morayma finally appeared in her room.

'Come,' was all she said. 'The master wishes to see you.'

'At last! Here you are,' Catherine cried as she followed her. 'I have been waiting for you all day ...'

'Silence!' the old Jewess interrupted rudely. 'I am not allowed to speak to you. And don't try to escape. You would not have a chance.'

At the threshold to her room, ten eunuchs armed with scimitars were waiting to escort her. Morayma saw to it that she was closely veiled.

'Be as humble as you can, Light of Dawn,' she remarked. 'I am not taking you to the Architect's Garden this time but to the Mechouar, the palace where the master reigns. He is very wrathful. I am sorry for you, because you will have to face his anger.'

'I am not afraid,' Catherine retorted proudly. 'Lead on. I am following you.'

Closely escorted by the eunuchs, Catherine was led through the harem to the palace doors reserved for the Caliph. The women thronged about her, curious, full of hate. She heard them laughing and joking. She saw Zorah's green eyes glitter as she spat at her. As they passed out of the Court of Lions, the crowd of women was so dense that they had some trouble forcing their way through. The women refused to make way. There was a scuffle, and Catherine suddenly heard a voice whisper, in French, in her ear:

'He has been taken to the Ghafar. It won't happen just yet!'

She smiled gratefully, catching a glimpse of Marie vanishing in the throng. It could only be her! And she felt better. So Arnaud had been taken to the Alcazaba keep ... he was in no danger of immediate execution.

By wielding their scimitar handles and hippopotamus-hide whips, the eunuchs finally succeeded in forcing a way through to the door between the two parts of the palace. The Moorish guards were on duty there, helmeted, holding their lances in one hand, solemn and threatening figures ... the advance guard of justice ... On the other side of the door they stepped into a majestic sort of royal cloister, a lacy white marble building standing around a carpet of green water enclosed by a double hedge of sweet myrtle. No tender plants or welcoming shade there, as in the Architect's Garden; only rank upon rank of armed guards as far as the grandiose chamber, reached through a massive square tower at the far end, and a crowd of servants and sumptuously-dressed dignitaries. The escort, and even Morayma, left Catherine at the entrance to the Ambassador's Hall. A dim light fell like lead through the narrow coloured-glass windows upon the huge throne of jewel-encrusted gold where the Caliph sat watching Catherine approach.

The ruler's head was covered with a green silk turban, pinned by a huge emerald. He carried a sceptre in one hand, a long curved bamboo covered with gold. And Catherine noticed, with a tremor of fear, that there was not a trace of gentleness in the icy gaze that enveloped her.

Two servants wearing long green robes took her by the shoulders as she entered, and forced her down on her knees before the throne. At this she lost her last shred of hope. She could expect no mercy from this man, who was actually treating her as if she were guilty. She stayed motionless, waiting for him to speak, but looking boldly into his face.

With a wave, he motioned everyone to leave. When the last servant had retired, he commanded: 'Take off your veil. I want to see your face. Besides … you have no right to wear it. You are not one of us.'

She obeyed gladly, and at the same time she stood up, determined not to lose any of her dignity. If she could not save Arnaud, she was determined to oblige Muhammad to send her to join him. The white veil she wore fell about her like a pale cloud, and her eyes met the ruler's angry face.

'Who gave you permission to stand?'

'You did. You said, "You are not one of us." I am a free woman, and I come of a noble family. In my country, the King speaks to me with respect.'

Muhammad bent toward her, his full lips curved in a mocking and contemptuous smile.

'And has your King slept with you too? Well, I have … Why should I respect you?'

'Was it to tell me this that you sent for me, O Mighty Caliph? I do not see the point, unless you find pleasure in insulting a woman.'

'I could easily have sent you to your death without a word, but I wanted to see you once more … if only to find out how skilful you are at lying.'

'Lying? Why would I bother? Question me, Lord: I will answer you. A noblewoman does not lie.'

There was silence. Accustomed as he was to servile slaves, and the indolent, docile creatures whose greatest delight was to be summoned to his bed, Muhammad gazed with annoyance mingled with astonishment at this woman who dared to stand before him, without a sign of fear, without arrogance, but with a simple pride and dignity that ignored her present danger.

The turn their discussion was taking gave the young woman renewed courage. If she could only go on speaking to him like this, almost on equal terms, there might be a chance … But Muhammad suddenly launched an attack.

'They say that the Frankish prisoner … the murderer of my beloved sister … is your husband?' he remarked, with a show of indifference.

'That is true.'

'In that case, you have lied. You are not a slave bought in the markets of Almeria.'

'They lied to you, Lord. I did not lie, because you never asked me. Now I am telling you of my own accord: my name is Catherine of Montsalvy, the Lady of the Chataignerie, and I came here to take back the husband your sister stole from me.'

'Stole? I met this man many times. He seemed well enough pleased with his lot ... and the insane passion which Zobeïda conceived for him.'

'What prisoner does not try to make the best of his lot? And as for love, my lord, you who take women at your pleasure without following the dictates of your heart, you must know that men find it easy enough to do these things.'

The Caliph abruptly threw aside the sceptre that, though adding majesty to his position, was something of an encumbrance, and shifted about uneasily. Catherine noticed a shadow of melancholy pass through his pale eyes.

'Is that the way you see things?' he asked bitterly. 'I gave you so much love in a few days that I expected a little more warmth on your part. I really believed for a moment that I had found in you the one I had despaired of finding. So you were only a slave in my arms, like all the rest?'

'No, you made me happy,' Catherine admitted, frankly. 'I did not know you, and I was surprised, agreeably so, to find you the man you are. I expected someone terrible, and you were gentle and kind to me. This memory you evoke ... why shouldn't I admit that it was a pleasant one and that our night together was a sweet one? I promised I would not lie to you.'

Muhammad stood up with a swift, supple movement and came near to Catherine. There was a high colour in his cheeks and his eyes gleamed.

'In that case,' he murmured, in a low, urgent voice, 'why not take up the poem where we left it? Everything can stay as it was. You belong to me and I can easily forget the bond that attaches you to this man.'

Catherine trembled to hear the passion that vibrated in the Caliph's words. Love was the one place where she could not follow him, because she could not possibly surrender to his passion now. She shook her head, and answered with a weary gentleness:

'But I couldn't. He is my husband, as I told you. Our marriage was blessed by a priest in our country. I am his wife till death should part us.'

'And that will not be long in coming! Soon you will be free, my rose, and you will begin a new life here that will make everything you have known look like a bad dream. I will make you my Sultana, queen of all that lives and breathes here. You will have all that you desire, and you will rule more truly than I, since you will rule over my heart!'

All of a sudden Muhammad had recovered the passionate face he had had in the garden with the singing fountains. Catherine realised, with great sadness, that he genuinely loved her, that he was prepared to make all manner of sacrifices for her – except, no doubt, the one she really wanted from him. It would have been easy enough to have lied and let him believe in a feigned love, but she was fairly certain that this would not save Arnaud and that he would never forgive this last betrayal. She had promised him to be frank, so she would be honest to the bitter end. Perhaps, after all, this man whom she had always known as just and kind still had enough generosity of soul to behave magnanimously …

'You did not understand me, my lord,' she said sadly, 'or perhaps you did not want to understand me. To have come all this way, through so many dangers, must mean that I love my husband … more than anything in the world!'

'And I told you that he would not be your husband for much longer!'

'Because you have sworn to kill him? But, Lord, if you love me as you say you do, you could not want to reduce me to despair. Do you believe I could love you when he was dead, accept the caresses of hands still red with his blood?' An idea came to her suddenly; a mad but generous idea. Arnaud's desperate plight left her no choice. She had the right still to sacrifice herself for him, and this man had enough love to accept what she would now offer him.

'Listen,' she murmured urgently, 'you cannot wish to place such a terrible memory between us if you really love me. Let my husband go free! Have him escorted safely to the frontiers of Granada … and I will stay with you, and be your slave as long as you want.'

This time she was deliberately withholding the perfect honesty she had promised, because she knew quite well that if he accepted, she would do everything possible to escape; and that, for his part, Arnaud would attempt everything to reclaim her. But she needed to gain time and above all to deliver Arnaud from a speedy execution. She went up to Muhammad, gently, so that her perfume swept over him, and even went so far as to lay her hand on his arm. To the devil with scruples! Arnaud's life came first!

'Listen to me, Lord, and do what I ask,' she implored. 'Pardon my husband!'

He answered coldly, without looking at her, his gaze lost in the green garden beyond.

'I have not the power to pardon him. You forget that the woman he killed was my sister, and that the whole kingdom is clamouring for his blood.'

That the whole of Granada wished to be revenged for the death of the universally-hated Princess was a thought that made Catherine smile inwardly. But she said nothing. This was not the moment to debate the dead woman's popularity. She had felt Muhammad tremble when she touched him, and that was enough.

'Then … let him escape. No-one could blame you for that!'

'Escape?' This time he looked at her, and Catherine saw that his eyes were cold as steel. 'Did you know that the Grand Vizier in person has appointed himself as his jailer? Do you know that besides the twenty Moorish guards who watch over him, there are a whole troop of the Great Cadi's men hidden close to his dungeon? For Allah himself demands the blood of the murderer of a princess of Granada. To let him escape, I would have to get rid of all those people – and that would be a danger to my very throne.'

As he spoke, Catherine seemed to lose all hope. She suddenly realized that this battle was in vain, that he would find every pretext possible for refusing a pardon he did not wish to grant. He hated Arnaud, rather because he was her husband than because he had killed Zobeïda! However, she made one last effort to soften his heart.

'Your sister wanted to hand me over to the slaves,' she said clearly, 'expose me naked on the ramparts and then hand me over to her Mongol executioners. Arnaud killed her to save me, and you, you refuse me his life … yet you claim you love me?'

'I told you I could not do it.'

'Come now. Are you or are you not the master here? And what was Zobeïda but a woman … one of these women so much despised by the men of your race? You want me to believe that the Great Cadi himself, the Holy Man of Granada, demands my husband's blood?'

'Zobeïda came of the blood of the Prophet!' Muhammad thundered. 'And he who spills the Prophet's blood must die! The crime is all the worse when the murderer is an infidel! Stop asking the impossible of me, Light of Dawn. Women do not understand men's affairs.'

Catherine started at the contempt in his voice. 'If you wanted to … you, whom they say are so powerful …'

'But I don't want to!'

He turned towards her and took her arm, bruising it in his rage, and brought his flushed face close to her own.

'Don't you understand that your prayers only increase my wrath? Why don't you say everything you have in mind? Why don't you say: free him because I love him and I shall never renounce him. Free him because I have to know that he is still alive somewhere … at any price … even if it means submitting to your kisses? Madwoman! Can't you see that it is your love for him rather than the desire to avenge my sister that makes me hate him? Because I do hate him now, do you hear … I hate him with all my powers, with all my strength, because he has succeeded in obtaining the thing I value most in all the world! To be loved by you!'

'And do you think that you would succeed better by killing him?' Catherine asked coldly. 'The dead are more powerful than you suppose.

You might succeed in keeping Arnaud of Montsalvy's wife as your slave, but you will never possess his widow! First because I will not outlive him. And then because your crime would appal me if I were to live ...'

She shook herself free and stepped back, staring at him defiantly. It was strange how anger made all men alike. In that man's exasperated countenance she seemed to see the reflections of other rages, those of all the men she had loved or fought. And she had always emerged victorious in the end. The moment he stopped appealing to her heart or her feelings, she felt strong in the face of an angry man. But she was wrong in supposing that this anger, this weakness, would put Muhammad in her power. All those other men had been of her own race. He was different. There was a whole world between them, over and beyond which their minds could never meet.

The Caliph regained his self-control with a visible effort. He turned his back on Catherine and sat down on his throne again. He picked up his sceptre once more, as if seeking in this emblem of power a defence against this too seductive woman. Catherine stiffened, suddenly uneasy before his sidelong glance and the thin smile that curled his lips beneath the blond beard. Fear crept through her now. Muhammad's fury was less alarming than his smile.

'You will not die, Light of Dawn,' he began softly.

'Stop calling me that!' she protested. 'I hate that name. My name is Catherine.'

'I am not used to these barbaric names, but I will do as you wish. Very well then, you will not die ... Catherine ... for I will see that the means are not provided. And I will possess you whenever I want to ... No, don't protest! And I will not have his blood on my hands ... for it is you yourself who will kill him!'

Catherine's heart missed a beat. She thought she must have heard him wrong, and she cried anxiously: 'What did you say? I don't understand ...'

'You will kill him with your own pretty hand. Now listen. Your husband is in a dungeon at the moment. He will stay there till the day of his victim's state funeral, which will take place at sunset a week from now. That day, he too will die, so that the slave may accompany his mistress and so that Zobeïda may have the pleasure of contemplating the bloody remains of her assassin in her grave. Till then he will not drink, or eat, or sleep, so that the people may see the wretched thing my rage can make of a Frankish knight. But what he endures till then will be nothing compared with the world of pain he will suffer before death. Before God, and before the people, the executioners will make him regret a hundred times that he was ever born, unless ...'

'Unless?' Catherine whispered, her throat suddenly dry.

'Unless you yourself curtail his sufferings. You will be present, my rose, attired as behoves a Sultana. And you will have the right to cut short his sufferings by striking him, yourself, with the weapon he himself used to kill.'

So that was the way he had chosen to make her suffer? By giving her the appalling choice of herself killing the man she adored, or hearing him scream for hours on end under torture! My God! How could she ever put an end to that life on which her own depended? Sadly, pitifully, she murmured, almost to herself:

'He would bless the death my hand brought him.'

'I doubt it. For he would know that you would belong to me afterwards in all legality. He will be informed that I am to marry you the same evening.'

Catherine turned away in disgust from the cruelty depicted on the Caliph's handsome face. 'And they said you were good, noble and generous …! They don't know you! But don't rejoice too soon. You don't know me either. There is a limit to how much I can suffer.'

'I know. You said that you would kill yourself. But not before the day of execution; because then nothing could save your husband from the tortures he deserves. You will have to stay alive for his sake, fair lady!'

She gazed at him with swimming eyes. What sort of love did this man feel for her? He thundered his passion at her, and then the next minute tortured her with cold cruelty … But she was incapable of reasoning or fighting anymore. She had reached the end of her reason! Yet it seemed impossible that, somewhere in the depths of this man's, this poet's heart, there wasn't a small corner that could still feel pity … She sank slowly to her knees and bowed her head.

'Lord,' she murmured, 'I implore you! See … I am kneeling at your feet. I have no more pride, or self-love. If you have any love for me at all, you cannot let me suffer so. You cannot condemn me to the torment of the days to come, you cannot wish me to break my heart slowly under the same roof as yourself! If you will not, or cannot, spare my husband's life, then at least allow me to be with him. Let me share his sufferings and his death, and as God is my witness I shall bless you with my dying breath.'

She held out her hands imploringly and raised toward him her lovely face, touching in its beauty, her eyes swimming with tears; but contrary to her expectations, Muhammad's rage only hardened.

'Get up,' he said curtly. 'It is useless humiliating yourself. I have spoken.'

'No, you cannot be so cruel! What use to you is a body whose soul is elsewhere … Don't make me suffer … Have pity on me!'

She hid her face in her hands. Outside, the sun sank in gory splendour, and from the neighbouring minaret came the shrill voice of the muezzin arose calling the faithful to prayer. The sound drowned Catherine's piteous sobs, and Muhammad, who might have been hovering on the verge of pity, took hold of himself again. He pointed to the door with a violent gesture and cried harshly:

'Now go! You are wasting your time and your tears here! You will get nothing from me. Go back to your room. It is the time for prayer.'

At once a gust of rage dried Catherine's tears. She sprang to her feet and darted a look of burning hatred at the Caliph.

'You are going to pray?' she asked, with withering contempt. 'So you know how to pray? Pray don't forget to tell your Allah, my lord, about your plan to destroy the union between two of your fellow creatures, and to make the wife murder her own husband. If he approves, it can mean only that he is a very different creature from the one true God, and that men get the gods that they deserve!'

She picked up her white veil, draped it hurriedly around herself and left without turning back. Outside she found Morayma and her escort. The long green courtyard was emptying rapidly. All the men were going to the mosque. Only four gardeners remained, nonchalantly pruning the myrtle bushes. One of them, a gigantic Moor, coughed as Catherine went past him. She turned to look at him unthinkingly, and gave a slight start of surprise. The face between the white turban and narrow black beard was Gauthier's!

Their eyes met. But she could not react, or linger there. She had to continue on her way while the disguised gardener made his way with the same lagging steps as the rest, toward the mosque. Yet Catherine felt her heart somewhat lightened by the encounter. She could not imagine how Gauthier came to be there, mingling with the Al Hamra servants, but doubtless it had something to do with the good offices of Abou-al-Khayr. He had no doubt passed himself off as a deaf mute, which would be the safest disguise for a pseudo-Muslim. The thought that he was there, close beside her, was so comforting that Catherine could have wept for joy. It was good to know that he was in this accursed palace too, watching over her as best he could. Josse on the other hand was in the Alcazaba, with the soldiers ... or perhaps in the Ghafar itself, near Arnaud. Then anguish seized Catherine again. First he did not know Arnaud, and secondly what could he possibly do to alleviate the prisoner's torments? Muhammad's words resounded in her ears again: 'He will not eat, or drink, or sleep for a whole week ...' What poor wreck of humanity would Arnaud be reduced to after seven days of torture! And would Catherine really have to strike him, in the heart, with the same dagger that had so often saved and protected her? She felt her throat go dry at the very thought, and her heart fail her. She knew that she would suffer, hour after hour, day after day, in her imagination, alongside the man she loved ...

One slightly comforting thought came to her. 'After having stabbed him, I will stab myself,' Catherine sighed.

When Catherine reached her room, Morayma, who had not spoken a word to her, threw her a doubtful glance.

'Now rest. I will come and fetch you in an hour ...'

'What for?'

'To take you to the baths. You are to share the Master's bed every night henceforth ...'

'You don't mean that he ...'

Indignation choked her, but Morayma merely shrugged, with the fatalism of her race.

'You are his property. He desires you ... What could be more natural? When one cannot avoid one's fate, the only wise thing is to accept it without complaint ...'

'And you think I can accept that?'

'What else can you do? You are beautiful. The master loves you after his fashion. You might succeed in averting his wrath ...'

A ferocious glance from Catherine showed Morayma the futility of such arguments, and she left the room. When she was alone, the prisoner sank onto her bed, almost sick with rage at the thought of what still awaited her. To think she had once trusted this Caliph, who now treated her with such icy cruelty. He was indeed a fitting brother for Zobeïda! She found in him the same arrogance, the same savage jealousy, the same total egotism. Zobeïda had believed that Arnaud would let Catherine be put to death, and would forget her in the Princess's arms; now Muhammad dared to try to possess her at the same time as he was condemning her husband to unspeakable tortures! Naturally Catherine was determined to defend herself fiercely, but she knew his executioners had the means to render her helpless. He would only laugh at her attempts to resist him ... and she did not yet have the right to kill herself. She took the little phial of poison that Abou had sent her and that she had hidden behind a loose tile, and contemplated it sorrowfully. If she could only smuggle half of it to Arnaud, she would cheerfully swallow the rest ... but it wasn't possible!

The gliding footsteps of the dumb eunuch of the morning, bringing her another tray of food, made her jump. She hid the phial in the hollow of her hand. She watched the slave set the tray down beside her on the bed instead of on the little table as was his usual custom. She was about to push away this meal she did not want when a significant glance from the Negro caught her eye. The man drew a thin scroll of paper from his sleeve and dropped it on the tray. Then he bowed to the ground and left the room backwards, as protocol demanded.

Hastily unrolling the note, Catherine was overjoyed to read a few lines that her little friend the doctor had written:

'The one who sleeps soundly is unaware of pain, grief and any outward circumstances. The rose-petal sweets that will be brought to you each evening will make you sleep so soundly for several hours that nothing, and no-one, will be able to wake you ...'

That was all, but Catherine's heart sent up a fervent prayer of thanks to the loyal friend who still managed to watch over her so closely, by means known to himself alone. She understood what he meant: every evening, when she came to fetch her, Morayma would find her so sound asleep that the Caliph would be forced to abandon his designs upon her. And who would ever think of suspecting those innocent little rose-petal sweets that were served with every meal in Granada?

Catherine hastily put the phial of poison back in its hiding-place. She must eat something else in order to allay suspicion. This was a real effort, because she was not in the least bit hungry, but somehow she managed to force herself to eat something off several dishes. At last she ate several spoonfuls of that celebrated scented jelly and then went and stretched out on her bed, with a feeling of triumph. She trusted her old friend Abou too much not to follow his commands to the letter, and she was almost positive that the little doctor's attentions would not be confined only to herself. He must know all about Arnaud's dreadful plight too. Gauthier's presence among the Al Hamra gardeners was almost proof of this. Little by little, Catherine's taut nerves relaxed. The mysterious drug was taking possession of her body …

14: The Drums of Allah

The crowd started massing at the foot of the red double keep and the Gate of the Seven Stages as the heat of the day subsided. There was a great open space there where the Caliph was wont to inspect his troops, and where great public festivals were held. Wooden platforms had been set up at the foot of the Al Hamra ramparts for the people, and stands draped in coloured silks for the Caliph and his dignitaries, but there was such a gigantic crowd that the platforms were soon packed tight with men and women and a large part of the townspeople had to remain standing.

All the previous week the priests and beggars had been up and down the length and breadth of Granada proclaiming the news that the Commander of the Faithful would hold a great festival on that day to commemorate the funeral of his beloved sister. During the festivities the infidel who had murdered her would himself be put to death. The whole town came at the appointed hour: men, women, children and old folk, all packed together in a seething, restless, noisy, shrill, colourful mass. The countrymen had come down from their neighbouring mountains, mingling the brown hues of their earth-coloured djellabas with the red, white, blue and orange robes of the citizens. There were a few groups of mercenaries from the Mahgreb, their long, plaited hair sticking out over their black tunics with the scarlet lozenge on the back, while others were dressed in dark blue and veiled like women. They carried curious shields of painted hide, and their strange appearance made them more formidable even than the Moorish knights with their glittering helmets.

All the inhabitants of the upper town were present, in their best clothes, shimmering with gold and silver in contrast to the immaculate white robes of the imams who were already crowding into the Cadi's stand. The giant Sudanese slaves from the palace were wandering about in the throng, strikingly handsome figures in their garishly-coloured robes and the slave's ring in one ear, laughing like expectant children at the thought of the spectacle to come.

The atmosphere of the place was something like that a fairground. All the entertainers and jugglers of the town had come to the empty parade ground, sure of finding an audience there before the spectacle began. There were tumblers; storytellers who accompanied their tales with short tattoos on their drums; hairy black snake-charmers brandishing their dangerous partners in a frenzied dance, acrobats even more supple than the snakes themselves; witches foretelling the future from willow baskets full of black and white shells; nasal-voiced singers chanting out verses of the Koran or love poems in the shrill tones of the nightly muezzin; old black-skinned clowns with grey beards going through their antics to a gale of laughter from the crowd; industrious beggars with over-agile fingers – all these mingled together in the fine red dust that smelt of horses' dung and straw.

Several men appeared high on the battlements above the gate to the Al Hamra. One of them, a tall man dressed in a striped orange robe, stepped out in front of the rest, who stood with their hands respectfully folded as if awaiting his orders. The Caliph Muhammad was just taking a last look to make sure that everything was in its rightful place and that the spectacle could now begin. All around the immense parade-ground the troops of horsemen in their pointed helmets and white turbans were moving into position … Up on the Al Hamra towers a group of storks stood, dreaming, perched on one leg …

Meanwhile, in the Sultana's apartments, an army of women servants, directed by the agitated Morayma, were preparing Catherine for the evening's spectacle. She appeared quite unconscious of what was happening around her. She stood in the middle of the room, in a gorgeous sea of veils, silks, open caskets, precious stones and flagons of scent, and let herself be dressed by them, without a word or a gesture, like a statue whose eyes alone were alive. The only sounds to be heard in the room were the exasperated cries of Morayma, eternally dissatisfied with the way her orders were being carried out, and the servants' irritable sighs.

The mistress of the harem had the air of a priestess carrying out some ancient ritual as she harried the women gradually covering Catherine from head to foot in gold. The fine gilded slippers embroidered in gold thread and gems were gold; gold too were the wide gauze trousers, and the short brocade jacket that covered her breasts. The remainder of the costume consisted of a mass of jewels: bracelets reaching halfway up her arms, heavy anklets, a thick collar dripping huge emeralds over her bosom, all but revealed by her plunging neckline, and finally a superb and massive belt, a masterpiece of Persian workmanship, studded with diamonds, rubies and emeralds, which Morayma fastened about the young woman's hips with an almost religious awe.

'In sending you this belt, the master proves his desire to make you his wife. This jewel was made for the former Caliph of Baghdad, Haroun-al-Raschid, for his favourite wife, and it is the pearl among all his treasures.

After the sacking of the palace in Baghdad, the Emir of Cordoba, Abd-er-Khaman II, bought it for the women he loved, and then it was stolen. The Lord Rodrigo de Bivar, the Cid, gave it to his wife, the Lady Ximena, but the belt was taken back again after her death. All the Sultanas have worn it on their wedding day …'

Morayma fell silent. Catherine was not listening. For the past week she seemed to have been living in a dream, a somnambulist lost in a waking nightmare, and this had soon filled not only Morayma, but the whole harem, with a sort of superstitious awe. The strange, deep sleep into which she had fallen every evening since her husband's capture had enraged Muhammad to begin with, and then plunged him into a slightly fearful astonishment. Nothing could dispel those slumbers of hers, which lasted several hours, till daybreak, and it was as if the hand of Allah himself had closed her eyelids.

At first drugs had been suspected, but nothing about the young woman's behaviour had struck her captors as being at all unusual or abnormal. Muhammad had been brought to believe that this must be a sign from heaven. He must not touch this woman, wife of a murderer, so long as her legitimate owner was still alive. And he had not sent for Catherine since the third evening. But Morayma, who was intensely superstitious, and somewhat given to belief in the black arts, was inclined to think of the new favourite as an abnormally endowed being. Catherine's silence, her long hours of taciturn refusal to speak, struck her as the marks of a spirit invaded by invisible powers.

To tell the truth, the effects of Abou-al-Khayr's drug were gradually taking hold over Catherine's mind. She passed the day in a sort of twilight state, her mind full of misty vapours that had the advantage of blurring her anxiety and soothing her pain. Had it not been for this she might well have been driven mad by the thought of Arnaud tortured by hunger, thirst and sleeplessness in the lugubrious dungeons of the Al Hamra keep. All the same, she had not touched the rose-petal sweet on the past two nights, because she was alarmed to find her mind and her reflexes slipping out of control, and she had simply feigned sleep instead. She wanted to be in full possession of her faculties on the day of execution.

One last touch of kohl on her eyelids, and then Morayma wrapped Catherine in a veil woven and embroidered in gold, which gave her the look of some strange, barbaric idol.

'It is time now …' Morayma whispered, offering Catherine her hand to help her across the threshold. But Catherine refused it. She was certain that the journey she was making now led only to death, that she had not much longer to live, and that all these fabulous clothes and ornaments with which they had decked her were the festive attire of a sacrificial victim. In a short while she would stab Arnaud to death to spare him long and appalling tortures, and then, swiftly, she would turn the weapon against herself. Her soul, and his, would ascend into this warm blue air, bathed in this radiant sunshine that was about to plunge behind the snowy mountain peaks, and then they would be reunited forever, free of pain, doubt, jealousy, leaving nothing but a scrap of inert flesh behind in the executioners' hands. All in all, this was a great day for Catherine, because, like Arnaud himself no doubt, she looked forward eagerly to the long peacefulness of death.

When the future Sultana appeared, surrounded by women and escorted by a powerful troop of eunuchs, the Caliph and his suite were already in their places in the high stand, hung with gold and green, that had been erected for him. The countless entertainers had stopped their antics, but the people were still making as much din as a cageful of parrots, and the general excited hubbub was deafening. The young woman's appearance silenced them for a moment. She stood out amid the tender pastel veils of her womenfolk, blue, pink, almond-green, saffron; she was both sparkling and mysterious, for the delicate cloud of golden gauze both hid and revealed the splendour of the jewels beneath. Silently Catherine ascended to her own stand, which was placed beside and somewhat lower than the Caliph's. It was hung with blue silk, and a flight of steps led down from it to the improvised arena.

Muhammad too was silent, nervously fingering his blond beard as he watched the young woman approach. Their eyes met, and it was Muhammad who looked away first, struck by the flash of anger in Catherine's gaze. He frowned and turned his attention back to the arena, where a troupe of young Berber dancers had just appeared, to the accompaniment of plaintive, sing-song music. They wore long white robes covered with massive jewellery, their faces were painted like girls, and there were red ribbons tied about their waists and foreheads. These pretty youths had faces of exquisite delicacy, languishing eyes and inscrutable smiles. They thumped the ground with their bare feet, writhing voluptuously, miming the very movements of love in a strange ballet with complicated steps. Some among them were singing, in high-pitched shrill voices, to the accompaniment of ear-piercing rebecs, and others clacked bronze castanets between their fingers to the rhythm of their steps.

These ambiguous dancers displeased Catherine, who turned her head away, a movement that provoked glances of hatred from them; but she found it hard to watch their mannered movements and the limp femininity of their poses at this death feast. For this was indeed the festival of death. This crowd was here to enjoy the smell and sight of blood! High up, in the royal mosque, the drums began a sinister tattoo. The rolling passed like a wave over the dancers, who prostrated themselves on the ground, panting, and stayed there motionless till the furious thunder had ceased. Slowly the heavy portals of the Gate of Seven Stages swung open and a solemn procession emerged. The embalmed body of Zobeïda, a red, rigid outline beneath the long crimson veil covering her from head to foot, appeared, carried on a silver litter by twenty slaves and preceded by players of fifes, raitas and tambourines. The body was surrounded by a group of white-robed priests. Then came a great troop of black eunuchs, led by their chief, a gigantic Sudanese with a bronzed face, carrying his scimitar upside down in token of mourning.

The appearance of her enemy woke Catherine from the sort of disdainful indifference in which she had armoured herself. Zobeïda was dead, but her hate lived on, and Catherine felt it passing into her. A cold fury washed over her at the sight of this cold corpse to which she would shortly be forced to sacrifice her husband and herself. The slaves meantime laid the litter upon a sort of low table in front of the Caliph's stand. Muhammad stood up and stepped forward, followed by Banu Siradj and several of the dignitaries, to pay tribute to his sister's remains. Once again Catherine would have liked to look away, but something seemed to force her to keep watching. She had been conscious of an almost unbearably persistent stare trained upon her. Instinctively, she turned to look, and then she suddenly recognised Abou-al-Khayr in the Caliph's suite. The tall, solid figure of the Captain of the Moorish guard had kept his slender silhouette concealed till then. The little doctor was staring at her intently from beneath the immense orange turban he habitually wore, and when their eyes met at last, Catherine noticed that he gave a furtive, hurried smile and then turned his head a fraction as though indicating that she should follow the direction of his eyes. Then she saw Gauthier standing in the front row of the mob, towering above them with arms folded, giving a fairly convincing impression of an idle sensation-seeker. He still wore his gardener's cap, a sort of red felt cone pulled down almost to his eyes, and he looked as calm and cheerful as if he were attending the liveliest of festivals rather than an execution.

Then Abou-al-Khayr's eyes moved a little farther off, to where a group of Moorish cavalry stood at attention, and Catherine recognised Josse beneath a pointed golden helmet. She took a little time to find him though, because with his swarthy skin, his fine black beard and the lance in hand, sitting upright in his saddle, he offered just as savage and military an appearance as any of his companions. There was nothing to distinguish him from them, and Catherine could not help admiring the skill with which the Parisian beggar played his role. He appeared quite indifferent to what was going on in front of him, more concerned with keeping his horse in line. The animal seemed unusually nervous and kept curveting and prancing about. Had it not been for Josse's expert handling, it would doubtless have caused some trouble and confusion in the crowd.

The sight of her three friends revived Catherine's failing hopes. She knew they were brave and loyal and capable of anything when it came to trying to save herself and Arnaud, and this determination she sensed in them breathed new spirit into her ... How could one ever entirely lose hope with men like these as allies?

A long ceremony followed the arrival of the Princess's body. There were songs, ritual, solemn dances, followed by an interminable address delivered by an imposing old man with a long, snowy-white beard. He was as tall and withered as a poplar tree in winter, and from beneath their bristling white brows his eyes gleamed with a fanatic's fire. Catherine already knew that this was the Grand Cadi, and she dug her nails into her palms as she heard him invoke the wrath of Allah, and that of the Caliph, against the infidel who had dared to raise a sacrilegious hand against a descendant of the Prophet. When he finally fell silent, after one last burst of execration, Catherine knew that Arnaud's last hour had come, and her own with it. The faint gleam of hope that her friends' presence had kindled, faded ... What could they possibly do? What could three men do faced with a whole multitude? There was the crowd of townspeople, the Court, the soldiery ... and so much hatred for the infidel everywhere, such a fierce joy at the thought of his approaching death! ... God alone could help them! Catherine addressed a silent prayer to the Saviour; another to the Virgin of Puy, whose protection she had invoked before; and lastly a rapid but fervent prayer for help to Saint James of Compostela.

'Give me a little more strength, Lord,' she beseeched. 'Make me strong enough to stab him!'

Once again the drums had started rolling high up on the ramparts. Catherine's soul trembled at the sound. She seemed to hear a threat with every muffled beat; it sounded like the slow pounding of a dying man's heart. It was funereal. At the same moment, the Caliph's executioners stepped, two by two, through the palace gates. They wore blue jackets with rolled-up sleeves, and wide billowing trousers in yellow material embroidered in red. They marched round the arena, carrying a strange assortment of bizarre-looking instruments that made Catherine go pale, and arranged themselves in a circle, pushing back the crowd that the guards were having some difficulty in controlling. Meanwhile a troop of half-naked slaves hastily assembled a large, low scaffold just in front of Muhammad's stand, with a wooden cross upon it, similar to the one that had once stood upon a hill in Jerusalem, but much lower, so that the executioners charged with torturing the condemned man could work more easily. More slaves brought in smoking braziers, into which the torturers plunged a whole assortment of iron rods, hooks and pincers. The crowd stood enthralled, scarcely breathing, as these sinister preparations were made; but they sent up a roar of welcome on the appearance of a huge, hunchbacked Negro, as withered as an ebony-tree, who strolled calmly into the arena. He carried over one shoulder a carpet-bag in which the dead man's head would be placed, to be presented to the Caliph, before being fixed on a spike on the

Tower of Justice. This was Bekir, the chief executioner, and an important personage, as his silver-embroidered crimson robe proclaimed. He climbed with a solemn air onto the scaffold and stood there without moving, arms folded and head thrown back, to await the arrival of the condemned man.

Once more the drums rolled. Catherine felt as if she were suffocating beneath her golden veils. She bit her hand to prevent herself crying out aloud. Her nerves were strung to breaking-point. Her eyes despairingly sought out Abou-al-Khayr, but the little doctor stood with his head on his chest and seemed to be asleep. He looked so tiny, so frail in the midst of this vast crowd that Catherine began to panic. Could he and the other two really be planning some sort of rescue? It would be madness if they did, because not one of them would escape with their lives. They must not try …! No, it would be better for her and Arnaud to die! But quickly …! She looked round at the crowd.

Gauthier stood in the same place, as immobile as a statue, but Catherine saw him stiffen slightly when the Al Hamra gates creaked open for the third time. The condemned man appeared at the foot of the red walls, between the immense iron-barred gates …

Catherine sat up with an exclamation of horror that she could not control. Arnaud was pale, almost naked but for a cloth tied round his loins and heavy chains on his feet and wrists, and he staggered in the sunlight like a drunken man. His arms were tied behind his back, his face was covered by a straggling beard and his eyes were dreadfully sunken; but in spite of everything he seemed to be making a supreme effort to retain some dignity at this crucial moment. Then he tripped over a stone and fell to his knees. The guards had to pull him back on to his feet. Lack of sleep and food had wrought their ravages, and the guards had to half carry him down the slope.

Morayma clutched desperately at Catherine's arm, trying to drag her down into her seat again, but the young woman neither saw nor heard what went on around her, oblivious of everything but the long brown body that the Moors were dragging to the scaffold. Her whole body was rigid with pain. Now Muhammad's sombre gaze fastened upon her, and in a whisper Morayma pleaded:

'I beg you to take hold of yourself, Light of Dawn. The master is watching you.'

'Let him!' Catherine burst out angrily. 'What do I care?'

'His wrath might fall more heavily upon the condemned man …' the old Jewess suggested timidly. 'Please don't defy him openly. Great men know how to make people pay dearly for their humiliations. My people know that only too well.'

Catherine said nothing, but she understood. Suppose the Caliph, in his anger, decided to withdraw the appalling concession he had offered her? Suppose he prevented her from sparing her beloved the terrible tortures that the executioners' ugly pile of instruments seemed to portend? She slowly let her knees bend and sat down again, but her whole body shook convulsively. She felt as if she were dying herself, and she had to fight against the creeping, growing weakness that froze the blood in her veins. Her whole soul, her very life itself, was concentrated in her eyes, fixed unmovingly upon the man about to die.

The executioners hoisted Arnaud onto the scaffold and stood him against the cross. They did not fasten his hands to it but held them open against the wooden timbers. At once something whistled through the air, received with cheers from the crowd and a faint moan from Arnaud. Two archers standing at the foot of the Caliph's stand had drawn their bows and aimed with devilish skill, pinning his hands to the cross with their arrows, right through the palms. Arnaud went white with pain, and sweat trickled down his face. The hysterical cry of 'You! You!' rose from the women into the warm, violet-tinged air. Catherine sprang to her feet with a cry. One of the executioners had drawn a long, red-hot brand from the brazier and was now approaching the condemned man, cheered on by the mob.

Catherine, wild with fury, tore herself from Morayma's restraining grasp and ran down into the arena till she stood face to face with Muhammad. The crowd fell silent at once, and the executioner paused in his work, mouth agape with astonishment. What did she want, this gold-veiled woman whom the whole town rumoured was to marry the Caliph that very evening? Catherine's voice rang out, high and accusing.

'Is that what you promised me, Caliph? You are not going to break your word to me, surely? Or do you not know what that means?'

She spoke in French, in a last attempt to conciliate this man who had them both in his power. If she were to humiliate him in front of his people, he would surely never forgive her ... The Caliph's smile gleamed thinly in his blond beard.

'I just wanted to see how you would react, Light of Dawn. You may perform the *coup de grâce* I promised you, if such is your wish ...'

He stood and stared commandingly round at the mob.

'Listen all of you, loyal subjects of the Kingdom of Granada. This evening the woman you see here is to become my bride. She has won my heart. As a wedding present I have granted her the privilege of killing my sister's murderer with her own hand. It is right that he who killed a woman should die by a woman's hand.'

The growls of rage and disappointment from the mob lasted no more than a moment. The company of archers in front of the Caliph's stand raised their bows threateningly. No-one dared protest after the Caliph had finished speaking.

Catherine's eyes sought Abou's anxiously, but the little doctor had not moved. He certainly seemed to be sound asleep. She felt bitter ... How could he abandon her at such a moment? He was just like all the rest; his own safety meant more to him than friendship ...

Now a slave knelt down in front of Catherine, holding a golden platter on which the Montsalvy dagger gleamed sinisterly. Catherine snatched it up almost eagerly. The silver sparrow-hawk fitted comfortably into the palm of her hand, like a pet bird. At last she had the means to deliver Arnaud, and herself too!

She drew herself up and flashed a steely look at Muhammad. Then she tore the veil defiantly from her face.

'I am not of your race or religion, Sultan! Don't forget that!'

With this she turned on her heel and walked proudly toward the scaffold. Courage! This was to be her greatest hour! In a brief moment, her soul and her husband's would escape together toward that gold and crimson sunset that flamed above the arena, freer even than those birds floating high above them ... The crowd fell silent, reluctantly impressed by the sight of this beautiful woman advancing proudly, with death in her hand, toward the crucified man ... It was a rare and splendid sight, and in the eyes of this refined and civilised people it equalled the barbarous pleasure afforded by the sight of a man put to the torture.

But now Arnaud raised his head upon the cross. His eyes, strangely clear and determined, met Catherine's first and then the Caliph's.

'I refuse this supposed act of mercy, Lord Sultan! The speedy death you have allowed this woman to bring me is nothing but dishonour! What knight worthy of the name would consent to die by a woman's hand? And by *her* hand, above all? Apart from the dishonour to me, you would be making her responsible for your crime, in forcing her to murder her own husband! Hear me, all of you!' And now the man's voice swelled, and rolled over the crowd like thunder. 'This woman dressed in gold, this woman whom your Sultan plans to take to his bed tonight, is my own wife and the mother of my son! And know too that if I killed Zobeïda, it was for her sake, to save her from death and violation, so that the mother of my son should not be sullied and dishonoured by vile slaves! I killed Zobeïda, and I am proud of it! She did not deserve to live! But I refuse to die by a woman's hand! Leave me, Catherine ...'

'Arnaud,' the young woman begged, in despair. 'Please, for the sake of our great love!'

'No, I command you to leave me ... and I command you to live ... for the sake of our son!'

'Live? Do you know what you are saying? Let me strike, or ...'

But two guards seized her arms. Muhammad had guessed that she intended to kill herself. But her angry cry was drowned out by Arnaud's voice. It was not so powerful now, for pain had shortened his breath, but it rang out as clear and inflexible as ever.

'Bring on your executioners, Caliph! I will show you how a Montsalvy dies! May God protect my King and have mercy on my soul!'

Catherine sank to her knees in the sandy arena, too weak to do more.

'I want to die with you! I want ...'

At an angry sign from the Caliph, the executioners went back to their instruments of torture. The mob was seething like a storm-tossed sea. On all sides, people commented on the condemned man's brave words, there were exclamations of astonishment and admiration, almost of pity ... And suddenly, behind the red walls of the Al Hamra, the drums started to roll once again ...

Every head turned, and everyone's movements hung suspended, for these drumbeats were quite different from the ones they had heard before: this was the fierce, rapid drumming-out of a sort of tocsin in a new, warlike rhythm. Then came screams, angry shouts and moans from the palace: cries of rage, pain and triumph. The Caliph's Court and the huge crowd waited, frozen in amazement, not quite knowing what this new development could mean. But Abou-al-Khayr had suddenly decided to stir from his apparent stupor. Ignoring protocol, he gave an enormous yawn ...

Instantly Josse gave free rein to the spirited mount that he had so much difficulty in controlling, and it began galloping wildly about in all directions, creating havoc in the orderly ranks of guards. At the same moment, Gauthier pushed back his stupefied neighbours, struck down the guards restraining the crowd behind him and ran full tilt toward the scaffold. The giant was unchained. Inspired by the sacred rage that took hold of him in the hour of battle, he speedily dispatched the men guarding Catherine, the executioners themselves. Even the gigantic Bekir fell, spitting out teeth, under the wildly lashing hooves of Josse's horse. Catherine became aware through her daze of astonishment that someone had taken her by the hand.

'Come,' Abou-al-Khayr's voice spoke quietly. 'There is a horse here for you.'

With this, he pulled off her gold veils and threw over her shoulders a large dark mantle that had surprisingly appeared from under his robes.

'But ... Arnaud!'

'Let Gauthier take care of him!'

The giant was busy pulling out the arrows that fastened Arnaud to the cross. Then he slung the man's inert form over his shoulder like a bundle of clothes and sprang down the steps of the scaffold. Josse had more or less succeeded in mastering his horse by now, and he surged out of the crowd near Gauthier, leading by the rein another powerful animal, a sort of massive warhorse with an enormous rump. The giant leaped into the saddle with amazing agility for a man so heavily burdened. Then he dug in his knees and spurs and the great horse sprang through the astounded crowd like a cannonball, taking little heed of the people trampled underfoot ...

'You see,' the little doctor's tranquil voice remarked, 'he doesn't need us.'

'But what is happening?'

'Nothing much: a sort of little revolution! I will explain it all to you later. In any case, it seems to be keeping our Caliph busy for the moment. Come, now is the moment. No-one is interested in us now.'

By now the entire arena was thrown into the greatest alarm and confusion. The mob of women, children, tumblers, old folk and vendors of one kind or another were fleeing wildly in all directions, trying to escape the horses' charging hooves. The palace guards were at grips with a troop of horsemen dressed and veiled in black, who had suddenly materialised, from where no-one quite knew. Fighting was going on in the stands as well, and Catherine saw that Muhammad was acquitting himself valiantly in this hand-to-hand struggle. The cries of the dying mingled with angry shouts and the moans of the wounded. The black birds were closing in, up in the mauve sky, and their flight swooped lower and lower …

The centre of this human whirlpool, the leader of the black-clad riders, who had till now been holding themselves in check amid the crowd, was a tall thin man with a swarthy countenance. He too wore black, but his face was uncovered and a magnificent ruby flashed in his turban. His scimitar flashed like the Archangel's sword, striking off heads like a reaper scything corn. The last thing Catherine saw, as Abou-al- Khayr led her off on a horse that had appeared as if by magic, was the death of the Grand Vizier. The bloody scimitar of the black knight swept off his head, and a moment later it was hanging from his victor's saddlebow.

And still the drums continued their thunder from the rooftop of the royal mosque of the Al Hamra …

The town was in an uproar. While Abou-al-Khayr led the way through the winding alleys between windowless walls, Catherine kept seeing incidents that reminded her of the Paris of her childhood. On all sides, men fought each other and blood flowed. It was dangerous to pass below a terrace, because a rain of various projectiles was falling from them, and here and there, in the panic-stricken crowd, the macabre silhouette of one of the black-clad horsemen surged up and was lost again. Then a scimitar flashed in the lamp-light, for it was growing dark now, and there was a scream of agony. Abou-al-Khayr refused to stop.

'Hurry,' he said. 'They might close the city gates.'

'Where are you taking me?' Catherine asked.

'To the place where the giant has taken your husband. To the Alcazar Génil, the residence of the Sultana Amina.'

'But … why there?'

'Patience for a moment. I will explain everything later. Now hurry …'

Neither the din, the danger, nor the cries could diminish Catherine's heartfelt joy. She was free, Arnaud was free! The whole nightmarish scene of torture had vanished as if by magic, and her horse's prancing steps echoed the joyful beating of her heart.

At length they broke into a gallop, oblivious of the people knocked flying by their horses' hooves. The south gate was fortunately still open, and they crossed it at full gallop, hoof-beats drumming over the little Roman bridge that spanned the clear, foaming waters of the Génil river. Soon there appeared, beyond a clump of palms, the white cupola of a large wall surrounding green treetops and a sort of tower topped by a mitre-shaped roof. It was flanked by two pavilions and fronted by an entrance supported by slender pillars. Ghostly figures were passing to and fro before the gate, which was hurriedly opened as Abou-al-Khayr clapped his hands to his mouth and gave a strange, piercing cry. The two horses and their riders galloped on under the gateway and did not slow down till they stood safely before the jasmine-festooned columns of the palace entrance. Behind them the massive outer gates were shut and barricaded fast.

Catherine slid down from her horse and almost collapsed into Gauthier's arms. He caught her and held her away from him at arm's length, so overjoyed that he forgot his usual restraint.

'Alive!' he cried. 'And free …! Praised be Odin and Thor the Victorious for returning you to us! We have been half alive these past few days.'

But she could not keep back her impatience and anxiety another minute.

'Arnaud? Where is he?'

'Not far away. They are taking care of him …'

'He isn't …' She dared not continue. She seemed to see Gauthier pulling the arrows from his pierced hands, and the blood streaming from his inert body as the giant slung him across his shoulder.

'No. He is weak, of course, because of all the blood he has lost. And Master Abou's skill will be most welcome.'

'Come, let us go,' said the doctor. He slid from his horse and set his turban squarely back on his head with a triumphant gesture. He took Catherine's hand and followed Gauthier across a huge room magnificently decorated with a marquetry pattern comprised of thousands of brilliantly-coloured flowers, a fantastic motionless blossoming that would never fade. They entered a long gallery with little arched windows. The black marble floor gleamed underfoot like a dark lake all around the archipelago of scattered rugs. Beyond was a smaller room, where Arnaud lay on a silk mattress, an unknown woman on one side of him and Josse, still wearing his military uniform, on the other. When the Parisian saw Catherine he smiled broadly, but Catherine paid no attention to him, or to the woman, and sank down on her knees beside her husband.

He was unconscious, his face drawn and pale, with dark mauve shadows beneath his closed eyes. Blood from his pierced hands had stained the green silk mattress and the carpet, but now it had stopped flowing. His breathing was shallow, rapid.

'I think he will live,' said a grave voice close to Catherine's side. She turned and met a pair of eyes so black, so mysterious, that it seemed impossible to read them. She examined the woman who had spoken for the first time and saw that she was young, very beautiful, with a gentle but proud face, the golden skin of which was marked with curious painted signs in dark blue. Noticing her surprise, the woman smiled briefly.

'All the women of the Great Atlas are like me,' she explained. 'I am Amina. Come with me. We must leave the doctor to care for the wounded man. Abou-al-Khayr does not like women to interfere with his work.'

Catherine could not help smiling. First because Amina's friendliness was contagious, and then because her words reminded her of the first time she had met the little Moorish doctor, in the inn on the road to Peronne. That had been the first time he had tended Arnaud, whom Catherine and her uncle had discovered lying unconscious by the roadside. She knew of her friend's prodigious skill. So she let herself be led away, as Gauthier murmured:

'I will stay with him ...'

The two women went and sat down beside the narrow canal that crossed the garden. A double rose-bed surrounded it, and fine jets of water arched and crossed overhead, bringing a delicious coolness that dissolved the heat and weariness of the day. Heaps of silk cushions, their colours blending with those of the roses, were massed along the margin of the pool. There were great lamps of gilded bronze and big gold trays covered with cakes, sweetmeats and every sort of fruit. Amina motioned to Catherine to sit down beside her, then sent her women away, their pale veils blending into the garden shadows or into the lighted house.

The two women stayed silent for a while. Catherine was drinking in the fragrant tranquillity of this beautiful garden almost unconsciously, still unutterably weary from her day's experiences. And she savoured the serenity of this woman sitting beside her. After such horrible terror, grief and pain, after having all but died of fear many times over, Arnaud's wife felt as though she were almost in paradise. Death, fear, even anxiety seemed to have dissolved. God would never have saved Arnaud so miraculously only to snatch him away again. He would be cured, saved ... She was certain!

The Sultana watched her visitor and respected her silence for a while, before pointing to the trays of food.

'You are tired, exhausted, I am sure,' she said gently. 'Rest, and eat.'

'I am not hungry,' Catherine replied, with the ghost of a smile. 'But what I would like to know is how I come to be here. What has happened? Can you tell me now, after welcoming me so generously?'

'Why should I be anything but welcoming? Because my lord wanted to make you his second wife? Our law allows him as many wives as he wants … and as far as my personal feelings are concerned, I have had nothing but indifference for him for a long time.'

'Yet they say that you are still very close.'

'Outwardly perhaps. It is possible that he still feels fond of me. But his incredible indulgence toward Zobeïda, the ease with which he accepted her worst extravagances and crimes, including her attempts to murder me, has slowly killed any love I might once have felt for him. You are welcome here, Light of Dawn, and particularly so now that I know what you have endured. It is noble and fine in a woman to risk so much for the man she loves. I was moved by your story. That is why I agreed to help Abou-al-Khayr in his project.'

'Forgive me for insisting on this point, but what exactly has happened?'

An amused smile revealed Amina's little white teeth. She picked up a fan, the delicate palm fronds of which were gilded and painted, and waved it softly with her slender, hennaed hands.

'Just at present Lord Mansour-ben-Zegris is engaged in seizing the throne of Granada from Muhammad.'

'But … why?'

'To avenge me. He believes I am dying. No, don't look at me like that,' Amina went on, laughing. 'I am perfectly well, but Abou the doctor has spread a rumour that the Grand Vizier, enraged by Zobeïda's death, has had me poisoned so that I might accompany my enemy into death and be deprived of the pleasure of rejoicing in her demise.'

'And Mansour-ben-Zegris believed that?'

'He raced round here this morning like a madman. He found my womenfolk tearing their veils and my servants howling with grief, and myself stretched out on a bed as pale as death.' She stopped to smile at Catherine, then added, forestalling her question: 'Abou-al-Khayr is a great doctor. Mansour saw me only from a distance in any case, and he was quite convinced. That decided him to attack the Al Hamra. Abou, who knows Mansour well, suggested that the time of the execution would be the most favourable one for an attack, because then the Caliph, his Court and a part of his troops would all be outside the fortress. They laid their plans, and when the royal drums sounded a warning, Abou-al-Khayr yawned as a signal to his servants. You know the rest …'

Now Catherine understood. Abou had fomented a revolt led by Mansour so that the condemned man's escape might be contrived under cover of the general agitation.

'Heaven be praised,' she sighed, 'for giving my husband the strength to endure so much pain without dying!'

The little doctor's high voice, speaking from behind, made her turn round. Abou-al-Khayr carefully rolled down his sleeves over his freshly-scrubbed hands and then sat down on the cushions.

'Your husband was not half as weak as he appeared to be, my friend, but he had to act the part!' he said, fastidiously picking up a honey cake with his fingertips and conveying it to his mouth without losing a single drop.

'What do you mean?' Catherine asked, unthinkingly dropping into French.

'He may not have eaten much, but he had quite a bit to drink, thanks to Josse, who was on guard in the Ghafar. And above all he was able to sleep. How did you like your rose-petal sweet these last few days?'

'It was excellent. But I thought the guards were forbidden to let the prisoner sleep at all, and that the Grand Cadi sent men to make sure the orders were carried out?'

Abou-al-Khayr started to laugh. 'When a man sleeps so soundly that nothing on earth will waken him, and one is under strict orders not to let him sleep, the wisest course if one does not want to be punished or made to look foolish is to conceal the fact. The Cadi's men are as anxious for their skins as most mortals. Your husband slept soundly on three consecutive nights.'

'But not because he ate rose-petal sweets?'

'No. It was thanks to the water Josse brought him, in a little phial hidden in his turban. It certainly wasn't enough to quench his thirst fully, but it was enough to keep his wits clear.'

'And now?'

'He is sleeping, guarded by Gauthier. I made him take some goat's milk and honey and then some more of the sleeping-draught. '

'But what about his hands?'

'One does not die because one's hands have been pierced, so long as the bleeding is stopped in time and the wounds tended. Now you must get some rest too. You are safe here, whatever the results of the fighting.'

'Who will win?'

'There is no knowing. Mansour's attack was prepared somewhat too hastily perhaps. On the other hand, he took Muhammad by surprise, and his desert warriors are the bravest fighters in the world. But there are few of them, and the Caliph has many guards. However, they say half the town supports Mansour.'

'But suppose one of them – Mansour or the Caliph – should die?' Catherine exclaimed, horrified. 'You haven't stirred up the hatred between these two men just so that we may be saved? We don't deserve to have so many lives sacrificed for us!'

Amina laid her hand soothingly over Catherine's.

'The fighting between Mansour-ben-Zegris, my cousin, and the

Commander of the Faithful never ceases! It takes very little to set it going again. And then it dies away again for a while! It may turn out that the Caliph has to go away for a time to allow the town to calm down. But Mansour can never take the throne so long as he is alive. The priests would never allow it ...'

'But if Mansour were conquered? What would be his fate?' Catherine asked, her interest aroused by this doubtless cruel and bloodthirsty man who had nevertheless saved her own life and her husband's. She could not help feeling guilty about the subterfuge that had been played on him.

Abou-al-Khayr shrugged and picked up another cake. 'Don't worry! He would not be so foolish as to let himself be captured. Besides, his life is not in such great danger. If he were defeated he would escape, cross the sea and travel to Fez, where he owns a palace and lands. Then, after a few months had elapsed, he would return, more arrogant and powerful than ever. And it would begin all over again. Except that this time he would have Banu Siradj to contend with. Zobeïda's death seems to have driven him almost crazy.'

'The Grand Vizier is dead,' Catherine cried. 'I saw a knight dressed in black with a huge ruby in his turban slice off his head and fasten it to his saddlebow.'

She was astonished to see a broad smile of contentment spread over Abou's face. 'The sage tells us that it is evil to rejoice in the death of one's enemies ... but I have to admit that I shall never mourn the passing of Haben-Ahmed Banu Siradj!'

'If only Mansour had been able to destroy the rest of his family along with him,' the Sultana cried, with sudden violence. 'But these people seem to swarm everywhere like ants ...'

'Let us be content for what we have achieved already,' said Abou, 'and hope that ...'

The sounds of urgent hammering on the palace gates interrupted him. Shouts and cries arose beyond the walls. Then the curious howling noise that Abou himself had made on arrival at the palace. Slaves ran to the gates. The huge bronze-studded portals swung open without a creak, but the slaves only just had time to leap back to avoid the onrush of a group of veiled horsemen. Catherine recognised at their head the man with the ruby, and she turned away. The Grand Vizier's head still dangled, with eyes closed, from the saddlebow. Amina stood up, without the slightest show of surprise, and waited beside the rose bushes. She merely drew her gold-embroidered mauve veil over her face. Her gaze seemed to petrify the knight. Catherine saw that he had a beautiful, cruel mouth outlined by a fine moustache, and fierce eyes set in a thin, melancholy bird face.

Mansour-ben-Zegris sprang from his horse, came toward Amina and stopped short, three paces away. 'You are alive?' he breathed. 'What miracle saved you?'

'Abou-al-Khayr saved me,' the Sultana answered calmly. 'He is a great doctor. One of his drugs overcame the poison.'

'Allah is powerful!' Mansour exclaimed in a voice so rapturous that Catherine almost smiled. This warrior with the fanatic's face seemed to have a touch of childlike credulity! It seemed to be the easiest thing in the world to get him to swallow the most absurd tales! Still, Abou-al-Khayr certainly had a great reputation.

But now Mansour's black eyes turned and fastened upon Catherine, although she too had covered up her face. Something about this woman's figure seemed to impress him, because he asked:

'Who is this woman? I have never seen her before.'

'A fugitive! This is Muhammad's white-skinned favourite! While you were fighting, Abou managed to rescue her, together with the condemned man, the man who killed Zobeïda, who is her husband.'

Mansour's face did not conceal his amazement. Evidently he knew nothing about Catherine and Arnaud.

'What is this strange tale? What does it all mean?'

Catherine sensed that Amina was smiling behind her semi-transparent veil. She obviously knew her alarming lover inside-out, and managed him with consummate ease.

'It means,' she said, with a touch of solemnity, 'that the Caliph was intent on breaking the holy law by seizing the property of another man. This woman travelled here from her distant country, through great dangers and perils, in order to take back her husband, whom Zobeïda held captive. Her beauty awoke the Caliph's desire. And it was to defend his wife, whom Zobeïda threatened to kill, that the Frankish knight killed the black panther.'

This little speech made a deep impression on Mansour. His reasoning in general seemed to follow one simple pattern: any enemy of the Caliph's was necessarily his friend. His eyes lost their ferocity and grew gentle and friendly.

'Where is the Frankish knight?' he asked.

'Here. Abou-the-doctor is looking after him. He is resting.'

'He must flee from here. Tonight!'

'Why?' the Sultana asked. 'Who would think of looking for him here?'

'The Caliph's guards. The death of this dog here, whose head hangs at my saddlebow, together with the loss of his favourite and the condemned man's escape, have thrown Muhammad into a terrible rage. Tonight all the houses in Granada, even the country dwellings … and your own palace, O Princess, are to be searched!'

A shadow passed across the Sultana's expressive eyes. 'You failed, then?'

'What did you suppose when you saw me arrive here? That I had come to place the Caliph's crown at the foot of your bed? No, I came to cheer on my men, and rest a little myself before fleeing from here. The enemy have taken my palace. I am happy to find you alive, but I must make my escape as soon as possible. And if your protégés want to escape from Muhammad they will have to leave Granada this very night, for the Caliph is even more anxious to find them than he is me!'

Catherine had followed this brief exchange with understandable dismay. As she grasped the meaning of what they were saying, a terrible weariness descended upon her. Must they go on escaping and hiding then … and under such appalling circumstances? How would they ever manage to smuggle her wounded, drugged husband out of Granada? She was about to ask Amina when the Sultana spoke again. Her voice was as soft as ever, but Catherine sensed that it was vibrating with controlled anger.

'So you are leaving me once more, Mansour? And when will I see you again?'

'All you have to do is come with me. Why stay with this man who has brought you nothing but disappointment and grief? I love you, as you know, and I can make you happy. The Great Sultan would be happy to receive you …'

'He would never welcome an adulterous wife. While Muhammad lives, I have to stay here. But now we must think how best to place the sea between you both. Which road will you take? Metril?'

The black knight shook his head. 'Too simple. That is the first place they will look for me. No. Almeria. The road is longer, but the Prince Abdullah is a friend of mine, and I have a ship in the port.'

'Then take the Frankish knight and his wife with you. If they go alone they will be easily captured. But if they travel with you they stand a better chance of escaping from Muhammad's men.'

'Do you believe that? Messengers must be leaving even now for all the ports and frontier towns with a full description of them both … No, I think I can escape myself, because I have allies, friends and servants everywhere. But I would not give much for their chances.'

Abou-al-Khayr intervened at this, without letting Catherine get a word in. 'One moment, Lord Mansour. Only take them with you and I will make certain that they are completely disguised. I have a plan in mind. Moreover, I will accompany you too, it you will permit me. Until my friends here are safely beyond the reach of the Caliph's executioners I shall not return home.'

The little doctor spoke with such unaffected nobility and simplicity that Mansour dared not refuse. While Catherine squeezed Abou's hand gratefully, Mansour growled: 'Very well. Do as you please, Abou-the-doctor, but remember this: in half an hour I must leave this palace! Just the time it takes to feed my men and horses. If your protégés are not ready to accompany me by then, they will have to remain here. That is all.'

Abou-al-Khayr bowed silently. Mansour turned on his heel and went back to his sombre troop of horsemen waiting by the gates, holding their reins, like a black wall pierced by gleaming eyes. Their chief said a few words to them, and then, one by one, they wheeled their horses about and filed off in the direction of the palace. Then the doctor turned to Catherine and Amina.

'Come,' he said, 'we haven't much time.'

As they entered the palace, a thought suddenly struck Catherine. She tore off the fabulous belt of Haroun-al-Raschid and handed it to the Sultana.

'Take it,' she cried. 'This belt belongs to you. Nothing on Earth would induce me to take it with me.'

Amina's slender finger stroked the huge gems for a moment, and there was a hint of sadness in her voice as she said: 'The day I wore this for the first time I thought it was really the chain of happiness ... But I gradually came to realise that it was only a chain, nothing more ... and a heavy one. I hoped that the bonds were broken tonight ... Alas, they are still there, and this is the proof! Never mind! I am grateful to you, all the same ...'

The two women were about to enter Amina's private apartments behind the doctor when two large, powerful black slaves in brown-striped robes appeared, half carrying, half dragging a small woman dressed in black, who was struggling like a fury.

'They found her at the gates,' one of them explained. 'She kept shouting that she wanted to see Abou-the-doctor, and that they had told her to look for him here ...'

'Release her,' Abou commanded. Then he turned to the woman. 'What do you want?' he asked.

But the woman did not answer. She had just recognised Catherine. With an exclamation of joy, she tore off her black veil and ran toward her.

'I have found you at last! And you promised that you would never leave without me!'

'Marie!' Catherine exclaimed, half delighted, half ashamed, for in the excitement of her escape she had quite forgotten Marie and her promise to her. 'How did you manage to escape and find me here?' she asked, embracing her warmly.

'Easy! I was with all the others for the ... execution. I never took my eyes off you for a second, and I saw you escaping with the doctor. There was such an uproar in the square that I was able to slip away in the crowd as they scattered in all directions. The guards and the eunuchs had too much to do to keep an eye on all of us. I went to Abou-al-Khayr's house, hoping to find you there, but they told me he was attending the Sultana Amina and must be at the Alcazar Génil. So, here I am! You ... you aren't cross with me for coming?' the girl added, suddenly anxious. 'You know I do so long to go back to France! I would much rather wipe my children's noses, cook stews and wash platters than yawn away my life amid the velvet and silk of a gilded cage surrounded by half-crazed women!'

By way of an answer, Catherine hugged the girl again, and laughed. 'You did the right thing, and it is I who must ask you to forgive me for breaking my promise. It wasn't entirely my fault ...'

'I know. The main thing is to stay together ...'

'When you have quite finished with the formalities,' Abou's mocking voice cut in, 'would you care to remind yourselves that time is short and Mansour will not wait?'

15: *Magdalene*

The silent troop that left the Alcazar Génil half an hour later bore no resemblance to the one that had entered it a short while before under the impetuous leadership of Mansour- ben-Zegris. The dark horsemen with veiled faces had been transformed into members of the Caliph's regular guard, their black robes replaced by the white burnous. Mansour himself had left his costly, gold-embroidered costume and fabulous ruby with Amina, and was now dressed as a simple officer. Gauthier and Josse rode with the soldiers, their turbaned helmets pulled down to their eyes, and kept close guard over a great litter with tightly-drawn silk curtains, which journeyed at the heart of the cortege.

Arnaud lay, still unconscious, in the litter, tended by Abou-al-Khayr, Catherine and Marie. The two women were dressed as servants of a rich household. Marie fanned the wounded man with a feathered fan, while Catherine sat holding one of the bandaged hands in her own. The hand burned with fever, and Catherine watched the sleeping face anxiously. It was unveiled for the moment. Abou-al-Khayr had hit upon the cunning scheme of dressing Arnaud in magnificent women's clothes of the largest available size. Swathed in voluminous draperies of dark-blue satin striped with gold, his legs attired in wide pants and embroidered slippers, the knight passed well enough for the elderly, sick noblewoman he was supposed to be. This quaint disguise had relaxed Catherine's high-strung nerves a little. It added a note of humour to this strange and precipitate flight of theirs. Best of all was the mere fact of departing, leaving behind this strange and dangerous city that a little while before had seemed unlikely to free them alive. So she spoke quite calmly to Mansour as she took her place on the mattress of the litter.

'What are we to say if we meet any of the Caliph's men?'

'That we are escorting the old Princess Zeinab, grandmother of the Emir Abdullah who reigns over Almeria. She is on her way back to her palace after a visit to our own Sultana, who is a long-time friend.'

'But will they believe us?'

'I think they would be afraid to disbelieve us,' Abou-al-Khayr interrupted. 'Prince Abdullah, who is the Caliph's cousin, is so touchy that the master himself is very careful in his dealings with him. Almeria is our most important port. As for me, being a doctor, it is quite in order for me to escort this noble lady,' he added, making himself comfortable on the cushions.

By now the troop were pressing on through the night, their muffled hoofbeats making next to no noise. The nearby town still seemed to be in an uproar. All the lights were lit, huge fire-pots flamed on the ramparts and Granada glittered in the night like a huge colony of glow-worms. The picture that met Catherine's eyes as she peered through a crack in the curtains, with curiosity tinged with triumph, was a dazzling one; but the cries and shouts overflowing the high walls lent it a sinister undertone. In there, people were groaning, dying, long leather whips cracked over backs stooped in terror ...

Mansour's voice reached her, growling: 'The Caliph is settling his accounts! Let us make haste! If I am recognised we will have to fight, and there are but twenty of us!'

'You seem to have overlooked us, my lord,' Gauthier remarked in a curt tone. He rode so close to the litter that Catherine could have touched him by stretching out a hand. 'My friend Josse is no coward. And for my part, I have the strength of ten men.'

Mansour's dark eyes scrutinised the giant, and Catherine guessed that he was smiling faintly as he replied calmly: 'Very well then, shall we say that there are 31 of us, and may Allah go with us!'

He rode up to the head of the little column again and they were soon swallowed up by the darkness of the countryside. The lights of Granada were receding little by little. The road, which would have been hard to follow for those unfamiliar with it, grew steeper and all of a sudden as the town vanished behind a massive shoulder of rock.

'The road will be difficult,' Josse remarked from the other side of the litter. 'We have to cross some high mountains. But it will be easier to defend ourselves.'

A brutal order rang through the night, and the troop stopped. Catherine anxiously parted the curtain, after a quick glance at Arnaud, who slept on happily oblivious of what went on around him. The rocky shoulder lay behind them, and Granada was visible again. Also visible was Amina's palace, the lamps of which glowed at the top of the white battlements. Mansour's voice reached Catherine, who was prey to an attack of acute uneasiness.

'Look there! We were only just in time!'

A troop of white-robed horsemen could be seen galloping in a cloud of dust across the Roman bridge. They carried torches that scattered clouds of sparks through the night, and when they reached the gates of the Alcazar Génil they reined in hard. The Caliph's green standard fluttered at their head, held by a lieutenant. The entire troop disappeared within the massive gates. Catherine shivered. He was quite right. If they had stayed in the palace a few minutes longer it would all have begun again: nightmare, fear and finally, death!

Mansour's voice rang out again. 'We are too far away for them so see us. Allah be praised, for we would have been outnumbered five to one.'

Catherine looked out between the curtains at the tall figure of their leader. 'But will Amina be all right?' she asked.

'What has she to fear? They will not find anything there. Our clothes have all been buried in the garden and there is not one of her slaves or servants who would not prefer to have their tongues cut out than betray her. Even if Muhammad should suspect her of having helped me, he would never imagine that she had helped you too. He will not touch her. The people adore her, and I think he still loves her. But the day is coming when he will give her up to me,' he finished, with a brief outburst of rage. 'I will return more powerful than ever, and that day I shall kill him. By Allah, my return will see him draw his last breath!'

Without another word, the rebel Prince spurred his horse and galloped up the first foothill of the sierra. The rest of the troop followed suit at a much slower pace. Catherine let the curtain down again. The litter was quite dark inside, and it was so hot that Abou fastened back the curtains on his side.

'We are in no danger of being recognised. So we may as well breathe,' he murmured.

In the paler darkness, Catherine saw his teeth gleam and knew that he was smiling. The smile comforted her. She felt for Arnaud's forehead anxiously. It was still hot but less dry than it had been. A faint sweat was forming on it, and his breathing seemed regular and stronger. He was sleeping peacefully. Then Catherine folded herself into a ball at her husband's feet with a feeling akin to joy in her heart, and fell asleep.

The attack took place two days later, toward sundown, in the heart of the sierra. The fugitives had climbed up the long Génil valley and were now pressing up the flank of a narrow gorge where a path wound sinuously above the foaming waters toward the high peaks. The heat, torrid near Granada, had lessened considerably. Soon they would reach the snow level. The path seemed to be making for a sort of natural amphitheatre, with steep vertical walls of rock crowned by three mighty peaks. Mansour pointed to the highest of these.

'That one is called the Mulhacen, because the Caliph Mulay Hacen is buried there. The only creatures that live there are the eagles and vultures and the followers of One-eyed Faradj, a famous bandit.'

'We are too numerous to fear a bandit!' Gauthier declared contemptuously.

'Don't be too sure ... When Faradj is short of money he sometimes enters the Caliph's army, and when he is reinforced by frontier guards he becomes formidable.'

The last slanting rays of the setting sun lit up the white burnouses and gilded helmets of the Caliph's pseudo-guards, who stood out in strong contrast to the black rocks. Suddenly there were fierce shouts and such piercing screams that the horses shied. One of them reared and bucked and threw off its rider, who vanished with a scream of agony into the gorge below. From behind every rock a man sprang out ... and the whole mountainside seemed to come alive and fall like an avalanche on the little troop. They were mountain people, raggedly and dirtily dressed but carrying knives as sharp and polished as their white teeth. A small, crooked man, with a bunch of eagle feathers in his dirty turban and a grubby bandage over one eye, led them into the fray with the most dreadful howls of encouragement.

'One-eyed Faradj,' Mansour shouted. 'Post yourselves around the litter!'

The soldiers' scimitars flashed. Gauthier spurred his horse to the head of the column, beside Mansour, calling out to Josse: 'Guard the litter!'

But the litter curtains parted as if blown open by a whirlwind and Arnaud emerged, pushing Catherine aside as she tried to cling on to him and begged him to stay where he was.

'A weapon!' he cried. 'And a horse!'

'No,' Catherine cried. 'You mustn't fight yet ... you aren't strong enough ...'

'Who says so? Do you think I'm going to stand by while they cut these beggars to pieces and not take part? Get back in there and stay there!' he commanded roughly. 'And you, friend Abou, watch over her and don't let her do anything silly!'

He tore off his blue draperies, almost wild with impatience, so that he was left wearing nothing but voluminous trousers and a scanty jacket that barely covered his wide shoulders.

'A weapon, and a horse!' he repeated.

'Here is a weapon,' Josse said calmly, handing him his own scimitar. 'You will know how to use it better than I. And take my horse.'

'What will you use?'

'I am going to catch the horse that belonged to the soldier who fell into the ravine. Don't worry, I shall be all right ...'

'Arnaud,' Catherine cried pathetically, 'please ...'

But he wasn't listening. He sprang into the saddle and kicked his horse's sides with his bare heels till it came alongside Mansour and Gauthier, who were already engaged in a furious battle with ten men against each of them. His appearance had the effect of a cannonball. This great fellow draped in women's veils who rode to the attack with the most ferocious roars produced a moment of stunned amazement in the enemy. Mansour, suppressing a violent urge to laugh aloud, took advantage of this. As for Catherine, this vision was momentarily too much for her, and she burst into clear, joyous laughter: Arnaud looked so funny in his pantaloons! But her laughter did not last long. In a moment she sank back against the cushions and turned desolate eyes to Abou.

'He is mad,' she sighed. 'How can he survive this fighting when only two days ago …'

'He has eaten and drunk and slept during those two days,' said the little doctor, calmly fingering a chaplet of polished amber beads. 'Your husband is a man of uncommon strength. Do you seriously imagine that he could have heard the clash of sabres without joining in? The fierce battle cries are like the music of lutes and harps to his ears.'

'But … his hands?'

'The wounds are closing, as you saw. And he knows that if they bleed, I can yet again stop the bleeding.'

Abou smiled at her encouragingly and fell to silently invoking the intercession of Allah, and his Prophet Mahomet, in the combat that Catherine was now observing with alarm, her brief moment of gaiety quite forgotten. There seemed to be a horde of brigands. They swarmed upon Mansour's men, and they were soon hidden behind a forest of flashing blades. But the men of the Grand Atlas were courageous fighters, and more than equal to the mountain bandits. They stood in a rock-solid formation around the litter, and Catherine felt as if she were in the vortex of a whirlpool of whirling scimitars.

Mansour, Arnaud and Gauthier fought magnificently. Men fell like flies beneath their blows. Catherine heard Arnaud laugh in the midst of the mêlée, and this gave her a moment's annoyance. He was really in his element out there; he had found himself again at last. 'He is never so happy,' she thought sadly, as in the thick of battle. He does not find the same complete satisfaction even in my arms …'

A loud, shrill voice reached her: 'You won't escape me, Mansour-ben-Zegris! When I heard of your escape, I knew you would try to reach Almeria over this mountain pass, and you walked straight into my trap …'

This was Faradj taunting his enemy. The little man himself was a prodigious fighter, and the duel between him and Mansour was a ferocious one.

'Your trap?' the Prince answered disdainfully. 'You do yourself too much honour. I knew you would be lurking in these hills, and I am not afraid of you. But you will be disappointed if you hope to capture gold or jewels – we have only our weapons!'

'You forget your head! The Caliph will pay me ten times its weight in gold, and I would be received back into Granada as a hero!'

'The only time you will contemplate Granada as a hero will be when your own head is mouldering on a spike on the city walls!'

The remainder of the dispute was lost in the din of the fighting. Catherine sat huddled against Marie, and the two women watched the battle anxiously.

'If we are recaptured,' the young girl murmured, 'you will be all right, because Muhammad loves you … but I will be delivered to the executioners and impaled!'

'We will not be recaptured!' Catherine asserted, with a confidence she was far from feeling. The dark was closing in fast. Only the snow caps above were still rosy with the setting sun. The hillsides were growing black with shadows. Death had cut great inroads into both camps. Every now and then a horse and rider would crash into the river below with a despairing cry. Mansour, Arnaud and Gauthier fought on, and the brigands had lost many men, whereas only five of the others had fallen. But the fighting still raged, night was drawing in, and Catherine had to dig her nails into her palms to stop herself screaming aloud from nervous tension. Marie sat, scarcely breathing, beside her, her eyes glued to the fighting, the consequences of which could be so terrible for her. Abou-al-Khayr was still praying

And then two cries broke out, so rending and terrible that Catherine sprang from the litter, heedless of danger. Arnaud's flashing scimitar had just struck off One-eyed Faradj's head, and the man's body crumpled to the ground with a thud. But Catherine scarcely noticed this, because her eyes were drawn to another, dreadful sight: Gauthier, still astride his horse, mouth open in an endless cry, with a lance driven full into his chest.

Catherine's eyes met the giant's for a second, and in them she seemed to see a look of immense astonishment. Then, like a lopped oak, the Norman crashed to the ground. 'Gauthier!' the young woman cried. 'Oh, God!'

She ran toward him and knelt down, but Arnaud had already dismounted and pushed her aside.

'Leave him. Don't touch him!'

Abou-al-Khayr came running up, and frowned. He knelt down and laid his hand over the stricken giant's heart. A thin trickle of blood ran from the corner of Gauthier's mouth.

'He is still alive,' the doctor said. 'We must take the weapon out gently … very gently. Can you do that while I hold him?' he asked Montsalvy.

By way of reply, Arnaud stripped the bandages from his hands, in case they slipped on the lance shaft. Then he seized the shaft while Abou carefully held open the mouth of the wound and Catherine wiped the blood away from Gauthier's lips with a corner of her veil.

'Now …' said the little doctor. 'But gently, gently; we could kill him in removing the lance.'

Arnaud pulled, and inch by inch the murderous blade slipped out of the depths of Gauthier's chest. Catherine held her breath, afraid that each breath the giant drew might prove his last. Her eyes filled with tears, but she bravely kept them back. At last the lance was out, and Arnaud flung it angrily away. The doctor hastened to staunch the wound with such bandages as Marie had been able to fabricate hastily from the cloths that came to hand.

There was silence around them. With their leader dead, the bandits had fled, and Mansour was not bothering to pursue them. The survivors of the battle closed in round the wounded man in a silent circle. Mansour quietly wiped his weapon clean and thrust it back into his belt before bending over the wounded man. His dark eyes met Arnaud's.

'You are a valiant fighter, Lord Infidel, but your servant too is a warrior! By Allah, if he lives I will make him my lieutenant. Can you save him, doctor?'

Abou, who had cleaned the wound with his accustomed skill, now shook his head doubtfully, and Catherine noticed, with a pang of fear that his brow stayed creased and anxious.

'Save him,' she begged. 'He can't die … not Gauthier!'

'The wound is deep,' Abou murmured. 'I will do my best. But we must move him from here. It is too dark to see.'

'Take him to the litter,' Arnaud commanded. 'I am damned if I will set foot in it again!'

'You are almost naked, barefoot and you still aren't cured yourself,' Catherine lamented.

'Never mind. I will take the clothes off one of the dead soldiers. I refuse to go on wearing this naked woman's costume – it makes me look grotesque. Can't we have a little light?'

Two of the soldiers, still panting from the battle, came up with torches, while four more lifted Gauthier from the ground with infinite care and carried him to the litter, where Abou had stowed away all the provisions and medicines under the cushions.

The snowy summits stood out like gigantic ghostly shapes against the night sky. The wind was rising, howling through the ravine like a sick wolf, and it was growing cold.

'We must find shelter for the night,' Mansour's voice said in the darkness. 'It would be suicide to try to follow this road at night and we no longer have anything to fear from Faradj's men. Clear the path, you men!'

The mighty splashes that followed this order told Catherine that the dead were being tipped into the river below, friend and foe united in their last journey. Arnaud, who had vanished briefly, now reappeared wearing a white burnous and turbaned helmet, dressed from head to foot.

The icy wind from the snow crests threatened to blow out the torches. Lit by the torch-bearers, the party set out again, but with redoubled precautions, along the steep and dangerous road. Mansour led the way, leading his horse by the bridle-rein, searching for some kind of shelter. Then came the litter, as slowly as possible so as not to jolt the wounded man, whom Abou was tending with the help of Catherine and Marie.

Soon the black mouth of a large cave yawned in front of them. It was big enough to transport the litter inside once the horses had been unyoked. The men and animals huddled forward. A fire was lit, and once Abou had finished with her services, Catherine came to sit beside it with Arnaud. After bandaging the wound, Abou had given Gauthier a soothing potion to make him sleep, but his fever was rising and the little doctor could not conceal his pessimism.

'His extraordinary constitution might just pull him through,' he told Catherine, who looked pale with misery. 'But I haven't much hope ...'

Stricken to the heart, she sat down beside her husband, huddled closer to him and laid her head on his shoulder. He put his arm round her tenderly and then forced her to look at him, gazing into her eyes, which were heavy with unshed tears.

'Weep, my sweet,' he murmured. 'Don't control yourself. It will make you feel better. I understand your grief. You know ...' He paused for a second, and Catherine felt his grip lighten. Then he made up his mind, and went on firmly: 'I don't mind telling you that I was jealous of him once ... This dog-like devotion of his, and his unwearying protection of you used to annoy me ... But the moment came when I realised the worth of his feelings ... We might never have found each other again, but for him... and then I knew that I was wrong: that if he loved you, it was with a quite different love from the one I had suspected ... something like the veneration one offers a saint ...'

Catherine shivered, and she felt her heart pounding. She suddenly remembered that frenzied night at Coca, and the memory was so fresh suddenly, so raw, that a wave of remorse and shame engulfed her. She felt like ridding herself of it forever, confessing that Gauthier had been her lover and that she had found happiness in his arms. Her lips parted.

'Arnaud,' she whispered, 'I must tell you ...'

But he swiftly closed her lips with a kiss. 'No. Don't tell me anything ... This is not the moment for memories, or regrets ... Gauthier is still alive, and Abou may work the miracle that can save him. Who knows?'

His great burnous enveloped the mingled warmth of their two bodies, like a sweet, safe roof over them both. But Catherine's heart was heavy inside her. If she spoke the truth, what would Arnaud say, what would he do? He would reject her at once, throw her out into a cold world that would chill her to the soul, and she was so happy there beside him! It was so good to feel him next to her, protecting her with all his renewed strength, with all this love that he alone could inspire in her. She seized one of his hands passionately. The wound had reopened but the bleeding had stopped. She kissed it fervently.

'I love you,' she whispered. 'Oh, I love you so!'

He did not reply, but held her closer, gripping her so hard it almost hurt; and Catherine knew that he was fighting against the need to possess her completely. His dark eyes went from face to face of the silent warriors of the desert grouped about the fire, expressionless, silent. They made up a strange, hermetic, enigmatic circle clustered round the fire, the light from which flickered and gleamed on their swarthy countenances, reflecting back a tinge of blue from the dark tunics they always wore. No-one looked at them. Those who were sound of limb were caring for the wounded. These men of war were still vibrating with the excitement of the recent fighting; but so accustomed were they to a life of danger since early childhood, that none of them lost a moment in recuperating their energies. For who could say if they would not be fighting again that very night?

The strange, almost unreal picture they presented was one that remained for a long time in Catherine's mind. This night in the bowels of a foreign mountain was like a stop in some cave peopled by djinns, those genies of eastern legend whom Fatima and others had told her about in the harem … But soon afterwards Mansour's tall shape appeared beside the fire. He murmured a few words to his men, in a dialect Catherine did not understand, and then walked calmly around it and came to sit down beside Arnaud. One of his two servants appeared, carrying bananas and dates on his outspread palms. The Moor took some and offered them, with a fleeting smile, to the Frankish knight. This was the first courteous gesture he had made toward him, but it was enough to show that Mansour recognised him as his equal. Arnaud thanked him silently with a slight inclination of the head.

'The lords of war recognise each other at the first clash of arms,' Mansour explained simply. 'You are one of us.'

Silence fell again. The men were eating, but Catherine could not swallow a thing. Her eyes kept straying toward the litter that stood near the mouth of the cave. An oil lamp made it look somewhat like a large lantern inside, where Abou was still engaged in tending the wounded man. From time to time she heard a groan, and her heart smote her grievously each time. In a little while, Arnaud would be taking over from the little doctor so that Abou could get some rest, and she would go with him. But she already knew this was going to be an ordeal, and this dreadful weakness and helplessness she felt could only grow worse at the sight of the giant who was so badly, even fatally, wounded …

A wolf howled on the mountainside and Catherine shivered. Another bad omen ...

Arnaud guessed at her distress. He bent toward her and whispered, in a voice that was soft but passionate: 'You will never have to suffer again, sweetheart. You will never go hungry or cold again, and you will never be frightened! As God is my witness, I swear I will spend the rest of my life making you forget what you have suffered!'

When the rebel troop reached Almeria five days later, Gauthier was still alive, but it was clear that he could not last much longer. In spite of the determined, concerted efforts to save him made by Abou, Catherine and Arnaud, life was slowly ebbing from his giant frame.

'There is nothing more to be done,' the doctor finally admitted. 'All I can do is prolong his existence a little. He would undoubtedly have died the night he was wounded if it had not been for his exceptional strength. And yet,' he added, after a moment's thought, 'he does not seem to want to live. He is not helping me!'

'What do you mean?' Catherine asked.

'That he does not want to live! You might say ... yes, you might say that he is happy to die! I have never known a man wait so tranquilly for his own end.'

'But I want him to live!' Catherine protested, with a burst of almost childish anger. 'You must make him live!'

'There is nothing you can do. It is written so. I believe he feels his mission on Earth is accomplished now you have found your husband again.'

'You mean ... that he doesn't care about me anymore?'

'I mean that he cares too much, if anything! And that is why I think he must be happy to die ...'

This time Catherine did not reply. She understood what the little doctor was saying. Now that she was back with Arnaud, Gauthier felt there was no longer any room for him in her life, and perhaps he did not feel brave enough, after having stood beside her through the dark days, to witness their new happiness ... She could understand that, even while she still reproached herself for that mad night they had spent at Coca. In saving him from madness she had done something irreparable to them both. Whatever happened, Gauthier felt he must leave Arnaud of Montsalvy's wife ...

'How much longer can he live?' she asked.

Abou shrugged. 'Who knows? A few days, perhaps; but I would be inclined to say a few hours. He is sinking fast ... and yet I was counting on the restorative effects of the sea air!'

The sea! Catherine gazed at it, almost incredulously, from the hill-top. It stretched out to the farthest horizon, silky, sparkling, a deep sumptuous blue in which the sun kindled countless diamonds. It circled a beach as golden and soft as a woman's hair, and beside it stood a huge town of dazzling whiteness, crowned by a stronghold of equal whiteness. Below lay a port where boats fluttered their coloured sails. Huge palm trees swung their dark green crests slowly in the sea wind against the backdrop of a blindingly blue sky.

The town stood at the mouth of a wide valley full of orange and lemon trees, and Catherine thought she had never seen a more dazzling sight. The sea she had known before, when she had contemplated it with a sort of superstitious awe at the side of Duke Philippe in Flanders, had been quite different: green and grey, threatening, crested with whitecaps, or flat and calm, the colour of dead grass beyond the dunes where the sea wind whipped up the long grasses. She clasped Arnaud's hand, forgetting her sadness for a moment.

'Look! It must be the most beautiful place on Earth! Wouldn't it be wonderful if we could live here together?'

But he shook his head, and the hard lines Catherine knew so well appeared at each side of his mouth. The look he swept over the radiant countryside below was almost resentful.

'No. We could never be happy here. It is too different from the places we are used to. We are not made – particularly I – for these countries of softness and grace, their charms concealing cruelty and vice and brutality and a belief in a god that is not our own. To live in Islam one would first of all have to conquer and kill and destroy, and then one might be able to rule. Only then would life be possible for people like ourselves … Believe me, our old, bleak Auvergne, if we ever see it again, will give us more real happiness.'

He smiled at her disappointed face and dropped a quick kiss on her eyes. Then he went to join Mansour. The whole troop had halted on this shady hillside for a sort of council of war. Catherine left Gauthier's side for a moment, slipped out of the litter and went over to the men. Mansour pointed to the white fortress that dominated the city.

'That is the Alcazaba. Prince Abdullah rules from there. He usually prefers it to his palace by the sea. He is only 15 years old but he lives for war and feats of chivalry. You have nothing to fear from the Caliph on his lands,' he told Arnaud. 'What are your plans?'

'I want to find a boat to take us back to our own country. Do you think that will be possible?'

'I have two of my own in the port. One of them will take me back to Africa, to plan my revenge. The other will take you, and your people, as far as Valencia. Ever since the Cid drove us out,' he added bitterly, 'the ships of Islam cannot enter the port, even for commerce, although we welcome foreign ships in our own ports. The captain will put you off on the coast at night. You should have no difficulty finding a boat at Valencia to take you to Marseilles.'

Arnaud nodded agreement. At Marseilles, which belonged to Queen Yolande, Countess of Provence, he would be almost home, and Catherine saw, from the way he smiled, how much this thought delighted him. He was going back to the old life, after believing it lost to him forever; the life of comrades-in-arms and wars. For she doubted deep within herself that he would ever be happy with the peaceful life of the Château of Montsalvy, which the monks were even now rebuilding … But then Arnaud's smile vanished, and he frowned anxiously.

'Can we leave tonight?'

'Why so much haste?' asked Mansour. 'Abdullah will greet you as warmly as I would do myself if I could take you with me to the Mahgreb. And that way you would take a pleasanter memory of Islam with you.'

'I am grateful to you. Rest assured that I shall take away pleasant memories, if not of Islam, then at least of you, Mansour. Heaven was on my side when I met you, and I am deeply grateful. But there is the wounded man …'

'He is going to die. The doctor told you so.'

'I know. But he might last until we reach France!'

Catherine's heart swelled with a great wave of tenderness. This mark of consideration on Arnaud's part toward the humble Gauthier touched her deeply. The Norman was going to die, certainly, but Montsalvy did not want to leave his body in pagan ground. She raised grateful eyes to her husband. After a moment's reflection Mansour said slowly:

'He will not live that long. But I understand your thinking, brother! It shall be as you wish. My ship will set sail this very night … Now let us be off.'

He climbed back into the saddle. Catherine returned to the litter to find that Gauthier had momentarily regained consciousness. His breathing was growing more laboured every minute. His huge body seemed to shrink all the time, and his face grew ashen, already touched by the shadow of the angel of death. But he recognised Catherine when she leant over him, and smiled.

'Look,' she said, pulling aside the curtains so that he could see out. 'There is the sea that you love and that you have so often told me about. It will make you better.'

He shook his head, and a faint smile curved his pale lips. 'No … It is better this way … I am going to die!'

'Don't say that,' Catherine protested, then added fondly: 'We will all look after you and cure you …'

'No. There is no point in lying. I know … and I am glad! You … you must promise me one thing.'

'Anything you want.'

He motioned her nearer, and Catherine bent over so that her ear almost touched the dying man's mouth, and he whispered: 'Promise me ... that he will never know what happened ... at Coca! ... It would hurt him ... and it was only a kindness on your part. It wouldn't be worth making him suffer for that ...'

Catherine sat upright and clasped the burning hand on the coverlet with a sort of passion. 'No,' she said vehemently, 'it was not out of kindness, but love! I swear to you, Gauthier, by everything I hold most precious in the world: I loved you that night, I gave myself to you with all my heart, and I would have gone on if you had wanted me to. Look,' she went on, in a lower voice, 'you made me so happy that night that for a moment I was tempted to stay there, forget about going to Granada ...'

She stopped. A look of inexpressible joy smoothed out Gauthier's ravaged features, giving them a look of gentleness, a beauty they had never worn before. He smiled like a happy child, and for the first time since that famous night, Catherine saw the same passion in his grey eyes.

'You would have regretted it, my love,' he whispered, 'but thank you for saying so! I shall go happily now, so happily!' Then, as Catherine opened her mouth to protest again, he murmured, still lower, in a voice that grew steadily weaker: 'Don't say anything more ... Now leave me! I want to talk to the doctor ... and I haven't much time left! Farewell, Catherine ... You are the only person in the world I have ever loved!'

The young woman's throat ached with sudden grief, but she did not dare refuse his request. She gazed at his face for a moment, with its closed eyes that might never open again. She bent forward once more, and softly, with infinite tenderness, pressed her lips to his dry ones. Then she turned to Marie, who had been silently sitting at the far corner of the litter, witness to this last meeting.

'Call Abou. He is not far away ... I am getting out.'

Their party was now moving forward slowly, because there was a great crowd along the road into the white city. It must have been a market day, adding to the bustle and activity of the busy port. Marie gave a sign of understanding and called to the doctor, while Catherine climbed down from the litter to hide the tears that were coming thick and fast. Arnaud was riding a few paces ahead, beside Mansour. She called to him, with so much pain in her voice that he stopped dead and stared at the pretty face drowned in tears. Then he bent forward and gave her his hand.

'Come,' was all he said.

He lifted her off the ground, placed her in front of him and wound his arms about her. Catherine buried her head against his breast and cried like a child. Arnaud said merely:

'Is it the end?'

She nodded, unable to speak.

'Then weep for him, sweetheart,' he said. 'Weep as long as you want. You cannot mourn too long for a man like that!'

At last they reached the crowded harbour with its countless fish stalls, and vendors of shellfish, oranges, vegetables, fruits and spices sitting cross-legged on the ground next to their bulging sacks, clamouring to the people to come and buy their wares. Mansour's men forced a way through the crowd for the litter where Gauthier lay dying. They were heading for the quayside, and the boats. Fishing boats of all sizes were tied up alongside the quay, and among them there were a few large merchant vessels and two Barbary ships, lean and deadly as leopards, crouched low amid the bulky commercial boats. Mansour pointed them out.

'Those are my ships ...'

Arnaud smiled. He had just realised that the bulk of Mansour's fortune, apart from his properties in the mysterious Mahgreb, came from the proceeds of piracy. Those were ships for hunting and killing, and he felt somewhat uneasy at the thought of Catherine and Marie setting foot on those sea-going beasts of prey. How could they be sure that the captain, once safely out to sea, would not steer his vessel for Alexandria or Candia or Tripoli, where the fairest lady of the West would undoubtedly fetch a good price in the thriving slave-markets? Gauthier's imminent death changed many things. He and Josse would be the sole defenders of these two women against an entire crew, now that Abou had decided to return to Granada ... Once they had passed the outer harbour of Almeria, there would be no Muslim voices raised in defence of these 'roumis' against the Barbary men. Arnaud did not doubt Mansour's good faith, but still a pirate was a man used to lying, deceiving and persuading. The captain in charge of this ship of prey would only have to report that he had fulfilled his mission, and no-one would give another thought to the fate of the Montsalvys ...

Preoccupied by these sobering thoughts, Arnaud instinctively drew Catherine closer to him. But for once she did not respond to the pressure. Her eyes were round with amazement as she gazed at a ship that had just entered the harbour, and as she stared at it disbelievingly she kept wondering whether she was seeing straight or merely dreaming.

This boat was unlike the others in the harbour. It did not have triangular sails pointed like spearheads, but one immense square red-and-blue-striped sail, which the sailors were now lowering, because manoeuvring into port was the work of the oarsmen. This boat was a massive galley with a swelling keel and a rear castle pitched high and carved as elaborately as a wooden coffer. It was not the lines of the vessel that drew Catherine's eye so much as the pennants streaming in the wind at the stern. One of these, which was of azure banded in silver, bore a crest of three sable cockleshells and three hearts gules. She knew that coat of arms well.

'Jacques Cœur!' she cried. 'That must be his ship!'

Arnaud was now watching the handsome boat as well, but it was the other pennant that he seemed to be staring at, thunderstruck. It was longer and bigger than the first.

'The lily of Anjou, lambel of Sicily, pales of Aragon and cross of Jerusalem!' he breathed. 'Queen Yolande ... That boat must be carrying an ambassador.'

Their two hearts beat fast with joy. This ship alone seemed to stand for France, and for friendship, for loyalty, nobility ... The bright colours shimmered in the hot sun. They would feel quite at home on that ship ...

'I don't think you will have to supply us with one of your ships after all,' Arnaud told Mansour. 'That one belongs to a friend, and it would appear that it brings an ambassador from our own country ...'

'A merchantman,' Ben Zegris remarked, with a touch of disdain, only to add, a moment later, 'but well armed!', for the gaping mouths of six cannon had just come into sight.

The *Magdalene*, as the ship was called, was not seeking to tie up at the quayside. When she reached the centre of the harbour she dropped anchor, and a small skiff was lowered into the water, while an army of turbaned functionaries and sightseers swarmed along the quayside to meet it. Mansour's troop and the litter were swallowed up in this tide of humanity that pushed and squeezed and struggled for a better view of the unexpected newcomers.

The little skiff was being rowed swiftly to the quay, and it carried three personages on board, one wearing a turban and the other two embroidered hoods. But Catherine had already recognised the taller of the two hooded men. Before Arnaud could stop her, she had jumped down from his saddle and was elbowing and pushing her way through the crowd so vigorously that people were obliged to make room for her. She managed to reach the water's edge just as the skiff landed. As Jacques Cœur sprang up on to the quay, she almost tumbled into his arms, laughing and crying all at once ...

He did not recognise her at first, and would have pushed aside this dusty Muslim woman who clung to him, but then he saw her face and suddenly grew pale.

'Catherine!' he cried in amazement. 'It can't be! Is it really you?'

'Yes, yes, my friend, it is ... and I am so happy to see you again! Good God, it must be heaven itself that brought you here! It's too wonderful, too unbelievable, too ...'

She hardly knew what she was saying. The delight that flooded her was enough to turn the strongest head. But now Arnaud came forward through the crowd. He dismounted, and he too almost fell into Maître Jacques

Cœur's arms. The good merchant was astonished to find himself being embraced by a Moorish officer. Then he recognised him.

'And Messire Arnaud!' he cried. 'What an amazing stroke of luck! Fancy finding you the moment I step off the ship! Did you know that my business here is now ended?'

'How is that?'

'What did you think I came here for? I came to find you. Haven't you noticed the royal arms on the boat? I am ambassador to the Duchess-Queen, and I have come to claim the Lord of Montsalvy and his wife from the Caliph of Granada ... returning in exchange one of his bravest captains, who was unfortunate enough to be captured along the coast of Provence. A commercial transaction ...'

'But you would have been risking your life!' Catherine protested.

'Hardly,' said Jacques Cœur, smiling. 'My ship is well armed, and the people of these countries treat ambassadors with respect and are also interested in trade. I get on well enough with the children of Allah since I took to buffeting and trading round the Mediterranean!'

The pleasure the three friends found in rediscovering each other seemed well nigh inexhaustible. They all laughed and spoke at once, quite oblivious of everyone around them. Their questions followed each other so thick and fast that there was no time to answer them, and yet they each wanted to know everything, and at once. It was Catherine who came to her senses first, however. Her eyes went beyond Arnaud and Jacques Cœur, who were still thumping each other enthusiastically on the back, to where the litter stood with Abou-al-Khayr's head thrust anxiously out between the curtains. At once she was guilt-stricken to realise that in the excitement of the meeting she had momentarily forgotten her dying friend. She seized Jacques by the arm and shook him.

'Jacques,' she begged. 'You must take us away from here, at once ... at once!'

'Why?'

She explained briefly, and the joy faded from the merchant's tanned face.

'Poor Gauthier,' he murmured. 'So he was mortal after all! I own that I would never have believed it. We will take him on board immediately, so that he can breathe his last on his own soil ... Even a wooden deck would be better than this heathen land!'

He turned toward the men who had accompanied him, a little fellow with a lively face, who appeared to be a secretary, to judge from the writing-case hanging from his belt, with its little parchment scroll; and a turbaned knight who stood silent and motionless behind him, apparently indifferent to the scene played out before him.

'Lord Ibrahim, you have arrived home! There is no need to discuss the terms of your freedom further, because I have already found my friends.

You are now free.'

'Thank you for your courtesy, friend … I knew I had nothing to fear from you; you have been a jailer such as few prisoners have the good fortune to meet. That is why I came with you quite fearlessly.'

'I had your word that you would not try to escape, and I trusted you,' the merchant replied. 'Farewell Seigneur Ibrahim.'

The prisoner bowed low and then vanished rapidly into the crowd. Mansour and his men were pushing back the throng now to make way for the litter. Jacques Cœur's sailors lost no time in lifting out the dying man, unconscious now, eyes shut. The bright sunlight lit up the emaciated face hollowed by ghastly shadows, and the men gazed at him in superstitious awe. They laid Gauthier in the skiff, and Abou sat beside him.

'I will remain with him till the end,' he said. 'You do not plan to set sail at once, do you?'

'No,' said Jacques Cœur. 'Not till the day after tomorrow. While I am here I want to take the opportunity of loading up with silks and marble inlay work, spices, tooled leather, gilded pottery and those fine gazelle-skin parchments from the Sahara that this country specialises in …'

Catherine suppressed a smile. While Jacques Cœur had certainly come there to find them, and while he might be flying an ambassador's pennants, nothing could quench the mercantile spirit in him – it prevailed over everything. This voyage might have been undertaken in friendship, but it would be a waste of time …

While the little skiff sped off toward the merchantman, whence it would shortly return to collect them, and Arnaud was making his formal farewells to Mansour, Catherine turned to Jacques and demanded: 'Now, my friend, tell me how you knew we were here.'

'It's a long story. But, to put it in a nutshell, you owe my presence here to your old friend, the Dame de Châteuvillain. You abandoned her halfway up a mountain, it seems, but you also left her with a squire of Messire Arnaud's on her hands, and she had no difficulty in worming the truth out of him. With that she made a half turn, rushed off to Angers, to the Duchess-Queen, and told her everything. Madame Yolande sent for me, and together we planned and equipped for the journey.'

'Incredible!' Catherine cried, in astonishment. 'And to think that same Ermengarde wanted to carry me off gagged and bound to her Duke!'

'But only for as long as she believed it really was the best thing for you. When she found that you were quite determined to pursue Messire Arnaud … she resolved to help you. She wants your happiness more than anything else, and you cannot imagine the fuss she made before I set off. I had great difficulty in getting out of bringing her with me!'

'Dear Ermengarde,' Catherine murmured, touched. 'She is an amazing woman. But what a risky undertaking! How could she be sure that I would find Arnaud again, and that I would even reach Granada?'

Jacques Cœur shrugged and smiled mockingly. 'I suppose she knows you well. If your husband had been held prisoner in the heart of darkest Africa you would have found some way of rescuing him. Though of course I should have had to make a longer journey then ...' he added.

Gauthier died in the darkest hour of the night, the one just before dawn. He lay in the rear castle of the ship, where Jacques had had him placed ... and his face was turned toward those high seas that he would never cross ... His death agony had been a terrible one. His damaged lungs took in air with the greatest difficulty, and it was the giant's amazing constitution, his great physical strength, that prolonged the hopeless and exhausting duel with death, making it all the more cruel.

Catherine, Arnaud, Abou-al-Khayr, Josse, Marie and Jacques Cœur remained with him, helplessly and sorrowfully looking on at this last agonising struggle the unconscious Gauthier was making to cling on to a life that had already rejected him. They huddled together, weary and drawn in the smoky taper-light, and prayed for death to silence the tormented tongue that babbled on in an unknown tongue, sending up curses, laments and entreaties to the mysterious Nordic gods whom the Norman had worshipped all his life. Outside, the crew stood waiting, not quite knowing what to expect, but aware that some kind of drama was unfolding in that closed cabin.

Finally Gauthier gave a last convulsive movement, a sigh that sounded like a death rattle, and the massive body was still. Now that the laboured breathing had ceased the silence that fell was terrible. The anchored boat, the gentle rocking of which had cradled the giant's dying agony, creaked eerily, and the sound was taken up by the harsh cries of seagulls.

Then Catherine knew that it was all over. Stifling a sob, she placed two fingers gently on Gauthier's lids and closed her friend's wide-open eyes for all eternity. Then she turned and ran to Arnaud, who held her close against him to hide her weeping face. Jacques coughed, trying to hide the emotion that shook him.

'When the sun rises we will bury him at sea,' he said. 'I will say the prayers ...'

'No,' Abou-al-Khayr interrupted. 'He asked me to arrange his burial. No prayers, but I will tell you what must be done.'

'Then come with me. We can give the orders now.'

The two men left, and Catherine heard Jacques' voice calling out orders from the poop deck, followed by the hurrying footsteps of the crew. She looked at her husband, but now he led her to the bed where Gauthier lay. One after the other, Catherine and Arnaud knelt to pray, with their whole hearts, to the all-merciful God in whom this good man had never believed. Silently, Josse and Marie came and knelt on the other side ... and even through her grief Catherine noticed that the Parisian's eyes were full of tears, but that he never let go of little Marie's hand. He seemed to have taken her beneath his wing. It occurred to her that this might be the start of a new happiness, and that these two, who had come from very different lives, were now discovering each other. Now Arnaud's grave voice spoke up, reciting the prayers for the dead, and Catherine joined in.

Three hours later, with the whole ship's crew standing to attention on the bridge and the ship's bell tolling a funeral knell, Arnaud of Montsalvy proceeded with a strange ceremony in accordance with the instructions passed on to him by Abou-al-Khayr. The ship moved slowly toward the harbour mouth, towing a sail boat behind it. The boat was piled high with straw, and the Norman's body lay upon this, covered with a sail. When they reached the harbour entrance, Montsalvy sprang into the boat and hoisted the sail, which bellied in the wind. Then he climbed into the *Magdalene* and cut the cord that tied the little sailing boat to it. The boat leapt forward as if pushed by an invisible hand and soon overtook the red-painted galleon, whose oarsmen sat motionless. Those aboard the ship watched for a moment as it sped by, carrying the long white wrapped body with it. Then Arnaud took a large bow from Abou's hands, fitted a blazing arrow to it and drew back the bowstring ... The arrow whistled and buried itself in the midst of the straw, which instantly caught fire. In a moment the little boat became a vessel of flames. The corpse vanished behind a curtain of fire while the wind, fanning the pyre, drove it slowly out to sea ...

Arnaud dropped the bow and looked at Catherine, who had followed this strange ceremony uncomprehendingly, her throat tight with unshed tears. She saw that two tears shone in her husband's dark eyes. Then he spoke, hoarsely:

'It was thus that the captains of the snake-ships used to travel the swan's road into eternity. The last of the Vikings has had the burial he desired ...'

And then, because his emotion was choking him, Arnaud of Montsalvy turned and hurried away.

The next day, at dawn, the *Magdalene*'s red and blue sail swelled in the fresh morning wind, and Jacques Cœur's galleon sailed majestically out of the port. Catherine stood for a moment clinging to Arnaud under the cape that enveloped them both, and watched the white city in its green setting vanish from sight, still hoping for a last glimpse of Abou-al-Khayr's absurd turban amid the bustling throng that lined the quayside.

Her heart had been heavy within her to leave this other old friend so soon after Gauthier's death, for she felt she owed her newfound happiness to him. But the little doctor had cut short her faltering farewells.

'The sage has written, "Absence exists only for those who do not know how to love. It is a bad dream whence one awakens one day and instantly forgets." One day perhaps I shall come knocking at your door. I still have many customs to study in your strange country!' And he had turned on his heel and left without another word.

When there was nothing left to see, when the town was no more than a white blur where the gold roofs of the mosques shimmered faintly, Catherine turned toward the ship's massive prow. It cut through the blue deeps with a sound like tearing silk. Far away on the horizon, the blue of the sea merged into that of the sky. White gulls wheeled overhead. Over there, beyond this infinite space, lay France, the native land; Michel's laughter; Sara's kindly face; the knotted hands and faithful eyes of the people of Montsalvy. Catherine looked up and saw that Arnaud too was staring toward the horizon.

'We are going home,' she murmured. 'Do you think this time it will be forever?'

He smiled at her in his tender, mocking way. 'I think the Lady of Montsalvy has had enough of the high roads, sweetheart! Study this road well, it will be the last ...'

The *Magdalene* was reaching the open sea. The wind freshened, the ship took on all its sail and then, like a freed bird, sped forward across the blue billows.

PART IV: EPILOGUE

16: A Time for Love

Ever since dawn, two lay-brothers had been ringing the great bell of Montsalvy Abbey in a joyful pealing suited to so happy an occasion. Their arms were so weary by the time High Mass finished that the Abbot Bernard of Calmont had to send reinforcements. They could not have managed another stroke; yet they had never felt happier in their lives. Meanwhile the trumpets blared triumphantly and with ever-increasing volume from the high ramparts.

It was three days since the great procession of litters, riders, chariots and men-at-arms, pages and servants had started arriving before the gateway of the great new château, the white towers of which soared above the deep cleft valleys. The whole village was on tenterhooks. It was rumoured that Dame Sara, who ruled over the serving-women, chambermaids and cooks at the castle, had been at her wits' end, despite her vast experience, and had finally been forced to take over the Abbey guest-house and even a few of the village houses to accommodate all these new arrivals. But now everything had been sorted out and the happiness reigning over the brilliant procession that wound out of the church toward the castle was without a flaw. The whole village was decorated, from cobble-stones to chimney-pots. The villagers had brought out the finest hangings and coloured clothes from their marriage-chests, and decked their homes with these, and with flowers and brilliant autumn foliage. Everyone was proudly wearing their Sunday best, of fine wool or sturdy linen, often embroidered. Wool caps were perched jauntily on the men's heads while the women's linen headdresses, so fine and airy, looked as if they might instantly take flight. The young girls wore new ribbons plaited into their hair, and the youths had a way of pulling their caps down over one eye and ogling them, that suggested that when the dancing was over not a few young couples would be stealing off into the nearby woods.

In sum, it was the greatest day Montsalvy had known for several decades. They were celebrating at once their new-found prosperity, the opening of the new castle, the return of the Lord and Lady of Montsalvy to their estates, and finally, the baptism of young Isabelle, the little daughter who had just been born to Catherine of Montsalvy.

All the nobility for twenty leagues around had come for the festivities. The villagers respectfully pointed out the great nobles from the Court who had come to present their compliments to the rulers of this little city, together with the King's captains who were there to celebrate the return of their old comrade-in-arms with a delight all the more exuberant for having believed him dead these many years. But the greatest wonder was reserved for the godfather and godmother who headed the glittering procession, immediately behind Dame Sara, dressed from head to toe in crimson velvet and Brussels lace, who carried the baby proudly in her arms. At their approach, all the good people of Montsalvy went down on one knee, a little bewildered and slightly uneasy, but above all immensely proud of the honour conferred upon their little city. It is not every day one has the chance to salute a Queen and a Constable of France in the heart of the Auvergne! For the godmother was none other than Queen Yolande of Anjou, beautiful and dignified beneath the glittering crown that secured her gold-embroidered black veils, and the godfather was Richemont, dressed in gold and blue velvet, a hood strewn with immense pearls framing his scarred features. He led the Queen by the hand along the carpets that had been laid down on the road, under a veritable storm of flower petals and leaves that the young girls were strewing over them. They both waved and smiled at the cheers of the enthusiastic crowd, enchanted by this country festival, to which their presence lent something of the glamour of a royal occasion.

Then came the ladies, surrounding Madame Richemont, and it looked as if a fragile forest of sparkling, colourful steeple head-dresses was on the move. And after them the lords, with their rugged faces. People pointed out the celebrated and formidable La Hire, who was doing his best to look amiable, and the splendid Poton de Xaintrailles, richly apparelled in green velvet lined with gold. But the fairest of them all, so the good people of Montsalvy agreed, with a trace of justifiable pride, was Dame Catherine herself.

In the few months since she had brought Messire Arnaud triumphantly back to the land of his fathers, her beauty seemed to have bloomed as never before, and it had acquired such polish and perfection that it made every movement a poem, every smile an enchantment. Ah, yes, happiness suited her! In her blue and gold gown, beneath the cloud of muslin that billowed from her head-dress, she looked like a fairy ... She was by far the loveliest lady of them all, and Messire Arnaud, who led her proudly by the hand, seemed deeply convinced of the fact. He himself wore a simple black velvet suit, with no ornament other than a heavy chain of rubies, as if he wished to set off his wife's beauty all the more effectively by the simplicity of his own attire. And the kindly peasants were quite moved to see them looking into each other's eyes and smiling at each other just like a pair of young lovers.

To tell the truth, Catherine had never been happier in her life. This October day of the year 1435 was the finest she had ever known, because it had reunited around her those she loved. As she descended the garlanded street of Montsalvy, holding her husband's hand tightly in her own, she thought how her mother, whom she had rediscovered again after all these years with a joy almost too strong to be borne, awaited her at the castle. And there too was Uncle Mathieu, greatly aged but still sprightly. He had spent every day since his arrival trotting about the countryside accompanied by the old bailiff, Saturnin, who had become his inseparable friend. Only her sister, Loyse, had not come; but a cloistered nun no longer belongs to this world. The new Abbess of the Benedictines of Tart had merely sent her blessing to the infant, through a messenger ...

'What are you thinking about?' Arnaud asked, after contemplating his wife with a smile for a moment or two.

'About all this about us! Would you ever have believed that we could be so happy? We have everything: happiness, beautiful children, wonderful friends, a family, worldly honours ... even a great fortune ...

The latter they owed to Jacques Cœur. The proceeds of the fabulous black diamond were becoming, in his skilful hands, the cornerstone of a great fortune. In the midst of the grandiose plan he had conceived for the restoration of his country's wealth, the furrier from Bourges, who was on the road to becoming Lord Treasurer of France, had found time to pay back a hundredfold to his friends such favours as he had received from them in his darker days.

'No, I should never have believed it possible,' Arnaud admitted frankly. 'But don't you think we have done a little to deserve it, sweetheart? We have suffered so much; you particularly ...'

'I never even think of that. My only regret is that your mother, Dame Isabelle, is not with us ...'

'She is not far away. I am certain that she sees and hears us from that mysterious place where she has met the great Gauthier again ... Besides, haven't we reincarnated her?'

It was true. Little Isabelle did not resemble her mother in the least. She had her grandmother's blue eyes, the imperious profile of the Montsalvy family in general and the black curls of her father in particular. According to Sara, she seemed to have inherited his irascible, untameable character as well.

'When she has to wait for her milk, even for a second,' the former gypsy, now promoted to governess, had sighed pathetically, 'she howls loud enough to bring the walls crashing down.'

Just now, young Isabelle slept soundly in the good woman's arms, amidst the silk and lace of her exquisite robes. The sound of oboes, pipes and fifes all around her seemed not to disturb her in the least. She lay with one of her tiny hands curled round Sara's thumb, and it seemed as if she could sleep through the sound of cannon fire without so much as opening an eye.

But it was a different story when the baby and her escort entered the courtyard of the castle where servants, men-at-arms and maids were waiting to pay their respects. As soon as she appeared, two figures rushed to her side: one was a little boy of three, whose golden hair shone in the sunlight, and the other a big, stout old lady dressed in crimson and gold: her brother Michel and her honorary godmother, Ermengarde de Châteauvillain.

In spite of Sara's respectful but firm remonstrances, and the screams of protest from Michel, who also wanted to carry his baby sister, Ermengarde snatched her up by main force and carried off her now-bawling trophy to the immense white tapestry-hung hall where a banquet had been laid. The rest of the company followed hard on the heels of the godparents, and in a moment the castle was overflowing with cries and laughter, and the music of lutes played by the minstrels who were to accompany the feast.

Later on, after countless dishes had come and gone – pâtés, venison, fish, peacocks served in all their plumage, boars presented on a bed of apples and almonds, with their horns and flesh stuffed with rare spices – the valets brought in tarts, sweetmeats, nougats, creams and many other desserts, accompanied by wines of Spain and Malvoisie. At this point, Xaintrailles stood up and called for silence. Holding a brimming goblet in one hand, he saluted the Queen and the Constable, then turned toward his hosts:

'My friends,' he said, in his most resonant voice, 'with the permission of the Queen and Milord Constable, it is my pleasure to tell you of our great happiness in being present at the resurrection of Montsalvy, which coincides with the resurgence of France. War recedes throughout the country, and the English are being driven out pell-mell. The treaty our King has just signed with the Duke of Burgundy at Arras, while it may not be a model of its kind, at least has the virtue of putting an end to a merciless war between fellow-countrymen. There are no more Armagnacs and Burgundians, only loyal subjects of King Charles the Victorious, whom may God preserve in health and strength!'

Here Xaintrailles paused for breath and to let the applause die away. He glanced around him quickly, and then his brown eyes lit upon Catherine and Arnaud, who sat smiling at him, hand in hand. 'Arnaud, brother,' he went on, 'we thought you were lost to us, and you have returned, and that is well and good. I won't tell you what I think of you; you know all that; we will pass over that … But to you, Catherine, who braved great dangers and perils to go and snatch your love back from the very gates of death, who fought bravely in Montsalvy's place for the downfall of our evil genius, La Trémoille, who helped us complete the work of the Blessed Maid of

Domrémy, I wish to speak of our great love and our pride and joy in being your guests today.

'Few men could have equalled your courage, and few men would have been capable, either, of the faithful love that has stayed burning in your heart these many years.

'The dark years, of which you have known too many, are ended. You have a long life of love and happiness before you … and the happy task of setting a whole new generation of thoroughbred Montsalvys on their feet! Gentlemen and ladies, I ask you to rise now and drink to the happiness of Catherine and Arnaud of Montsalvy, a long life, and great times to the bravest of Christian knights and the fairest of the West!'

The great ovation that greeted Xaintrailles' last words echoed round the vaulted roof of the new château, and was taken up by the joyful cries of the villagers below. For a moment the little fortress-town was one great shout of love and joy. Catherine, pale with emotion, tried to get up to reply to this speech, but it was all too much for her. Her legs refused to support her, and she had to cling to Arnaud's shoulder to stop herself falling.

'Oh, it's too much,' she murmured. 'How can one be so happy and not die of joy?'

'I think you will soon get used to it,' Arnaud answered with a laugh.

It was late in the night when the ball ended and Catherine and Arnaud finally reached the chamber they had chosen for themselves in the south tower. Harassed servants were sleeping on their feet all over the château, wherever tiredness had overtaken them. The Queen and Constable had retired to their respective suites long ago, but here and there, in distant corners of the castle, groups of impenitent revellers were still engaged in celebrating so memorable a feast. There was dancing going on still in the courtyard round the dying embers, accompanied by lusty singing.

Catherine was as weary as everyone else, but she did not feel sleepy. She was too happy to want the day to end just yet. She sat at the foot of the great bed with its blue damask curtains and watched Arnaud unceremoniously shooing away her women.

'Why are you sending them away?' she asked. 'I'll never get out of this dress by myself.'

'I am here,' he said, with a mocking grin. 'We'll see what an excellent chambermaid I make.'

He pulled off his doublet and flung it carelessly into a corner of the room. Then he set himself to taking out all the pins that secured Catherine's tall steeple head-dress. He did so with a delicacy and skill that made her smile.

'You are right. You are just as clever at it as Sara.'

'Wait, you haven't seen anything yet. Stand up …'

She obeyed, and began pointing out the ribbons and hooks he would have to undo to remove her dress. But Arnaud took hold of her dress by the neckline and ripped it so that the blue satin tore from top to bottom, and her fine lawn petticoat with it. Catherine found herself standing there as naked as the day she was born, but for her blue silk stockings. She gave a cry of annoyance.

'Arnaud! Are you out of your mind ... a dress like that!'

'Exactly. You should never wear this dress again. It has been a day of triumph; keep it as a souvenir. Besides,' he added, taking her in his arms and fastening his lips over hers, 'It really would have taken too long to unfasten.'

The 'souvenir' sank to the floor and Catherine, with a sigh of contentment, surrendered herself to him.

Arnaud's mouth was warm, and it smelled a little of wine, but it had lost none of its skill in rousing Catherine to a turmoil of desire. But he kissed her slowly, deliberately, seeking to awaken the passion that turned her into a shameless uninhibited Bacchante. He held her against him with one arm, and with the other hand he slowly caressed and stroked her back, her hip, then slipped up toward one breast and then down, over the smooth curve of her belly. And Catherine was already vibrating like a harp in the wind.

'Arnaud,' she murmured, falteringly, against his lips, 'please ...'

He took her head in both hands, plunging his hands into her long silken hair, and tipped it back to the light.

'Please what, my sweet? Please make love to you? That's exactly what I'm about to do. I am going to love you and love you, Catherine sweetheart, till you are breathless and cry for mercy ... I hunger for you as though you had never borne me two children.'

With that, he bent her back till her knees gave way and she sank beneath him onto the great bearskin in front of the fire. Then he clasped her tightly in his arms.

'There. Now you are my captive, and you will never escape from me!'

She wound her arms round her husband's neck and sought his lips with her own. 'I don't want to escape from you, my darling. Love me now; make love to me till I forget that I'm not part of you, till we are one.'

She saw the brown face close to her own twisted in the almost agonised expression that desire gave him, and she pressed herself against him so that he could feel every inch of her body under his. Then it was Arnaud's turn to lose his head, and for a long while the only sound in the great warm room was the soft moaning of a woman in love.

As Arnaud dozed off, later, during a break in their love-making, Catherine asked suddenly: 'What was La Hire saying to you during the ball? Is it true that you will have to leave here in spring, and go back to war?'

He half opened one eye, shrugged and pulled a corner of the bearskin rug over himself and over her. 'The English still occupy some of our strongholds. As long as they remain here we have to fight ...'

She began to tremble, suddenly a prey to all the old fears that had tormented her so much in the past. Was it all going to start again? 'I don't want you to go away, I don't want you to leave me again. I got you back, I want to keep you ...'

She tightened her arm round him in a childish gesture, as if she was afraid that he would disappear instantly. Tenderly, he stroked her cheek and softly kissed her. She saw his white teeth gleam in the half light and knew that he was smiling.

'Do you think I want to leave you again and spend night after night without you; without your eyes, your body? I am a soldier and I have to do my duty. But when I go away, you shall come with me ... The campaigns last only six months, and there are many castles behind the lines. You shall wait for me there, and we will never be parted ... never again. The time for tears, for suffering and pain is over for you. Now the time has come for us to love. And we won't waste a single minute of it.'

About the Author

Juliette Benzoni was born Andrée-Marguerite-Juliette Mangin on 30 October 1920 in Paris, France. She spent her childhood in Saint-Germain-des-Pres until she was almost 15 years old, when her family went to live in Saint-Mandé. She was educated at College d'Hulet, then at the Institut Catholique, where she studied philosophy, law and literature. In 1941 she married a doctor from Dijon, Maurice Gallois, and was soon mother of two children, Anne and Jean-François. In her twenties, she spent many hours in libraries, studying the history of Burgundy in Medieval times. One day she came across the legend of the Order of the Golden Fleece, which would later inspire her to write the *Catherine* series.

After her husband died in 1950, she went to Morocco to visit a relative of his, and ended up staying for two years, joining the editorial staff at a radio station called Radio-International. She then met Colonel André Benzoni, who in 1953 became her second husband. After her return to Paris, France, she launched into journalism, writing for several newspapers. At the beginning of the 1960s, a literary editor who had seen her make a television appearance invited her to write a historical romance in the style of Anne Golon's *Angelique*. The outcome was *Catherine: One Love is Enough* (original title, *Catherine, Il Suffit d'un Amor*), the hugely successful first entry in what was originally intended to be a five book series.

Next came another big success with the *Marianne* series, set during the Napoleonic period, beginning with *Marianne: A Star for Napoleon* (original title, *Marianne: Une Étoile Pour Napoleon*). Juliette was then asked if she would write two additional *Catherine* books, due to their sensational popularity. She agreed, and the series' seventh and final entry, *La Dame de Montsalvy*, appeared in 1979.

In 1983, the French company Antenne 2 adapted *Marianne: A Star for Napoleon* for television, directed by Marion Sarraut. This led, three years later, to a television adaptation of all seven books in the *Catherine* series, again directed by Sarraut; the end result pleased Juliette far more than a substandard movie version produced in 1968.

Juliette died on 7 February 2016.

For more information about Juliette and the *Catherine* books, see this official website: www.catherinedemontsalvy.ch.

Other Titles from Telos Publishing

Printed in Great Britain
by Amazon

82225704R00173